Chateau de Bitremont in Bury (circa 1850)

Lydie of Peruwelz

A Love Affair That Outlived Separation, Insanity, and a Nicotine Murder

Richard Burack, Sr., MD

Lydie of Peruwelz
A Love Affair That Outlived Separation, Insanity, and a Nicotine Murder

Copyright © 2016 W. Richard Burack 1989 Trust

Certain characters in this work are historical figures, and certain events portrayed did take place. However, this is a novel. All of the other characters, names, and events as well as all places, incidents, organizations, and dialogue in this novel are used fictitiously.

The major characters in this book are historical figures whose every word uttered in a trial about a murder—its planning, performance and outcome—were described under oath. All words were recorded by a stenographer with a telegraphic printer (as published by Théophile LeRoux in Procès du comte et de la comtesse de Bocarmé devant la Cour d'assises du Hainaut. Mons, Belgium, 1851. 277 p.) Many of these same characters later took part in fictional events. Their imagined experiences, dialogue, and travels enrich the book, although its core remains the murder and its life-long effects on their lives. These storybook lives contain most of the fictional persons and events that perforce make Lydie of Peruwelz a Historical Novel.

iUniverse books may be ordered through booksellers or by contacting:

iUniverse
1663 Liberty Drive
Bloomington, IN 47403
www.iuniverse.com
1-800-Authors (1-800-288-4677)

ISBN: 978-1-4917-4378-2 (sc)
ISBN: 978-1-4917-4380-5 (hc)
ISBN: 978-1-4917-4379-9 (e)

Library of Congress Control Number: 2014916230

Print information available on the last page.

iUniverse rev. date: 10/11/2016

To my wife, Mary

Contents

Acknowledgements

I wish, first off, to thank Ms. Holly Starley, an immensely gifted Senior Consulting Editor.

I am grateful to Mrs. Lucretia McClure, retired as Special Assistant to the Director at Countway Library, Harvard Medical School in Boston; formerly Director and Associate Professor of Medical Bibliography at the Edwin G. Miner Library at University of Rochester Medical Center. She copied, and sent historical medical publications to me from Boston for more than twenty years. Many were old and rare. She invariably accompanied them with friendly, encouraging words. Without her motivating influence, I may not have written anything.

I am deeply indebted to a friend and former colleague, Dr. Paul Foreman. It was his imaginative idea to radically change what was initially a dry, academic discussion about the history of laboratory studies of the nervous system, especially about nicotine's isolation. His encouragement and support, including insertions of illustrative chapters, educated me how to use hard, historical facts as the core of a book which also contains relevant fictional material. He taught me the gist of novelizing; putting one's imagination into words. Despite his magnanimity, he refused the offer to join me as coauthor. Description of his counsel as "helpful" would grossly understate its importance. (See Background).

Had it not been for the expertise of Ms. Nancy Dickinson, an executive secretary, we might never have completed a pre-publication manuscript. Her oversight was essential to its realization.

The finished book owes its existence to Madame Marie-Clotilde Boël, a kind lady of Roucourt, a suburb of the small city of Peruwelz, Belgium. In 1997 she gave me a rare volume containing a stenographic recording of courtroom proceedings in an 1851 murder trial. The sessions of hearings in the Court of Assizes, in the large city of Mons, are the floor on which this book is based. It is regrettable that Madame Boël did not live long enough to view the fruit of her generosity.

Aside from her work as a historian, people respected Madame Boël for her extensive charitable work. Except for the elegance of her home's exterior, there was nothing pretentious about Madame Boël who, Mary and I later discovered, was a scion of one of Belgium's most distinguished families. We visited her twice and discussed, along with much else, her reaction as a youth to Nazi occupation of Roucourt during World War II. She excused herself briefly and reappeared with an ingenious self-sewn skirt composed of English, German, and American flags. If she saw Germans in the area, she turned it so the swastika showed; another turn made it an American Stars and Stripes skirt, and another showed a St. George's Cross. She made turns in a dancing manner, all the while laughing. She seemed still to be a young woman.

For a variety of reasons, I extend appreciation to Mrs. Gertie Johansson, librarian of the Hagströmer Medical-Historical Library in the Karolinska Institute, Stockholm, and to Dr. Ove Hagelin, its director at the time. Mrs. Johansson provided many old, rare German publications for the unpublished antecedent of this book.

The late Dr. Paul Draskóczy, a close friend, laboratory colleague, and gifted psychiatrist, reassured me that my portrayal of neurotic and psychotic behaviors is not grossly incorrect. Dr. Draskóczy died after a brief illness in December, 2014. He is missed.

I am grateful to Dr. Edgar Estes Folk III, a fine physician, bibliophile and friend since 1946 when we met as entering medical students at the Wake Forest University School of Medicine in Winston-Salem, North Carolina. He examined an early version of this book and gave me a green light to continue the project. The present version contains far more than he read but his approval was encouraging.

My daughter, Anna Burack Wilson, author and editor of scientific reports for more than thirty years, has guided prepublication reviews of the manuscript. Her tutelage has been useful as well as kind. Every effort has been made to follow her advice rendered from a distance of two-thirds of the continent. She cannot be held responsible for failure on my part to follow every detail of her remote oversight.

Background

In 1992, after retiring from a full-time career in medicine, I began to write a historical account of study on the human nervous system. It began, for practical purposes, with observations of extracts from tobacco leaves carried out between 1492 and 1826. Many inquisitive people, most of them unknown, made concerted efforts to improve the extracts' purity and potency because smoking tobacco leaves or drinking its water extracts influence human behavior. In 1826, two skillful German medical students isolated nicotine from the leaves, clarified its chemical structure and showed that it is the active, highly poisonous agent that their inquisitive predecessors sought for more than three centuries. Studies of nicotine's effects eventuated in present-day knowledge about impulse transmission between nerve cells.

The Heidelberg medical faculty briefly celebrated the students' isolation and study of Nikotin (nicotine) as merely a *chemical* achievement. However, an unknown faculty member injected a minuscule amount of the pure nicotine into a vein of a large, healthy dog. The animal suffered an immediate convulsion and was dead within a minute. The students drank half an ounce of the highly diluted chemical every morning for three weeks but had to quit because they developed disabling, chronic nausea.

Hence, the students classified nicotine as a violent poison, probably unfit for use as a tool in medical investigations. They were chemists, not pharmacologists. By categorizing nicotine as a poison, they may have retarded its study in physiology and pharmacology research laboratories mushrooming in German and French universities from 1830. Nicotine's rarity and cost were also major obstacles to its use. Several decades passed before it caught the attention of German scientists.

Because literary agents believed that too few general readers would find it engrossing, I did not allow distribution of that long manuscript describing old, basic, often lengthy studies of tobacco's toxicity.

***

There has not, to my knowledge, been a published monograph in pharmacology/physiology literature analyzing reasons for the long delay in the use of nicotine as a laboratory tool. That job suddenly became a project for someone other than me to pursue as a result of a "final" library search for articles on early studies of tobacco leaf contents.

One day in 1994, out of curiosity, I *did* revisit the rare books department of the Countway Library of the Massachusetts Medical Society at Harvard Medical School, to look for any relevant publications about nicotine that I might not yet had found. Mrs. McClure advised studying every card in a long pre-computer-age drawer marked "Nicotine." One card referenced a library holding previously unknown to me—a small, brittle, and yellowed shard snipped from an unknown 1850 English language newspaper. Its three lines announced that a man had recently died of nicotine poisoning in Peruwelz, Belgium. The shard contained no other information. It was a puzzling bit of information, if 1850 was truly the date.

Only a handful of university chemistry professors knew of the 1826 Heidelberg synthesis, and few, if any, were anxious to deal with the substance. Not until 1860 to 1870 did scientists in Germany's foremost medical research laboratories (Leipzig and Berlin) dilute a minuscule amount of nicotine one-thousand-fold and inject it into dogs' veins, to observe whether it had nonlethal physiological effects. It transiently rendered certain nerves temporarily nonfunctioning but caused no deaths. The findings were a signal contribution to neuroscience research.

***

Setting all mention of neuroscience aside, it is remarkable that despite nicotine's dangerous properties, rarity and exorbitant cost, an English language newspaper would report that, in 1850, a man died of nicotine poisoning in Peruwelz, an obscure Belgian town.

When my wife, Mary, asked if the library visit had been fruitful, I told her the puzzling information I'd uncovered. "One has to wonder," I mused out loud, "how and why was there access to nicotine in a small Belgian city in 1850?" Anyone with a basic knowledge of nicotine's history, its rarity, and *exorbitant* cost had to wonder. In 1994, there was no feasible way for me to delve into the intriguing story.

Mary loves atlases. She found Peruwelz, a dot in central-western Belgium, practically touching the French frontier. It is far from any medical laboratories in Belgium, France, or Germany.

***

In July 1997, Mary and I began a European vacation. Our intention was to drive through a part of France in a rental car, with maps and a Guide to inexpensive rural hotels. After fleeing crowded Paris in early morning, we drove eastward trying to find roads leading to the Maginot Line, which to this day attracts visitors.

At about noon, we lost our way and stopped briefly in the French village of Conde, to orient ourselves. As I reached for maps in the glove compartment, Mary spotted a small directional sign approximately thirty feet ahead, "Peruwelz One Kilometer."

"Isn't that where that nicotine poisoning took place?"

"Yes! Your memory is excellent. By all means, let's go there and inquire about the 1850 poisoning."

A short, tree-lined avenue enters Belgium and, after a few yards, becomes the main street of Peruwelz, a small, provincial city. On a narrow side street was a sign, "Police," with an arrow. At the police station, one officer understood my poorly-spoken French questions.

He told me to wait while he made a brief telephone call, and then Officer Philippe Ankaert of the Brigade de Peruwelz jumped into his police car as he called out the French for, "Follow me."

We sped a couple hundred yards to the end of Main Street, drove over a bridge, made numerous right and left turns on small roads, and eventually traveled a long, straight, paved street on which we suddenly slowed before a very large, manicured lawn within a perfectly circular driveway leading to a red-stone castle with a weathered, green turret.

***

A pleasant, plainly dressed, welcoming woman invited us in. She spoke a few words of English, but her sister and a brother-in-law were visiting her, and both spoke it well. The welcoming woman was Madame Marie-Clotilde Boël[1] of Roucourt, one of two small suburbs of Peruwelz. The long, straight street she lived on was Avenue Lieutenant Boël, named for her brother. He died fighting with the Belgian underground during WWII.

Her distant forbear, Léopold Boël, was communal secretary of the region at the time of the poisoning, which I quickly discovered was a murder when Madame Boël[2] mentioned that he "testified at the trial about what he knew of the accused man's character."

Madame Boël informed us that Peruwelz, which is large in area, has two small suburbs—Roucourt and Bury. The murder took place in 1850 in Bury in the sixteenth-century Chateau de Bitremont, the ancestral home of the de Bocarmés, one of Belgium's prestigious families.

---

[1] Madame Marie-Clotilde Boël had written several volumes about the history of the region and was, we later heard, reputed to be the area's leading intellectual figure.

[2] Madame Boël died several years ago. Many in the region must still miss her.

Madame Boël anticipated, perhaps from something Officer Ankaert said when he telephoned her, that I might be searching for a copy of a book containing a stenographic recording of the entire 1851 murder trial. She had, therefore, already called ahead to the single stationery store in Peruwelz with a copier large enough to reproduce its invaluable pages of very small font and half line spacing. She wanted to be sure the stationer was open for business.

I had no previous knowledge of verbatim stenographic recording in the mid-nineteenth century. I learned later that stenographers used telegraphic printers to record all conversation and that the method was widely used in Western Europe in the mid 19th century. To read more about stenography dependent on telegraphic printers, see the Addendum to this work.

***

Madame Boël emphasized that the book contains all audible words spoken during the 1851 nicotine murder trial, but is very rare. She owned only one copy. She asked, "Would you like to have one, too?"

Indeed, I did. She then trusted us, complete strangers, to drive, with her invaluable volume, back to Main Street of Peruwelz, have it replicated, and then return it to her. We did that gladly. We asked if there were a charge for permission to copy her book. She smiled, frowned, shook her head, and said, "No, of course not." Hers was a typical French gesture.

Those 277 pages of crowded French words, font size 8 (footnote size) with half-spaced lines, needed a magnifying glass to read.[3] The content made possible completion of this book. The words voiced by courtroom officials and defendants during sessions of the trial held all of Europe's rapt attention in the year 1851. To my knowledge,

---

[3] Procès de Bocarmé. (The Bocarmé Trial). Printed by Théophile Leroux, editor and publisher, Mons 1851. No copyright is claimed.

the trial may be the first to deal with the dreadful issue of brutalized "captive wives." More than one hundred and fifty years later, the ugly problem continues to blemish even the world's most advanced nations.

***

On returning home to New England from France, I used certain sections of the book that agents told me would not interest many people. I believed that what I saved of it might be the basis of a thinner book that would be easy to write quickly. It was of course also necessary to begin to translate the trial notes obtained from Madame Boël. The French spoken during the trial was generally uncomplicated.

In blocks of time, while resting from the tedium of using the magnifying glass, I completed the thin book about nicotine's history and was on the verge of sending it for publication. I showed it to friends with science backgrounds, three of whom but one urged its publication.

The dissenter was Dr. Paul Foreman, an erstwhile colleague whose specialty is Biology and whose good sense I have always admired. After he read it, he found no fault with the verbal composition but boldly asserted that it was another dry, academic book. He felt it was unlikely to attract general readers and might even meet with nitpicking by professors of neuroscience. He asked, "Why waste your time on a chemical when you hold a rare stenographic copy of a mid-19th century murder trial? There has to be deep interest in learning the motive for the murder, the work of those who investigated it, the person or persons accused of it, how authorities conducted the trial, and how testimony of witnesses determined its outcome."

I knew that Dr. Foreman was right. He suggested removing a hundred and forty footnotes, minimizing reference to neuroscience, and novelizing *around* the murder and trial, which would be the core of the story. He was thoroughly convincing.

Dr. Foreman politely refused to join me as a co-author: "This is *your* book—I'll be as helpful as I can be." He made that promise nearly 20 years ago and has patiently kept it.

He gifted more than a half dozen usable chapters to this book in which a romance wraps around a notorious, historic murder trial, which is the central story element. Each of his chapters described events that one may reasonably expect to encounter in the unfolding of a love story.

Novels about romantic love are usually based on three elements: serendipitous discovery, distressing rupture, and unanticipated restoration. Dr. Foreman's chapters were especially helpful in developing the first two elements. The third contains some essential measures of a mended romance, to wit, the degree of its bilateral fulfillment and how long it lasts. Part Three of the book deals with this third element.

Prologue

On the bright morning of July 21, 1851, a gleaming, black, horse-drawn prison vehicle, surrounded by sixteen police on horseback, arrived with military precision in the large cobblestone city center, or Grande Place, of Mons, Belgium. Within the prison vehicle was Alfred-Julien-Gabriel-Gérard-Hippolyte-Visart, Count de Bocarmé, who was condemned to death for premeditated murder. The eerie entourage halted before the gilded provincial government headquarters, where a guillotine was standing on a scaffold erected for the occasion.

The Grande Place was, and still is, an impressively beautiful, oval area, large enough to be a park. Carefully tended, richly colored flowerbeds and brightly blossomed shrubs bordered the narrow, red clay paths through and around the oval. The facades of handsome, gray, and light brown buildings with Mansard roofs, none more than five stories, formed a harmonious perimeter. At one end was the only tall structure, a spired Gothic cathedral. Its white exterior blended well with all else.

Mons, close to the French border, is the capital city of the Belgian province Hainaut. It is still ranked one of the most beautiful and pleasant cities in Belgium. Its locale is among gorgeous green rolling hills and rapid, clear streams.

***

At the scheduled decapitation of a psychopathic criminal, the condemned man's every step to the scaffold would be closely followed by an American clergyman, the Most Reverend John Purcell, Archbishop of Cincinnati. He would chant prayers for the soul of the condemned, kneeling as near as possible to the head of the scaffold with eyes closed and hands supplicating as his lips would barely audibly recite last rites.

1

The archbishop had been finishing a visit to Rome, where he read about a sensational murder trial in Belgium. Unexpectedly, he received an anguished telegraphed request from a Brussels uncle of the man sentenced to death by guillotine. "Would you be willing to detour through Mons on your return to America, to accompany a pitiable nephew to his death on the scaffold in early morning July 21?"

The archbishop readily consented to accompany the reprobate member of a noble Belgian family to his execution. The uncle of the condemned Hippolyte Visart, Count de Bocarmé, had been forced to make this request because his nephew so utterly detested anyone associated with the Belgian judicial and prison systems. This included its resident priests, with all of whom he refused to communicate. Hippolyte did agree to speak with the archbishop but refused to discard his insistence that confession, even to an archbishop, was tantamount to admitting that he was guilty of having committed a heinous murder.

Archbishop Purcell, deprived of sleep during the long trip from Rome, arrived in Mons late on the morning of July 20. Tired as he was, he quickly went to Hippolyte's cell, introduced himself, and shook the frightened prisoner's cold hand. The count took awkward advantage of the handshake to lecture the gentle archbishop about lack of mathematical proof of God's existence and then to insist, repeatedly, that he was an innocent man.

The archbishop sized him up at once as deranged and mercifully allowed him to avoid the confessional, to attend Mass, and even to receive communion. As he drank the wine and chewed the bread, Hippolyte was deep in thought. A few words of Latin meant nothing to him. He occupied his small mind planning an insipid arrangement to ensure that he would go directly from the scaffold to heaven, in case there really was such a place.

The timeworn "deal" he envisioned was to offer an insanely enormous bribe to the keeper of purgatory's gates. Although he was many thousands of francs in debt, he was certain that no one with an ounce of brains would turn down the enormous pension benefit he intended to offer. He never thought about hell as an alternative because he did not believe in its existence.

***

In early evening of the same day, the count received two visitors accompanied by two strong guards. One visitor was a hunchbacked, gnomish executioner and the other a doctor. The little man stepped forth to introduce himself as Monsieur Jan Willems, who politely wished to apologize for what his occupation obliged him to do.

The count had nothing to say, but Willems stepped back, bowed, and said in a goatlike, nasal voice, "May God have mercy on your soul."

The doctor, who introduced himself impersonally as "a doctor," remained silent for some seconds before asking in a flat, toneless voice, "Do you have any questions?"

"Yes!" shouted Hippolyte in his ugly, loud gravel voice. "Is it painful? Be sure the blade isn't dull. I heard of someone who had a nervous executioner who couldn't hit the mark. He struck the back of the man's head three times, and crushed it before he chopped through his neck. The thought of that is frightening. Be sure that doesn't happen to me!" His harsh, loud voice was too commanding for the doctor to tolerate. With condescension, annoyance and impatience, he replied with heavily intoned words, "Don't be ridiculous! It doesn't hurt!"

He immediately turned his back on the prisoner and, with the executioner and their two guards, exited, as a jailer outside quickly checked the security of the two locks of the cell door.

***

The jailer sat outside the cell for a minute or two and then stood, revealing a slightly hunched upper back. He took a step closer to the prisoner, who could now better see his thin, heavily lined face. He was older than any jailer who had monitored the death-row cell located at the end of a dimly gas lit corridor. His appearance had evidently caught Hippolyte's attention; he stopped pacing and, for the first time, made eye contact with a prison employee, although he did not abandon his glum expression. Old as the jailer seemed to be, he was a clean-shaven man with a freshly ironed uniform, the collar of his blue shirt open.

He took immediate advantage of the eye contact, quickly using it to remark mildly but factually, "You're in a bad situation, one that I wouldn't want to be in. Other jailers have told me about your predicament, and I've thought a lot about it. You can't have been a jailer for as long as I have been without trying to help prisoners, or you'd become a senseless, unfeeling excuse for a human being."

Hippolyte stood almost at a standstill, shifting his weight from one leg to another on the heavy wooden cell floor as he listened to the old man say, "I was lucky to land my job thirty years ago, or I might have ended up a prisoner myself. Things were a hell of a lot worse out there then. If I hadn't landed this job, I don't doubt that I'd have had to steal, maybe kill. I badly needed a little cash to feed my young wife and a newborn son. But I'd have been caught and put away for years, maybe for life, especially if I killed when I didn't mean to."

The prisoner took a step closer to the cell bars to get an even closer look at the old man's deeply lined, thin face. The move made the jailer feel that he had now caught the so far silent count's attention, and he did not want to lose it.

"I want to tell you an absolute truth. I've been thinking a lot about the bind you're in. It's a tough one, but I think I can tell you how to deal with it. I don't intend to be brief; there's a lot to say."

The duplicitous count interrupted with a fatuous proposal. "Tell you what. Hand me the keys and lemme punch your face a few times so it looks like we had a fight. I can get out o' this place, and you'd have an excuse."

The old man smiled benevolently, sat down again, and calmly replied, "You know I can't do that. At the very least, I'd lose my pension, and you'd be quickly caught. So let's talk sensibly about how to help you. You wouldn't be the first prisoner I've helped deal with the establishment's quirky rules."

"What does 'establishment' mean?"

"It means those legal bigwigs in Brussels—whatever it is you call the group of them. They've written a code that demands a particular punishment for certain crimes. Judges are not free to ignore the code when a jury finds someone guilty of a crime listed in the code. I'll bet that it never occurred to any one of those bigwigs that the cruelest sentence they can inflict for any crime is permanent life imprisonment. No question about it—that is by far the cruelest sentence they could impose on anyone. I have seen all too many lonely lifers suffer miserably slow deaths.

"I don't want to get into what trouble you may have had, and I don't care to know. All I want to do is help you think straight. I never had any fancy education, but I pick up useful words here and there. I mean to say that I want you to think *rationally*—reasonably and wisely—about the sentence the bigwigs imposed on you and the best way for you to manage it. *The point is, you can use that sentence wisely, and I'll tell you how.*"

The count narrowed his eyes skeptically, but the old jailer was prepared. "If you don't already know it, the guillotine is the easiest, painless way to put you permanently to sleep. No one denies that; it's common knowledge. It's why the rich French, the ones the revolutionaries didn't like, paid a hell of a lot of money, sold their homes and their estates, and gave away their life savings for the privilege of letting the guillotine anesthetize them instantly."

Hippolyte knew nothing about the French Revolution or *any* history. He didn't get the point the old jailor tried to make.

The jailor saw the confused expression on the condemned man's face. Standing and speaking eye to eye with the doomed count, the jailor repeated, "The people who were in trouble in France and faced execution were grateful to a man who invented the guillotine. They knew that, without that invention, they could suffer a slow, gruesome and painful hanging, with their feet six inches from the ground. Worse, they could be strangled by a strong-armed thug, a professional executioner. Thugs were hired imports, usually from India, where the name for one of these brutes was actually "Thug."

"Thugs wore black masks and used enormous muscle strength to tighten a hempen rope twisted 'round the victim's neck. It had a big knot in its middle. With their thick leather gloves, they yanked on its ends so violently at about every fifteen or twenty seconds that they were able to break the victim's neck as painfully as possible. It might take up to five minutes. Then, depending on how much they were paid for minutes of their time, they could prolong the agony for a while before putting the tortured screaming, or moaning prisoner to death with such hard, prolonged tightening of the rope that he died of strangulation."

(Hippolyte, a perverted sadist of the first order, listened *very* closely, although it is difficult to know *exactly* why. Lacking any empathy, he may have been fascinated to learn of a unique form of cruelty. But he *was* fearful of decapitation by an executioner wielding an axe).

"Obviously, rich people would pay a lot of money to avoid a slow hanging or death by a Thug. Today, in 1851, the two major sentences demanded by the code are either sudden sleep by the guillotine or very slow death after a long life imprisonment. The guillotine gets most of the publicity supposed to frighten people from breaking laws. If the authorities really want to frighten the public not to break laws, they ought to be using more honest words to describe the nearly unbelievable horror and torment of life imprisonment. My hunch is that you're a person who may never have thought of that.

"The way to take advantage of that punishment they handed you is by gladly letting them give you eternal anesthesia in a fraction of a second with absolutely no pain. The alternative is so much worse that I can hardly describe it. It means years and years of seclusion in a cell in a poorly heated prison, where you have a single, thin blanket that can't keep the cold out, so you can't sleep. Other prisoners in adjoining cells go crazy and scream. *You* would go crazy too, sooner than you think. You cannot help screaming when you're so miserable and helpless. You rot, and you die a long drawn-out death. It's the cruelest punishment ever devised."

"So, what do you want *me* to do?" asked Hippolyte, shifting his stance a little.

"Tomorrow morning, I want you to shave, ask for a clean prison uniform, comb your hair, and look as good as you can."

"Why should I have to go to all *that* trouble?" asked the unshaven count in a slightly hostile tone.

"Look here; listen to me. They make a ceremony out of the proceeding, including a constant drumroll to make the police and the military think they're attending a grand, important event in their careers. That's how shallow their minds are. If you purposely fail to look at the drums, people will center their attention completely on *you* because they will automatically aim their eyes on where you aim yours. Be smart; use that attention to your gaze to convince nearly everyone that *you* are the center of interest.

"From the moment you exit the back of the police wagon, I want you to hold your head high and look straight ahead like a sternly disciplined soldier. Under no circumstances are you to show any fear because there really is nothing to fear. And do not make any speeches! That's exactly what the bigwigs and the local prosecutors want you to do. Don't give them the satisfaction.

"Pay no attention to the riffraff who will be there. They're ignorant fools who've come to gawk at you, hoping to see you quivering with fear, screaming your innocence, and resisting the police. Let them know, without doubt, that you are the strong, courageous man you've always been and that you still *are* strong and courageous.

"My hunch is that you don't realize what a famous person you are these days. All of Europe knows about you but have never seen you. If you follow my advice, the people will *never* forget you. I want you to know that!

"All the newspapers in Europe will describe every little part of your behavior tomorrow morning—the expression on your face, your posture, and how you walk. I guarantee that the newspaper reporters will write up your courage for history. The public will respect you and be as impressed by your bravery as your family will. That is *my* advice. You can take it or leave it.

"I don't know if you're a religious man—maybe there's a heaven, maybe there's a hell—who knows? In any case, if a clergyman wants to follow you up the scaffold and whisper prayers, be polite and let him. It cannot hurt you. Actually, it may make many people form a permanent good image of you. The newspaper reporters will write it up that way. They would enjoy getting readers to imagine you as a handsome, God-fearing man. Word will get around, and lots of people will say, 'He wasn't as bad a man as I thought because now he has God on his side.'

"You may feel indifferent about religion; but that's none of my business. All I know is what route I would take if I were in your shoes. I would black out any fears right this moment and play an unexpected trick on the legal system that, I promise you, they will never forget."

"What kind of trick?" asked the intrigued, but suspicious, Hippolyte de Bocarmé.

"One day, those in the legal system will wake up and realize that the only value of emphasizing a guillotine is to frighten anyone who might give thought to committing a crime. The system is using this fear to spread the word that when they catch you, they will dispense the harshest possible sentence. That's thickheaded misinformation because a guillotine works so quickly and painlessly that it's a useless way to get even with those who commit the cruelest kinds of crimes.

"You can do a great thing for this country tomorrow, *one that will grant you a heroic place in Belgian history.* You are in a perfect position to hasten the day when the legal system wakes up and spreads the honest word that compared to suffering a living death in a prison, the guillotine is a box of candy.

"Remember, I have been a jailer for thirty years. I have had experience with a hell of a lot of poor, miserable human beings who have been in your place or have undergone inhumane imprisonment for years and years because of a regrettable mistake made a long time ago. For those men, life imprisonment is too cruel a punishment. Six months or a couple of years is enough punishment for most of them.

"Criminals who do the very worst things should be the lifers because the punishment ought to fit the crime. If the system wants to harshly punish a criminal who's committed an especially vicious crime, he should, without doubt, *be in prison for life.* There is no 'justice' in letting him off easy with a guillotine."

"Yeh, but I won't be alive to enjoy that day!" Hippolyte continued to look glum, but the jailer was ready to tell him more.

"I have to add a little. There's one more special cruelty about being a lifer that I haven't told you. There'll come a day when you are old, sick as hell and *truly* dying, but there won't be anyone there to comfort you, hold your hand, get you a cup of water because your mouth is dry, and tell you how much they love you for the things you did for them before you were arrested.

"Almost all of them will be dead or too old and sick to get there and be with you. If you have any little kids, they probably will not even know you are in prison because, when they were very young, the family was too ashamed to tell them.

"Do you *really* think that any jailer is suddenly going to turn into an angel and take care of you like a nurse? When you're too weak to get up and you crap your sheets, or soak them and your thin blanket with your piss, do you think jailers are going to run to clean you up, give you new bedclothes, a comfortable extra pillow, and a clean, warm blanket? You know better than that."

"Yeh. Most jailers are sons of bitches," mouthed the count.

So, stand up like the strong man you are, make your family and country proud of you; have an easy good-bye and an untroubled permanent sleep. The only angry and disappointed people will be the bigwigs in Brussels, who stupidly asked the jury to give you what they mistakenly thought was the worst possible revenge for whatever you did.

"Your case will make them eat their hearts out for the rest of their lives as the public learns, and begins to realize, that putting someone out of the way with the guillotine is a pleasant vacation compared to the living death of life imprisonment."

The thirty-two-year-old deranged count, who listened spellbound to the old man's every word, said nothing in return. Hippolyte de Bocarmé didn't know enough to say "thank you" when he should.

***

Obviously, the kind but wise jailer gave this advice to Hippolyte from safely outside the cell, beyond possible reach of his long arms and powerful hands. The old jailer did not trust Hippolyte, and he did withhold information from him. He did not tell him that he had followed every word of the long trial and was convinced, beyond doubt, that the count had murdered Gustave Fougnies, his brother-in-law, with unsurpassed cruelty.

The jailer knew that Hippolyte was a conscienceless psychopathic killer, unable to imagine the horror he's caused someone else because something in his brain doesn't function as it should. Yet these conscienceless psychopaths are often terrified when threatened with death.

All the nameless jailer wanted to do was combat the horrendous fear felt by a human being who, he firmly believed, had no business being free in society. He meant much of what he argued, but with respect to this particular prisoner, he believed that, when the guillotine permanently removed the Count de Bocarmé in the morning, society would be safer without this murderer, who was also a sexual deviant and pathological liar.

When it came to understanding emotions, the jailer had a heightened sense of empathy, meaning that he could sense the fear others felt, while Count de Bocarmé had no empathy at all, the hallmark of a conscienceless, psychopathic personality.

***

At the execution in the morning, storekeepers pulled their shades. A small number of rabble from surrounding villages and a few newspaper reporters gathered behind a roped-off area to watch Count Hippolyte Visart Count de Bocarmé emerge tall, and apparently composed, from the haunting prison vehicle, his wrists tightly tied behind him, as a muffled drumroll began.

He mounted the thirteen steps to the scaffold with his head held high. He walked with agility, gazed straight ahead, and lay prone at once. He placed his chin in a small indentation, which assured he was in the proper position for beheading. He did not turnto glimpse at the gleaming, slanted knife sixteen feet above until a few seconds later, when he lifted his head to tell Monsieur Willems, the executioner, that his wrists were too tightly tied to flex them; Willems immediately loosened them.

The count used the moment to observe his surroundings, replaced his chin and flexed his wrists, the signal that he was "ready." Instantaneously, the eight hundred pound-weighted blade, razor sharp, fell and severed his head from his body painlessly in two one-hundredths of a second. From his position, he had been unable to see a wire basket set to catch his detached head. Monsieur Willems had tawdrily decorated it with flowers.

The archbishop, intensely concerned with the fate of a soul, was oblivious to the ear-splitting crash of the knife when it reached its terminus, but not the multitude of pigeons that suddenly arose in a crowd from their roosts in all surrounding buildings, their wings loudly flapping.

The pigeons remained aloft for minutes, even as the city groundskeepers had begun to clean up the bloody mess. It would take laundresses almost as long to clean the blood splattered on the archbishop's starched surplice.

***

The next editions of European newspapers reported how fearlessly the Hippolyte Visart Count de Bocarmé, "a tall, attractive man," had met his death in a way that his "distinguished ancestors" would have approved. The reporters paid great credit to Archbishop Purcell of the United States for his unsurpassed ability to provide solace and comfort to the condemned man; for having imbued in him "the moral courage to meet with his God" and then prayed to Him to reward the condemned's unqualified penance with absolution that would cleanse his soul of sin. As predicted, many readers added their prayers for the Count de Bocarmé's forgiveness.

No one could report the old jailer's remarkable feat bracing a terrified, homicidal maniac with psychopathic personality disorder to meet death with seeming dispassion. It was impossible to publish anything about the creative man's persuasive influence; he had not told even his wife what he had engineered.

Judge Lyon, who sentenced Hippolyte as the legal code demanded, personally detested him. Yet, he was empathetic and compassionate; he knew that the "old jailer" had a reputation within the prison system for calming excessively frightened prisoners; he hoped the count might be induced to behave on the scaffold in a manner that would not distress his esteemed relatives.

The Visart family in Brussels knew that Hippolyte had already blemished their reputation, but after all, he was ill with a dementia that caused him to lack a conscience. In the last analysis, he was brave and God-fearing.

***

The *not guilty* verdict, which the jury delivered for his wife Countess Lydie Fougnies de Bocarmé, disconcerted much of the public, who had read only newspaper accounts of the trial's day-to-day progress and considered her at least as guilty as her husband. Unknown to them was that the jury and the count, along with his two lawyers, had covert access to testimony Lydie gave under oath to Judge Lyon in a perfectly legal, highly confidential [*in camera*] session. The count's lawyers chose not to refute her credible description of her despicable husband's cruel character and controlling, deranged personality. She pled that she had acted involuntarily under highly unusual circumstances. Lyon twice reminded the count's lawyers that they and their client had a fair chance to enter a rebuttal, but they twice refused to use the opportunity. The jury energetically favored Lydie's complete innocence.

The quick and painless execution of Hippolyte Visart, Count de Bocarmé, did not allow him time to think of his freed wife. That was a blessing. He would not have been pleased to know how she was currently disporting herself.

Part One

CHAPTER 1

The Essay

In the week before the widely and eagerly anticipated trial of the Count and Countess de Bocarmé (which would begin May 27, 1851), the justice department accused each defendant of premeditated murder of Gustave Fougnies, the countess's younger brother. Widely distributed posters entitled "Act of Accusation" summarized the charges against the couple. As details of the planning and enactment of the murder leaked, public opinion ran strongly against both of the accused perpetrators, who faced the death penalty, if found guilty as charged.

Tickets for admission to the trial were nearly impossible to obtain. A few seats were kept open for a handful of those who, during the night, slept on the sidewalk close to the courthouse entrance. All other seats were occupied either by political figures, office assistants, and their friends. The inadequate number of seats did not prevent the daily accumulation before the courthouse entry of large, unruly crowds that spilled out and blocked the street.

***

During this same time, an essay describing Hippolyte's "Early Life" appeared in one of Mons' popular newspapers. Four other newspapers had refused to publish the piece, even if paid to print it. The fifth agreed, for a substantial sum, to print it, keep the sum confidential, and omit mentioning that it was, in fact, an advertisement. The author was Ida Chasteler de Bocarmé, Hippolyte's mother.

She told of a sick, troubled child and adolescent whose conduct was, at very least, perversely antisocial. How much of her description was false, incomplete, exaggerated, or embellished was impossible to say. Ida was shrewd. She made public her son's deficiencies, adding his iconoclastic view of religion, possibly trying to induce a significant number of the populace to believe that he was just a badly neglected child and a mixed-up person, one who ought to be pitied not censured. Unless *all* of the *jurymen* chosen from the populace pitied her son, a guillotine would censure him, and she was aware of that. Motherly love is nearly limitless in the extent to which it will go to help an endangered child.

Ida's Advertisement, for which she paid an unknown sum to an unnamed newspaper, read:

Hippolyte de Bocarmé is a count because in the previous century during an uprising against the Dutch Republic, Louis-François Visart, a General of the revolutionary Spanish-Hungarian army was honored with the hereditary title of count. The title passed to his cousin Julien Visart de Bocarmé, whom I married. I am Marchioness Ida Chasteler de Bocarmé niece of a general who fought bravely on the Spanish and Austrian sides, during the series of complex battles that eventually freed our nation from Dutch control.

Count Hippolyte de Bocarmé was our first child and only son. Julien was in Belgium's diplomatic service; and in 1819, he received orders to go to Java to represent Belgium in its East Indies colony, whose largest island was Java, where its capital lay. I underwent a month-long, hair-raising passage to Java on an old sailing ship L'Eurinus Marinus. It made little headway during a violent three-week storm it encountered at the Cape of Good Hope.

Unfortunately, I was pregnant with Hippolyte and found the passage to Java uncomfortable. I was terribly ill with seasickness, especially during the storm. Count Alfred Hippolyte Visart de Bocarmé was born soon after the ship made port.

Hippolyte was a sickly child from birth. He cried incessantly when awake. Native Javanese women had to try to sooth him because I proceeded to have more children—three girls—in quick succession.

At age seven, he developed a febrile illness with diarrhea, a sickness endemic to the tropics that forced me to return to Europe with him and his three sisters. In Belgium, we lived in the city of Tournai. Hippolyte's health improved, but he refused to play with his siblings or other children.

He remained motionless on the floor for lengthy periods and refused to utter more than a few words. He displayed temper tantrums if asked to do anything he wished not to do, tumbling to the floor and holding his breath long enough to become slightly blue until he briefly lost consciousness. [4]

He refused to go to school and did not learn to read or write. I was at my wit's end, when Julien unexpectedly finished his term of duty and returned to Tournai. Although gruff and unsympathetic as always, he saw that his son needed an elementary education. He sent him to a school where his classmates were younger but normal children. Hippolyte allegedly behaved well and tried hard for eighteen months to learn to read and write. The teachers wrote me that he had made progress in reading but failed to learn to write. Simple arithmetic was his favorite subject; they claimed that he was moderately good at it. In demeanor, however, he remained "distant and taciturn." They wrote that other children tried at times to torment him physically, but invariably regretted it because he fought back fearlessly and effectively.

***

---

[4] Note that breath holding and losing consciousness is common in strong-willed normal children as well. Perhaps Ida did not know this.

Count Julien retired at age fifty. He was well to do because of good investments and a government pension. This gave me a sense of security, but I had no idea that he found the company of people in his social circle in Tournai "monotonously dull." He found everyone, including me, "boring." One day, without prior discussion, Count Julien told me of his intention to leave Belgium, to immigrate to the United States of America as soon as possible, and to take thirteen-year-old Hippolyte with him.

I refused to follow him, as he undoubtedly expected. He announced that he had acquired well more than two thousand acres in Arkansas County in southeast Arkansas. I certainly would not accompany them. Imagine living in so primitive and poorly populated a place.

I remained in Tournai with my daughters. My financial situation immediately deteriorated because he left me only his pension. His investment portfolio was much larger. He kept all of it for himself.

Count Julien had to find someone to build a rustic house for him because I never knew him to use his fingers for any purpose except to shake East Indian hands. The nearest town was faraway DeWitt, the capital of Arkansas County. It contains the only post office, through which Julien and I exchanged rare letters.

He learned to cultivate tobacco on the rich land between the Arkansas and White Rivers, while Hippolyte occupied himself for more than three years almost exclusively with hunting. He became proficient with a bow and arrow, and then his father gave him one of his rifles. However, his father never gave him love, education, or religion.

Hippolyte mingled with indigenous people and learned their ways, including a love for swift horses. He became friendly with young men of three tribes which occupied the area between the rivers. It was their homeland as well. The Caddo Tribe comprised sedentary farmers who grew beans, corn, squash, and tobacco and raised sheep. The other two tribes were less domesticated hunters. My son's association with natives provided his first contact with tobacco cultivation, as well as the making of cigars. He enjoyed growing tobacco and smoking it.

Hippolyte was especially intrigued by the Caddo use of a mucoid tobacco extract smeared on the tips of arrows. They caused almost sudden death to wolves that attacked the Caddo sheep. The wolves quickly fell to the ground, had convulsive spasms, and died. The phenomenon left a deep impression on Hippolyte.

Hippolyte spent too little time with his father, who was preoccupied with learning to cultivate tobacco. As a result, Hippolyte grew to be too independent and too self-concerned, with little or no thought about the welfare of other human beings unless he suspected hostility toward him.

His sole interests were his own few needs. He carried a rifle to hunt wild animals for food, a knife to skin and eviscerate them, and matches to light fires for roasting their flesh. There was too little oversight for a boy of fourteen.

A knapsack held ammunition, blankets, and miscellany. With these provisions, Hippolyte was able to wander from his father's house for a week or more, communing with nature and observing animal life, as he trod on the thick grass of Arkansas's fertile prairie. Now and again, he sighted a distant native hunting game with bow and arrow.

I can say with reasonable assurance that the cause of Hippolyte's predilection for guile, and a tendency to question the motives of others, was his constant need to be on guard to defend himself from threatening forces, whether dangerous animals or hostile natives. That young man grew so strong that he once killed a ferocious jaguar with his bare hands.

During his fourth year in Arkansas, Julien wrote that Hippolyte had developed an illness with daily fever. After "some months," it had debilitated him. It took his father that long a time to become concerned enough to send him back to Europe for me to care for him. I knew that Julien was not stupid. I knew also that he was self-centered and thoughtless about the welfare of others, including his own children. Those daily fevers had to have affected my son's mind.

The wealthy Count Julien gave his ailing son just enough money to pay for a one-way voyage to Europe. He had no emergency funds. Perhaps Julien thought anything more than the minimum might end up in my pocket to pay for additional medical care in Belgium.

Hippolyte had to hook a free ride on a grain barge sailing south on the White River that empties into the Mississippi River where Arkansas borders Louisiana. The Mississippi River ends in the busy port of New Orleans, where he boarded a ship that took him across the Atlantic to Le Havre, a three- to four-week sail. From Le Havre, he found his way by newly built railroads back to me in Tournai.

I was alarmed when I saw my son. He was so thin that I thought he might be close to death. The doctor came and emphasized that he needed as much good food as possible.

He acted primitively, with very little speech and with a severely limited vocabulary. "I'm hungry," he'd bellow. "I'm cold." And I'd fetch him a blanket and some food. Never did he thank me.

At times, he trembled and sobbed but never complained. When he recovered his physical health, a fair amount of vocabulary also returned. It was apparent that he was unable to read. Although usually silent, he would occasionally blurt remarks that made me wonder about his sanity.

He literally stank. He refused to bathe and would not change any of his garments. When I told him it was essential to bathe and wear clean clothing, he was reluctant to obey, arguing that his clothes were not torn and he smelled no worse than a stableman.

I saw him slowly recover his physical health, but still he could not read well. This observation so unnerved me that I thought I needed spiritual guidance. I planned to attend Mass the following morning and take Hippolyte with me. I mentioned the plan to him and was overwhelmed by his response.

His response was remarkably clear and complex, compared to anything he had had to say since his return home to Tournai.

I was appalled by what I heard. I was astonished to hear him say loudly and bluntly, "I don't give a damn about God. Only if someone could prove the existence of God by mathematical means would I become a believer!"

I cannot find the words to describe how sick his language and comments made me.

He would argue frequently with me about the impossibility of the existence of an omnipotent, merciful, and loving God, often repeating that only a hateful power would allow disease and natural disasters to take the lives of innocent people.

"Why would a loving God allow sickness, starvation, earthquakes, hurricanes, and tornadoes, if he had the power to prevent them?" he would demand of me.

When I failed to provide a satisfactory answer, he would tell me, "I would have to throw away everything that makes sense, if I had to believe in your God. Your God is superstitious. I will not go to any superstitious Mass."

Comments like these frustrated and infuriated me because I had no rational way to reply. I learned to avoid any discussion of God or religion with my son. But, I wondered how he learned these lines and could express his arguments with verbal ease, as if memorized by rote. Frankly, I wouldn't trust his father Count Julien. He would often say awful things about religion when he had his government job. But he was careful never to express them even in the presence of close friends.

***

Hippolyte was seventeen years old when I sent him off to a boarding school in Lille, where he behaved himself, conscientiously trying to improve his speaking and writing skills. He learned to read but poorly. He showed interest in arithmetic and technical subjects but made almost no progress learning to write.

He was nineteen when he left the school at Lille. Shortly after that, I moved with him to Germany, where I tried to encourage a young woman of my acquaintance to marry him, thinking she might provide a healthy, continuing educational influence. The young woman, who knew from the outset what I had in mind, let me know after a few weeks that she could never marry anyone as "bizarre" as Hippolyte. I tried to find out what she meant by "bizarre," but she was bashful and reluctant to say very much.[5]

---

[5] It would be of interest to know if he was sexually aggressive toward her. However, Ida would likely have omitted this useful information. Note that she omitted saying whether he spoke German and is vague about his length of stay in Germany.

Frustrated by the failure of that project, I sent him to live with his cynical grandfather at his Chateau de Bitremont in Bury, a rural suburb of the small city of Peruwelz. All who knew the old man understood that he was, at least, a difficult person. A few people considered him detestable. He purposely lived alone, and at a distance from his children, because he could not put up with them and none of them could stand being around him. I feared that he would pick on Hippolyte and make his life miserable, but I truly had no other choice.

Grandfather employed fifteen gardeners to cultivate flowers, vegetables, and tobacco on his large estate, where he kept several domestic helpers and a valet. He also had horses, which he stabled. His relations with his employees were no better than with his children; he was forever finding fault with their work, whether it was growing vegetables or doing house-cleaning jobs.

A back door led from the chateau to a large barn that housed the horses needed to pull plows. Horses need a good deal of care, but grandfather was never pleased with the care the stableman took in washing them down. He also accused him of feeding them too many oats, whereupon he would rail about the high price of oats. He found some fault with each of his employees.

Grandfather used one of the walls of the barn to hang certain tobacco leaves. He chose them from his large annual crop. His purpose was to protect them from frost during winter nights. He would use these selected leaves in the spring, to make his favorite pipe-smoking tobacco. All of his gardeners and domestic help had a feeling of relief when grandfather was fully engaged in growing tobacco because he paid less attention to them.

23

Although raising a large tobacco crop needed no great skill, it did require oversight in sowing the seeds and constant care of the developing plants. Hippolyte had seen his father grow tobacco in Arkansas, but his grandfather became his real teacher. As long as grandfather had fifteen strong men acting as gardeners, he was free to grow tobacco year after year, because there was so much fertile land in the fields surrounding the Chateau de Bitremont.[6]

***

Parenthetically, in a discussion of tobacco cultivation, Count Julien comes naturally to mind, although he communicated very little with his son because Hippolyte was unable to write and could read only poorly. There is a salient reason to think of Julien. His decision to emigrate from Belgium to live alone in a foreign country has the mark of an eccentric decision. Available Arkansas County Records list him as one of the "early newcomers to Arkansas County (1830)."

---

[6] The biggest problem facing farmers who grew tobacco was the length of time it takes to do so. Tobacco farmers planted the seeds as early in the year as possible after the frost had disappeared. In Grandfather's and Hippolyte's part of the world, March planting would yield a harvested crop in early November.

Between sowing and harvesting, there is need for a moderate amount of hard work and careful attention. To protect seedlings from unexpected chills, the farmer covered them before transplanting them to mounds of soil. As the plants grew, it was necessary to remove any worms. Using a finger to pull them off was simple. It was important to excise the tops of plants to prevent their using energy to grow flowers. It was necessary to crop leaves growing too close to the ground, and everyone hoped for occasional rain because water was essential. Eventually, the plants grew to seven feet or more. Fortunately, the selected leathery leaves held up well when protected from bitter cold.

A single word, "mysterious," describes him in the records, which give his year of death as 1850.

Some psychiatrists are inclined to think that "a parent of a psychopath like Hippolyte is not uncommonly a person with an eccentric personality." The source cannot speak for all of his colleagues, nor does he know the inclination's source. Nevertheless, a gratuitous and serious comment by an expert seems germane.

***

Curing handpicked, green tobacco leaves took several months. From Hippolyte's later imitation of this practice, we know that Grandfather watched patiently as those he selected hung in the barn, slowly losing their immature aroma and darkening to a special hue. We know, too that after carefully removing the midrib of each leaf, he put the soft leaves in a hand-operated meat grinder, slowly mixing them with honey and ground cinnamon. When the resulting tobacco grounds had dried to the degree of dampness he wanted, he stored them in glass jars, from which he would remove small quantities to pack his pipes for smoking. From the same source, we know how Grandfather treated the ground tobacco. Grandfather's way of preparing smoking tobacco was extremely deliberate. Few people, not even Hippolyte, shared the pleasure of joining the old man when he smoked his authentic blend. Reclining in an overstuffed chair by a fireplace, the old curmudgeon inhaled the aromatic fumes in solitude, a faint smile and half-closed eyes signaling deep satisfaction. Smoking seemed to be the only real pleasure available to the old misanthrope. (After Grandfather's death, Hippolyte told guests that *he* devised the process.)

Grandfather lived for two years, providing Hippolyte with room and board and a chance to learn much about tobacco that his mother was unable to include in "The Essay."

***

Hippolyte's mother wrote:

I know that there was no warm greeting, not even a smile on Grandfather's part when he met his grandson Hippolyte. Aside from relegating him to the most uncomfortable bedroom available, Grandfather made no effort to speak with the young man. His room was so hot and humid in the summer and so cold in the winter that even the valet had refused to occupy it. Yet my son often remained there, uncomplaining and silent, for hours at a time, seeing his grandfather only at meals.

I learned that Hippolyte ate so little that his grandfather accused him of wasting money by wasting food. However, one redeeming feature to the arrangement was its freeing Hippolyte to occupy himself in gardening. He had his own ideas about how best to cultivate plants, and he enjoyed being out-of-doors in the countryside working the land.

Hippolyte spent a lot of time improving his reading ability, but he never learned to write better than a scribble. He confined his reading to books about horticulture. Remembrance of experiences when he smoked cigars with natives when he was fifteen led to inquisitiveness about varieties of tobacco, a subject with which he became familiar. He found dusty volumes of books about horticulture in the columned living room of the Chateau de Bitremont. Grandfather had bought them years before, but he never read them. He forgot he owned them.

The sole topic his cranky grandfather would discuss with Hippolyte was tobacco cultivation, an opportunity for Hippolyte to learn as much as he could about it, and which he enjoyed discussing. Grandfather was impressed with his grandson's knowledge of the crop in which he had invested his time and money for many years. He was always willing and eager to listen whenever Hippolyte shared information he had just read in the old horticulture books that he forgot he owned. Hippolyte improved his reading ability in the process.

Grandfather flattered himself as a talented mentor, pleased that his grandson enjoyed learning about tobacco, the only substantial matter they discussed at dinner. When he died two years later, he left the chateau to me, and I purposely retained the fifteen gardeners as a way to keep Hippolyte usefully occupied.

***

Unable to stay permanently at Bury, and not wanting to leave my son alone in the large mansion because he couldn't find his way in this world, I again sought to find Hippolyte a wife. I found two possibilities—one rich, the other poor but both distinguished by their education and their piety. Both refused to marry Hippolyte.

CHAPTER 2

Joseph Fougnies and Lydie Fougnies

Joseph Fougnies's children were two—Lydie (named after her grandmother and her mother) was born in 1818, in Peruwelz. Her younger brother, Gustave, was born in 1821.

In the city center of Mons, Joseph opened a small grocery store in an easily available, prominent location. His extremely hard work and fair pricing for good produce drew an increasing clientele. He added a butcher shop, increasing both clientele and income. His store, where he worked long hours, became a remarkably remunerative business.

Joseph expected to remain in Mons for the remainder of his life, but the owner of a chain of large grocery stores in other Belgian cities was well aware of the store's present worth and, more importantly, its future value. He offered Joseph a surprisingly large sum for his business. The two men bargained in a friendly way, and Joseph agreed to accept his final grand offer. He lived modestly while he shrewdly invested most of the money, including the sum his wife's wealthy father had given them when they married. He invested the greater part of it in fast-growing French equities and government bonds.

It would seem that a large portion of the money must have belonged to his wife, the former Lydie Tabary. It happens that, when she abandoned him and her children, she again became a French citizen. Therefore, her suit for half of his quickly growing fortune was drawn out for several years, and her unexpected death invalidated her suit.

Joseph Fougnies became the busy manager of a fast-growing financial portfolio. He attributed his initial success to good luck. Eventually, he transferred most of the holdings to safer French government bonds.

When he had enough reliable and continuously replenishing income, he returned to Peruwelz and occupied a large apartment in an unusually large brick building belonging to his brother, the real estate tycoon of Peruwelz. The building contained three identical large apartments. Each would better be described as a large home occupying as much floor space as one would expect to have in a three-story house. His brother occupied one of the other "apartments," and the third was rented to an unknown person with a large family. The individual entry door and roominess of the living area made it an ideal place to live and raise children, but it required M. Fougnies's employing full-time home helpers and a cook. He could easily afford it.

Perhaps the size of her new home and fear that she would be unable to manage it overwhelmed M. Fougnies's wife, a woman who, sad to say, was probably correct. She did not have the ability to oversee a cook and kitchen and five other full-time household employees.

Her husband, Joseph, was a quiet man of few words, who was forced to raise his voice from time to time because she could not do the arithmetic to help him keep track of simple household expenses. The dispirited, depressed woman chose one day, without notice, to leave her husband and children, to return to live with her family in France.

***

M. Fougnies, as he was now known, loved his two children. The elder, Lydie, had dark hair and blue eyes and was energetic and friendly, with a reputation as a supremely good student. Her father, sensibly generous to his children's needs, sent her to board in private grammar, junior high, and high schools in Tournai, rather than attend neighborhood schools in Peruwelz. Lydie took her scholastic work seriously but maintained a pleasant demeanor. A grammar school principal, who recognized that she was exceptionally bright, allowed her to skip the fourth grade.

Beyond high school, her education continued at the esteemed, eighty-year-old Belgium College, also located in Tournai. The college was a substantially endowed institution for young women able to obtain high grades on a competitive entrance examination. The fee for permission to take the examination and the high cost of tuition with room and board gave the college a reputation as an educational institution for daughters of the comfortably wealthy and the rich. Its costs were effective barriers to entry for most of Belgium's middle-class, public high school graduates.

Lydie, then, was a rare middle-class student because kind members of the admissions committee knew a good deal about her from their friends who taught at the private elementary schools she attended in Tournai.

Young women from other countries formed a disproportionately large segment of the student body. Most of them had attended private high schools with demanding standards. In choosing a roommate for Lydie, the administration purposely chose an open-minded young woman from Italy from an open-minded upper middle-class family. The chair of admissions had had an opportunity to meet her and her parents, who were temporarily residing in Belgium. At the well-run institution, even the small secretarial staff was alerted to be protective of the bright youngster from nearby Peruwelz.

Lydie, therefore, received a degree of education and culture that few European women enjoyed in the nineteenth century. The curriculum was demanding, the instruction excellent. The bright young woman worked hard and graduated with highest honors in English and History of the English Language. The faculty, who universally liked her, voted for Lydie to receive the Perfect Student Award when she graduated.

Lydie's single, unusual habit while attending college was to buy large quantities of candy, which she disbursed freely to her classmates.

She was well able to pay for the candy, and the significance of her generosity may become evident when we read about her adult life. Her purpose was clearly to ingratiate herself with fellow students in the only way she knew how. She had experienced this materialistic form of friendliness and generosity from her well-to-do, laconic father.

Lydie's habit seemed necessary to her because nearly all of her college classmates came from wealthy aristocracy, but Lydie's provenance was middle class. The public deemed the middle class lower in social status than the nation's small aristocracy, regardless of wealth. This stiff social classification existed in most western European nations, whether or not their political structure claimed it to be democratic. Belgium, for example, was a "democratic kingdom." Classification based on birth was especially strong in England, where more than a residue of it exists to this day.

Lydie shared her dormitory room at Belgium College with Angelica Bregosi, a young woman from Italy who was mature for her age, strikingly attractive, and wore a nearly constant smile. Angelica and her parents had come to Brussels for an extended period. Her father, Antonio, wanted to study Belgian business practices, although his specific purpose was unclear. Signore and Signora Bregosi occupied an apartment in Brussels and sent their only child, Angelica, to the highly recommended Belgium College. Angelica became Lydie's closest friend.

Vanessa Buckingham, a sociable, well-mannered English girl a year older than either Lydie or Angelica, occupied an adjacent dormitory room. Vanessa's permanent home was Chipping Camden, in the lovely Cotswold country west of London. Her father owned a large machine tool manufacturing company in the outskirts of nearby Evesham. Vanessa was the only daughter and younger child of Mr. and Mrs. Thomas Buckingham, who were living temporarily in Liège, Belgium's major manufacturing center and home of a world-respected university. He was assisting in setting up a new company for the manufacture of machine tools.

Angelica stimulated Lydie's interest in music, which later became essential to her mental health. Vanessa assisted both Lydie and Angelica in their study of English and the history of the English language. When the three completed the demanding curriculum at the college, they returned to their homes. Lydie had the least distance to travel; she returned to live in provincial Peruwelz nine miles distant. The young women missed one another's company and remained in contact thereafter by exchanging letters. They knew each other well enough to share most details of their personal lives. Lydie and Angelica were especially close.

While at school, Lydie attended classes in fictional writing. The freedom to use one's imagination to hatch a plot or tell a good story and to introduce and maneuver characters, whose varied backgrounds, experiences, and speech interweave and comprise an interesting tale, seized her attention. She found an obscure English novel entitled *The Tale of Adeline Kelney* or *Memories of a Young Woman* and began to try her hand at fictional writing before she graduated. With generous help from Vanessa, Lydie diligently translated and radically modified the story to produce a new fictional book that she mailed to a reputable Parisian publishing house. The editors read it and were initially inclined to publish it. After a second read, they decided that it was a little too amateurish to print. The editor in chief and owner of the company was kind enough to return the manuscript with a most encouraging letter. No other publishing house than his was willing to give it the same attention, which disappointed Joseph Fougnies. He questioned the taste of Parisians.

Lydie sent the manuscript to the Society of Arts and Letters of Hainaut Province. A commission reported favorably on it, noting especially that so young an author wrote with such maturity. When they complimented her and offered editorial advice, which she incorporated, Joseph Fougnies suddenly forgot the Parisian affront and had the book sent to a publisher in Lille, who wanted to print it. Sadly, its publication never materialized because of a squabble over ownership of its copyright. A publisher in Brussels claimed to have read the book before the editor in Lille. The high cost of litigation made printing impractical.

The literary world of Hainaut generously offered Lydie heady wine of encouragement, for the kind letter the society sent to her encouraged her to try again. She began writing an entirely new novel, but for reasons unknown, she never polished it. Entitled *The Barber of Bernan County*, it got no farther than her desk drawer, where it joined a later manuscript of her memoirs. Both are lost.

***

Lydie was good looking and had a fine feminine figure. She had adequate money to buy tasteful clothes that fit her figure well, and she was usually well poised. She had an undeserved reputation in Peruwelz as a coquette who tantalized adolescent boys to the point where they secretly harbored sexual fantasies about her. She was wholly unaware of this, but she did, at times, try kindly to urge younger people to use proper grammar. Lydie was a bit of a pedant but was always pleasant. She was inordinately idealistic and sincerely wanted to help those who had not had the educational advantages she had. This idealistic pedantry, as we shall discover, would trouble her life.

It is worth emphasizing that Lydie was, in no way, an overbearing, intellectual show-off. She was much too mature and worldly to act that way. She knew that she had had the good fortune to have a fine education, and she had the good sense and discipline to make full use of it. Her education taught her to think independently and rationally.

In any society, there are those with narrow minds who resent others who think independently and misconstrue their conflicting views as unjustified, a violation or threat to their own strongly ingrained beliefs. These bigots can be dangerous, if given a little power. The truth is that Lydie, although an independent thinker, kept "controversial thoughts" to herself. She was actually thin-skinned and cared deeply what others thought of her. If others found her distant, it may have been her intention to fend them off lest they get too close. She was a very private person.

To escape into privacy, Lydie relished time alone, reading good books, writing two of them, and exchanging letters with people in the literary world and her dispersed college friends. In these periods of solitude, her curiosity also roamed to an interest in art history and the origins of eighteenth- and nineteenth-century music, which she enjoyed at rare musicales in Tournai. She especially enjoyed Haydn and early Beethoven symphonies and sonatas. Lydie investigated music history with fascination. Angelica had introduced her to the sweet melodies of operatic refrains from Italy (*La traviata* was a good example). Her accumulation of information about musical history urged her frequent attendance at musicales and other intellectual events in Mons, Ghent, and Bruges.

There is every reason to conceive of Lydie Fougnies as a highly intelligent, learned young woman, although few realized that she was neurotically insecure because of her middle-class origins. Stratification by social class seriously tormented her.

***

Her years of attendance at good schools had been a maturing experience. She met a mix of young women from educated families. Their views added to and broadened multiple frames of reference. She became aware of cultural differences that undoubtedly excited her interest in the structure of novels whose production required worldliness and imagination, as well as discipline. Lydie took seriously advice from several literary people beyond Peruwelz in connection with the one book she was nearly able to publish.

She had the ability to listen carefully and critically to what others talked about. Paradoxically, this ability saddened her because the population of Peruwelz with whom she mixed during the year after she graduated from college seemed bereft of interesting people in her age group. Nevertheless, as an attractive young woman with a reputation for worldliness, the upper middle-class social set of little Peruwelz warmly accepted Lydie into its ranks. Within these ranks, she sought to find male companions with whom she felt at ease but never found one. The contemplative young woman realized that she would be happier living elsewhere.

In truth, Lydie was glad to have a well-to-do father. In contemplating her future life, she liked to suppose that she would continue to enjoy his financial support. It would provide ways and means to add to her fund of knowledge and stay above the prevailing level of worldliness she found in Peruwelz. She gave thought to working hard to become a respected author of novels. In any case, she decided never to live out her life in Peruwelz. It was clear that she wanted intellectually uplifting friends, companions and perhaps lovers.

When she was little, her father chanced to instill in her a cockeyed concept of upward mobility. He would readily interrupt his usual laconic mood to remind anyone who would listen, that toward the end of the French Revolution, his father had bought a section of land known as Wiers, near Peruwelz, within which are the villages of Garenne and Bois. He inherited that land and itched for the day when officialdom would name him Baron du Bois. In the meantime, he often referred to himself, unofficially, by that title. Lydie understood, even as a child that he was reaching: grocers and butchers were rarely "titled." Thus did Lydie learn about titles. Trouble was, although raised as an aristocrat, she was still "middle class" and seemed destined to remain at that level for life, unless she shone outstandingly in some scholarly pursuit.

***

Lydie came home on some weekends and never heard her father scold her mother out of impatience. She did know that her mother was incapable of doing elementary arithmetic and that her father had been patiently tutoring her mother for many years. She did not know that he'd finally lost some of his patience and chided his wife.

A likely scenario is that Joseph Fougnies was a guileless, unsophisticated high school graduate. Lacking social pretensions, he wanted a simple, unpretentious wife but forgot to test her skill in simple arithmetic. His prospective wife's father and mother, who knew her deficiencies better, were delighted that a sober young man, ambitious and hard-working, asked permission to marry her—so pleased were they that they showered money and valuables on the couple.

Lydie's mother later sued her husband for half of his fortune. Because she had hastily renewed her French citizenship, her case lingered in neglected piles of legal documents for four years, when she fell ill and died. The suit died with her.

CHAPTER 3

Gustave Fougnies

Gustave was born three years after his sister, Lydie. As he grew, he never sensed Lydie's displaying any special warmth for him. Gustave was bright and sensitive, and he thought that Lydie might be ashamed to let the world know that her sibling had only one leg and used crutches. He was wrong about that. She reeked of empathy and kindness, if you got close enough to her.

The quiet boy thought Lydie was too concerned with what people thought of her. Also, he thought that the criteria she used to evaluate others were too rigorous. He imagined that Lydie was, for an unknown reason, aloof—unable to imagine herself in the place of less fortunate others or to feel sorry for them.

Gustave's evaluation of his sister was wrong. She was, after all, three years older and, for the greater part of his early life, she had a full-time distant world of her own at college with other engaging girls and young women her age.

However, one can understand the feelings of a homebound, lonely, preadolescent youngster living in an age when there was no telephone to invite a school friend to come over to play a game of checkers and who had no radio with which to listen to serial dramas or the news.

It was easy for him to have confused inattentiveness with lack of empathy in his sister, a bright young woman who had her own exciting life, given to learning and exchanging ideas with a small number of contemporaries. For much of her brother's life from age twelve through sixteen, Lydie lived primarily at school. She was home only on occasional weekends.

***

37

More to the point, Gustave had his very special problem. While he was a normal infant at birth, he had a serious misfortune during his infancy. The wheel of a heavy, horse-drawn wagon ran over his leg and fractured his right thighbone. The fracture was severe; a sharp segment of broken bone extruded through the skin. Street dirt, including particles of manure, dirtied the bone, and the wound became chronically inflamed. A surgeon had rinsed the bone and wound well but could do no more than wait, patiently hoping that any wound inflammation would clear up spontaneously and that the fracture would heal. Gustave's painful, disabling illness naturally affected the quality of his life. He became a chronic invalid. When he was a small child, a servant pushed him around the town as he lay in a carriage. It was a way for him to breathe fresh air and have exposure to sunlight. Sympathetic passersby thought it a pitiful sight.

Medical doctors were leery of the surgical belief, for in that era, medical doctors were captives of a prevailing opinion that chronic inflammation will inevitably cause death by causing other organs to deteriorate. Not surprisingly, the youngster became frightened and sad. (Bacterial *infection* was unknown in 1837).

Walking was agonizing, but he forced himself to do it. His father made it possible for him to attend eight grades of a local elementary and middle school. He hired a man to push his son there on a reclining carriage. He tried to walk a little, but doing so was painful. The boy became increasingly self-conscious about his awkward gait because it drew embarrassing attention to him. He was, incidentally, the most talented pupil in each of his eight grades.

While the common folk in Peruwelz were sympathetic and spoke kindly to him, Gustave tended to avoid carriage trips into the city center after he finished the eighth grade, when he was eleven (1832). Overcome by introspection, pain, and embarrassment, he elected not to enter high school.

Getting up from a bed or chair and getting back into them were excruciatingly painful. Nevertheless, he forced himself to rise each morning and each afternoon for breakfast and lunch and to sit in a chair to read newspapers and an occasional simple book. He was a lonesome, bright teenager with little to look forward to except occasional visits to his home by school friends. He wished they would visit more often. He felt isolated and became introspective.

Complicating his dismal outlook on life was his father's benign arthritic limp. It exacerbated his self-consciousness about his own infirmity. His father did what he could to lessen his son's suffering, even arranging for doctors from distant Paris to help, but to no avail.

***

Gustave was also aware of his mother's unhappiness. He witnessed his father gently admonish his mother now and again. He was twelve when his mother left their home to return to her family in Cambrai, in France, although he did not know why she left. She was demoralized because after years of her patient husband's sympathetic tutoring, she still was unable to do the elementary addition and subtraction necessary to keep track of household expenses.

Gustave shed tears but noticed that his sister, Lydie, who was a very young fifteen-year-old and had entered Belgium College two days before her mother left, did not, three weeks later, manifest signs of emotion. This surprised twelve-year-old Gustave. Young women at fifteen are not fully matured socially, but they usually know that deeply felt emotions need not be accompanied by visible body language such as crying or accusing the mother of having deserted her children.

Without full knowledge of why his mother left, he irrationally likened Lydie's lack of tears to her lack of response to the sharp, fleeting pains he felt at the sight of his unhealed fracture when he walked a few steps without crutches. He sometimes screeched with brief, sudden pain and felt that Lydie paid no attention. He considered her uncaring, although these sharp pains were common. They came

39

and went suddenly when she was studying. She heard him shriek, looked up, and saw him getting back onto his bed, heard no more sound of discomfort, and went on studying. She had heard these brief shrieks often enough to know that they were fleeting. The first few times she heard his yell, she'd rushed to help, but when she reached him, the pain had always disappeared.

CHAPTER 4

Gustave's Second Injury

In the summer of 1837 when Gustave turned sixteen, his father arranged for him to have a vacation in the countryside near Leuze, not far from Peruwelz. Joseph Fougnies may not have warmed the cockles of the hearts of some denizens of Peruwelz who envied his unexpected financial success, but he did love both his children dearly. Gustave was deeply touched when his father presented him with a pony, apparently trained and gentle.

With his father watching, Gustave had the good sense to speak softly and warmly to the pony, pat his nose gently, and offer him oats with the flat of his hand. After ten minutes, Gustave smiled broadly, placed his one good leg in a stirrup, and raised himself to the saddle. But the animal reared and threw him to the ground. It was a serious fall because, unluckily, his bad leg struck a small outcrop of rock where his old lesion was located.

At first, medical doctors believed him to be incurably infirmed, but his surgeon in Peruwelz disagreed. It would be possible to amputate the extremity at mid-thigh level above the old fracture, and hope for the best. At least, there would be no inflamed (infected) fracture to deal with. Moreover, chloroform anesthesia was now available at the hospital in nearby Vieux-Conde, in France.

The surgery went well, but slight postoperative inflammation appeared in the new stump a few days later. The medical doctors' opinion was that it was a new inflammation (infection)which would become chronic. They still believed dogma that chronic inflammation anywhere in the body would inevitably cause other organs to dysfunction.

Gustave's saddened father had no choice but to believe them. Dr. Semel in Peruwelz and Dr. Lambris in Tournai, medical doctors, shared the same view on this matter. It was an era when medical doctors were thought to be intellectuals of the profession. Surgeons were merely technicians.

As if the prognosis were not enough to cause Gustave to be frightened, the doctors ordered the sixteen-year-old to abstain from wine or beer. Gustave had just begun to sample varieties of both, which he drank in small amounts, and found that they relaxed him and relieved his anxiety. He was never a heavy drinker of alcoholic beverages, but he enjoyed finding, collecting, and tasting beers and wines from different breweries and wineries in Belgium, an epicurism he adopted independently. He was not, after all, short of money. His spending money was generous.

Remarkably, he soon sensed improvement in his stump, accompanied by a general feeling of better health, which helped his disposition, too. He did not want to be ill and pitied. A healthy Gustave had a gentle disposition, which made him likeable. As he continued to feel better, he dared to leave the house on crutches. It seems that, this time, the surgeons were right.

When Gustave met people on his short walks, he felt more at ease speaking with those from the working class. He spoke the language of the common people, whose knowledge of the outside world was simple, and these folk were generally disposed to being decent to him.

Although he never knew that he had any artistic talent, Gustave began spending entire days drawing and painting landscapes and flowers. He asked for carriage rides to specific locations, to sketch outlines of wild flowers that he later copied to wooden panels and painted.

Gustave had practical sense, too. He realized that, although his long illness had prevented him from continuing his education, he was not yet seventeen. He was young and curious enough to want to delve into high school studies. His father agreed and arranged for tutors from Tournai to visit him each week, bring books, and assign lessons.

A serious student, Gustave enjoyed mathematics through trigonometry, studied French grammar, and read enough about French and European history to whet his appetite for more history and, notably, short stories. He obtained nearly all the books he asked for from nearby Vieux-Conde. He threw himself into these studies enthusiastically for three years, to the delight of his tutors. While they were unable to obtain a formal high school diploma for him, a private institute with which they were associated granted him a special, sealed certificate signed by the institute's director.

All the while Gustave was being tutored, he felt as though his health was improving. His energy increased and his appetite returned; but he did not want to declare openly that he was much cured, lest he seem critical of Drs. Semel and Lambris.[7] He was feeling so much better that dared to leave the house one or two evenings a week to repair several of his old friendships.

Gustave was now regularly disobeying doctors' orders. He and old schoolmates enjoyed sensible, relaxed conversations. All of them were old enough now to sip the local favorite beer, which was almost universally called "houblon." The brew had no adverse effect.

---

[7] Otherwise healthy bodies frequently overcome bacterial infections.

CHAPTER 5

Felippe Van Hendryk

Lydie regularly visited the art museum in Mons on Saturday mornings and wanted one day to view a particular painting by the Flemish artist Pieter Bruegel the Elder. The world is indebted to Bruegel for painting the droll behavior of Flemish peasants of the 1500s enjoying their lives—dancing, eating, arguing, and making love—long before there were candid cameras to copy the scenes for us. An unknown young man came to view the same painting a minute or so after Lydie began to view it. The two struck up a conversation and chuckled together as they studied the antics of the peasants.

The question of whether Bruegel was born a peasant and discovered he had a knack for drawing, took lessons, and then traveled the world before returning to Antwerp and Brussels was the beginning of their conversation. The two laughed a great deal together as they studied the large canvas and played a game of finding instances of unusual but normal behavior of the peasants before the other did.

Laughter and good fun came of their game, in which both showed themselves to be sharply observant people.

"Those men at the table seem to be having quite an argument," said the young man.

Lydie laughed and responded, "They've had a little too much beer, don't you think?"

"That's what I was thinking, but I didn't want to jump to a conclusion too quickly. I might spoil their reputations with their neighbors by implying that they seem to have been bibulous by noon."

Lydie had a good laugh. "I cannot recall when I last heard the interesting word 'bibulous' trip so easily from anyone's tongue. It's a word whose origin is interesting."

The young man realized that the attractive young woman with a good sense of humor was probably scholarly. He wanted to know who she was.

Having had enough of Bruegel, the unknown young man—who was himself cultured, as well as quite good looking—asked Lydie if she would care to join him for a walk in the gardens behind the museum. It was a picture-perfect summer day without a cloud in the sky.

The two young and attractive people walked slowly past a hedge of mountain laurel speckled with white flowers. The hedge gave way to a patch of bright red roses interspersed with large, yellow sunflowers. They maintained a space between them that one would expect of a brother and a sister strolling together, but the young man was determined to close the space.

When the polite young man and the intriguing young woman at his side were still examining the Bruegel, he'd seen that she had good taste in clothes. She wore a striking, cobalt blue dress with a small, white collar. The dress fit her height exactly, hardly touching the ground as she walked. Her hat was white with a brim of medium width and a delicate, cobalt blue ribbon. She wore thin, white gloves. As far as Felippe could see, her facial features could not have been more alluringly composed. She had a ready smile and the low-pitched, well-modulated voice of a cultured woman.

As they walked they came to another break in the hedge that revealed a stunning luxuriance of lilies. The beauty of the flowers brought them closer, to admire their various colors and unforgettable structure. Lydie's partner was quick to take her hand and hold it as they took pleasure from the scene. She smiled, looked into his face briefly, and tightened the hand clasp minimally.

He took immediate advantage. "I may earlier have referred to myself in a careless, mumbling way, but I do want to introduce myself to you properly. I am Felippe Van Hendryk."

Lydie's response was immediate. As she continued to hold his hand, she told him, "I am Lydie Fougnies."

Felippe looked directly into her very blue eyes and commented, "Fougnies is an extremely old name, and probably Celtic. One almost never hears similar names these days. You are, indeed, as French as it is possible to be. Do you visit the museum often, Lydie?"

"I visit it almost every Saturday morning."

"So do I!" answered Felippe, who was pleasantly surprised.

Lydie volunteered to say that she was from Peruwelz and was not expecting to hear him say, "I know it very well."

They continued to hold hands as they finished their stroll. Each found the other's conversation seemly and cultured and both looked forward keenly to what would become regular Saturday meetings.

Felippe accompanied her to the train soon to depart for Peruwelz. From within the car, Lydie watched him walk a short distance to a blue cabriolet and pat the waiting horse's nose but lost sight of him as her train lurched and began quickly to move.

***

After their next meeting, Felippe said that her living in Peruwelz could be advantageous to them. Without telling her exactly where he lived near Peruwelz, he suggested that he could easily take a carriage to her home. He explained, "I have access to horses near Peruwelz, and we could ride into the countryside and have picnic lunches."

Lydie was surprised to find that Felippe had a detailed acquaintance with the area around Peruwelz. It was on one of these picnic lunch days, when he came to pick Lydie up at the spacious Fougnies home, that he first met young Gustave, the younger brother of his alluring female friend. He had not yet undergone his second operation. The older, mature Felippe, who was twenty at the time, empathized at once with sixteen-year-old Gustave, chatted with him, and encouraged him. Gustave, young and unsophisticated as he was, could tell that this fellow Felippe was a "nice guy."

Gustave found Felippe's fund of knowledge surprisingly interesting and broad; he especially enjoyed their time together. Felippe so inspired Gustave to educate himself that, young and ambitious as he was, the lad actually read some of Dumas' Parisian Scenes. He liked especially Dumas' novelette *La Duchesse de Langeais*, a sensational, captivating story of unrequited love. Gustave recognized the author's extraordinary ability to write with remarkable power. His appreciation of the novelette is an indication of his refined taste for good literature, at an early age; a trait he shared with Lydie.

***

As for Lydie, she began to hunger for Felippe's company and had no interest in being with anyone else. He felt the same. The affinity they had for one another grew to the point that they were together as much as possible. Felippe regularly brought Lydie to his home and introduced her to his mother, who smiled courteously and shook Lydie's hand but made no conversation. If Madame Van Hendryk seemed cool, she had no effect on the ardent mutual affection that bound Felippe and Lydie. They craved one another's company.

Lydie and Felippe were experiencing a deep infatuation. The magnitude and character of their relationship are impossible to describe. Even *divine rapture* is an inadequate term. Their infatuation—their love—is a human experience too splendid to paint with words.

Lydie was now twenty. Felippe, at twenty-one, had not yet applied for university. If Lydie thought Felippe's mother might be indifferent to this, she was mistaken. Felippe's parents, especially his mother, took notice of his procrastinating.

***

The Van Hendryks owned a magnificent home and estate on the outskirts of Brussels, a comfortable estate on the periphery of Peruwelz, as well as an inviting country home in Pipaix, a quaint village near Peruwelz, where they kept their horses and often spent weekends. The level of wealth to which Felippe was accustomed was new to Lydie. She was unable to discuss horses, skating, swimming, travel, or the use of a country home, as Felippe could. She had visited Brussels only once, when she went with her class on a school trip. Felippe soon discovered this, and it mattered not at all to him. If anything, he admired her even more because she had developed into a warm, thoughtful person without the trappings he had always taken for granted.

It was obvious to Felippe's parents that their son had developed affection for a young, French-speaking woman who, they believed, did not have the "right pedigree." While they were not vocal about this, they tried subtly to imply to him that Lydie would be an unacceptable permanent companion for him.

Felippe detected their hints, but he had his own mind. He was mature beyond his age and could read Lydie far better than they could. He was certain that he loved Lydie for her loyalty and good sense as well as her attractiveness, warmth, and respect for his mind.

His attention flattered her, and although his background and family wealth intimidated her at first, they became tolerable issues as her fondness for him grew. She was convinced that she loved Felippe deeply and always would. If he continued to love her, she told herself, his parents' coolness to her would disappear.

The young lady, whose fine education and an association with many friends born into the aristocracy, had led her in the past to wonder about her ultimate societal position. Her main goal had become achievement of personal happiness with the companionship of a man whose interests were not focused on accumulation of wealth. (She realized that Gustave and she were likely, at a distant date, to receive inheritances from their father.) She admired Felippe's deep concern for the welfare of poor and unfortunate fellow Belgians.

Felippe talked about his interests in animal welfare too—horses in particular—going so far as to mention studying veterinary science at university. He spoke, too, about obtaining a degree in international relations and law, which would allow him to contribute to improving relations between Belgium and other nations. His parents preferred discussing his future as a lawyer specializing in international relations. They knew he was a good student and was, they calculated, more suited to play this role than most young men because he was *their* son, one of privileged parents like themselves, people with connections at the top echelons of Belgium's government. They hoped that he might eventually exert important influence in governmental and societal issues. Lydie tended to agree with his parents but thought it prudent not to express her opinion. She would follow Felippe in whatever life he chose to live.

Felippe introduced Lydie to horses. The two would ride for hours in the countryside near and around Peruwelz and Bury, especially when Felippe visited with his parents on weekends at Pipaix. As the young couple rode among the rolling hills around Peruwelz, Felippe would tell Lydie his dream of protecting lands like these throughout the country so that future generations of children—she silently hoped he meant their children—could enjoy the unspoiled countryside as they were doing.

Lydie savored Felippe's company. She appreciated that he never made her feel self-conscious about the differences in their backgrounds. He flashed intuitive, understanding smiles when needed. This had to be the true love she'd always craved.

Felippe invited Lydie to garden parties that his parents frequently hosted at their country estate. Important, well-known politicians, diplomats, actors, and writers from Brussels attended these impressive events. When Felippe's father had his fiftieth birthday, an important anniversary celebrated to this day in many European families, the king of Belgium attended as a weekend guest of the Van Hendryks.

Lydie and Felippe had not yet seriously discussed marriage during their chaste relationship. Felippe was a responsible person, and he respected Lydie too much for their romance to become more intimate than it was already. They were both sensible to Felippe's need to enter university, presumably in Belgium, and prepare seriously for a career.

Premarital love was not the same as married love; they both knew that. Felippe knew it all too well, for he had friends who'd pushed the bounds of lovemaking too far and ended up with quick marriages they had not been prepared for, and with children for whose care they were not ready. These unfortunate instances were usually destructive. More often than not, they destroyed professional careers.

His friends and their young wives often discovered that they were less temperamentally compatible than they'd thought they were and, naturally, wanted mutually agreeable divorces. They found that divorce was becoming very difficult to obtain in Belgium. A powerful political party held it to be a violation of religion and aimed, in an upcoming election, to establish a national law barring all divorce. In the meantime, an increasing degree of red tape was already a serious hindrance.

Felippe, and nearly every considerate person he knew, disliked the cruelty and unfairness of that growing barrier. The vast majority of enlightened people admired the young United States, whose founders created a Constitution that protects its soundness by forbidding the establishment of a national religion.

Lydie was determined not to let happen to Felippe what had happened to his acquaintances. She sensed when it was time for her to go home. She distanced herself a little, gave him a smile that smacked of regret, kissed his forehead, and stood up. He always followed suit and drove her home. Nevertheless, Lydie hoped, if not assumed, that eventually she would become Felippe's wife and bear his children. She was content to leave their relationship as it was; she considered it sublime and was patient. She did not imagine that the possibility of Felippe's ultimate marriage to her was a front and center issue in the minds of his parents.

Friday night came upon Peruwelz, and Lydie prepared to go to bed early, dress smartly in the morning, and catch the early train to Mons to spend the day with Felippe.

All went well the next morning as the train arrived in Mons and she walked to the bottom step of the museum where Felippe would soon meet her. To her surprise, Madame Van Hendryk was already there.

"Good morning, Lydie." She smiled. "How lovely you look in that dress, and what a beautiful morning it is. Felippe will be on his way shortly, but he will be a little late since he has a meeting with his father this morning."

"Good morning, Madame Van Hendryk. This is quite a surprise seeing you, and thank you for admiring my dress," Lydie remarked.

"I wanted to take advantage of this time to meet with you privately and to inform you of a decision my husband and I have made. We have decided that Felippe needs a change that will allow him to meet different people, and we have arranged for him to go to university in Switzerland. He will leave Belgium at the end of this month. I know it will be difficult for him to tell you, and I thought it would be easier on him if I gave you the news."

Lydie was speechless, and thought it insensitive that Madame Van Hendryk would not allow her son to be the one to break the news to her. Lydie had always known that she was not who the Van Hendryks would have chosen for their son, and it was now clear to her that they wanted her removed from Felippe's life. Belgium and nearby nations offered excellent universities, but she had made "meeting different people" a priority.

Madame Van Hendryk had nothing more to say. She left abruptly, the clip-clop of her horses' hooves on the cobblestones quickly disappearing.

Lydie sat on a nearby bench in a state best described as stunned. She was angry, too. *How dare that woman snub me because I don't speak her Germanic Flemish?*

It was a moment when Lydie hated *herself* too, because she was middle class and spoke French. She knew no Flemish. She hated that woman. Naturally, her first thought was about what would happen to her relationship with Felippe.

Felippe looked pale when he ran toward Lydie minutes later. He was trembling with anger because he had seen his mother while on his way to meet Lydie and she had told him that she'd announced to Lydie the plan for him to go to Switzerland. He had wanted to tell her himself.

"I don't want to leave you, Lydie, but I don't know what to do. I love you dearly, Lydie, and want to stay with you. I know my parents are snobs, but never in this world did I think they would see you as anyone but my warm, dearest, beautiful love. They have always preferred having Flemish friends, but I never imagined they would be upset because you are French. Their friends are all rich Flemish families in Brussels and Antwerp, and they can't seem to understand that money isn't everything in life."

Lydie bit her lower lip hard before saying, "You must go, Felippe. Your life will be miserable if you stay in Belgium. You know that. Your parents will never accept me, and they will make your life unbearable if you stay. More than anything else, I want *you* to be happy."

She managed to hold back her tears to continue. "If we cannot be happy together today, then perhaps we can be at some other time. I must leave you now, but I will never forget you. My heart will always be with you."

Lydie swiveled much too quickly and ran away much too swiftly in a sudden flood of tears that she had been holding back, certain that she had seen Felippe for the last time. She felt rudely and hurtfully insulted by Felippe's mother and, for the first time, knew to her core that she and Felippe had different mind-sets than his parents. Felippe ran to find her, but she had already entered one of the railcars, and he failed to discover her.

As she sat in the train to Peruwelz that was preparing to leave, she repeated through her tears, "He said, 'I love you.'" She sobbed softly, "I love you, too, Felippe, and I always will."

The year was 1841.

CHAPTER 6

Loose Ends

For the next few Saturday mornings, Lydie visited the museum in Mons, hoping that Felippe would be there; but she gave up when he left Belgium for Switzerland.

The turn of events in Lydie's life was particularly difficult. Her sadness was overwhelming and inconsolable. While she might once have harbored some interest in being titled, if given the choice now, she would rather have a peaceful life with the first man she could fall in love with and raise his children.

Memories of Felippe very slowly faded until, several months later, an announcement in Brussels newspapers mentioned Felippe's engagement to the daughter of an immensely wealthy Swiss banker.

The announcement had a deeply traumatizing effect on Lydie. She was again profoundly depressed, unable to sleep, and had no appetite for food. After several days of feeling sorry for herself, she tried to get a grip on her emotions, rationalizing that she need not self-destruct "merely" because of Felippe's upcoming marriage into the highest station of Swiss opulence. Actually, she was fighting a deep sense of depression that she stood little chance of overcoming.

The Lydie we knew before she met Felippe made an effort to return to her former self—an ambitious, young student eager to learn. Regardless, a deeply entrenched, inerasable degree of vengeful feeling took its harmful toll. She recurrently conjured up recollection of her last, brief meeting with that Van Hendryk woman, whom she held in utter contempt. As she gradually felt less and less emotional stress over her loss of Felippe, she found it more and more difficult to erase from her memory the contemptible, boldface snub she had suffered on a bright Saturday morning as she'd stood on the sidewalk in front of the Mons Museum. She imagined every sort of retaliatory

54

action she might have taken—even slapping the high-and-mighty woman's face. *"How good it would have felt to trip her with my foot and see her fall on her face and bleed on the sidewalk from a few crooked teeth,"* she mused.

Lydie was a very angry young woman, time and again wondering why she had not been quick enough to ask, *"Who in the world do you think you are, speaking to me so condescendingly?"*

Publication of the appointed date of Felippe's marriage on the society page of a Brussels newspaper aggravated the contempt she felt for Mme Van Hendryk. So quickly did Lydie's anger pitch into action when she read it, that she fancied facing that woman and speaking her mind, *"If I'm not good enough for you and your ilk, I'll make it a point to marry someone just as aristocratic as you think you are—perhaps more so!"* She knew no such man at the time, but the thought was real.

Immediately after this fanciful impulse entered her head, she realized that she was on the verge of becoming too angry, which she knew was self-destructive. She probably did not realize that she was concomitantly suffering an overwhelming amount of anxiety with her marked hostility. She rationalized that none of these intensely angry reactions was individually abnormal and felt good, but that excess cumulation of anger would be catastrophic to her health. Wise enough to recognize the danger of too much sick thought, she took account of the resources available to her.

Hoping to divert her mind from previous sick thoughts that were beneath her dignity, she decided to immerse herself in music and theater to the extent she could. Peruwelz, she felt, was an intellectual desert compared to Ghent, Bruges, Brussels, or Tournai. Those cities contained enough people to support adult evening entertainment— music in the form of string quartets, Shakespearian dramas and lighter plays, as well as an occasional opera. They had bookstores and dress shops galore. They had fine restaurants and hotels.

Since she was, fortunately, never short of funds due to her father's generous living allowances, Lydie decided to take advantage, to the extent she could, of the cultural events these cities had to offer.

In the back of her mind was the possibility that she might meet interesting people, for it was undoubtedly true that she knew no one in Peruwelz with whom she could have an enlightening conversation. There were certainly no mature and worldly young men there.

Lydie bought the newspapers of the cities that interested her; discovered what seemed the most attractive activities scheduled in coming days and weeks; and planned a busy, potentially stimulating and felicitous schedule of activities. She asked her father's permission to stay overnight, from time to time, in cities such as Bruges, when there were evening events that sounded attractive. She would take a morning train, arrive early enough to have coffee and a light lunch, browse in bookstores, buy an occasional dress that appealed to her, and have dinner alone in a good restaurant. She would then attend a play, musicale, or other worthwhile event and stay overnight in a convenient hotel.

Her father consented. He knew she was a responsible young woman who would behave appropriately and carefully; he believed that she needed no chaperone.

Lydie read of an English theater group, which would very soon perform Shakespeare's *Romeo and Juliet* in Bruges. She sent a letter to purchase a ticket and received it a day later. She told her father what she had done and again he gave her permission to attend the performance and stay at a hotel before returning to Peruwelz the following day.

He had been aware for many weeks that she was depressed and presumed that something had hindered her relationship with Felippe, a young man he genuinely liked. Laconic Joseph Fougnies chose to say nothing about his observation.

CHAPTER 7

Bruges

The following Friday afternoon, Lydie went to Bruges, where she had a small lunch, browsed in a bookstore, and bought one on the history of French music. She purchased a new dress and attended the play.

During an intermission between acts, she'd wandered into the lobby to walk about on its comfortably thick, red wall-to-wall carpet, when she found herself face to face with Rose LeBrun, a Belgium College classmate whom she knew well. Their dormitory rooms were on the same corridor.

The two, pleasantly surprised, hardly knew what to say except, "Hello!"

Rose made conversation impossible because she wanted Lydie to meet her parents as quickly as she could. Rose had always held Lydie in high regard as an excellent student and a pleasant person. She had even told her parents about her.

Rose introduced Lydie to her parents, Dr. and Madame LeBrun. He and his wife were having a glass of champagne and asked, "Would you care to join us with a little bubbly?"

She smiled as she said, "No, thank you."

Mme LeBrun cordially shook her hand and sought to make conversation by asking how she liked the performance of the first act.

Lydie responded, "The English is spoken beautifully, but if I had not previously reviewed and studied the play, I would not have been able to understand certain of Shakespeare's lines." She cited the phrase "Dun is in the myre," explaining that she now understood it to be a proverbial expression used in an old rural sport, meaning, "We are at a standstill."

The depth to which Lydie had studied English impressed Dr. and Mme LeBrun. Mme Lebrun was curious to know where she intended to spend the night. "Surely you have no way to get back to Peruwelz after the performance."

When she heard that Lydie intended to stay at a hotel, Mme LeBrun briskly remarked, "I won't hear of it. Won't you come home with us, have some coffee, and have a chance to chat with Rose and us? We have plenty of room. You could return tomorrow on the noon train."

Lydie readily took advantage of her generosity. "Thank you, I'd like very much to accept your invitation."

A bell rang just then to alert people in the lobby that the next act would begin shortly.

***

Conversation was interesting in the comfortable home where Rose lived. Lydie learned that Rose was an only child and that, at the moment, she was at a loss to know how to spend her time, now that she was no longer a student. Lydie found her to be all that she remembered of her—affable, considerate, and a little shy.

Dr. LeBrun asked, "Are you a frequent visitor in Bruges?"

"No," answered Lydie. "In a way, I am in a state something like Rose's. However, where Rose has all of the culture of Bruges to occupy her, Peruwelz is much more provincial. I didn't realize how lonely a place it can be until recently, when my closest friend left the country to attend university in Switzerland.

"Frankly, I miss him. My father gave me permission to travel to this cultural event in Bruges to divert my mind from the loneliness I feel."

She knew she was talking to a doctor, who listened carefully to what she was saying.

His suspicion was that the loneliness of such an attractive and bright young woman on the heels of a broken relationship with a male friend might be a serious matter. Although he had no reason to know the provincial atmosphere of Peruwelz, he divined that having to travel all the way to Bruges to seek intellectual stimulation was unusual. As he rose from his chair, he remarked, "That's interesting, very interesting. Let's talk more about it tomorrow morning; I'll not have to be in my office until noon."

Many Belgians were in the habit of having a cup of coffee before going to bed. Rose had briefly gone into the kitchen to brew some while Lydie was chatting with her mother and father. He left, and Mme LeBrun joined him to walk upstairs. They were retiring for the night. She told Rose that she was leaving it to her to show Lydie to her room "whenever you more energetic youngsters decide that you have to get some sleep."

Lydie was glad that Dr. LeBrun was a medical professional. She fully intended to be frank with him in the morning. Perhaps he would know of someone she might visit for counseling. Rose and Lydie stayed up for another hour, sipping coffee until midnight, talking mainly about letters each had received from other members of their class in the year since graduation. Rose told her that she had had a few dates that amounted to nothing. Without saying so, Lydie wondered if Rose were lucky not to have to go through the agony that she had to deal with.

Lydie was actually younger than Rose but felt that she was, somehow, older. Rose was pretty. She had delicate facial features and a less filled-out figure; they made her seem younger.

As they climbed the stairs to their bedrooms, Rose said, "Whenever you come to visit in Bruges, don't hesitate to let us know. There is always a place here for you to stay overnight. I want you to know that."

Lydie thanked her and added, "I'll be sure to take advantage of it."

CHAPTER 8

A Warning

Having had a long and pleasant day, Lydie was tired and had a good night's sleep. She arose early, bathed, dressed, and went downstairs to the living room, where Dr. LeBrun was sitting alone, reading a French medical journal. He explained that he was originally from Paris, where he'd attended medical school and that he was in the habit of rising early to study until Mme LeBrun came down to have breakfast with him.

He told her that his specialty was neuropsychiatry, and he went directly to the point, saying, "I don't know if you were aware that I am a neuropsychiatrist, but your remarks about loneliness being associated with loss of a male friend struck me as a possible cry for help.

"You are a very attractive, intelligent young woman. A close male friend doesn't usually abandon someone like you."

"Thank you, Dr. LeBrun. You've readily put your finger on it. His parents pressured him to do it. He was very angry with them, and so am I. Now he is in Switzerland where, within less than a year, he has become engaged to someone else.

"I can't blame *him* for the severance, but I am filled with sickening hostility toward his mother. It is an unhealthy mind-set. I am so filled with hostility toward her that it's eating me up inside. I'm drowning myself in too much anger directed at her and with too much solitary study, without laughter and joyful moments."

Dr. LeBrun wanted to tell Lydie to relax and take a seat. Noting her continuing wish to talk, he had not interrupted her. He now had a chance to ask her to relax in a nearby overstuffed chair. "Was that mother of his ever warm? Did she ever invite you to dinner or have a substantial chat with you over the kitchen table?" asked Dr. Lebrun.

"No," replied Lydie.

"And yet, as a strong idealist, you trusted her implicitly?"

"I thought she was as human as I am and that all would work out eventually," Lydie said despondently.

Dr. LeBrun laughed softly and reassuringly, "Well, we'll come back to that. Anyone who has the intelligence to analyze her immediate problem as neatly as you have has a good prognosis. Did I hear something about your having had a roommate from another country? I think her name is Angelica?"

Lydie replied, offhandedly, that Angelica had been her roommate, but she returned to her previous thought—that she had caught the fact that he was a doctor but had not known his specialty, adding that he was remarkably insightful.

"Yes," she said. "You have found out exactly what I'm dealing with. I have given serious thought to seeking a professional who might provide me with counseling. There is no doubt that I am depressed. I suppose that going to such effort to keep my mind off the injury by seeking solace solely in serious intellectual stimuli—books, music, such very academic interests as history of French music— rather than laughing and having hours of fun-filled experiences is the giveaway. Serious study and no play are not good for me."

"If you have been able to realize that, you are bound to repair the trauma you've suffered, bound to work your way out of this. Is your father in a position to support some travel for you?"

"Yes. Fortunately, I think he is."

"Wasn't there some mention that your roommate was from Italy? Rose has mentioned her to me. She thought the world of her—a bright, supportive person."

"Yes. Angelica Bregosi," Lydie acknowledged.

"Write her a letter. Ask her if she would be in the mood for a visit. The experiences of travel, meeting new people, and dealing with new and different cultures can divert the mind from a transient problem. Mind you, I don't mean to minimize the trauma, but your great calamity is extremely common." He rose to move closer to where she was sitting.

"Yes, I see it every day among young people like you—especially in idealistic people who too easily trust everyone. They are unaware that someone in a position of power, who happens not to like you for some foolish reason, might be plotting to take you down. Nonetheless, the prognosis for recovery is very good. The brain is a resilient organ."

"Thank you ever so much, Dr. LeBrun. Traveling is an excellent and exciting idea! I'll gladly accept that travel advice. Actually, I thought about taking a long trip but wondered how difficult it might be for a single young woman to do it without a chaperone."

"Lydie, you are so innately sensible. Yes, it would be good to have a chaperone, but you're mature enough to make it on your own, provided of course, that there are actual people to visit. Frankly, I don't see a good reason for you to seek counseling. I don't think you need it."

The doctor paused for nearly half a minute as he stared at the ceiling and returned to his focus on Lydie. He continued, "The only other advice I have for you has to do with your trusting, idealistic side. Thus far, it may have kept you in the dark about a few unpleasant facts.

***

"Are you aware that aside from your intelligence, you are a physically attractive woman—enough so to make many men turn their heads for another look?"

"No, I'm not," said Lydie curtly. "My male friend, I am certain, was attracted to me because we thought similarly about things and had good conversations and good times together. I was grateful to him for introducing me to healthy outdoor sports. He taught me how to ride a horse. We would ride for hours in the countryside, stopping for a picnic lunch. He was respectful, thoughtful, and our relationship never went further than hugs and kisses. He had good sense."

"I fully understand why you miss someone so bright and decent. You are quite mature and probably would be careful. Yet, unless I am wrong, which would not be the first time for me, your knowledge of the world seems to be that of a cloistered academician. Are you certain that you don't realize that you are a young woman whose physical presence and carriage attracts the attention of men?"

"No. I'm not homely. But I think that Felippe, my male friend, enjoyed my *company* as much as I enjoyed his. I don't recall his ever telling me that I am beautiful or whatever you mean by 'attractive.'"

"Still," insisted Dr. LeBrun, "you're very idealistic, and, I suspect, you might be *too* trusting. Keep in mind that there are individuals out there, especially men, who might turn out not to be as interesting, decent, and capable of truly caring as they may seem.

"Be wary of those who might merely care to have a physical relationship. If you do take a long trip by yourself, see to it that you have a definite, safe place to go and be careful on the way."

"Yes, I will, I assure you. I *do* intend to travel and *will* be extremely careful."

"A lot of young women, and young men, too, come to see me. They are down in the dumps because of a lost or broken relationship. Many are not as fortunate as you. They haven't the wherewithal to make a long trip, which is a wonderful way to help heal the trauma.

"Often, they react unwisely. They feel compelled to involve themselves in a new pairing, with someone else who seems to be interesting, but it turns out to be an unhealthy relationship that does further damage. The wise thing to do is accept the reality of the loss and use it as a teaching experience. Life is not necessarily going to be a bed of roses.

***

"It should be reassuring to you to hear that the feeling of sadness or loneliness almost never lasts forever. The brain of an otherwise healthy person is, as I said, resilient. The parting is a lesson about life that has taught you a maturing fact." The doctor gesticulated with his palm at his side as he spoke.

"That's good advice, Dr. LeBrun. I'll be careful. It isn't like me to rush quickly into a hurried relationship. In a way, I may have been lucky that I knew no individual in Peruwelz with whom I'd care to have had a hurried relationship." She laughed when she said this.

"All right," said the good doctor, "send a letter to this good friend of yours in Italy, tell her briefly that you've had an unexpected severance of a relationship, that you'd like to get away on a long trip and meet new people and so forth. Well, you're bright enough to know how much detail you want to give her; you know her."

"Yes, I do know her very well."

"Bear in mind that it is essential that you go to places where you know people and that you travel directly and safely. If you must make stopovers, be especially careful.

"I say this because I do not think it's a good idea for a young woman, especially for one like you, to be traveling around alone— staying alone at hotels overnight without having been warned that it's hazardous. There's too much latitude for naively becoming acquainted with unhealthy, even dangerous, people. There are people out there with serious personality disorders, some who would try very hard to get to know anyone as attractive as you."

"Excuse me, Dr. LeBrun. Haven't you already warned me about that?"

"Lydie, I wanted to lead into specifics. There are people who might seem to be normal but who, unfortunately, have a severe and sinister personality disorder. What they bear in common is a complete lack of conscience—an inability to understand the discomfort, pain, or emotional trauma that they enjoy inflicting on others. They have

64

what, in this era of our medical ignorance, we have chosen to call Moral Insanity.

"The average person is not likely to suspect that a total stranger who wants to make conversation in a hotel bar or restaurant, train, or elsewhere, might be a person without any conscience whatever.

"They are usually men looking for something they crave. Very often, they are seeking good-looking women or young girls or children of either sex to use them immorally. These people are artful, clever, and can be either impulsive or preoccupied with developing a scheme to steal; rape; or, rarely, even to murder."

"I've heard this mentioned but not in so serious a way," Lydie remarked.

"Oh, it's a very serious matter. The vast majority of these men have an ungovernable sexual drive; that's of course why women have to be on guard. It's why desirable women have to be careful of strange men who want to make conversation. They may seem friendly but they have unfriendly motivations.

"Never agree to join a stranger over a conversation and a drink. His aim may be to find out your name, where you live, and perhaps to show you something interesting in his hotel room. You would be surprised at how many young women would naively say, 'Yes, sure,' and feel flattered by the invitation.

"Peculiarly, once he has raped a woman, a man capable of performing so heinous a brutality has no more interest in her, unless he chooses a means to kill her, if he thinks she might report the incident to the police. Then he will lurk elsewhere for the next woman.

"Those victims are idealistic, just as you are. For some reason, no one taught them that there are certain situations where their natural tendency to trust must be weighed in. Your idealism is a wonderful trait. Even if it were possible to remove it, I never would.

"All I want you to realize is that it is essential not to be *dangerously* trusting and that there are certain times when you should be especially on guard. I don't want to leave you feeling that you must avoid all men, but there is reason to believe that those with what we call Moral Insanity are not as rare as was once believed.

"When I studied with the pioneering psychiatrist, Professor Charcot in Paris, at the Salpetrière Hospital, we tried to discover a neurological basis for this disease but lacked the means to do so.[8] We studied a group of men who police officers had arrested for suspicious behavior, and we were astonished that the police, members of the judicial system, and even most practicing doctors were unaware of the existence of men with Moral Insanity. The police had to let them go free after they had questioned them about their suspicious behavior. These individuals are such clever, pathological liars that they can easily manufacture convincing alibis.

"There is also enormous ignorance on the part of the general public about the prevalence of these individuals and their antisocial proclivities. Because they can hide their ugly side for weeks or months, an appealing woman can be tricked into marrying a man who is morally insane. These poor wives find out, too late, that their husbands enjoy slapping their faces, or much worse.

"A morally insane husband can force his wife to obey his commands, even though she knows they are often illegal. At times, such a man can even threaten to kill his wife, if she fails to follow his frightening demand to help him kill someone else. These individuals are very dangerous."

"I was not aware of this." The information disturbed Lydie.

"In a society where stigma is attached to divorce or it is illegal, the unlucky wives who marry these men want to run away but often cannot because they have borne children and cannot manage to slip away with them."

"How awful," cried Lydie. "Those poor trapped women!"

---

[8] LeBrun and Charcot were nearly the same age.

"What is worse, some of these pitiful wives, after years of having to live with these brutal men, may have no choice but to concede and follow their commands out of absolute fear of what could happen to them if they resist.

"Sometimes, the wives undergo seriously strange psychological changes and, at times, even feel grateful to their insane husbands for not having killed them. These women will go as far as to voluntarily help their men indulge in criminal acts to avoid being beaten. They can be intelligent women."

"That *is* sad; it's awful," uttered Lydie. Her face contorted into an expression of disgust.

"Regrettably, the vast majority of medical practitioners are unaware of the lives of these pitiful women. Practically no one in a position of authority has any knowledge about the psychological dynamics in the relationship between these unfortunate wives and their brutal husbands.

"I lecture as often as I can, at medical society meetings, about Moral Insanity. Of all insanities, I believe it is the most dangerous and antisocial."

Lydie nodded her head and furrowed her brow.

"I don't want you to have sleepless nights worrying about every man you'll meet or cause you to avoid all men or marriage. There is no reason for it; you are aware, alert, and stable. Men with conscienceless personality disorders, who chronically beat their wives, may be unusual, but keep in mind that reliable statistics about their frequency don't yet exist. The fear of these wives to make their situations known is an unfortunate fact that keeps us in the dark."

"*That's* terrifying!" said Lydie, almost shouting.

"Yes it *is* terrifying. Mind you, though, that there are also *men* who genuinely need assistance because a harmless trait or something in their upbringing made it hard for them to learn to socialize normally. These men deserve help. However, that help should always come from a doctor or another man, never from a woman who feels sorry for one of them. It's a *long* story, and I haven't the time to go into more detail, but it is worth mentioning and worth your keeping it in mind."

***

Mme LeBrun appeared and then Rose. The four had a hearty breakfast. It was a beautiful day in a beautiful, small city. The sky was blue, and the sun was shining on a pleasant summer day.

Rose planned to take a good walk with Lydie along a canal leading to the sea. Lydie delayed their walk for a few minutes. She explained that she wanted to speak briefly again with Rose's father. She had failed to bring up an important point with him and wondered if he might available to chat about items unrelated to what they discussed earlier.

Rose said, "By all means, go do it. I can wait."

Having found Dr. LeBrun, Lydie returned to take her walk with Rose. They had a good brisk walk, and returned home.

CHAPTER 9

Continuing Advice

Everything that Dr. LeBrun had taught his daughter's college friend to this point was correct. However, he may not have realized the degree of suffering she felt but had no time to explain to him. Otherwise, he may (or may not) have suggested serious counseling. He correctly spent time educating her about Moral Insanity, but awareness that his wife would be joining him momentarily made him rush, and he forgot her initial complaint.

"Dr. LeBrun, all of what you taught me is, as I told you, extremely interesting and useful, but I am not sure that it deals with what ails me most. As I told you, I'm drowning myself in too much anger directed at Mme Van Hendryk, Felippe's mother. It's eating me up inside. I feel agitated and constantly restless."

"I beg your pardon, Lydie. I was carried away by what I recognized as your deep idealism, and it led me astray. Certainly, we can discuss your agitation and restlessness. These are common complaints, but they lie within one of the poorly understood areas of psychiatry at the present time. Nonetheless, we could discuss the possible significance of your symptoms tomorrow. It's Sunday; we'll have the entire day to chat, if we happen to need a lot of time.

"Would it be possible to have dinner with us tonight; spend tomorrow here; and, depending on your schedule, take the train to Peruwelz either tomorrow or on Monday morning?"

"You are very kind, Dr. LeBrun. Thank you, I *would* appreciate more time with you."

"All right, I shall telegraph an explanation to your father immediately to tell him that you have extended your visit until tomorrow or Monday."

M. Fougnies, once satisfied that Lydie was safe, agreed and politely thanked the doctor for his continuing interest in helping his daughter.

***

Dr. LeBrun made a Saturday evening dinner reservation for Mme LeBrun, Rose, Lydie, and himself at a nearby small restaurant. Once seated, he noticed that Lydie's hands and forearms were trembling, a sign of anxiety or fear. He urged her, in spite of her numb-nose history with wine, to sip freely of a goblet of champagne before they placed their dinner orders. Dr. LeBrun joined her, but he sipped some burgundy wine. The alcohol in the champagne relaxed her and eliminated the trembling.

To temporarily change the subject from her medical problem, he purposely asked if Lydie had any interest in Belgium's national political situation and history. He found, in her response, that her grasp of Belgium's history was surprisingly detailed.

"Let's see," she said, "I believe I know the high points of our history at least as far back as the War of the Spanish Succession. The 1713 treaty of Utrecht assigned the new nation's first name— Austrian Netherlands. The Austrian ruler I most admire was the broad-minded Empress Maria Theresa. She did much for education, established the Belgian Academy of Sciences and other forward-looking institutions. You wouldn't want me to recite many more details than that, would you?"

The troubled young woman had confirmed for him that her mind was clear. "All right, I'll express an *opinion* about a 'high point' in our history. I believe we would have a more progressive culture, if the *good* features of the Napoléon Code were still the Law of the Land. The French invaded us in late 1792 and ruled us for five years. During that time, Napoléon's Code made sure that government workers were those who were truly qualified for the jobs they held—not just sons of politicians. Also, the code encouraged schools, employers, and the government to treat the rich and the underprivileged equally insofar as it was possible. It would take time to achieve a broad educational system effective enough to enable those born poor to attain the same level of knowledge as those born rich. Still, much of the disparity of wealth and its associated cultural inequalities would eventually disappear. And the code also ensured separation of religion and government."

"Lydie, you're a hundred years beyond your time," said Dr. LeBrun with a broad smile. To himself, he thought, *clearly, her brain is not diseased. I hope it's not a serious ailment that's bothering her.*

They had a good dinner at the intimate, candle-lit restaurant, which had opened recently.

***

The next day, Sunday, Dr. LeBrun met confidentially with Lydie and opened their session by reading notes he had taken the day before, "Your basic complaint, as I wrote it, was 'I am filled with hostility; it's eating me up inside—I feel agitated and constantly restless.'"

"Yes, I believe I did say that. *I am frustrated because I want to get back at Mme Van Hendryk* in a way that forces her to regret what she did to my life and dreams."

Dr. LeBrun quickly opened his eyes wide, looked directly into hers, straightened his lips, and nodded his head twice. "What is bothering you is a common ailment we see in neuropsychiatry clinics. It is one of the hardest to treat. 'Agitation' is often a sign of hostility. So is 'get revenge.' *Frustration over an inability to 'get revenge'* is less common but is a very serious matter. Its treatment always requires the sincere cooperation of the patient."

Dr. LeBrun continued. "So your feeling of what you called 'agitation' is probably a manifestation of deep hostility, and you have certainly emphasized your antipathy for Mme Van Hendryk.

"Let us speak frankly about 'hostility.' There are many types. For example 'fear' is a form of hostility. Hostility is *commonly* associated with a desire for ill-specified 'revenge.' *But it is not common to hear that a chief complaint is frustration over the inability to wreak vengeance.*"

Lydie interjected, "But I *do* feel frustrated because I *am* unable to wreak it."

He paused a few seconds and replied, "Before we get into hostility more deeply, I want to know something of your upbringing as a child. Do you recall being loved by a reassuring mother to whom you could always turn for advice and support?

"The honest answer, Dr. LeBrun, is absolutely not."

She gave him a synoptic account of her relationship with her mother, adding, "I know that children are expected to love their mothers, but I'm a rare exception."

"No. You're not as exceptional as you think. Others are afraid to admit similar bad relationships with their mothers. Still, I'm sorry to hear of it.

"What about your father? Has he been supportive?"

"Yes, very much so. He is an observant man of very few words. He understands that something is bothering me but lacks the inclination to discuss it.

"On the other hand, he is a self-made, wealthy man, who is materialistically extremely generous and kind. I love him dearly. He has always been farsighted; I owe the extent and level of my education to him."

"I'm happy to hear this. I think I would like him. You owe a great deal to him," said Dr. LeBrun.

Lydie added, "My father was a grocer and butcher. He sold his large store for a good price, invested the money wisely, and became wealthy. He also owns land with two inhabited villages on it, and has always wanted to be titled a baron. As a child, I knew this was impossible because former grocers and butchers are rarely titled.

"His talk about being titled was what made me conscious that I'm middle class, and frankly, *this social classification of the population deeply bothers me.* I felt as though I was the only student from the middle class in Belgium College and had to hide it. I confess that one of the reasons I love Felippe is that he is an aristocrat who loved me in spite of my background. It was never an issue in the front of my mind, but I was conscious of his egalitarianism.

"I thought the issue of 'class' had been settled, but *Felippe told me outright, 'My mother is a snob.'*

"She destroyed our dreams purely and simply because I am categorically 'middle class. I didn't crave to be reclassified; I loved Felippe, and without doubt, he loved me. As we parted, his last words were, 'I love you.' His parents forced him to go to law school in Zürich, *'to meet other people.'* He was completely dependent on them financially, and he had to obey."

"The *hostility* you have for Mme Von Hendryk is straightforward, except that it is accompanied by a strong desire for revenge. Do I have that right?"

"Yes."

"Lydie, I'll not mince words with you. You have the right to *think* about revenge but *no* right to perform a vengeful act," answered Dr. LeBrun in a resolute voice. "I must tell you — hostility, when associated with a desire for revenge, can be gravely dangerous. Perhaps you are not aware of the unhealthy effects that ceaseless hostility generates in you, not counting the time it wastes from the constructive use of your mind.

"If you occupied yourself with writing a book, the anger would dissipate more quickly than you are unable at present to imagine. Authoring is something you've already done with some success. Perhaps you may ingeniously invent some other constructive way to occupy your mind; you *are* a person with talents. Your education makes you fit to be a teacher. You may have other talents to put to good use. I don't know all of them."

"Thank you, but I think you may be overrating me."

"*No*. It's not a good practice for a doctor to overrate a patient; he may actually *believe* the doctor and develop a superiority complex on top of whatever else is bothering him." He made a truncated laryngeal laugh but maintained a resolute visage.

Lydie had not seen this side of him before now.

"What I failed to emphasize," said Dr. Lebrun, "is psychological trauma's effect on physical health and longevity. In my experience, *angry persons* don't live as long as happy ones. I find it intriguing but have no idea of the reason why."[9]

"*Lydie, you are harboring a sick obsession, and it is a dangerous matter.* The anger, especially the desire for revenge, must stop. It is more than antisocial—it could be criminal—and I will be so bold as to tell you, as your doctor and an admiring friend, that *I consider it inappropriate.* What, exactly, would you do to 'get revenge,' if you had Madame Van Hendryk 'pinned to the mat,' to use wrestling terms?"

"I don't *really* know, to tell the truth. I was not thinking of causing physical harm. I would like to be situated or *positioned above my middle class status to enable me to blacken her name.*"

"Lydie! Each of us has, at some juncture in our lives, been rejected. We did cover this point earlier when we spoke about the danger of naive idealism. You mistakenly took Felippe's mother for granted, but she rejected you.

"If it were possible to wave a wand and make Mme Van Hendryk join us at this very moment, what action—what *lawful* action— would you take to sate your thirst for revenge?

"Tell me; or tell Mme Van Hendryk *through* me; I will play her role."

---

[9] Hostility promotes release of neural signals that elevate the blood pressure, which damages the vascular system of the heart, kidneys, and brain.

74

Lydie paused. "I would tell her that she had arbitrarily, that is, for *no sound reason*, destroyed her son's and my love affair and *ought to be ashamed* of herself."

"Imagine that haughty woman's response were something like this: 'Felippe was not yet *worldly enough to decide for certain on a marital partner.* He had met too few people to make that choice. I wanted him to meet a variety of young women with backgrounds similar to his, and I wanted it to be in a university *known* to attract academically ambitious young women who have a variety of talents. They are numerous at the graduate school of the University of Zürich, in Switzerland.

"I wanted, as best I knew, to ensure that *the mother of Felippe's children* would conduct herself by the same standards of conduct as Felippe, his father, and I were exposed to in our pre-university years. When we toted up *your pros and cons*, you were not in the league *we wanted for him.*

"*Come now*, young lady," declared Mme Van Hendryk imperiously and condescendingly, "Felippe's father has served as friend and advisor to King Leopold. He was *never* a grocer or a *butcher.*"

"So," said Dr. LeBrun, returning to his own voice, "Mme Van Hendryk finally revealed herself as a snob. It's not an amiable quality, but it's not illegal to be a snob. All right, Lydie, *how would* you respond?"

Lydie was silent and then wept until she could respond to the phantom Mme Van Hendryk. "*You* fancy yourself as *someone special. You are only a snob.* That is what Felippe called you when he came running to me on the museum steps moments after the departure of your carriage. You're *no good*! Felippe *told* me that he *didn't want to go to Zürich—that he loved me* and wanted to stay with me."

"Young woman, your behavior and unmasked hostility, *especially* when you speak to your *superiors*, is proof enough to me that you were *not* the right person to marry my son. You don't have as much '*class*' as you *think* you do. I have to leave now. The marriage of

Felippe to *Ula Frissen* is only five days away. There is a great deal to do when you expect *more than eleven hundred invited guests*."

"Notice," said Lydie, "that she had to insert the Frissen name. Ula's father is perhaps the wealthiest banker in Switzerland. She's not above *boasting about wealth*. That is not 'upper-class' behavior. Nor is the presumption that she is *my* 'superior.'"

"You are right about that, Lydie. She's *not* a likeable character."

***

Yet, Dr. LeBrun felt he had heard enough. "Lydie, you had your chance to demonstrate how you would 'get even.' You made no significant points with Mme Van Hendryk, although I can easily see why you dislike her. I want to assure you that the idea of confronting you with her phantom was certainly not cooked up to embarrass you. I merely wondered what a face-to-face meeting could produce.

"Any other attempt to hurt her by spreading rumors about her are either likely to fail or draw the attention of police detectives. They take rumor-mongering *very seriously*, especially when the alleged victim is friendly with the king; and we *know* that the Van Hendryks are his friends. *You* attended that fiftieth birthday party they threw for King Leopold.

"If this little act isn't enough to convince you to drop your desire for revenge, I don't know what will. You may still hate the woman, but you *must* drop the desire for revenge.

"As a friend who admires you, I feel the right to tell you that the way you're thinking about her is more 'middle class, *or lower*, cultural behavior' than you realize. It is puerile. It is *far* beneath your dignity. It is never too late to begin *to learn to accept setbacks* as part of life.

"I *have* had a slight change of mind. I am *not* going to force the decision to have counseling. If you care to get back to me within the coming week to tell me your decision on that matter, I'll try to

76

help you find a counselor. Note that I am relying on *your* judgment because the decision to act like a mature adult woman is yours. *No* counselor can possibly help you if you refuse to drop your desire to be vengeful in illegal ways.

"Now!" He paused. "Do you *still* harbor a need for revenge?"

"You did show me that meeting her might be useless, and I appreciate that certain kinds of revenge might be illegal. Certainly, I'll give serious thought to your advice about biting my lip and facing up to reality like an adult. Perhaps there *is* nothing to do but use the therapeutic passage of time in hope that the deep sore will heal. As for seeking a counselor, I have to *think* about that one.

"Anyway, I am *extremely grateful* for the important advice you gave me. I'm a fortunate person to have had the chance to speak with *someone of the caliber of Dr. LeBrun so openly and fully.* Please don't give up on me, sir. Some way or other, sooner or later, all of this will be as transient as a bad dream, if I can keep my mind usefully occupied."

***

Dr. LeBrun had come to know more than Lydie realized. He concluded that she was sick but unaware of it. When she left his office, his gut feeling about her future happiness was far less optimistic than hers. He regretted—*I have no medicine to treat her. Medical doctors have no understanding how to treat what is clearly a deep sickness of her mind. If she ever gets into serious trouble one way or another, it will be because her brain was muddled, not because she intentionally did something wrong. All that my generation of doctors knows about the brain is that it has cells, but what they do and how they interact is pure mystery to us. Two hundred years from now, they may know more. Meanwhile, we'll have to be satisfied with accepting a sad fact—the mysterious brain is the body's most important organ, But we haven't the slightest way to understand its thought processes, let alone how to redirect them.*

***

Lydie caught the afternoon train back to Peruwelz.

CHAPTER 10

Letter Writing

Lydie decided to share her woe with Angelica. She deemed her a little warmer and less rigid than Vanessa. Good sense told her that her description ought to contain no mention of wealth, aristocracy, and grand parties attended by the king of Belgium.

Better to describe Felippe as a wonderfully thoughtful person, the victim of a socially rigid mother, his anger at his parents' brash decision to send him far away to university for reasons that evaded her understanding, because there are very good universities in Belgium and adjoining countries.

She *did* write that she cried often and was depressed and that worse than anything was Felippe's admission as they parted, of his love for her. Nevertheless, he had not written, for reasons that are now obvious—the recently published announcement of his intention to marry a Swiss woman "who must be the happiest woman in the world." Once she read of the engagement, she dared not write to him for fear of causing him any complications—she loved him too much to cause him any possible upset.

Lydie added that she had to get this tragedy off her mind by sharing it with trusted, close friends and asked if Angelica had any suggestions that might hasten the day when she would be able to put the worst of the grief, mixed with anger, behind her (read depression, anxiety and revenge).

She felt better when she posted the letter. It was the first time she had bared her emotions to anyone, and she wondered what advice Angelica might offer.

It happened to be a Tuesday. In Ghent, a musicale was scheduled—an all-Beethoven evening and she would attend it. She still needed the solace of music.

79

CHAPTER 11

Letter from Genoa

A week and a day passed. On Wednesday morning, Lydie awoke a little later than usual because she had stayed up late the evening before and then tossed and turned in her bed for a while, until she eventually fell asleep in what she imagined to be the early hours of the morning. She bathed, dressed, and entered the kitchen at about nine thirty to ask the household cook if there were any black coffee.

The Fougnies' cook was a middle-aged man who was always in a good mood and ever willing to be helpful. As he poured her coffee and added a warm croissant, he remarked that the day's mail had come and it was in the sitting room table near the piano.

Lydie went to fetch it and was surprised to see an overseas letter with Italian stamps. She set it aside, hoping to read it after she had eaten her little breakfast because she wanted to read it alone in her room.

She quickly finished eating and disappeared into her bedroom, where she added the extra pillow of her double-sized bed to the pillow she slept on, propping herself up to read what must be Angelica's reply. On her bedside table there was always a knife to open letters. The letter looked long. The return address was Angelica Bregosi's. Lydie could hardly wait to open it.

***

Dear, dear Lydie,

The news in your letter was not what I expected. It filled me with grief. I feel so much the anguish you are undergoing. You describe your lovely relationship with Felippe and how it ended. Your words made me cry for you.

80

However, you must be strong and do every possible thing to win back your senses. I have never yet had such an experience, but somehow I know in my heart what love is and how much it must hurt to have it torn out.

I hope you don't mind; I showed your letter to my mother, and she was horrified that a bestial woman could cause such heartache in a young woman so coldly. My mother—you met her only once in Tournai—expresses her sympathy in so many words I cannot describe them in English.

This evening my father read your letter too. My papá is almost never an angry man, but he was angry with Mme Van Hendryk. He has a mind that is good for meeting situations that are not good and declared that it is not enough only to send you sympathies and other kind words. He says they are empty because they express only our feelings for you.

When he met you that one time at the college in Tournai, he decided that you were mature and gifted but are now badly hurt and cannot get the best help because your city is so small. He says it is not a good place for you to recover. It is his idea that you have lived too long in a small city. He declares, therefore, that we must act more decisively by inviting you to come to Genoa. It is not such a hard trip to get here, as I will tell you, if only you can go to Antwerp. He has cargo ships that sail from Antwerp to Genoa.

My mother said that a young woman needs a chaperone. He told her that one of his ships is on the way to Antwerp and the captain is his trusted friend Emilio Campanella. Emilio's wife, Vittoria, is with him. They have no children, so Vittoria often accompanies him on his trips. The captain's quarters have an extra bedroom.

The ship should arrive in Antwerp within the next three days, so my papa says that you should take a train to Antwerp in the next day or two, not later. Take a room in the Railroad

Hotel next to the dock. It is important that you walk to the dock, find the dockmaster, and tell him who you are. He's a nice man. Ask him to send a message to the hotel asking them to let you know when The Angelica—he named it after me!—comes in from Genoa.

My papá is also sending an explanatory letter to his English friends in Dover by a small fast ship, asking them to forward the letter to the dockmaster and another letter to the Railway Hotel. There is no way to contact Captain Campanella and Vittoria at sea. When they arrive in Antwerp, the dockmaster should be able to let them know that you are a guest of my father's and are invited to return with the ship to Genoa. Vittoria and Emilio Campanella are very good company.

Bring mostly everyday clothes, except maybe one or two of your better dresses because they sometimes do dress up a little for special occasions. When you get here, we will go through your wardrobe, and if you need anything, I'll know where to get it. You and I will visit other interesting places and museums, and my father will cover all the expenses. I will not give you a chance to say "No, thank you." Cancel all your appointments beyond tomorrow at noon and take a train to Antwerp.

We are so looking forward to seeing you. Keep your courage up and try not to think of that terrible woman, but I know it is impossible to remove Felippe from your mind. Papa says that time and new sights can do miracles.

Love and a hug to start,
Angelica

***

The letter boosted Lydie's morale enormously because she had been thinking that travel to another part of Europe was probably the medicine she needed to distract her attention from her problems.

In the afternoon, she visited a bookstore and found a travel book with a short description of Genoa on the Italian Riviera. "Genoa," she read, "is one of the busiest of Italian seaports, where commercial shipping is a prominent business."

Many thoughts ran through Lydie's mind. Important ones related to Angelica's father. He must be a sensitive man to realize that expressions of sympathy were inadequate. Lydie thought Angelica lucky to have such a discerning father.

When she heard that the train might take seven hours to reach Antwerp, she bought a book of short stories to while away the time.

Lydie told her father that evening, at dinner, about her invitation to visit Genoa, and he nodded his head in approval, without comment or questions.

Gustave said nothing during dinner, but he wondered why, of all places, Lydie would be visiting Genoa rather than Rome or Florence. He didn't care to be intrusive and ask.

On the other hand, her father remembered well that her college roommate came from Genoa and assumed that she was going to visit her. In all likelihood, he thought it was Lydie's business and did not care to discuss it with Gustave. Typically, he said not a word.

***

Lydie wrote a short note to Angelica thanking her for the invitation and adding that she would take the train to Antwerp next day. Not knowing exactly what day *The Angelica* would reach Antwerp, she was anxious to get there as soon as possible. Moreover, she badly wanted to get out of Peruwelz.

It was normal that, as she prepared to leave, she remembered happy occasions of Felippe using the knocker on the front door to catch the attention of the butler when he came to pick her up for picnic lunches in the countryside. The sight of the ample entrance hall where she met and hugged Felippe, and the living room where they would chat for a few minutes before leaving together, were other normal memories. She sincerely hoped that all of them, as much as they now may hurt, would fade into blue obscurity.

As she was about to leave, her father appeared in dressing gown and slippers. He gave her a hug and a kiss on her cheek and handed her a fat envelope. With the envelope came advice: "In case you find yourself stranded or short of transportation, use this. And please stay in touch with me wherever you are."

He was a perceptive, cagey, and kind man, no matter what anyone else thought. She thanked him, kissed and hugged him, and was quickly out the door. She had to walk to the station, and the butler accompanied her, wheeling her luggage on a cart.

***

Lydie took the train to Antwerp. The trip was a little longer than seven hours. At a point when she wanted something to do, she remembered her book of short stories. She was well into one that caught her attention until she realized that it had to do with a murder. Murder and death turned Lydie off. She set it aside, returned to watching the out-of-doors as it passed by, and her mood returned to very good, even celebratory, thanks largely to Dr. LeBrun.

Her short stay in Antwerp proved exciting and informative. Lydie enjoyed the food in the hotel restaurant. She would never forget ordering oysters on the half-shell "with a glass of the coldest, best white wine available." The oysters were excellent, but the wine made her nose numb so quickly that she could drink very little of it. She did not discover until later that the wine, a Pouilly-Fuissé, was the most expensive in the hotel's cellar.

She had an exceptional tour of the art museum and found that buildings in the city center had a distinctive style resembling nothing she had seen before. (She had never visited Holland, which had transferred ownership of Antwerp to Belgium a few years earlier, at England's demand.)

Lydie began and ended the first day of her adventure abroad in a relatively good disposition. She eagerly anticipated the upcoming voyage and her stay with the Bregosi family.

The Angelica proved to be a sturdy ship with a kind, experienced captain and crew. Captain Emilio Campanella and his wife, Vittoria, were wonderful companions before and during the voyage. She spent two days ashore in Antwerp with these close friends of Antonio Bregosi. Mealtimes with them were especially interesting. They were warm, worldly-wise people who spoke three languages. They preferred English. Like Angelica, both were born and raised in Genoa.

CHAPTER 12

Genoa

The big cargo ship slipped into the newest dock in the deep Genoa Harbor on a sunny early morning on the fourteenth day since it departed Antwerp. Angelica was there waving to Lydie, who stood on the foredeck in summer clothing, aside Vittoria. Lydie blinked away tears as she waved back to Angelica.

Lydie and Angelica hugged, sitting behind a cab driver who made little effort to force his two horses to hasten up a steep mountain lane to its "high point." Both Lydie and Angelica laughed where a left turn put them at the beginning of the so-called 1600 thoroughfare. Angelica felt the urge to cry laughingly, "I can hardly believe that we are together again."

The horses ran faster on the flat thoroughfare and eventually took two or three right forks; climbed a steep, slightly narrower paved street; and, near the top, turned into a flagstone driveway with a stable at its end. Beyond the stable, large enough to hold three horses, Lydie saw acres of lush pasture. Angelica introduced Lydie to her parents, who warmly welcomed her. Lydie could not help sensing that she was among demonstratively warm people. Their behavior was unlike that of northern Europeans. They were unexpectedly informal, relaxed, and very friendly.

***

Angelica had already decided to keep Lydie's mind so occupied taking in the sights and people of Genoa, Florence, Rome, and several other cities that she would not have time to think about matters that had been causing her so much heartache.

86

Signore Bregosi, a handsome, friendly man, put an arm around each of the young women, gave them hugs, and asked Angelica what her traveling plans were for Lydie and herself. He thought that her plans were moderate and sensible.

Then he changed the subject. "I don't want to frighten you attractive ladies, but today's newspaper carried an unpleasant story that I think, nevertheless, you both ought to know about.

"A young, pretty woman of your age, a tourist from the United States, was staying at one of the four-star hotels in Florence. Its name isn't given. She had apparently come alone. The bartender noted that she accepted an invitation to sit at a table and have drinks with a man who'd introduced himself to her. At some point, the young woman and her new-found friend left the bar area. This morning the maid was making beds and found her raped and choked to death in a room assigned to the man, who was using an alias. There is no trace of him, and her bed was never slept in the night before.

"Obviously, he's a dangerous nutcase, but I want to be sure that both of you be wary in conversations with strangers, let alone their invitations. Your names and where you are staying are your personal business."

"We'll be careful, papá, we promise," replied Angelica as Lydie, who had taken several half steps back, trembled.

Signore Bregosi turned to Lydie and asked if anyone had personally warned her about "friendly strangers."

Lydie, who was seriously bothered by the story, told him, "I know about these conscienceless men with Moral Insanity. Young women who are idealistic and trusting are especially in danger. They must be warned ahead of time that there are definite limits to trusting people, especially unknown men."

Antonio gave her a strong hug and told Angelica that she was lucky to be traveling with someone so well informed. He added, "Stay together. Questions in museums are to be directed only to the guards who wear uniforms." Then, he again thanked Lydie.

CHAPTER 13

Florence

The following morning, Angelica and Lydie left, by train, for Florence. They enjoyed themselves immensely, savoring the food served on the train and enjoying the attention shown by all the young men who saw them.

Angelica and Lydie had a good trip, ate a good dinner, slept well, and had hearty breakfasts the following morning. As they passed the front desk to return to their room, Angelica learned that she had a telegraphic message from Genoa. It was in a sealed envelope. She decided to read it when they returned to their room, where Lydie sat comfortably by the small desk and prepared to write a short letter, again to her father, on paper with a hotel letterhead, to let him know she was now in Florence.

She did not notice the concerned expression on Angelica's face; nor was Lydie aware that Angelica held the note for nearly a minute before interrupting her. Angelica had no choice but to tell Lydie that the message was about her father in Peruwelz. It had somewhat unpleasant news that she could not keep from Lydie. She read it to her:

Please inform Lydie of receipt, minutes ago, of telegraph from Dr. Semel: "KINDLY INFORM LYDIE FOUGNIES HER FATHER SUFFERED SMALL STROKE YESTERDAY. CONDITION STABLE. MIND CLEAR. LEFT ARM WEAK. NOT YET ABLE USE RIGHT LEG. OUTLOOK VERY GOOD. REASSURED M. FOUGNIES AND GUSTAVE. STILL, FATHER WISHES LYDIE HOME SOON AS CONVENIENT. REPEAT: THERE WILL BE RECOVERY WITHIN WEEKS. PLEASE REPLY TO ME."

***

Lydie was at first silent, and then she cried. Angelica tried to console her by emphasizing the good prognosis and hugging her shoulders, as she remained sitting. "I don't want you to be overly disappointed that our trip has to be ended this way. Please, do not. We can take it up again when your father is improved. While I think I know how you feel, you must be realistic. You should be pleased that this is only a mild stroke, common in older men. You and he are fortunate that he is alert and will improve so much that he will once again be practically normal." Angelica had not forgotten her proper conversational English.

Angelica handed Lydie a handkerchief to blot her eyes and blow her nose.

"Thank you very much," sobbed Lydie. "In a way, it's also fortunate that I learned of his stroke while I was with you. No one in Peruwelz could possibly have been so reassuring and supportive."

"That's what friends are for," said Angelica, who added, "I'll go to the desk and ask them to save places for us on the next train to Genoa. Once we get there, I am sure that my father will arrange the fastest way to get you back home. For the moment, you ought to lie down and digest the better sides of this information. Between us, I think your father is lucky, and so are you. As you explained to me, he has no more close friends in Peruwelz than you do. So, he needs you, to help him get better as soon as possible.

"You may want to hire a strong, attentive woman to help you care for him, in times when he needs to be lifted," Angelica continued. "Do I have your permission to send a message to Dr. Semel, asking him to hire a local nurse or nurse-practitioner to go at once to your home and stay there overnight until you're back in, let's say, about two weeks? Then you'll know he's in professional hands. It doesn't seem that he has to be in a hospital if he has help like that. Is that all right with you?"

"Yes, yes, of course, thank you. Please do that. I would be so frightened if I were home alone with him; I would not be able to think straight. He's been a wonderful father."

CHAPTER 14

Return to Peruwelz via Genoa

Angelica was able to get tickets for Lydie and herself in a private compartment on the train leaving Florence at 11:00 a.m. It would make no stops until Genoa and would arrive at 6:00 p.m.

"We can have dinner alone with my parents, unless they invite Vittoria and Emilio again; I suspect that they'll do that."

"By all means," replied Lydie. "That would mean a lot to me."

Angelica excused herself. "I'll check the desk again, to see if more mail has come from Genoa."

She returned very soon and announced, "Enough time passed between my first and last use of the telegraph office for the operator to tell me I had just received a new message via Genoa from Dr. Semel. He has hired a competent French nursing assistant to look after your father. Her name is Emerance Bricout. I also sent a message to my father suggesting he invite Emilio and Vittoria to dinner."

Lydie smiled for the first time since the early morning, gave Angelica a kiss on the cheek, thanked her with all the sincerity she could muster, and then said, "What are we waiting for? Let's get to the station."

Angelica agreed, and as they looked around the room to be certain they were leaving nothing behind, she said, "Oh, yes! There was a second late message from my father, saying he's giving thought to the fastest way to get you home. He'll tell you in the evening."

Thereupon, the two young women left the room and walked down the single flight of stairs to the lobby. Angelica put the bill on the Bregosi Company's standing charge—an arrangement of a sort Lydie never knew existed.

They took a cab and rode to the station. Angelica handed the driver some paper money that must have been of a quantity that pleased him because he seemed unable to thank her enough.

The seats in the compartment were comfortable. They heard no noise except the rolling of the wheels on the track. Lydie quickly began to feel a little better, now that she had fully digested Dr. Semel's optimistic prognosis for her father.

She looked forward to the comforting atmosphere and kind people in the Bregosi home. She would miss Angelica's company, but Lydie was eager to get back to her father to lend what comfort she could. She had not realized until now how competent a professional Dr. Semel was, and she was anxious to meet Mademoiselle Bricout.

The anxiety and fear Lydie felt when she'd heard that her father had suffered a stroke left her feeling exhausted. She fell asleep and woke up when the train was at the station in Genoa. She excused herself for sleeping. Angelica hugged her and told her, "You deserved some rest because it has been an anxious, frightening day that has wrung the energy out of you. It was entirely normal, Lydie"

***

Within minutes, they were sitting side by side in a horse-drawn cab and arrived safely at the warm, joyful Bregosi home in forty-five minutes. Signora Bregosi demonstrated her kindness and concern by giving Lydie a prolonged hug and a kiss on the cheek. The Campanellas arrived and much conversation was shared during dinner. A still tired Lydie asked to be excused. She went upstairs, still so filled with anxiety that she enjoyed only a fitful sleep. After she left the group, Signore Bregosi remarked that he had detected some disquiet in his daughter and wished to know what had caused it.

Explaining that she was not sure she could choose the best possible words to describe what worried her, Angelica related Lydie's reaction to the news of her father's illness:

"Even after she learned that Dr. Semel described the stroke as one with an excellent prognosis, Lydie seemed helpless."

Angelica could not have known that Lydie was having a severe nervous breakdown: an inordinate degree of anxiety, fear, and depression had caused her inability to think soberly and logically in a tight situation. She lacked assurance and confidence. [Nor could either young woman ever have known that scientific interest in nervous breakdowns would lead to deep study of the scientific boundary between normal and insane behavior.]

It would have been impossible for Angelica to describe more than she saw. She knew nothing about Lydie's early life—her lack of maternal love and support when she was a child and developing teenager. Throughout her developmental years, her father had loved her in the only way he was able, namely, with materialistic generosity. He demonstrated kindness by being generous with money.

Nor did Angelica know that, as a substitute for those "cold" developmental years, Lydie used academic achievement to draw warm praise. She had tried, unconsciously, to attract respectful attention to obtain the security that children normally acquire from maternal love. Trouble is recognition and reward for academic achievement may not substitute for normal mothering.

Angelica continued to answer her father: "It simply did not occur to her to make an effort to get a train ticket back to Genoa or to discuss with *you* the best way to return to Peruwelz quickly and safely. Her thinking wasn't clear and she tended to be hysterical."

Angelica went on, "It is clear that in Florence Lydie wasn't using her mind in the orderly way that she always had used it. I sincerely hope that this is not a permanent change." (Angelica's fear was unfounded because as Lydie's sort of illness improves, *the temporary abnormalities of behavior always disappear*. However, this detail, *reversibility of neurotic illness*, was known neither to Angelica nor to most persons or doctors in the first half of the 19th century).

It did not occur to Angelica or anyone one at the dinner table that Lydie's severe disorder of mood was a mental illness.

***

In the mid-19th century, when Lydie was stricken, the medical profession had not yet made careful study of numerous indispositions of the mind that do not rise to the level of insanity. They did not know how to deal with them.

In the 1860s, physicians at the elite Salpetrière psychiatric hospital in Paris encountered a significant number of non-insane persons with what seemed a concatenation of mental symptoms who continued to seek help from the hospital outpatient clinic.

In 1865, staff doctors could still attach no specific diagnosis to their miscellaneous complaints which were distressing enough for sufferers to continue to seek help. At the suggestion of Professor Charcot, the Chief-of-Service, senior physicians undertook an analysis of the patients' use of adjectives they used to describe their plight. The analysis led to the realization that the number of major symptoms was far fewer than was thought.

The major manifestations and symptoms were only five in number: an "anxious" feeling, thinking impulsively and inappropriately, insomnia, poor appetite, and mental depression (feeling dejected). The complaints were consistent with "mental breakdown," a broad descriptive category subsumed under neurosis. The use of *neurosis* was sensible—it happened to include Lydie's ailment in Florence. Hers was a neurosis.

Having established a good categorical term for an illness that to this day distresses many men and women, the Paris doctors were nonplussed. They knew of no established mode of treatment to relieve the patients' neurosis. So they thought.

It was apparent that the unhappy patients were anxious to talk with the doctors about their illnesses: it made them feel better.

Accordingly and wisely, the patients were discharged and referred to chosen practicing physicians, who were well educated, broad minded, and kind. They met with patients weekly and encouraged them to discuss what ailed them. Because the physicians were pleasant and nonjudgmental, most patients freely shared their inner forebodings and social histories.

Their histories of "psychical injuries" ranged from very personal problems to disillusioning adversities and insults encountered in the competitive environment of a bustling metropolis. Thus were neuroses added to the list of other recognized throes of the mind that can be effectively treated by conversational methods known to be restorative and to cause fewer complications than pharmaceuticals.

The doctors kept records of the length of time it took for patients' symptoms to recede fully. In the vast majority, resolution of situational neuroses happened within several weeks. A small minority of neuroses, so-called "border neuroses," needed treatment *on average* for a year or more. (It is now known that very rare cases may take as many as three years or longer to completely regress).

From the experience in Paris, which was too late to help Lydie, the medical profession in other advanced nations of Western Europe learned about the symptoms of neurotic "breakdowns" The dispersed information had to have been especially helpful and interesting in an exceptional and useful way, namely, the highest incidence of neurosis is found in men and women who are intelligent, educated, and emotional. (This is now recognized as a clue to diagnosis).

As a general rule, neurotic men and women present no threat to society and rarely require hospital care. They are usually expected to recover spontaneously and quickly.

***

Far less common than neuroses are psychoses. They are very serious illnesses. There are several classes of them. Each psychosis is a particular kind of insanity. (An example is schizophrenia.) Psychoses are not related to neuroses, although they were once mistakenly *thought* to be related. Some psychoses may be symptomatically modified with medication, but none is curable. Some psychoses pose an immediate danger to society; they often require prompt institutional confinement.

From nearly the beginning of contemporary recognition of the difference between neuroses and psychoses there has been curiosity whether severe prolonged neuroses might actually *be* psychoses. Most psychiatrists doubted it. Doubt usually centered only on certain rare neuroses: ones that may take a year or longer to recede. (In the 19th century, they were named "border-neuroses." It was a less than good choice of words: "border" on what?)

During the early twentieth century the psychiatric world was shocked by a published study of a very few patients with border neuroses. The study suggested that a handful drifted into what were called psychoses rather than into normality. Thus, it was claimed that neuroses and psychoses must represent phases of the same illness! Leading lights of the profession were dubious of the small study's result or the interpretation of it without further investigation.

The significance of the alleged finding, if valid, threatened to have incalculable effects on brain research. Immediate re-study was imperative. In the short term, the validity of so radical a concept posed staggering problems for the future. The implication that neuroses and psychoses are parts of the same disease was, in fact, hard to believe.

A new study of "borderline neuroses" was of course undertaken at once and was meticulously prosecuted. It showed that if *all* patients with neuroses, including border neuroses, are followed long enough, all of them undergo spontaneous complete or partial remissions. None became psychotic. Need for meticulously perseverant execution of such an important study, and for the good care of patients during the study, were its essential features.

A point should be made that while official teaching is strong, and states a majority *view*, it is short of being categorical. Thus, the official teaching's holding that "the possibility that psychoses and neuroses are phases of the same disease is highly unlikely" is an *opinion* based on the observation of a limited number of patients. Therefore, the same majority *view*, namely, "a few fellow physicians had unwittingly, perhaps impatiently, given inadequate time to a few border neurosis patients, to allow them to recover partially or completely" is not compelling argument. Hence, the door remains open through a "barely visible crack" that neuroses and psychoses are manifestations of the same disease of the brain.

***

Signore Bregosi had arranged the easiest and fastest way to get Lydie back home, for which she was truly grateful. The next morning, after tearful good-byes and promises to stay in touch, Lydie left for Peruwelz.

Her trip home was largely by train and was uneventful. She was glad to see the butler waiting for her at the train stop in Peruwelz. They walked home together. The butler reassured her that her father looked well, had a hearty appetite and appeared to be on the mend. When he opened the door, she went directly to her father's bedroom, where he was sitting up on three pillows.

Lydie had never before seen her father cry, but tears flowed freely as he hugged her and thanked his "little duchess" for interrupting her trip and managing to return much more quickly than expected. He had thought it would take her at least three and a half weeks, maybe a month. She explained that she had come mainly by trains—all arranged by her college roommate's father, Antonio Bregosi.

"Be sure to thank him for me," he told her. And she said, with a smile, that she would do that.

Lydie then told her father that, when she'd fully comprehended that Dr. Semel looked forward to a complete or nearly complete recovery, the news cheered her up.

A tall woman dressed in a white nurse's uniform without the standard hat entered the room. She had a broad smile and plain but pleasant features. When she spoke, she sounded as though she was refined. She was poised and introduced herself as "Mademoiselle Bricout—Emerance Bricout."

Lydie held out her hand, and Emerance shook it gently as she told her, "Monsieur Fougnies is an excellent patient, and he is doing very well. Strength has returned to his left arm. In a few days, we'll see if it's true of his right leg. Dr. Semel will oversee that examination; if I can help him in any way, I will."

Lydie's father waggled a "come over here" sign to Mlle Bricout with his right hand, and when she came close, he put his right arm around her waist, kissed her on the cheek and said, "Emerance, you've been wonderful."

Lydie laughed, turned to Emerance, and asked respectfully, "May I call you Emerance, too?"

"Of course. I was hoping you would ask."

"You need not ask *me*. I am Lydie. I want to thank you ever so much for the kind, good care you've given my father."

"Lydie," said her father, "go say hello to your brother. Thank him for being so supportive when this damned thing hit me so suddenly."

"No sooner said than done," Lydie replied, as she turned toward Gustave's room.

***

Gustave was sitting in a soft chair with his nose in a book.

Lydie spoke first, "It must have been a frightening experience when papá had his stroke. I am sorry that I picked the wrong time to be away. He is grateful to you for your supportive role. So am I."

"Well, there really wasn't a lot to do," Gustave declared. "I woke up early, as I usually do, and expected to see him at the breakfast table, but he was not there.

97

"I thought that was peculiar, so I went into his bedroom. And he said, 'That's strange; I woke up and tried to get out of bed, but my right leg wouldn't move. Then I went to scratch my head with my left hand, and I couldn't move it.'

"I told him to stay where he was and telegraphed Dr. Semel, who was still at home. He came right over; examined Father; asked him a few questions, to be sure he had no mental trouble; and then told him, 'You've had a small stroke, Monsieur Fougnies, but you're going to have a nearly complete, maybe a complete, recovery in a few weeks.'

"Dr. Semel looked around and asked where you were. When he heard you were in Italy, he scratched his face and thought for a couple of moments. Then he said to Father, "There is no reason for you to go into a hospital. You just need a nurse or a good nursing assistant.

"Then he thought for another moment, and said there was a new nursing assistant in Peruwelz. She'd recently come from Paris and was looking for a job in the hospital. The hospital administrator had no need for her, but would gladly have hired her if they had had need, because her credentials were so good. She carried a fine letter of introduction from the director of one of the big Paris hospitals.

"Dr. Semel asked Father if he had permission to telegraph her. He sent her a message, and she arrived in less than half an hour.

"Emerance really knows her stuff, and she's nice to everyone. She has taken care of lots and lots of stroke patients in Paris. She told me this is a mild, not unusual one. It has a good prognosis. She asked if there is a room that she could stay in around the clock because father needs twenty-four hour supervision and help, so I put her in one of the guest rooms.

"Emerance is bright and speaks well. I guess the economy in France is bad right now, so she came to Belgium to find a job in a small town with a hospital."

"Thank you very much, Gustave. You handled it beautifully." Lydie bent over to plant a kiss on his cheek, which embarrassed him a little. "How about you; is all going well?" asked Lydie.

"Yes, but I miss those beer-drinking evenings out with Felippe. He taught me a lot."

"I don't like to talk about it, Gustave. Please, *don't* bring it up again," she pleaded. "He's at university in Zürich, and I think he'll be there for good."

***

Lydie left the room in a hurry because she did not want Gustave to see her cry. She went to her room and cried there, behind a closed door. She took a bath, which relaxed her, and she felt better. It grieved her to hear Felippe's name, and she felt like crying again. She thought she had passed that point, but apparently not.

There were letters to write—to Signore and Signora Bregosi, Emilio and Vittoria Campanella, and one directed to Angelica alone. However, she did not want to start now, as it was almost time for dinner.

Suddenly, she remembered that she had not gone into the kitchen to greet the cook, who had been so kind to her since she was a child. He was glad to see her. Lydie remembered that he had emigrated from Italy years ago.

"I've been away briefly in your homeland, Marco," she said cheerily. "I thought I'd check in with you to report that Italy is still there."

"Where did you go in Italy?"

"Just to Genoa and for only a day, Florence."

"That's a long way from Sicily, where I'm from. You were there a pretty long time."

Lydie laughed. "No. I was there four days; the rest was travel time."

"How did you get there?"

"On a ship from Antwerp to Genoa, where I have a friend."

"Ah! Genova, I think, is not such a good place. It was a joke in Italy to tell children who didn't mind, "I'll send you to Genova.""

99

Lydie laughed. She told him, "There's a section near the port that's still bad, but higher up on the mountain there's now countryside with open fields and gardens."

"Very interesting. Welcome home," said Marco again. "We missed you."

"Thank you." Lydie smiled.

***

She went to her father's room. Emerance was sitting and knitting. Her father appeared half-awake.

"What are you knitting, Emerance?"

"Winter will be here before you know it, and I may need a sweater."

"Have you been knitting for a long time?"

"Yes, I knit and sew almost anything. My mother taught me as a child."

"You're a talented lady. It's admirable."

At dinner, Lydie was pleasantly surprised to see that Emerance had the strength and agility to get her father into a wheelchair and push him to his usual position at the head of the table. The butler acted as the server.

Lydie was pleased by the way Emerance cut a slice of roast beef into safe-to-swallow pieces that her father ate with a good appetite. There were also small Brussels sprouts that she coaxed him to spear with his normal right hand and feed himself.

Having done that, she held and extended his weak left arm in the direction of another sprout. By steadying his wrist, he was able to spear another. She guided his arm, forearm, and wrist to his mouth, and he fed himself the sprout. He smiled with pride at the progress he was making. Only a week after his stroke, he did something he had imagined he would never again be able to do. Emerance, it was evident, had cared for stroke patients before and knew how to demonstrate the earliest signs of recovery—a maneuver that greatly improved her father's morale and pleased both of his children.

Lydie and Emerance became good, fast friends. Lydie insisted that she remain with the family as she had proved herself competent as an associate and her reward was a tenured position. Emerance was grateful and accepted the post gladly. She needed no directions to oversee the care of the house in a friendly, competent way that raised no hackles whatever from the other domestics, who were all male.

***

Emerance, the daughter of a small restaurant owner in Paris—a bistro (although the word was not used until the end of the nineteenth century)—had not a lazy bone in her body. She could cook, if Marco wanted time off; she could be the on-site nursing assistant for Monsieur Fougnies, should he become ill again; and she was an excellent all-around housekeeper. She made bright-colored slipcovers for the dark blue upholstered living room furniture and generally kept the home shipshape.

Emerance knew she was unlikely to be married and was pleased to accept the secure position offered to her by Lydie, with her father's strong approval.

It took Lydie the better part of a day to write the planned thank you letters. She included an additional one to Dr. Semel, thanking him for his professional service, emphasizing her father's appreciation of his prompt attention and that he anticipated his continuing oversight. She added that Emerance Bricout, whom he'd found for them, had taken excellent care of the patient and had earned universal admiration and trust. She was relieved to know that she could trust her father's care completely to Dr. Semel and Emerance.

Monsieur Fournies made steady progress. In six weeks, he was able to walk to the commode with minimal assistance from Emerance, and he was able to feed himself almost normally.

***

As for Lydie, time weighed heavily in Peruwelz because she had little to keep her busy and she could read just so many books or journals. She was bored because she had no urgent tasks worthy of her attention or interaction. She had no immediate reason to be temporarily distressed (except for Gustave's mere laudatory mention of Felippe, at which a short-lived exaggerated grief reaction afflicted her). To judge her as depressed at the time is probably exaggeration.

But, within the recent past she *had* experienced sudden onset of an illness that seemed to be caused by a frightening experience, namely, news that her father had had a stroke. Although described as "being mild with a good prognosis" she suffered a mental breakdown that, in retrospect, was a classic severe neurosis. In spite of the short, brisk initial phase of the illness, she *seemed* to have rallied adequately.

***

It is historically meaningful that from the day after she arrived home in Peruwelz, the subject of Felippe was not again raised during the following six weeks by anyone. Lydie *appeared,* in that non-threatening environment, to be neither convalescent nor indisposed. Accordingly, her father and brother thought she was well. But probably she was not well.

Conservative medical judgment a century and a half later holds that Lydie's length of convalescence during the weeks following her serious neurotic illness was inadequate. Hers was an unusually delayed, smoldering neurosis; perhaps a "border neurosis." Of retrospective importance is that Lydie's acute illness while in Florence happened some twenty or more years before recognition that nervous breakdowns were potentially serious illnesses. In reality, she was ill with a serious neurosis whose sudden onset dated to a traumatic incident on the steps of the Mons Museum half a year earlier. She was in need, at least, of an additional period of convalescence.

Most importantly, Lydie lacked a medical advisor at a moment when she had dire need of one. She, and her father and her brother, could not foresee that she was in imminent danger.

CHAPTER **15**

Lydie Meets Hippolyte

In eight weeks, Lydie's depression was again growing. Emerance had everything under control and. Lydie told her father that she would like to join the new Peruwelz Literary Society but only if he felt her occasional absences would not inconvenience him. He told her to join.

In truth, the presiding officer of the society had sent her a note inviting her to join and asking her if she would be willing to address the newly reorganized society on a subject she thought might interest its members. Among middle-aged older men and women in the town, the members of the Literary Society contained a small number of people who represented "the intelligentsia." Among them were several bright people for whom Lydie felt deep respect. They had known Lydie Fougnies from her childhood, so knew the extent of her education and her interest in literature.

Lydie agreed to address the society at its next monthly meeting. Her presentation, which she drew up carefully in the course of several days, was about the variety of talents that writers, novelists in particular, must sharpen if they expected their stories to hold readers' interests. The attendees responded to her fifty-minute lecture with almost universal congratulatory comments.

***

Marchioness Ida Chasteler de Bocarmé attended the meeting, as a visitor with permission to attend. She had spent a brief time in late morning visiting her bachelor son Hippolyte, who occupied the ancient de Bocarmé chateau in Bury, a small village suburb of Peruwelz.

Lydie Fougnies's edifying presentation impressed Ida. She praised her erudition, made small talk with her about Peruwelz and the value of the society, and then asked Lydie if she were married. Ida had a tendency to speak loudly, so nearly everyone could hear her conversation.

In the moment Ida asked if Lydie were married, there was a round of laughter in the tea-drinking assemblage. Lydie did not know its significance. When she told Ida, whom she did not know, that she was unmarried, Ida immediately said, "I would like to take you to see the Chateau de Bitremont in Bury My son, Hippolyte, occupies it. He's a busy bachelor and rarely has time to circulate in social circles."

Lydie heard more laughter but again did not pay attention to it. She was blind to its significance. She was only minimally acquainted with Bury, but she did know of the existence of the Chateau de Bitremont and took advantage of the opportunity to see it. She smiled, thanked Ida, and replied, "I would, of course, like to see the Chateau."

Ida immediately called a waiting carriage, and one hopeful mother and an attractive, idealistic young woman together rode the mile to Bury. Ida paid the cab driver.

Lydie saw nothing inappropriate in visiting an ancient chateau. She knew nothing about Mme Chasteler de Bocarmé or her son. She had no wish to disturb him.

Perhaps I have never completely tossed aside as unimportant my upwardly mobile instincts, Lydie joked to herself as she entered the sixteenth-century Chateau de Bitremont, which she associated with a distinguished family whose name she had never before known or heard.

***

She met Count Hippolyte de Bocarmé even before entering the ancient structure. He bore probably one of the most aristocratic names in Belgium. Everyone in Peruwelz seemed to know this, but

Lydie happened not to know it because she lived so much of her life in Tournai. On rare weekends at home, she invariably used the time to read or study. Ida's invitation merely made her curious to see the inside of a chateau. She had never visited one. She knew nothing of the place or who lived within it.

Hippolyte was in the garden behind the chateau. A tall, muscular man, he was dressed in well-worn work clothes. He appeared to show no particular interest at meeting her, an attractive, well-dressed young woman. At twenty-three, she was the same age as he, but he merely bowed his head briefly and held out a dirt-caked hand. Lydie had no choice; she had to shake it.

The three had entered the chateau through its rear door into the vestibule when Ida looked at her son and said to him loudly and imperiously, "I know you'll want to go upstairs and change your clothes, and then we can perhaps have a cup of tea in the Salon à Colonnes," a room so named because its ceiling was held up by sixteen columns.

From the commanding tone of his mother's voice, Hippolyte realized she had given him an order. He walked at once up the main circular staircase to the floor above, presumably washed and dressed, and met them again within five minutes in the salon.

He could not have washed himself adequately or changed into many clean clothes in five minutes, but he did manage to reappear in that short time. He sat down just as a young, very pretty housemaid entered with a teapot of hot tea and three cups and saucers on a tray.

Ida thanked the young maid, but before she could leave, the count harshly barked an order. "Bring us something to eat, too." He had an unpleasant, loud, granular and demanding voice.

Lydie noticed how the young woman nodded without looking at the count, noting that her expression did not change in response to the count's harsh tone. She left immediately to ask the cook to prepare a few butter and cucumber sandwiches.

Lydie had no reason to know that the count had tried hard to force the young woman, unsuccessfully, to let him have sex with her the evening before. Hippolyte disgusted her, and he was very angry for her using unexpectedly strong physical force to fight him off. (She was a student athlete). She'd also threatened to report him to the police, and the threat had caused him to loosen his hold on one of her arms. She had good reason not to speak to him and coldly to turn her back on him.

***

Ida's presence was obviously necessary to initiate conversation. "Well, Hippolyte, what were you doing this afternoon? I'm sorry for this surprise visit, but I have this young lady with me who wanted to meet you." Lydie had never told Ida that she "wanted to meet" her son. She had only accepted an invitation to visit the chateau. Ida's twist of the truth troubled her.

After a short pause, Ida repeated her question.

"What was I doing this afternoon?" Hippolyte parroted, and then answered with simply, "Planting tobacco. I usually plant local seeds because American Virginia seeds cost too much."

"Have you been planting tobacco for a long time?" asked Lydie.

"I learned about it in Arkansas," answered Hippolyte.

"You'll have to excuse me. I don't know where that is," replied Lydie.

"The United States of America."

"Oh," said Lydie, "now I know. You were in *A-r-k-a-n-s-a-s*! When were you there, and why?"

"My father lives there, and I went with him."

"How very interesting," said Lydie. How long were you there?"

"When I was sixteen."

Before Lydie could repeat her question to extract a straightforward answer, Hippolyte asked her, "What did you say your name is?"

She had no way to know that this was the first question the brusque count put to a woman he considered sexually attractive.

"Lydie, Lydie Fougnies. I was born in 1818, and I've lived in Peruwelz the greater part of my life."

The count remarked, "That's the same year I was born; only I was born in Java."

Ida interrupted to boastfully crow, "You were really born at sea,[10] as the ship passed the Cape of Good Hope. You were in Java to be with your father and me. Perhaps you were too young to know that your father, Count Julien Visart de Bocarmé, headed our Legation to the East Indies. Java was their main island. Unfortunately, you became ill a few years later, and I had to bring you home, along with your three younger sisters."

"Yeh, I came back."

Lydie brought the topic back to Arkansas. "Did you have contact with the natives?"

Hippolyte nodded and spoke in a disorganized way. "I had a lot to do with Indians. Some are hunters, and some live in little villages. They grow things. Some have sheep. There's a big difference. They use a bow and arrow, some have rifles."

"Do you want to return there?"

"Oh, yeh! I wish. This house is big. I can't leave, I hire many help. We have many acres. So we have horses." (Lydie noticed that his French diction was dreadful).

"What crops do you grow?"

"My favorite is tobacco. Sometimes I smoke it in cigars."

"Where do you get your cigars? I haven't seen many of them smoked in Peruwelz," said Lydie.

Ida answered, boastfully again, for her inarticulate son, "Hippolyte makes his own. He is very handy with his hands. He's an excellent carpenter and can fix anything that's broken. He also has a remarkable memory."

---

[10] He was born as the ship landed. Ida, reaching for drama, had him be born in a storm in the high seas.

She continued to "sell" him. "I was so proud of him when he was the champion at his school in games that need unusual brains; Hippolyte was able to beat even faculty members at bridge. He can remember every card someone else has turned and can practically calculate what cards others have not yet played. It's almost unbelievable."

"So you do have special talents," said Lydie Fougnies, "and they are truly remarkable. I congratulate you." She paused and asked, "Might I see the rest of this ancient home of yours?"

Ida answered her. "Of course. I'll be glad to show you around. Is that all right with you, Hippolyte?"

"Yeh, good. I can finish to plant tobacco seeds."

Lydie was bored, and her mind flashed back to Felippe. The meeting with this strange and apparently stupid or callow man could not fail to make her think of him. Felippe was irreplaceable.

***

Her ache for Felippe was a chronic sore. Yet she could not blame him because *he* had not severed the relationship.

Of greater importance was a train of thought in which she relived her unexpected humiliation by a woman whose own son described her as a "snob" and who had the injudiciousness to tell her, "We have decided that Felippe needs a change that will allow him to meet different people." Ten minutes later she'd learned that Felippe hadn't wished to go to Switzerland.

Her thoughts about "what might have been" had she not lost Felippe, flashed through her mind as she followed the overbearing mother of a half-witted son up the stairs of the lugubrious Chateau de Bitremont. For the first time, she experienced a momentary delusion. She thought that she saw Felippe, who asked why she had run so fast from him at the museum. He regretted her disappearing so quickly that he'd had no time to suggest that she take a train on weekends to see him in Zürich. It was a flashing delusion that seemed real for seconds. She did not know that such phenomena are symptoms of a serious neurosis. It came and went so quickly that she paid it no attention because she was unaware that it is a symptom of mental illness.

***

Lydie was seriously ill with her hostility-induced neurosis, although she had no idea that she was suffering an illness or of its extent. Nonetheless, she retained a degree of rationality. So it is not a surprise that, after having seen the grim upstairs of a home occupied by a count who was stupid, she concluded that, for the time being, except for its imposing mail address, the Chateau de Bitremont was a dreary habitation.

Afflicted with a major neurosis, Lydie was searching for an effective way to enter the aristocracy, for the single purpose of making Mme Van Hendryk regret how she had wounded her. She wanted to wreak a form of revenge that would cause her unable "ever again to have a decent night's sleep."

Lydie was not at first insistent that the only ineluctable means to accomplish her goal was by elevating herself to a high-titled position. She would not reject *any* method of aggression against Mme Van Hendryk except inflicting physical damage, libeling or murdering her. However, having given the matter a great deal of thought, the demand of her neurosis included almost no method that did not utilize an elevated social position. To "get even," she *had* to be a countess.

A lone exception might be writing a book that is a palpable public hit. She had once, in a hypomanic mood, envisioned writing an autobiographical work exposing and decrying the inequity of social stratification in a democracy. Her fame and her message, she thought at the time, would shame the woman who had spoiled her life.

I lack the energy to begin and to persevere, she told herself. She was correct. Serious depression and the weight of chronic anxiety made it nearly impossible to write a book.

Problem was, the only available unmarried count she was aware of, lived in a dreary chateau and was not particularly attractive.

Lydie sent a brief "thank you note" to Ida Chasteler, for showing her the Chateau but purposely made no mention of her son.

Nonetheless, something about her farmer son still interested Lydie because she was too ill to use good sense. She admired his size and strength; *he could be a protective man to "have around the house."* His need for education and willingness to be educated were other issues.

Her hunch was that his ignorance was due to very poor oversight of his upbringing. If so, his social and intellectual abilities should lend themselves to leaps of improvement, if he were serious about making the most of mentoring.

It was an easy step from that hunch to rationalize: *I am a learned person capable of teaching. I would mentor him, if he and his mother would permit me.* Associated thoughts consistent with the distorted delusions of a severely neurotic mind led her to believe she could mold, and occasionally to think she could actually see, a cultured Hippolyte enjoying theater, dressing in a way becoming a count, and appreciating Mozart and the subtleties of a Shakespearian drama. She had expressed her ambitious plan enthusiastically to six or eight of her friends in Tournai, and they'd concluded seriously that she was sick in her head, which she was.

Lydie's one available count would be a pushover to lead to an altar. She was certain of this. She was certain that, if she wanted to, she could snare this rustic farmer easily and become a countess. From an *objective* view, she might be able to accomplish this end easily because the rustic farmer she had in mind could never suspect that Lydie's mind was unsound.

Lydie had no suspicion that Ida's son was a wanton, vulgar individual. He was a conscienceless criminal, who was able to hide his malevolent antics for extended periods of time, if necessary to gain a criminal end. It is hard to believe that Ida, his mother, did not know of his police record. Naturally, she made no reference to it when she invited Lydie to visit the Chateau Bitremont.

Interestingly, if Lydie were able to "snare" the count, she told herself she would not introduce him to any of her friends: "Not until mentoring has taught him to conduct himself as a gentleman. He must have learned to be a socially acceptable member of royalty." Her attitude was a good indicator that she had not crossed the line that distinguishes neurosis from an irreversible psychotic illness.[11] Sick Lydie may have found the count intriguing on first sight, even though it was obvious to her that he was strange. Her sick mind led her to think "he could not be stupid if he plays bridge as well as his mother claimed.[12] *He's strange and unworldly*, she mused. *I would have to teach him how to greet guests and much, much more. He is just a simple, unsophisticated farmer, and I could probably put up with a farmer as a friend.* Her illness abetted her willingness to believe what Ida Chasteler told her in the sales pitch she'd made for her strange son.

Without doubt, Ida's son was as different from Felippe Van Hendryk as two men could be. It boggles the mind to imagine that Lydie, once the love of Felippe Van Hendryk, would consider Ida Chasteler de Bocarmé's son, the Count Hippolyte de Bocarmé, as a "male companion." Within the sick side of her conscious mind, she fancied that she could, by mentoring, convert "male companion" to

---

[11] Dr. Paul Draskóczy was a reasonable man, a sensible experienced psychiatrist with a solid background in scientific research. He thought it likely that the psychologically unbalanced Lydie found the large, strong man sensually appealing. (After a short illness in November of 2014, Dr. Draskóczy died. He was 88 years old).

[12] It is not unusual for men with his illness to have unusual talents.

112

"husband," once he met certain standards he presently lacked. She faced a question: How can he be edified?

Another sign that a rational streak was still alive in Lydie's mind was her constantly reminding herself of Dr. LeBrun's lecture about the need for care when meeting unknown men. She had no reason to believe that the count fell into the category of men Dr. LeBrun had warned her about. He was not an unknown man who had tried to make conversation with her on the street or in a hotel bar. His mother had introduced him.

Lydie believed that Hippolyte de Bocarmé fell into the category of men who, for "a reason," lacked social graces. The "obvious reason," she deduced, was poor upbringing during formative years in childhood and adolescence. If he is clever, as Ida Chasteler de Bocarmé claimed he is, he would fall into the category of those who need help and education.

She knowingly ignored Dr. LeBrun's advice that helping socially awkward men was kind, but should come from another man, preferably a physician, and "not from a woman who feels sorry for him." Her action was not a meaningless "afterthought." It was the explicit action of a sick mind.

***

When Dr. LeBrun warned young Lydie that women can willingly marry men with Moral Insanity, he ought to have more clearly emphasized an important point—that morally insane men are able to hide their insanity for lengthy periods.

On the other hand, certain imperfections are extremely difficult to hide. Due diligence by Lydie would have uncovered more than Hippolyte's poor ability to write, which could not conceivably be blamed on improper upbringing. She could also have discovered that he was unable to write his name and that he did not know the alphabet. Others argue that she could have inquired of Judge Messine or of the police themselves about his character. This view seems extreme; it would be grossly atypical for a young woman to have a police investigation of every man who interested her. One cannot imagine Dr. LeBrun demanding that his daughter obtain a police report of her every date in whom she showed an interest. LeBrun *meant* to warn about idealists who trust too easily.

However, it is highly unlikely that Lydie would have played with the notion of teaching refinement and social niceties to someone so primitively schooled were she not convinced that he belonged to one of Belgium's most nationally prominent families—was its "bad egg" but that he was in his present position because of ill luck and poor upbringing as a child.

She rationalized that the young Javanese women did not speak his language and had, themselves, enjoyed too narrow and limited educations to be able to raise him properly in his infancy and childhood, the most formative years of life. Were this the case, everyone would feel genuinely sorry for very many people raised in primitive societies who eventually move to literate cultures when they are grown. The plain fact is nearly all of them manage to accommodate easily.

Nevertheless, to imagine that even if it took a long time to do it, she could use her pedantry and mentoring to convert this particular "bad egg" into a refined individual was preposterous. To believe that she could cause such metamorphosis of his mind that he would love Beethoven and Shakespeare was absurd.

The hurt and grief she'd suffered when she'd read about Felippe's marriage to a Swiss banker's daughter may well have tilted the balance of Lydie's mind as much as had Mme Van Hendryk's action.

However, she *could* occupy herself as a mentor to the count. There were two advantages to acting as a mentor. One would be "protective coloration" to justify her being with the count so frequently. Second, her serious occupation as a mentor would help to divert her mind from the persisting grief she still felt about the loss of Felippe. His stability had provided shelter under which she felt secure. Alas, she had to learn to live without him. She was, after all, well educated and enjoyed teaching. Why not use these talents to help this awkward man, and do it in a serious systematic and organized way?

All of these thoughts raced through her mind within five or six days after visiting the chateau and meeting Hippolyte. Their substance indicates that she was leaning toward becoming a mentor for him.

While Lydie was thinking about the value of teaching Hippolyte to enjoy Mozart she had absolutely no reason to suspect that Hippolyte had a particularly retentive memory for special things, notably for attractive young women. It did not occur to her that he hoped to see Lydie again only because he craved the chance to have a sexual experience with her.

Seven days passed since she'd met Hippolyte before she received a note from Ida:

Dear Lydie,

I must tell you that Hippolyte so enjoyed meeting you that he would like to see you again. Apparently, he found you interesting and attractive. He insists that, if you visited him with some regularity, he could form an affectionate relationship with you.

To imagine her reciprocating Hippolyte de Bocarmé's "great affection," as Marchioness Ida literally described it at a later date, is a repulsive thought.

Lydie had not as yet seen or imagined Hippolyte's repugnant side. He was a conscienceless psychopath of the first order, afflicted with a common symptom of this character disorder—an ungovernable and diabolical sexual need driven by an abnormally frequent and compelling prurience.

The prurience is so frequent and demanding, that it necessitates satisfaction. The afflicted psychopath is devoid of any affection for the woman with whom he has a sexual encounter. In fact, once he has succeeded, he commonly loses interest in that woman.

If he has gained his end by raping a resisting female, who is outraged and would probably report his behavior to the police, he was likely to kill her— by choking her to death—to lessen the possibility of his being identified. Since a psychopath has no conscience, he would never suffer a moment of regret for his criminal behavior.

Although the treatment she'd received from Madame Van Hendryk was still deeply upsetting, and much as she wanted to "show her up," Lydie would never use prostitution to become a countess.

CHAPTER 16

Fantasy

A couple of weeks after her first meeting with Hippolyte, Lydie visited the chateau unannounced. Hippolyte was surprised, although he had no way to express his reaction verbally. Lydie and the count sat in the colonnaded living room, and she told him that she'd enjoyed her initial visit to the chateau. Conversation did not come easily to Hippolyte, so Lydie had to initiate it. She thought it important to let him know that she appreciated his commitment to farming.

"It is refreshing," she said, "to discover someone who works hard to earn an honest living and, in the process, benefits society." She clarified this for him by explaining that the production of food is an absolute necessity for all people.

He said nothing in response. Significantly, it did not occur to him to thank her or even to smile.

Then, she referred to his Javanese experience as a child and told him that those had been wasted developmental years. When he nodded his head slightly, she assumed that he agreed. She asked, "If you could, would you take advantage of an opportunity to try to make up for what you lost in the way of education?"

This time his answer was, "Yeh."

Lydie told him that she would be seeing his mother soon and would ask her permission for them to meet regularly for two hours, twice a week. Tuesdays and Thursdays were convenient for her; she asked if they were convenient for him.

He nodded his head once.

She wanted, she told him, to test his reading ability. A simple way to improve it would be to read newspapers together. Again, he nodded his head. Lydie said she would see him as soon after she spoke to his mother as she could.

117

Ida was at the next meeting of the Literary Society, where Lydie broached the issue with her. Ida considered it an excellent project and thanked her gratefully. Thus did Lydie naively enter into an extremely dangerous project, fraught from its outset with problems known to psychiatrists and psychologists as "Rescue Fantasy."

CHAPTER 17

The Game

In the beginning, Lydie spent one to two hours two afternoons a week getting Hippolyte to read parts of the daily Tournai newspaper. (Peruwelz had no local newspaper.) Naturally, the reading would begin after brief discussion about the state of his tobacco plants. Lydie was surprised at how many words were new to him but also gratified that he usually knew what most of them meant. For her part, she introduced synonyms for many of the words and discovered that he did have a fairly good knowledge of their meanings. She could tell because he used the synonyms properly, in whatever brief conversation she could coax from him by asking him questions about himself and the chateau.

About six months into the sessions, Lydie decided to test her pupil's ability to write and discovered, to her immense consternation, that the task exceeded Hippolyte's ability. Since spelling is essential to communication, she began by trying to teach him the alphabet, using large capital letters. To her dismay, he was unable to put the letters together to spell the numbers one, two, three, four, and etc. He could not even spell his name in capital letters. This discovery overwhelmed her. Any reasonably schooled citizen ought to be able to sign his name.

She wrote his signature for him and watched while he copied what was simply a complex picture to him and managed to remember it as a complex picture. He enjoyed "writing" *Count de Bocarmé* and thought it terribly humorous that *eau* had the same sound as a long *o*. Thus, one pronounced Bocarmé and Beaucarmé alike. Lydie did not realize, at the time, that she was contributing to his delinquency by teaching him that.

As several months passed, Lydie began to visit Hippolyte with increasing frequency. She found his social naiveté and innocent simplicity curious but innocently idiosyncratic. While she knew that the work would be challenging, she felt certain that he was honest. She would not admit it, if asked, but she did occasionally contemplate her possible future as a countess.

***

Lydie, who knew nothing of Hippolyte's sexual insanity, may have been thinking of marriage, but it was a subject far from the mind of her pupil. Hippolyte had cleverly tolerated her presence and feigned serious interest in her lessons but was always contemplating how to induce her to walk up the front staircase with him, enter his bedroom, and join him in his bed. Each time she left, his lust was at a maximum state. He relieved himself every day with the assistance of one of three promiscuous housemaids he had hired, who were willing to mollify him because they wanted to keep their jobs at the chateau.

CHAPTER 18

Restless

Lydie's attempts to impart knowledge were hardly useful to the psychopathic count, who continued to look upon sex with Lydie as the prize he had to obtain. His prurience in her presence, and after she left the chateau, was becoming irresistible. He had begun to consider raping her and the consequences.

Perhaps she would enjoy the experience and come back frequently for more of it; but more likely, she was a "proper" type who might be angered and report him to the authorities. That possibility would require his killing her, which would be easy, he thought, by simply pressing on her windpipe for a couple of minutes so she could neither breathe nor yell, and finding a place to hide her body where no one would ever think of looking. He prided himself on his ability to hide things. Of course, he would also have to slaughter her horse and bury him somewhere. Then he would dismantle her simple cabriolet and get rid of all the pieces. He thought that the rape, murder, and hiding all associated evidence would take him only two hours. Lydie may have been optimistic about diminishing his thirst for beer, but she'd failed to slake his insane thirst to have a one-time sexual experience with her with a plan to kill her.

One day, after one of their classes, Hippolyte could no longer tolerate the carnality she excited in him and he decided to rape her. The chateau was quiet. The cook was resting, and the horsemen were probably sleeping. The farm laborers were at work and knew they were never to enter the chateau without permission. He planned to pick her up, even if she were kicking and screaming; carry her to his bedroom; and rape her.

***

121

Seconds before he was about to pounce on her, Lydie remarked that he had never visited *her* at home, although she had been mentoring *him* for nearly a year.

Assuming that she lived alone, he quickly decided that it would be easier to rape her in her own bed, with no chance of anyone's being aware.

She indubitably saved her life, because he replied, "That's a good idea. Can we go *right now*?"

"It *is* a little early—but why not? You can follow me in your cab."

He followed her on the well-kept mile road to the center of Peruwelz, where she took a right turn before the hotel and then a left where a clearing of acreage marked the location of a projected Peruwelz Public Library. He practically smacked his lips with joy, thinking that since she lived alone at a distance from other houses, no one would hear her if she screamed. His demented optimism was short-lived.

Lydie's carriage climbed a steep hill, blocking sight of the road ahead. From its peak, one could see a building fifty yards ahead, and she came to a halt at the building, a large domicile of gray bricks. It appeared to be a single-family building, but actually it contained three very large apartments. Hippolyte followed Lydie to a door, where she knocked and a uniformed butler opened it. They entered and passed through an entrance hall into an orderly, spacious parlor.

A variety of framed paintings on white walls struck him first, and when he passed a polished, open grand piano on his right, he saw a large, blue upholstered sofa and two mahogany end tables. Each held a tastefully decorated oil lamp with a large incandescent mantle. Matching blue, overstuffed armchairs faced either side of the sofa. Next to each were a small table and an oil lamp with a medium-sized incandescent mantle. Sundry other tables and chairs were present, but none disturbed the harmonious arrangement of the room.

Within less than a minute another uniformed male attendant, Horace by name, appeared. He extended a warm greeting to Lydie, who was seated on the sofa, and he bowed faintly to Hippolyte, who occupied an armchair.

Lydie asked politely if she might have tea with milk, glancing at the count to see if he agreed.

He seemed uncomfortable and was mute.

Lydie asked if he would prefer a generous glass of burgundy wine. He nodded approvingly.

The orderliness and elegance of her home seemed to Lydie to have surprised and, possibly, overwhelmed him. She was correct, but only partially.

It was unfortunate that Lydie and Hippolyte arrived so early that both men of the house were having naps, which could be long ones. Lydie apologized to Hippolyte about their too early arrival, remarking that her father and brother might not rise for another hour. Hippolyte remained silent.

***

Hippolyte's intelligence was of a cunning and canny sort. While he was saying little or nothing, he was telling himself that he would have made one hell of a mistake if he had raped and killed her, although neither would have caused him a conscience qualm.

Next to an opportunity to sate their carnal lust, psychopaths crave money. He understood immediately that Lydie's father must be very wealthy, perhaps a millionaire; there was money available here.

He knew that Lydie was 'naïve', although he did not know that the word described her idealistic, trusting quality. He concluded that, if he saw her more often, he could get her to marry him. Curiously, he forgot his propensity for losing interest in a woman once he had copulated with her, and he gave no thought to the predicament marriage might force on him. Once married in Belgium, there was no chance for a divorce; a new law to prevent all divorce in Belgian was currently being offered by the religious party, which was likely to be the winner of an election soon to be held. Psychopaths are commonly impulsive; they tend not to think what their schemes might eventually entail.

Lydie finished her tea while Hippolyte, the Count de Bocarmé, gulped his wine, and there was no sign that her father or Gustave had begun to stir. She offered an apology for the bad timing and told Hippolyte they would have another chance next Tuesday. He shrugged his shoulders, said nothing, and left.

It is interesting that, in spite of having spent nearly a year trying to set an example for him, Lydie's rescue fantasy project had not improved his social skills one iota.

CHAPTER 19

Hippolyte, Gustave, and M. Fougnies

Gustave's questions to Lydie about her visits to the Count de Bocarmé's chateau had become too frequent to fend off with evasive, wiseacre answers. In truth, Lydie feared that Hippolyte had not yet developed the conversational and social skills necessary to warrant her brother's or father's approval. Nonetheless, to relieve their curiosity, which she felt obliged to do, she dared take a chance. She hoped, *if they meet Hippolyte, they may appreciate his dormant potential as an asset to the family.*

Lydie hadn't a clue why Hippolyte so readily accepted her invitation to visit her home again. She could not know that, when he found she lived in an expensively furnished home with her father, brother, and a retinue of uniformed servants, the orderliness and elegance had surprised, and possibly, overwhelmed him. He replaced his intention to rape and kill her with a scheme to marry her. His sudden increased interest in continuing the mentoring sessions flattered floundering Lydie, an ill and confused young woman.

***

Her demented suitor fancied himself an attractive, handsome individual, who enjoyed the admiration and friendliness of nearly everyone he knew. He believed that most women secretly thought him sexually attractive, and he harbored no doubt that the "millionaire" father of the woman he plotted to marry would enjoy enriching him with money. Delusions of grandeur were one of Hippolyte's insane afflictions. Devoid of empathy, he was unable to "read" others' reactions to his appearance and behavior.

125

Hippolyte's countless sexual dalliances with teenage housemaids working in his chateau left him with no reputation as a skilled lover. He would have been disappointed to hear this. The country-bred girls simply tolerated his abnormally brief ejaculation time as a few seconds of inconvenience, to protect their jobs. He imagined that marriage to Lydie would allow him to couple sexually with so good-looking a woman that his orgasmic sensation would have an especially ravishing quality.

In his ignorance, he never envisioned that marital sex is normally preceded by a period of endearing chat, caresses, and intimate fondling. The coupling and associated pleasure are not normally a perfunctory, animal like mounting, as with housemaids. Hippolyte had never heard of foreplay, and he lacked the wit to take part in it.

Gustave, who knew nothing of the count, wanted to meet the man. His father, asked if he, too, wished to meet the count, nodded his head approvingly. They would meet him in midafternoon next Tuesday, five days after he'd first entered the Fougnies' home alone with Lydie and smelled money underfoot. Sick Lydie's poor judgment imagined that Gustave and her father would find Hippolyte amiable.

***

Early Friday morning, she rode to Bury, where he was weeding. She asked him to wash his hands and follow her in his cabriolet. She stopped on Main Street in Peruwelz before Habits Parisien, the most expensive men's clothing store the town boasted. Hippolyte was uneasy, never before having been in an upscale clothing store.

Lydie, smartly garbed as usual, told an obsequious salesman, "Kindly dress this man with a suit—preferably dark blue. Include customary appurtenances, including stockings, garters, shoes, and simple shirts and a cravat or two. He needs a white, silk scarf and handkerchiefs as well. If he needs other useful accessories, please include them.

"Mind you, he's not going to meet the king, just businessmen who dress between formally *and* casually. Take your time to do it well. If there are questions, I'll be outside in a cab."

She left the submissive giant with the salesman, who worked for Habits Parisien, so by Lydie's standard of trust, had to be competent. She reentered an hour and a half later, by which time Hippolyte had persuaded the salesman to let him redress in his working clothes. Lydie was unsatisfied, but Hippolyte refused to don the suit again. She asked that the bill, which she guessed was considerable, be charged to M. Joseph Fougnies's account. The salesman accepted the request and added that "the gentleman should return on Wednesday afternoon to see the head tailor to make needed small fixes."

Lydie set the meeting for 3:00 p.m. on Tuesday, to allow Gustave and her father to have short postprandial naps before she arrived with Hippolyte. She drove first to the chateau to inspect the giant in his new suit. It was much too large.

"The salesman told me to see the head tailor, who works only on Wednesdays."

Lydie asked, "Are you wearing your underclothes, which might 'fill out' the suit?"

"I'm wearing underwear."

She found the cravat too formal. She replaced it with a shirt and had him wrap a silk scarf loosely about his neck over his shirt. She tied it with a loose knot, to add a touch of upper-class informality.

***

Her brother and father were in the sitting room awaiting them. Gustave, who used a special chair with an adjustable seat, located himself in front of the right sofa seat. M. Fougnies sat in one of the comfortable miscellaneous chairs facing the sofa but not far from it. The count followed Lydie into the room. She would occupy the far left sofa cushion, and Hippolyte would occupy the adjacent, soft upholstered chair.

However, Lydie had first to introduce Hippolyte to her brother, who rose on his crutches to shake hands with the count. Her instruction in social behavior had evidently not been complete. Hence, the count's meticulous, technical inspection of Gustave's chair was an appalling breech of etiquette. Lydie cringed into silence; she could find no words to stop Hippolyte's intensive inspection, which involved his lying flat on his back to inspect the adjustable mechanism underneath the seat.

When mortified Lydie recovered her ability to speak, she caught Hippolyte's attention by adopting a severe tone of voice as she introduced her primitive friend to her father.

M. Fougnies never considered small talk and hand shaking necessary. He nodded his head without changing his usual inscrutable facial expression.

The Count de Bocarmé's debut, having suffered an ominous start, Gustave wanted to help bewildered Lydie. He doubted that the count was conscious of Lydie's embarrassment and shifted the topic by putting friendly questions to him.

"Hippolyte, Lydie has told us about your experiences in the United States. You were there, weren't you, and for an *extended* period?"

"Well, it wasn't as hard as *that*! Yeh, my father grew tobacco, and I got to know some Indians." His excessively loud, gravelly voice made him seem vulgar.

"That sounds like the opportunity of a lifetime," said Gustave, leaning forward now in the chair he had retrieved. He smiled too, to simulate a friendly face. "Did you find their *culture* very much different than ours?"

"Naw—they raise vegetables, same way."

Lydie felt sick disappointment at Hippolyte's performance. She was grateful to Gustave for trying to help him after his initial, inexcusable behavior. She was certain that her father would never forgive him. She feared that he must by now consider her student an uneducable simpleton.

It was time now for Lydie, as the hostess, to make conversation in which Hippolyte could join, but her father interrupted her by asking, pointedly, if Hippolyte were feeling well. She repeated the question to Hippolyte, who had already heard it.

He answered harshly and coarsely, "Yeh, I'm healthy—and very strong, too."

Gustave noticed the alarm on Lydie's face and, acting intuitively, he modified his father's unqualified question by softening its quality and by smiling benignly as he spoke. "Hippolyte, I confess that I was tempted to ask you the same question about your health. You've been under pressure for a few weeks preparing for meetings with us, wondering what we might ask you. Like my father, I can see that you look like someone who has been under stress; your suit fits loosely. Have you lost weight?"

Lydie would have done anything to know how her socially awkward count could best reply to a question meant to be benign.

Hippolyte laughed loudly—too loudly and inappropriately. "No, I'm not sick! Lydie took me to a clothing store and bought me a bunch of fancy clothes that she thought I needed for this meeting, and it turned out the salesman's measurements were way off."

Hippolyte thought that the episode was so uproariously humorous that he plugged his mouth with part of the silk scarf he wore, to muffle his prolonged, unpleasantly loud laughter.

Problem was no one else laughed. Lydie blushed; lost her equilibrium; and, for several seconds, was unable to utter more than glottal sounds.

***

In those seconds, M. Fougnies understood the reason for the bill from the town's most expensive men's clothing store that had come in his morning mail. He saw that Lydie had spent more than one thousand francs to clothe this man, whom he had already decided was a "clown." He saw nothing humorous in what Lydie had done but said nothing. He considered it disgraceful for the count to have allowed a woman to buy him clothes, and that his daughter had made it possible. The indignation on M. Fougnies's usually inscrutable countenance required Lydie to attempt to explain.

She rose and continually faced her father as she addressed the small group, "Please remember that Hippolyte is a farmer, not a businessman accustomed to wearing suits. He wears worn clothes and oversees fifteen farmers; and with them he digs in soil and grows vegetables. The work of farmers is of paramount importance. They produce the food that we need to exist. Elegant clothes, suits, play no role in the lives of professional farmers.

"This reality struck my mind early Friday morning. I dressed quickly and drove to his home, where he was already at work weeding. I asked him to interrupt his work and follow me to a store, where he could outfit himself and dress properly for today's meeting. Please blame *me* if the tailoring was bad. I was outside when he chose his suit, and the salesman was careless in measuring. The head tailor will fix them tomorrow. He comes once a week—on *Wednesdays*."

Lydie had made the purchases four days earlier but had not courteously informed her father, who made no spoken issue of it. He loved his daughter too much to judge her openly.

"I know this wasn't a perfect first get-together," Lydie told the assemblage. "Perhaps the stars were misaligned. But before we go, we have tea or wine and miniature cakes and pies. I've asked Horace to take your orders."

M. Fougnies left at once for his office adjacent to the sitting room. He went to his desk and took twenty minutes to write notes that he locked in a drawer where he kept confidential papers.

Gustave asked Horace for tea, as did Lydie, who asked Horace, in a whisper, to bring an "oversized" glass of burgundy to Hippolyte.

Hippolyte didn't sip it; he slurped it noisily with a large bite of a small cherry pie and turned toward Gustave. Gustave kept his distance as "the farmer" masticated the "pie à la Burgundy" without closing his mouth and kept nearing him. The animated count wanted to deliver a discourse on the cultivation of tobacco. Gustave moved farther away on his crutches, to avoid a splatter of half-chewed food from the uncouth man's mouth.

Lydie unintentionally rescued her brother by announcing that there would be three more such "meetings" of Hippolyte with M. Fougnies and Gustave in the weeks ahead, adding her hope that they "will be more productive than today's has been."

***

Unfortunately, each of the later meetings added to the distance Gustave kept, in all respects, from the insufferable Hippolyte. Hippolyte could speak of nothing except hunting with natives and growing tobacco. The hunting tales were repetitious and immensely boring, as were his discourses on tobacco.

Gustave boldly interrogated his defensive sister about her toleration of Hippolyte even as a virtuous companion as, in fact, he seemed to be. "My God, how can you sit opposite him when he has a mouthful of food?"

Lydie reverted to evasive answers and registered her impatience.

Desperate for straight answers, Gustave candidly announced to her that Hippolyte was an "unsophisticated idiot."

Lydie acted as though she had been terribly insulted and refused to be further questioned.

Monsieur Fougnies could not tolerate Hippolyte. He avoided contact with him and refused to discuss him, even with Lydie. He instinctively distrusted Hippolyte, but his obvious dislike of the count did not encourage Lydie to have second thoughts about her relationship with him.

***

Joseph Fougnies speculated that Hippolyte had inadequate dependable income to support a wife. The quiet, observant man, whose wealth was considerable, concluded that an obnoxious individual wanted to marry his daughter in the hope of gaining financial benefit. He did not know that the count was an insane psychopath, and neither did Lydie. M. Fougnies believed that Hippolyte would marry Lydie, if she chose to marry him and that she *would* choose to marry him, if the count suggested it. M. Fougnies's intuition told him that there was a motive other than love in such a marriage but shared this instinct not even with Gustave.

Joseph Fougnies firmly believed that future access to Lydie's potential inheritance was Hippolyte's ulterior motive. Lydie's spending so much time and money on an individual of dubious integrity deeply concerned him. He could not understand his cherished daughter's motivation. He did not realize how sick she was, although he wondered about her poor judgment.

Lydie's desire to change Hippolyte never waned. It is a pity that Dr. LeBrun did not make clear to her that psychopaths can hide their true nature—a woman may be unaware of a serious reason to avoid marrying a scheming, conscienceless "lover."

Hippolyte's apparently innocent, childlike behavior released unhealthy Lydie's mothering instincts, and her determination to change him grew stronger in spite of the discouragement she received from her family and her college friends in Tournai.

Several of these old friends organized a small party and urged Lydie to bring Hippolyte with her. Once they met him, they were unreservedly shocked to hear Lydie describe the degree to which she was toiling to civilize a mentally deficient individual.

One of Lydie's closest friends had a whacky sense of humor. "Lydie," she said, "your attempt to educate your Count de Bocarmé reminds me of the lifetime goal of one of Jonathan Swift's less attractive characters. He was the pitifully demented man who labored for a lifetime to find a way to convert human excrement to its edible sources."

Everyone in the room except Lydie burst into hysterics.

Not Lydie. "How <u>dare</u> you say that!?" she retorted angrily. "Don't you ever again utter such calumny!"

Her friends eyed one another, as if to say, "Let's be careful what we say to Lydie. She is either in a very bad mood, or she is, without question, sick in her head." They did not quite understand the depth of her agony or the threat it represented to the mind of this sensitive and emotional young woman.

***

The explanation for Lydie's frame of mind was, undoubtedly, her compelling desire to become the Countess de Bocarmé. Of those who knew Lydie, the most unenthusiastic about her relationship with Hippolyte was Gustave. He had felt for a long time that she was overly concerned with how people viewed her, a hallmark of insecurity, but he never connected it to its ultimate cause, namely, despair about her middle-class origin. Not even Dr. LeBrun fully understood the basic cause of her discontent. He preferred to rationalize: "Every one of us has, at some juncture in our lives, been rejected." The role of mass class prejudice seemed beyond *his* ken, but not Lydie's.

Lydie knew that the *major* reason for the "rejection" suffered by countless millions of persons, including herself, was a *vicissitude of birth in all stratified social systems* in Europe, whether "democratic" or not. Lydie's tragic problem was not unique; some of it persists into the twenty-first century in different guises Passing laws against social discrimination is relatively ineffective and toleration of birthright aristocracy perpetuates it.

She was certain that Dr. LeBrun lacked her deeper understanding of the source of her middle class misery and must, therefore, be an aristocrat. He had never made it clear whether his family had been pre-revolution French aristocrats before he moved to Bruges and married a woman of the aristocracy. Lydie did not consider it appropriate to ask him if he had been "*classified*" at birth; it seemed an impertinent question. Regardless, what she took to be his superficial level of insight about the cause of her current inconsolable frame of mind convinced her that he was, or thought himself to be, an aristocrat.

She believed he *was* an aristocrat largely because he agreed that Mme Van Hendryk was a snob but he excused it because "being a snob is not illegal." She held that Dr. LeBrun *fully intended to accept as legitimate that dreadful woman's malicious and bigoted deed—the direct cause of my current wretched existence. Clearly, her calculated purpose was 'to destroy my little, less than aristocratic life by preventing my marriage to her son, who loved me as deeply as I loved him!'*

Put simply, Lydie was convinced that *aristocrats of a "democratic" nation falsely owed their "favored station" to a social system that purports to be "democratic" while it is manifestly not socially democratic.*

She insisted that if the neuropsychiatrist's lack of attention to the bigotry issue was purposeful; he must have thought bigotry so ingrained a part of the national culture that it has no space in a critical discussion of neurotic behavior. Whatever his reason for ignoring the subject, he left her resolute in the belief that one has an inherent right to escape bigotry. She needed only to minimally modify her plan to escape from the middle class. She must simply commit no crime.

Her objective, she told herself, was not to be confused with "social climbing." Rising in the social ladder to "settle a difference" was not a game for a *nouveau riche* adventurer. She intended to climb the ladder with a serious purpose. She never considered her project, tongue in cheek, as a wiseacre might speak of "my sick obsession" or "my sick-in-the-head idea."

The above does not completely disagree with an earlier statement that she had given thought to writing a book, a "palpable hit," about the injustice of class bigotry. Although she had abandoned this taxing project, she had taken on a lesser, but very personal, goal.

Severely neurotic Lydie did hold the view that individuals belonging to the aristocracy must accept the obligation to follow the rule of *noblesse oblige*, namely, to work voluntarily for public charities. She held another, distinctly self-serving view: she readily admitted to herself alone that the ability to enjoy a financially and socially comfortable position as an aristocrat would diminish her fear of competition, criticism, and danger of failure in the game of one-upmanship that she thought practically universal in the crowded, frenzied, and competitive middle class she had carefully observed and studied.

Although she was of the middle class, she had been a goal-oriented, hardworking, highly successful student *within the confines of a fine college*, where she'd won prizes and honors and was celebrated as a perfectionist. She was so proud of the perfectionist facade endowed on her that she believed it must never be endangered by discussion of issues with anyone critical of her.[13]

***

The sudden loss of Felippe was trauma *enough* to disturb a delicate personality. Dr. LeBrun, who was a very well-trained neuropsychiatrist of the era, recognized in an interview with her that she was not especially resilient. Without Felippe, she was grasping at straws, and marriage to Count de Bocarmé was the only available straw.

She was cognizant that the count was far from her intellectual equal. Although his lineage suggested refinement and good taste, Lydie observed for herself little about the man that made him attractive, even as a casual friend. Nevertheless, she continually

---

[13] Many perfectionist people dread the possibility of someone's detecting that they are not in fact "perfect." In the nineteenth century, all that was available to treat patients like Lydie were words and advice. We have little more to offer in the twenty-first century.

"surprised herself" by accepting Hippolyte's now frequent requests to spend time with her. Perhaps it was safe to be with Hippolyte because he lacked the wit to lacerate her perfectionist facade and she was, without question, attracted by the possibility of becoming a countess and automatically becoming an aristocrat.

CHAPTER 20

Dangerous Adventure

In 1844, the twenty-sixth year of her birth, Lydie was slowly becoming a less attractive candidate for marriage. She thought that she had resigned herself to spending the balance of her life without the love of anyone who could fill the void that Felippe had left.

Visits to Hippolyte's chateau seemed to Lydie to be proper and productive. His uncouth behavior provided an interesting social challenge for her. She continued to hope more than ever that, with sufficient time and attention, she could introduce him to good music and the theater. Lydie's disordered mind visualized a degree of transfiguration of his personality to one befitting his title of count. This is how she initially became a self-imposed victim of her idealism, and she remained a victim, unaware that her venture into educating an uneducable man for marriage could result in self-destruction.

Lydie knew what being in love was like and realized that she was not in love with Hippolyte. Nevertheless, she continually told herself, "I feel so sorry for him, and I am committed to helping him. I know I can change him."

***

The next annual meeting of the Peruwelz Literary Society was scheduled to take place in forty-eight hours. Ida attended, of course. She seemed somewhat reluctant to discuss the relationship of her son to Lydie. The essence of whatever brief words they exchanged was agreement that the sessions ought to continue, perhaps increase in number.[14]

---

[14] A brief description of what Lydie now set out to accomplish—even if it took two or three years—was shallowly alluded to in two pages in Chapter 16 "Fantasy." What Lydie undertook to do in the 1850s is now known to take place with some frequency. Brilliant young women lawyers defend criminals with whom they fall in love. Whenever possible, they visit them in jail, marry them when they have served their sentences, and then discover these men are beasts who keep them as captive wives whom they enjoy beating into submissive fear for their lives. Under those conditions, the wives suffer severe mental illness, including confusion about right from wrong. The psychological changes these once idealistic captive wives undergo are well known to psychiatrists of the twenty-first century. Lydie was not immune to it in the mid-nineteenth century.

In situations like Lydie's, the sick dream of a successful personality change acted as a magnet. Her success would be the reward of the title countess. Undertaking a rescue fantasy is usually associated with the hope that success will, somehow, provide a reward to the would-be rescuer. In Lydie's case, the reward would be the title of countess and, she unwholesomely imagined, an opportunity to thumb her nose at Mme Van Hendryk.

CHAPTER 21

Joseph Fougnies's Sober Decision

One day, Monsieur Fougnies announced that he felt so well that he wished to take a trip to the countryside around Leuze, to have a relaxing walk. He wanted to be alone with his thoughts. Gustave had no reason to discourage him, and Emerance thought the excursion a good idea.

***

M. Fougnies asked his personal driver to get him up that big hill and into the nearby center of Peruwelz. Instead of walking in the countryside, he asked a passing cab driver to take him to Tournai. He wanted to visit his attorney and notary, Monsieur Olivier Chercquefosse, at his office. There, M. Chercquefosse expressed his pleasure at seeing M. Fougnies looking so well and, naturally, asked the purpose of the visit.

Joseph Fougnies told him that Lydie, always the apple of his eye, was recently seeing too much of the Count de Bocarmé and might go so far as to consider marrying him. Admitting that it pained him to think of the possibility, he wanted to anticipate the worst; he wanted to modify his will. Although M. Fougnies had originally planned to leave his money in equal amounts to both children, he asked if an alternative will might be written, to become effective if the marriage should take place.

Certainly that can be done," answered Chercquefosse, "but the terms must be explicit. In your current will, you have enough wealth in bonds and cash in a fund whose interest, if split fifty-fifty, would provide each child with, at the very least, 2,000 francs per month. At a minimum, 24,000 francs annually is a good sum of money.

"Also, you have set aside special trusts to pay pensions to three of your present household personnel. That's very kind of you, an action rare in my experience."

"Those loyal people need a little financial security when they're old. I owe it to them to help."

"It's now up to you to tell me what to change, in case of the marriage you would rather not happen."

"Well, if she marries that count, whether or not he has wealth of his own, I would allow a new trust to dispense 2,000 francs to her annually, rather than monthly. How would that affect Gustave's income?"

"It's a little hard to say because bond yields do vary somewhat but, off-hand, it would nearly double his income to close to 50,000 francs per annum. However, I do want to remind you what the doctors have predicted about Gustave's longevity. If, God forbid, he should die young, to whom would the balance go? I take it you've thought about that?"

"Yes," replied M. Fougnies. "Between you and me, I no longer take the doctors seriously. Gustave's tenderness at the site of the second operation disappeared more than two years ago. He feels extremely well, and he has friends, including girlfriends. He gets around on crutches more easily than I can walk. As far as I am concerned, he will live a normal life-span, and we should bank on that. Those doctors haven't seen him in two years.

"I think he has enough sense to reinvest what he doesn't need; he is not a spendthrift. However, I want you to get in touch with him. His money is not going to Lydie, I am sorry to say, as long as she is married to that idiotic count. The best she could do for herself is to leave him permanently right now because, if the wrong party manages to win the majority in the national legislature in the upcoming election, there is not going to be any way whatever to get a needed divorce in this country. I am gravely concerned about her, but she is a grown-up, and I cannot order her around.

***

"Neither Gustave nor I can stand the count. My attitude is to be tough. I worked extremely hard to establish that business in Mons, which I sold for an honest sum, and I was careful to invest it carefully in France for the long term. But, I did not invest it for that insane count. In the highly unlikely event that the pessimistic doctors are right, Gustave will have a choice when he writes his own will about how to leave his estate.

"The industrial boom is presently good for equities. You can help Gustave out with his investments and his will. Keep in mind that I could not be more serious when I say that I do not wish one franc of my estate ever to be available to that count. Perhaps Gustave's share could become a trust, to be used only to educate Lydie's children, if he doesn't marry."

The two men, who had known one another for years, shared a sense of sadness. Lydie always had potential to be someone special, and her father had always been proud of his "little Duchess."

M. Chercquefosse felt very sorry for his friend Joseph Fougnies. "I'm genuinely sad that Lydie has got herself so involved with that count character. Would it do any good for me to have a frank talk with her?" he asked Joseph apprehensively.

"Thank you very much. But I honestly don't think so," said Joseph, shaking his head with his eyes briefly closed. "The more anyone tries to discourage the relationship, the more absolutely certain she is that she can educate and train that uneducable idiot. She is not acting normally. I hate to say it, but I believe that my lovely daughter has gone seriously out of her mind, and that's the kind of disease the doctors know nothing about. It's a very serious, sad matter."

***

There was an extended pause before Joseph Fougnies asked, "Is it possible for you to tell me, without breaching any major confidentiality, whether you happen to know much about this count?"

M. Chercquefosse said ruefully, "I won't be breaking my oath too much to say that he *is extremely bad news*, the worst possible. His mother, Ida Chasteler, is quite a piece of work, too. I've had some business to do with her. She wants to sue her husband for money, but there's no way to do it. It's his money, not hers. Her husband, who inherited the count title, left her and went to the United States to grow tobacco. He left her with a pittance of an income to care for her son and three younger daughters.

"The son is well known to the police, to Judge Messine, and to the courts. He's worse than immoral: he's amoral. He's been in prison for sex crimes. He's been playing possum with your daughter because, if she knew his full police record, she'd run a hundred miles from him. He's a thoroughly mean character with a dirty mind, to boot."

"That's what crossed my mind. When do you think you'll have this new will wrapped up? If I get a telegraph saying 'finished,' I'll know what it's about and get back over here the next day to sign.

"Please, bear in mind; it's neither child's business at this point. Be careful about that.

"Don't worry about that. He put out his hand to Joseph, who literally thought he might cry a few tears. He shook the hand warmly but briefly and managed to regain his poise.

"Thank you *very* much. If there is a marriage, please talk like an uncle with Gustave and guide him in his affairs. Emphasize need for confidentiality. Anything he tells Lydie about wills and money will go straight to the count's ears. He's crude, and he's anxious to get his hands on any money, if possible. *He could be dangerous*, too. Advise Gustave about investing wisely; you'll find that he's bright.

"I have a cabby waiting outside—didn't want to use my own cabby."

***

Monsieur Fougnies got the telegraphic message the following day, made a secret trip to Tournai, and signed the document. Thus would Lydie's financial state change radically if she should marry the Count de Bocarmé, although she had no way to know it.

CHAPTER 22

Father to Daughter

Although the count had the Chateau de Bitremont, Joseph Fougnies speculated that he might not have a reliable, adequate, and regular income stream. He doubted it but felt, nevertheless, that he had a responsibility to discuss this important matter with Lydie. He was, after all, her father and had a responsibility to warn her that a reliable income stream is essential to a working marriage. He urged her to ask her intended husband this question, and she said that she *would*.

M. Fougnies knew that his daughter was naive but was genuinely surprised to discover that she had never asked him these important questions.

A day later, Lydie told her father that she had spoken with Hippolyte, who'd informed her, "While I'm not rich, I expect to inherit a large amount of money when my mother dies because I'm an only child."

"Are you convinced that's the truth?"

"Of course. I've never known Hippolyte not to tell the truth."

The response did not reassure M. Fougnies, who now knew the brazen untruthfulness of the answer from a man whose veracity and character he distrusted. He did not ignore Lydie's avoidance of his "reliable income stream" question, and felt sick at heart about the situation.

***

It remains a mystery why he never confronted her with what he now knew about the count's police record. Without doubt, he thought to himself that she would soon find out some things about her betrothed and leave him. Surely, he also knew about the new stiff divorce laws in Belgium but thought he'd handle just one item at a time. A decision of the sort is no surprise; it fit his conservative laconic speech pattern—he took a situation one step at a time. He was a very conservative man, well aware now that his daughter was "sick" in her head and that openly drastic, tempestuous, or adamantly expressed opposition to the marriage might cause a hurtful, irremediable divide. He saw nothing but future trouble if he suggested that she see a doctor.

So little is written about M. Fougnies' personality in the Procès de Bocarmé volume that one can only speculate about his failure to act more effectively once he knew that the count had a serious police record. Probably it would not have helped. One must never underestimate the power of a severe neurosis. Lydie could justify the count's antisocial history by blaming his poor upbringing.

M. Fougnies told his daughter that he loved her deeply and wished her well, although he did have deep anxiety about her probable decision, adding, "However, you *are* an adult, and I have no power to control your decisions."

***

He ended the conversation by forthrightly announcing that, though it was difficult to tell her, he had firmly decided that, if she married the count and then found herself in any financial difficulty, she must not depend on him for help, adding that he appreciated her fine character and extreme idealism and, again, wished her well.

After this less than coercive attempt to change the mind of the daughter he deeply loved, Monsieur Fougnies still firmly believed that access to Lydie's potential inheritance was the ulterior motive in Hippolyte's aim to marry her. Even so, he decided that he would defray the costs of a proper wedding, when and if there was a marriage, and would pay for a lavish reception at the chateau.

***

144

Ever the trusting idealist, Lydie had had frank conversations with Hippolyte in late 1843, before her intended marriage in the coming June, about the rift between her father and mother when she was a teenager, about her private grammar school education, and about her matriculation at Belgium College. She told him about her trip to Europe on a large sailing ship and her interesting return by train but made no mention of the reason for the trip. He shook his head but could not have cared less.

It is unfortunate that she had forgotten Dr. LeBrun's warning about being too trusting. There was no good reason to tell Hippolyte in 1843 that her younger brother had been run over by a wagon, incurred a chronic bone inflammation and was destined to die at an early age, but she did! Lydie also told Hippolyte that Drs. Semel, in Peruwelz, and Lambris, the best-known diagnostician in Tournai, were certain that her brother would not live long, even though he had been feeling well for more than two years. She hadn't seen him for two years.

She did not know that Hippolyte made careful note of that information and intended to act on it. She did not know at the time that Gustave's condition had probably undergone a spontaneous cure. She had not seen her brother for a long time.

She did have a hunch, after listening to her father, that she would not inherit any of Gustave's estate if she married Hippolyte. Lydie knew that Gustave disliked Hippolyte as much as her father did, if not more.

Hippolyte had no realization of the shallowness of his own mind. He assumed without question, as we shall learn, that Lydie *had* to be Gustave's beneficiary, if her brother should die a bachelor.

CHAPTER 23

Premarital Minds

In January 1845, the count asked M. Fougnies for his daughter's hand in marriage and received his permission. After the marriage contract had been agreed upon but before the marriage had taken place, the count paid visits to Gustave's physicians in Peruwelz and Tournai, to inquire about Gustave's health and his probable life-span.

***

Based on belief of old and dubious information from Lydie, the Count de Bocarmé was convinced that Lydie had told him raw, truthful, and updated facts. His psychotic mind was at once convinced that, when Gustave died, Lydie would inevitably inherit a fortune, to which he would have free access. He felt good about that. What neither doctor knew was that Gustave's illness seemed now to have spontaneously disappeared. It had been two years since either one examined him.

***

As for Lydie, her mind was elsewhere. In her internal, unspoken dialogue, she anticipated with joy her inevitable admission to nobility. Not least of what secretly pleased her about admission to the aristocracy was the clearly sick thought that she would definitely "slam a door in Mme Van Hendryk's face."

It is true that during a short-lived period, with Felippe's love, Lydie had naturally assumed that she'd breached the barrier to aristocracy simply by acting as if she belonged there. It occurred to her fertile imagination that an evil Mme Van Hendryk had seen through what she considered a cunning intention. Therefore, she'd severely traumatized Lydie, perhaps for life.

Having self-indulgently dwelled for three years on the incident, she derived a warped pleasure in recalling and analyzing it. Her current analysis was as follows: Mme Van Hendryk had malevolently exposed her as nothing more than a cheap parvenu, a social climber of the first magnitude. Naturally, she loathed Mme Van Hendryk, but she loathed her "middle-class self" as well and, thereafter, felt more insecure than ever.

There was, after all, she confessed to herself, passive design on her part to cross a rigid social barrier using Felippe's help. This was undeniably artifice on her part. Therefore, the acutely sensitive young woman's humiliation also contained an undeniable sense of guilt. The mental trauma exceeded her breaking point, and Lydie entered further into the world of those who are badly mixed up mentally.

The few people who knew Lydie and had met the count continually discouraged her relationship with him, but she shocked them when she accepted Hippolyte's offer of marriage.

CHAPTER 24

The Marriage

The marriage ceremony for Count Hippolyte de Bocarmé and Lydie Fougnies took place at the cathedral in Mons on June 5, 1845, three years after she met him. Fewer guests witnessed it than one would expect at the wedding of someone of the Belgian aristocracy. More curious onlookers were outside the cathedral than there were invited guests within.

Hippolyte's bizarre, antisocial behavior had made him an aristocratic family's outcast. Family members in Brussels, Ghent, and Louvain received wedding invitations, but only a few found it convenient to attend the wedding or the reception in the evening gala at the Chateau de Bitremont in Bury. Those relatives who did attend the wedding displayed an air of indifference. They mingled only within their sphere of acquaintances, and never appeared festive. No doubt, the resistance to the marriage that Lydie's friends had made plain also added to the generally somber mood—even more somber than one expected in arranged marriages, which were common in the nineteenth century.

In spite of discouraging the marriage of his daughter to someone he disliked and did not trust, Lydie's father was polite and courteous and even gave the impression of pride when he presented his daughter to Hippolyte in the ceremony. Those who knew Lydie were convinced that she did not give the impression of being someone even mildly pleased about her marriage. She was clearly upset and angry that her brother, Gustave, did not attend. Although she knew that he strongly disliked Hippolyte, she viewed his absence unforgettably insulting. How much of this animosity was tinged by envy that he was now her father's favorite child and probably his sole inheritor was impossible to say. All emotional states have a touch of ambiguity in them.

The strained relationship of the siblings, known by those close to the marriage partners, was of no consequence to other guests. All of them enjoyed the champagne and fine French wines that were available in abundance. They dined on wild boar, pheasant, and ham from the Ardennes. Smoked salmon and French cheeses accompanied the excellent clarets and cognacs.

Hippolyte and his bride joined their guests, enjoying the music provided by a band of local musicians, who partook of the champagne, wines, and foods, the likes of which they had seldom, if ever, seen before.

Hippolyte drank too much. His drunken behavior took the form of gleefully pinching ladies' buttocks and approaching male guests and attempting to grab their genitals through their trousers, hoping to cause painful squeezing of their testicles. No one thought his behavior the least bit humorous except himself.

One guest told him, "Stop acting childishly. You're making an arse of yourself."

He responded by laughingly grabbing the guest's arm and twisting it, to produce as much pain as possible.

The man extricated himself and angrily told him, "Not even a drunk can be pardoned for what you just did. You must be crazy even when you're sober, you thoughtless idiot."

His response was, "If you don't like a little fun, get the hell outa here before I throw you out."

The man and his wife left, along with five other couples, who found the atmosphere intolerable.

Lydie was appalled by Hippolyte's antics, but although taken aback, she managed to rationalize her husband's behavior as an excess of normal celebration by a man on his wedding day.

However, she was not able to feel emotionally calm because she faced the unpleasant prospect of having to share her wedding night bed with a severely inebriated, foulmouthed husband.

***

149

After the last guests had left the chateau for the evening and the sounds of departing carriages had faded into the distance, the severely intoxicated Count Hippolyte de Bocarmé ordered all the servants to their quarters, shouting at them, "Get away from here! You'll need your energy to clean this place tomorrow. I'm sick of having to look at your ugly faces. Get out, now!" His words were slurred, and as he drank more, his ability to articulate became much worse.

Lydie was embarrassed to hear the count speak so impolitely to their staff, with such slovenly speech. In spite of his drunkenness, she felt that he should appreciate their servants, who had worked so hard preparing the chateau for a wedding reception. They deserved words of gratitude.

In the count's nonempathetic world, there was no room for gratitude. He had no sense of how the employees had toiled to the point of nausea, how much their muscles ached, or how much sweat exuded from their skins to enable him to drink himself into a stupor.

Holding a half empty champagne bottle, his eyes bloodshot, Hippolyte shouted to Lydie, "Get upstairs to our bedroom. I've wanted you in my bed for a long time, and tonight I'm going have you. I have looked at you and watched the way you behave, and I think that you believe you're better than most women are.

"Show me the difference. Believe me, I can tell if there is one. If you don't measure up, I'll let you know. But no matter how you perform, I will show you what real love is all about. Tonight you're mine, and you'll goddamn well perform your duty!" His speech was badly slurred.

Lydie listened to the drunken Hippolyte talk about consummating their marriage, like a lunatic whose only interest was a sexual conquest, without the warmth and tenderness that she had naively hoped might be associated with their wedding night. One might think that she knew him well enough by now not to hold so unrealistic a dream.

***

Hope changed to fright as she listened to her husband, who carried on as though he had become a raving, raging wild animal, wanting only to satisfy its sexual appetite by copulating with a timid, terrified, and uncooperative female.

Fear and revulsion and the loss of any interest in being physically close to the fiend she had agreed to marry a few hours earlier replaced whatever daintier fantasies Lydie may have entertained about her first intimate experience.

After a few minutes of shouting at her, mouthing words that made no sense, her former pupil fell onto a sofa in a semicomatose state and remained there in a drunken stupor. She was witnessing a rare situation, where a psychopath afflicted so badly with satyriasis would be physically unable to copulate.

Unfortunately, Lydie was too sick to make quick decisions. Faced with a fight or flight situation, although this was the perfect opportunity to flee from the chateau to her soft-spoken father's home in Peruwelz, she lacked the nerve to do it. Lydie was unable to imitate Angelica's decisiveness in making quick decisions and to act boldly and quickly to take appropriate action. All she had to do was find Alex Vandenberg or Gilles Van den Bergh to give her a ride to her father's house. Her neurosis was disabling.

Had she acted appropriately, the unconsummated marriage could easily have been annulled. Alas, Lydie could not impersonate Angelica. A healthy Lydie would have acted more appropriately. Instead, in a state of emotional paralysis, she watched her husband with combined pity and fright. She *was* frightened; she did not know what to expect from him when he woke up. She had never before seen Hippolyte act like this.

About an hour of sitting next to the sofa, she watched him struggle to his feet and walk carefully, as drunks do, toward the stairway that led to their bedroom, unaware that his wife was still sitting on a chair next to the sofa. He stumbled up the stairway slowly and entered his empty bedroom.

"Where the hell are you? Where is my wife? Have you forgotten what's expected of you on your wedding night? Are you hearing me? Where the hell are you? Come here now! Don't fiddle away time in taking your goddamn clothes off."

Nearly frozen with fear, Lydie walked slowly up the stairs, and as she entered the bedroom, Hippolyte slapped her face hard and shouted, "Why have you been hiding from me? Why have you kept me waiting for the reward a man should get from his wife?"

He pushed her onto their bed, and as Lydie tried to get up, he grabbed her and ripped her gown from her body. Lydie struggled to leave the room, but Hippolyte's strength made it impossible for her to escape. He held her arm with his right hand so tightly that it left a swollen, black-and-blue bruise visible in the morning. With his free left hand, he tore every remnant of underclothing from her. Lydie lay supine and terrified on the bed. She could hardly try now to escape by running through the door and about the chateau stark naked.

He leaned over and tried to kiss her. She found his alcoholic breath nauseating and moved her head. He struck her on the back of her head with the side of his left fist when she attempted to pull away.

He continued to hold her tightly with one hand as he removed his clothes with the other. He stood and undressed, breathing heavily but standing erect with all muscles flexed, to exhibit his muscular torso and his turgid organ. He said nothing.

The maneuver seemed a perverted form of self-admiration or glorification. There was no mirror behind the bed to observe himself, and Lydie kept her eyes closely shut. After nearly a minute, he suddenly leapt on her, and her many pleas to stop hurting her went unheeded.

Apart from the startle of the sudden but short-lived assault, for which she was unprepared, Lydie was horrified and confused. Was she really starting a new life with this man who showed such disrespect, selfishness, and strong force at a time that called for tenderness? How could her dreams have been shattered so quickly? How could she spend the balance of her life with this beast who was raping her on her wedding night? To whom could she complain? Feeling insulted and abused, she remained awake into the early morning hours while Hippolyte slept soundly, his loud snoring was the only sound interrupting the silence of the chateau.

Hippolyte awoke close to noon the next day and hit Lydie on the shoulder to wake her. She had finally fallen asleep, and although she was tired, she recoiled from his touch. The blood on the sheets made him realize what had occurred the night before.

Lydie sat up, kept her distance from him, and told him severely, "Last night, you were not the Hippolyte I wanted to marry. You were crude, and your roughness bewildered me. I became afraid of you, and your slapping me in the face still horrifies me. You are the first person ever to be so ignorant and cruel to me. That my husband would show such disrespect on the first night of our marriage is intolerable."

It is not unexpected that it never occurred to him to try to apologize. The lapse was consistent with his psychopathic inability to feel any empathy for Lydie's state of mind.

Lydie remained silent, with conflicting emotions of pity and hatred, while still—with psychopathologic idealism—wanting to preserve her urge to help Hippolyte become someone of whom she could be proud. Rescue fantasy, while it was an unnamed phenomenon in the nineteenth century and much of the twentieth, is almost never successful with sane people, but is destined to fail with a psychopath.

***

"Hippolyte, we must respect one another if we are to live under the same roof." She spoke sternly, but she could not rid herself of the fear she now felt for this crude man, knowing that he could repeat his behavior as a lunatic, at any time.

His response was, "No goddamn woman is going to tell me how I run my house! From here on, screw your goddamn mentoring sessions. You held them just to make me feel stupid."

Intuitively, Lydie now knew that she should henceforth be careful to avoid angering him and causing him to revert to lunacy even while sober. She did not immediately realize that the lunatic did not appreciate her severity. He had a long memory; she had now turned him into an implacable enemy. Too much alcohol had revealed Hippolyte's real nature. She saw it when he became sober. He continued to show the same disrespect that he had always displayed for the chateau staff.

For a few weeks, he made short-lived, suggestive gestures toward Lydie, usually in the afternoon, a signal that he wanted her to join him in their bedroom for a sexual engagement. These gestures became a predictable sign of his sexual need, and she tolerated these insults as the price she had to pay to transform Hippolyte de Bocarmé, as she had pledged, as well as to retain her title.

Conspicuously absent was any indication that her rescue fantasy had had any salutary effect or that it ever would. For the first time, she found herself convinced that she was likely to be in an untenable position. He again refused her offer to continue the twice weekly mentoring sessions, accusing her of having tried to hold him up to ridicule by tattling to her friends how humorously ignorant he was. Her situation epitomized the danger of rescue fantasy in its earliest stages. Worse was to come.

***

Hippolyte decided to treat Lydie as a lieutenant of the hired help, who conveyed his orders to them. Lydie despised hearing sharply worded commands from Hippolyte instead of polite requests. His rude and crude outbursts grew more frequent with time. The only difference between her and the other household help was that he felt

154

free to use *her*, at any time, as a sexual object. Lydie now absolutely despised him.

Sadistic beatings almost invariably followed their forced sessions of "lovemaking." Hippolyte complained that her performances were perfunctory and that she showed no interest in making them actively pleasurable for him. She submitted to his every need passively and without question or resistance and lost her self-respect completely.

She was now living with a selfish animal, who exercised nearly total control over her, and she grew ever more deathly afraid of him. As a means of self-defense, she carefully controlled her demeanor to suggest contentment because she had discovered that any expression or appearance of dissatisfaction, for any reason, incurred Hippolyte's anger and physical abuse. Lydie found a short-lived way of avoiding him from time to time; she would complain of various illnesses and her need to sleep. She desperately wanted to leave Hippolyte but did not know how.

She had now lost any resilience of character she might have had as a single woman, to withstand criticism from those who had discouraged her marriage. But largely, her "not knowing how to leave" was her retention of the psychologically sick interest in wanting to show Madame Van Hendryk that she could marry into the Belgian aristocracy.

***

Although they were not products of a loving, warm, and caring relationship, one stillborn and three living children were born to Lydie in the course of her marriage, which took place in June 1845. The three were born between autumn 1846 and early winter 1850. They were Robert-Gonzalès, Mathilde-Blanche, and Rose-Marie Eugènie.

In August 1851, Robert-Gonzalès was just over four years old, walking, and calling his father "Daddy." Mathilde was in a carriage, and Rose-Marie lay in a crib or a nursemaid's arms when bottle fed. Born so closely together, these children became the center of Lydie's life.[15] She frequently concocted the presence of illnesses in her children—illnesses severe enough to require her to sleep in their room.

She would insist to Hippolyte that she alone could provide the care the children needed at these times. When it became difficult to prove her children's illnesses, she complained that she was ill.

Lydie lived a frustrating, difficult, and sad life, compounded by serious financial problems brought on by Hippolyte's extravagant living on borrowed money he refused to consider repaying and her required complicity in this fraud.

She also knew of Hippolyte's extramarital affairs with certain of the domestic help, but felt that her silence and appearance of ignorance were worthwhile prices to pay, if it would lessen any physical contact with him.

---

[15] Their exact dates of birth do not appear in the records of *Procès de Bocarmé*.

CHAPTER 25

Chateau de Bitremont

The Chateau de Bitremont was one of the oldest residences in Belgium. In 1850, it was possible to travel from Peruwelz to the chateau by large and small horse-drawn vehicles. Its location was in Bury, a suburb of Peruwelz.

To travelers, the inn/tavern in Bury village was a pleasant sight that marked the center of the tranquil village known for its friendly and hospitable people and good beer. The favorite drink at its tavern was bottled houblon, a locally brewed good, cool drink.

The inhabitants of the area led agrarian lives. They cultivated their fields with diligence and good humor, and a few maintained simple bed-and-breakfast lodgings.

The residents of Bury demonstrated their religious devotion by decorating small areas around the town and along the moderately steep road leading to the chateau with statues of their favorite saints.

To reach the chateau from the village, one trudged up the steep road and passed a small church with a bell tower, and two hundred yards beyond, at the peak of a hill, the two towers of the feudal Chateau de Bitremont came into view.

***

In 1850, there were two ways to enter the chateau. A long, straight driveway bordered on either side by double rows of tall, Canadian poplars and flower gardens led directly to the front entrance. A second entrance road skirted the new wing, passing hundreds of acres of the chateau's farmland on its right as the road veered left to the rear of the imposing building. It ended between a pond and a large garden on the left and numerous stables on the right. A drawbridge allowed

157

horse-drawn coaches to cross the backyard pond to the rear entrance to the chateau. Both front and rear entrances, which were directly opposite, opened into a large entrance hall or vestibule.[16]

On entering through the front door, one was in a vestibule decorated with a plaster bust of the French playwright Moliere. On the right, a door opened to a square dining room with green- and black-striped wallpaper and an elegant oaken parquet floor. There were four windows, two facing the front lawn and garden. The other two, on an adjacent wall, were on the sidewall of the chateau. A narrow walkway separated the sidewall from a grassy extension of the front garden and courtyard.

A large, white, marble fireplace was located in the wall of the dining room to the right of the entrance from the vestibule. A round, cherry wood dining table and chairs occupied the center of an oaken parquet floor. At opposite sides were old hardwood armoires, one for storage of wine bottles, the other for wine glasses. A polished mahogany, three-level sideboard occupied wall space between the front windows and the far corner. It was a handsome room with handsome furniture, stunning wallpaper and an interesting, expensive floor, No carpeting hid its repetitious inlaid pattern of light within darker woods.

Opposite the dining room, on the other side of the vestibule, was a glass-paneled door through which one passed into "the old part" of the first floor. The doors opened into a sizeable room known as the Salon à Colonnes. Visitors to this room in the 1850s found it splendorous. Within recently painted, immaculate white walls were new, obviously expensive armchairs, colorfully upholstered sofas, fine hardwood benches, and a kneeler comfortably upholstered with soft velvet fabric. A crucifix and a clock with a large pendulum shared a wall with a coat of arms bearing the motto "I Protect the Weak."

---

[16] See cover photograph of the Chateau.

The next room was the Red Salon, so called because of the bright red tapestry that covered the walls. The furniture was as stylish and in as good taste as that in the Salon à Colonnes.

Altogether, one would have had the impression, prior to late November 1850, that the furnishings of the Chateau de Bitremont were so elegant and refined that the master of the house was of great wealth and refinement.

It would have seemed that no insignificant bourgeois family lived there and that life must be exceedingly pleasant for all its inhabitants.

***

Contrary to that impression, this was the home of the psychopathic Count de Bocarmé and his wife, the former Lydie Fougnies. The count had ordered his wife, who had good taste, to have the walls restored, as well as expensive furniture installed, in both salons and the dining room. He ordered her to have all this done, despite his immense indebtedness to those from whom he borrowed at least 250,000 francs, with no intention of repaying them.

In the gorgeous gardens that surrounded the chateau was a variety of flowers and esoteric plants. The count also used borrowed money to obtain them and had neither the intention nor the francs to repay the notary from whom he had received the large loan of francs.

Countess Lydie knew that this financial behavior was wrong and dishonorable, but she dared not disobey her husband, who would beat her sadistically if she failed to agree with him. The Chateau de Bitremont was, in 1850, a most unhappy house.

In the late nineteenth and much of the twentieth centuries, curious sightseers to the chateau had generally heard of terrible legends associated with it. Regardless of their accuracy, the hardiest visitors toured the chateau with some fear. These guests spoke in hushed tones especially about the dining room with green- and black-striped wallpaper and parquet floor, where, according to lore, an awful murder had once been committed.

During this period in the nineteenth and twentieth centuries, the once grand chateau fell into progressive disrepair. From time to time it sheltered homeless people, especially in winter. They burned furniture and furnishings to heat the interior. One hundred years after the "awful crime," animals and wild birds inhabited most of its rooms. Pigeons, once confined to the pigeon-house, had become so numerous that they occupied much of the bedroom floor and the entire attic. Once ornate gardens vanished and most of the many stately trees lay dying or dead from disease or neglect.

On June 2, 1989, flames incinerated the entire chateau except its stonework. The Peruwelz police attributed the fire to grand arson.

CHAPTER 26

Life at the Chateau

From 1846 to 1850, when jointly occupied by the count and countess, the chateau and everything in and around it was visible to the large, observant staff of domestic help. Almost all of them were born and raised in Bury. They told their family members and friends all that they saw and heard in the mansion, often exaggerating, embellishing, or misconstruing their observations.

The townspeople were mainly farmers, who lived modestly and were devoted to religion. Most would not have tolerated dissolute conduct if they reliably knew of it. Nevertheless, the ill-treated domestic help reported dissolute conduct within the chateau.

The domestic help magnified and extended the count's personal immorality to include others living at or visiting the chateau. Their reports represented most of the fodder for malicious gossip invented by Bury's younger male population when they gathered at the tavern.

The tavern tales became a favorite subject of discussion, especially when imaginations ran wild as the drinkers guzzled their beer. One has to suppose that the prattle provided more than a little vicarious thrill, especially for juveniles, whose undisciplined minds and mouths eased the way for rumors in Bury to spread to neighboring villages.

Truth is it was not unusual to see an out-of-town carriage or two pull up to the chateau on Friday evenings in summer and fall. They brought friends whom Lydie invited for the weekend. She retained her association with certain of her college classmates living in Tournai and welcomed their company even though painters were still at work refurbishing the original red wall color of the Red Salon and the white walls of the Salon à Colonnes. Hippolyte liked it when well-to-do and well-connected visitors came. He wanted them to think he was a wealthy count with no end of money.

161

Young men with lazy, dirty minds invented ugly tales when influenced by an excess of houblon. One of the worst was that these visitors eagerly took advantage of the apparent seclusion of Bitremont, and of its acres of grassland, to have intimate relations with their partners, unaware that members of the chateau's staff were watching them. All these tales were outright fiction. All of these visitors were refined and it would never occur to them to behave vulgarly.

Reports of Count Hippolyte de Bocarmé's sexual experiences with women other than his wife were common. It was impossible to confirm all details of *these* rumors. Nevertheless, they were the regular and favorite subjects of gossip from Chateau maids and converted to jokes when the drunk, younger Bury residents were into their beloved houblon.

Whether the count and countess loved one another was a common subject of discussion. Nearly everyone was convinced, correctly, that the count was unfaithful to his wife, but general belief was that, while it was she who hosted alleged weekend orgies, she did not, herself, indulge in any improper behavior.

Analysis of the count's conduct was what mattered most, because so much of it was true, although his mischief tended not to be a weekend activity. The presence of well-mannered guests inhibited him. Thus, there was general agreement that he was careful to give his prurient attention to female members of the chateau staff with utmost secrecy during the weekends. The beer drinkers seemed not fully to realize how weekend guests modified his behavior. This "guest effect" was little known.

More important was how Count Hippolyte de Bocarmé exploited his position as employer. He knew that jobs for young women were not easy to find in the area but still found an adequate number of young women (many were innocent young girls) applying for work as housemaids. Once he'd hired these girls, he crudely promised gifts and long-term employment in return for sexual favors from them.

When his subsequent propositions were rejected, as the majority was, he had no compunction about terminating a resisting young woman's employment on the spot, without payment of any salary she may have been due. There was, therefore, a high staff turnover at the chateau.

The high turnover did not bother the count, as it facilitated the hiring of fresh, potential candidates, some of whom would inevitably be willing to satisfy his inordinate sexual appetite. The sites of his fornication, quick lewd acts, took place in empty bedrooms, sometimes in the maids' bedrooms, or on a couch in the count's "office," whose doors could be tightly locked. The reports of Hippolyte's many affairs of the flesh were legendary. A constant feature was his premature ejaculation.

Tales of the count's beating his wife were frequent. Hippolyte knew that Lydie feared him, but Lydie realized that leaving her husband would cause her an extreme degree of embarrassment. She would have had to admit to her father, brother, and friends that she should have taken their advice.

However, a more critical suppression of her desire to leave him lay in her unbalanced mind; keeping her title as a countess was essential. Her neurotic need for the title was the real reason for her delay in planning seriously how to remove herself from the Chateau de Bitremont.

There were reports by the staff of hearing frequent sexual encounters of the count and countess during the day, accompanied by loud screaming. The domestics incorrectly interpreted what they heard, not realizing that the screams were not from orgasmic pleasure but, instead, were screams of the countess being sadistically beaten by her husband. This led the unsophisticated staff to question the mental stability of the count and, unfairly, of the countess.

***

It did not occur to the employees that the count was not the great lover he wanted others to believe. They assumed that Lydie was

163

"performing" satisfactorily during the couplings he insisted they have. The confused interpretation of the housemaids was probably due to their ignorance of the count's sick, sadistic side. They were aware only that the count was a sexual maniac of some sort. Common belief among them was that Lydie was aware of her husband's infidelities.

In truth, Lydie made an effort to avoid contact with her husband and accommodated herself to his seeking gratification in beds other than theirs. She more than tolerated Hippolyte's despicable use of other women as sexual objects; she welcomed it because he had less need to use her.

***

Most guests assumed that Hippolyte and Lydie were wealthy. None was aware that the Bocarmés had acquired all of their expensive furniture, oriental rugs, and other finery entirely on credit, soon after their marriage. The count exploited his noble title and ordered the countess to use hers to acquire what they, the count especially, wanted.

He was anxious to give an appearance of wealth. To very few, if any of the weekend guests at the chateau was it obvious that the count and countess lived above their means. The count did nothing to modify the extravagant lifestyle he insisted on showing guests. Although he owed many thousands of francs to notaries and banks, he had no intention of repaying them.

He ordered Lydie, who had good taste, to arrange the purchase of their expensive furniture, the construction of new stables, and even the hiring of additional stablemen to wash and rub down the horses every day. He wanted expensive new carriages of various sizes, too.

***

As Lydie's life grew increasingly unbearable, she learned news that crushed her heart. The bank that held her small inheritance in trust notified her that her father had died. The letter came after his funeral. Although she knew not to expect any financial assistance from him, the simple fact that he was alive had meant something to her spirit; perhaps a miraculous event would change his mind.

Hippolyte continued to demand that Lydie always accompany him when he sought vendors who would give them credit. They borrowed from anyone who was unaware of their reputation for not paying their bills or repaying loans. Since she spoke as one would expect a countess to speak, he remained silent, muttering a rare word. Cunning and unprincipled. After beating her daily, her husband used her charm to steal.

He indecorously tried to borrow money from servants at the chateau, with promises of repayment with interest "as soon as our funds, whose records were misplaced by a fool working in our Brussels Bank, are found and released."

Not one whom he importuned believed him. The count had no source of income ever to repay his loans but continued living in the grand style of the wealthy. The count ordered Lydie to mortgage some property that she happened to own, but, instead of using the money to repay debts, he insisted that she use it to entertain an increasing number of guests at the chateau, sometimes for up to a week.

He (and she) impressed the guests with first-class hospitality, which included supervised quail and grouse hunts. On one occasion, Hippolyte ordered Lydie to arrange an operatic performance of *La Traviata* in the chateau's courtyard. The cast of singers came from Brussels to Bury. The count and countess could ill afford this grandstanding that cost them more than 10,000 borrowed francs.

Hippolyte ordered Lydie to break the trust established by her recently deceased father. Its contents paid her [them] 2,000 francs annually. She obediently emptied the 40,000 francs in the body of the trust that paid 5 percent interest, but the count used none of it to pay debts.

The level of opulence with which the couple lived left many who worked at the chateau wondering how their employers could afford such an extravagant way of life, when they were unable to pay them their paltry wages on time.

Hippolyte also demanded of Lydie, after the marriage and while she was carrying her stillborn child, that she modify her will by naming him her sole beneficiary, and she complied. Later, she protested that she did so because he had already beaten her several times and she feared that he would beat her again if she hesitated. Hippolyte also demanded of Lydie, during one of the nearly daily beatings he meted out, to adopt his arrogant and demanding attitude in dealing with the chateau staff.

She feared being civil, which is why no one within the range of Hippolyte's sharp hearing heard a thank you for a job well done and why she treated small creditors in Peruwelz as haughtily as she did.

The staff at the chateau was always on call, and the count demanded that Lydie remain in bed late in the mornings, whether or not she was able to sleep. She was literally under duress to request that she be served breakfast in bed, after which she asked for her bath to be prepared. Preparing the bath was a difficult task for servants, who had to bring hot water from the kitchen to the master suite on the second floor.

Her husband ordered that excessive morning noise by the playing Bocarmé children invite her wrath, which she was to direct only at the nursemaids who looked after the children. Like the offspring of nearly all European nobility, the three Bocarmé children spent little time with their parents, who expected nursemaids to be their surrogates and to present the children to their parents briefly, at meal times only.

Countess Lydie often appeared sad and withdrawn, but she found some enjoyment and was affable with those around her when she made specialty cheeses at the chateau and gave them to guests who stayed there.

She developed a reputation among her social set, originally a few college classmates and enlarged by their friends, for what she named Brie de Bitremont, made from slightly salted, freshly churned butter, with black and white truffles harvested from the Bitremont woods.

The source of milk for butter and for her rich cheese was a small herd of Jersey cows that Hippolyte housed in new barns behind the stables. While the cheese was good enough to sell and fetch an attractive price, the countess's objective was more subtle. An ability to give her cheese freely to guests at the chateau would contribute to a false image of her and her husband's apparent wealth. It would promote and preserve an image of her as one of the Belgian landed gentry who preferred giving to receiving. Someone, she hoped, would repeat to him something like, "We appreciate your extraordinary generosity. The superb cheese Lydie makes of your dairy herd's milk is above and beyond what we have come to expect of you. Do thank Lydie, too, for her talent." He might beat her only once the following Monday. However, no words she knew would sate his sadistic beatings.

More guests thought Countess Lydie's cheese had such remarkable consistency and excellent flavor that they suggested she sell it. She told these guests, "Selling cheese is an occupation for the underclass. After all, there's more to a good life than making money."

She could not have meant to mouth so odious an antisocial remark had she not hoped that this comment, too, would reach Hippolyte and possibly save her from another beating. In truth, if she had sold cheese from the chateau, the income could have been used to alleviate a little of the out-of-hand financial pressures that the count and countess faced. The francs could have defrayed the cost of a couple of cases of claret they offered so generously to their guests.

***

167

Count Hippolyte grew tobacco and spent much of his free time tending a plot of plants, from which he cured handpicked leaves. When they lost their initial greenness and darkened to a special hue, he treated them as his grandfather had but told the guests that the recipe was his. He shared the qualities of this special tobacco with the guests. He would delight in telling new ones stories of making cigars with "Indians" in Arkansas. Those who had heard these stories on a previous visit usually left.

CHAPTER 27

Designing Murder

Hippolyte was determined to get Gustave's money and property. The only way to be sure of it was to kill him without alerting the police. After dinner one evening in late September 1850, as they sat in separate, upholstered lounge chairs in the Salon à Colonnes facing one another, he repeated to Lydie what she had heard him say several times before: "We need that sick little arsehole's money. He's living too long. I'm going to get my hands on that fortune of francs he's collected."

Lydie responded, "You keep repeating yourself. You've told me several times that you were going to kill him, and you know that I don't like to hear it."

"Sure. I've given this serious thought for a long time; I'm a practical man."

"Are you going to tell me anything new?"

"I'm telling you that I'm going through with plans to get our hands on the fortune that should go to us, not to that one-legged shithead."

"Please, darling, you don't have to shout. Hippolyte, the expression on your usually handsome face frightens me; it's too angry." She flattered him, hoping to avoid a slap in the face.

"Look here. What I happen to know, and don't dare ask me how I know, is that your goddamn brother is sick as hell. But the end isn't going to come soon. He has his good days and his bad days. I found out that, right now, he's well enough to sometimes leave the house after dinner and drink a little beer.

It crossed the count's mind that he'd like a mug of beer himself. But he was too busy giving what his purpose was—a threatening lecture to Lydie.

169

"Of course, that means nothing. His disease will catch up with him—that's certain—until he's bedridden for what might be years. *You* would have to take care of him when he can't take care of himself; ever think of that? He could live a hell of a long time before he dies; most of the time he's going to be in bed. What's he going to do with all that money when he won't be able to spend it?!"

Hippolyte liked hearing the sound of his own voice. Demanding absolute attention made him feel as though he were delivering a well-planned oration.

"He must know that he doesn't need it; he's selfish. He ought to turn it over to *us*. He knows he ought to, but he's too miserly and mean. I see a long future of pain and suffering for him and a time when he's going to need you, or someone else, to look after him. Hiring nurses will eat up a lot of his money, dammit. So we don't want that to happen.

"He's lived uselessly for too goddamn long. Now we even hear rumors that he talks about getting married in a few years. That's plain bullshit; it makes no sense. Not even a pipe-dreamer like you could believe that. The only kind of woman who'd marry him is a prostitute. He's not fit for a real marriage.

"You know as well as me, that the only thing about marriage that's worth anything is screwing. How in hell is he going to pull off a trick like that, unless he has a normal wife who's willing to twist herself into painful contortions to do it half right? Only a prostitute would agree to that."

"What *are* you talking about Hippolyte? You have a dirty mind. That doesn't make any sense."

Hippolyte jumped from his chair and slapped the left side of her face as hard as he could with the flat of his right hand. She held back her tears, although she felt seriously stinging pain.

Lydie now chose to be exceptionally careful about what she might say, as Hippolyte proceeded to lecture her with utmost conviction about frequent sex as the central necessity of a happy marriage. As he rambled, he informed her that a man with a missing right leg could enjoy a happy married life only if his wife's left leg had been amputated. He was very serious. She now understood better than ever the squalor that occupied his demented mind.

***

"You better goddamn well go along with my plan because it's going to need the both of us. I'll be giving orders, and you'll carry them out without a hitch."

He paused, looked sternly into her eyes without blinking, and warned her, "If you don't obey, I'll be forced to kill both of you. I'm determined to kill anyone who stands in my way. So, be careful.

"You asked me what I was talking about, so I'll explain it to you; but once you know, you keep it to yourself. That's a warning, understand? You know how I treat anyone, which includes you, who double-crosses or disobeys me.

"Whether you like it or not, wives obey their husbands. Everybody knows that. Don't ever double-cross me, stand in the way of my plans, or fail to obey my orders—never!—not if you want to remain alive.

"All right! You know perfectly well that I grow tobacco plants to make cigars and smoke in a pipe now and then. I've told you many times that, when I lived in Arkansas, I saw Indians kill wolves with a poison they put on the tips of their arrows.

"I didn't know how they did it, but I learned from one of them, who became my friend, that they make a gum from water they boiled tobacco leaves in; then they put the gum on the tips of their arrows. They killed wolves that attacked their sheep and cattle. The wolves stopped dead in their tracks seconds after the arrows struck them; they seemed to shake all over, fall to the ground, and die. I saw it happen."

"Hippolyte, excuse me dear, have you considered the role of the Belgian police? They have a good reputation."

"Hell with the police! The police don't know shit about Indians! I'm telling you, I am going to put the selfish little son of a bitch out of his misery. Your brother is an embarrassment to you, so why do you care whether he stays alive? No normal woman would ever marry him, except a prostitute.

"You want a prostitute to take our money? We're the ones who deserve what your brother has, not someone who's only known him for a short time. If your brother dies of poisoning, by something the Indians used, no one is ever going to know how he died."

She was afraid to tell him to shut up.

He stood before her and flexed his arms and his giant fists as he began another demented monologue. "Since the day I married you five years ago, I noticed that Gustave made no bones about his dislike for me and refused to attend the wedding. When the contract was signed, your two-faced bastard of a father had the rotten nerve to insult me by giving me a puny little income to add to what my grandfather left me.

"I almost told him to stick the contract up his arse and refuse to sign it, but I was patient enough to give him a second chance. I figured that, after he got to know me better, we'd naturally become good friends, like I get to be with most people. I waited until he died because I figured he'd leave his money to us, but he didn't. Your father thumbed his goddam nose at me by leaving the money to that little cripple who isn't worth a fat fart and has no use for it. Knowing goddam well he'll never marry, the cripple still tooked it and added it to his piggy bank—probably with a mean smirk. He must have laughed himself sick as he joked to himself, 'Don't worry, Lydie. It'll all belong to you, unless I recover and get married twenty years from now.'

"He's the same mean little bastard who called me some kind of an 'idiot'—you told me that—and he refused to go to our wedding. Isn't that right? Do you think for one minute that he's not going to pay the full price for that? No way! Even if it takes me two years to do it.

"He must enjoy playing games with us, trying to make my mouth water, like that poor, thirsty son of a bitch in the fairy tale. He kept climbing up a hill for a drink of water and, as he gets there, his mouth watering for a drink, the water disappears. That makes me mad.

"He ought to be decent and hand it over to us. Why in hell do we have to wait until he dies? He has a special love for money, like a king counting his gold coins three or four times a day."

He sat and put his hands on his knees.

"Okay! Now that you know that I'm serious, I'm laying the law down to you. *If you ever dare warn him what I'm going to do to him, I'll do the same to you.* Don't forget that you made me the sole and complete heir to anything you own, way back when you pushed out that dead baby. You signed it voluntarily; don't ever say that you didn't. And never try to find that signed agreement because you won't be able to. I'm good at hiding things.

"But I have to do some more research on this to be a hundred percent sure I hide the poison so it won't leave traces behind on the clothes he's wearing when I kill him.

"He's been sick for most of his life. Everyone around here knows that. His sudden death wouldn't surprise anyone, and we would inherit everything he owns—everything! Think of what this would do for us."

***

He pointed his right index finger and waggled it close to Lydie's face. "First goddamn thing in the morning, you write a nice letter for me to my father. Say all those little things you have to say in a letter before you ask for something. Then ask him for Virginia tobacco seeds. They're very small, almost as small as grains of pepper. He can get enough into an envelope to grow three crops of Virginia tobacco. We don't have any time to waste; it's already 1847, and we need the tobacco."

173

"Have you considered investigation by the police?"

"Naaah! For Crissake, I already told you that police don't know their own arses from holes in the ground."

"I don't know, Hippolyte; I'm afraid. Where would you get the poison? And how would you give it to Gustave? Would you put it in his food or in wine for him to drink?"

"That's for me to plan, not you. You just follow my orders, is that clear? Don't worry. I'm not stupid. Only you and I will know the truth, but if you ever told on me, you'd be easy to kill."

Hippolyte had the audacity to say this to the wife he had beaten with his fists almost daily since they married. He could simply punch harder and kill her.

***

Lydie now well understood that Hippolyte had a criminal mind; he enjoyed her fear of him. It made him feel good. Whether or not he had a suspicion that she was now doubly certain he was literally crazy and belonged behind bars is unclear. She could never persuade this lunatic to shut up and stop acting like one. She could not have told him that she could never and would never participate in any plan to kill anyone, and certainly not her brother. If she had, he would have treated her as he had done once before for not allowing him to engage with her in anal sex.

He'd explained at the time that he liked to "do what animals do when they 'fornicate.'" She hadn't dared tell him that he was using the wrong word to describe what he wanted to do. Within her mind, she heard what could have been Shakespearean banter but withheld the temptation to explain. He'd retaliated once before by rubbing her face in a pile of recently dug soil and would probably do it again. He was in no mood for humor.

For the first time since she had tried, with a kind heart, to teach him to act in a socially acceptable way, the clear, ineradicable thought came to her that, since Hippolyte was insane and extremely dangerous, perhaps she should try to escape.

***

He made it clear that he would kill me, and he usually means exactly what he says. He has no appreciation for all the good I tried to do for him. I even gave up the love of my father and brother to try to help him, she thought to herself. Thinking this way surprised her because it made her feel better. That she could develop this insight spontaneously in the presence of her insane husband was especially freeing. Had he left the room, she would likely have smiled, maybe laughed.[17]

She thought of escaping, but it was impossible. He watched her closely. How could she leave without taking their three children? Say she were to make it as far as the half mile to the village of Bury, who would protect her? Hippolyte was very strong. No one in the village would be able to fight him off. There was no police officer in the village. Her brother, frail and dependent on crutches to get around, could hardly protect her.

She considered all the possibilities, and none seemed feasible. Besides, she did like being a countess, and Hippolyte had said that it might take him two years before he would be ready to commit the murder. Her conclusion: *Maybe I still have time.*

This was not the only reason Lydie cooked up for procrastinating. Perhaps it would be safer to wait, she concluded. When the critical moment comes, he may not have the nerve to go through with the plan. She was still vacillating and contradicting herself.

---

[17] There is no scientific explanation for this inner change. The best current explanation is that she had subconsciously released most of her hostility for Mme Van Hendryk to Hippolyte, and diminishing hostility diminishes anxiety. In this case, the clearance was partial.

However, as she thought longer and harder about her situation, she reminded herself that she was in this horrendous situation because of a *foolish need to seek revenge on Mme Van Hendryk and because of my false values—I foolishly wanted so much to be a countess, and it got me nowhere.* Lydie was showing definite signs of improvement in her once seemingly fixed neurosis. Probably she had a way to go, to reach normality.

She compared her problem with a terrible nightmare. She had become ambivalent about the value of a title. She could think of no way to help herself, as she'd seen Angelica do for her in Genoa several years ago. The problem was, she was now a captive. She could think of no way to free herself and her children.

If she firmly announced to Hippolyte that she had decided to have nothing to do with his murder plan, there was a good chance he would kill her because she knew too much. Who would then take care of the children?

***

Early next morning, while having coffee with him, Lydie summoned the courage to ask, in a purposefully benign and innocent way, "Hippolyte, did you really mean it when you said you would kill me?"

She didn't like the answer.

"*Of course I would.* If you ever disobeyed or double-crossed me, or if I thought it might be in my interest to do it, I would kill you. Never forget that you signed over everything you own to me, in the event of your death, when you were not in such good shape pushing that dead kid out of that big, bloated belly of yours. *When all of Gustave's fortune comes to you, be certain you're not stingy with it. If you happened to die in an accident, it would all be mine.*"

He went off on a tangent. "Who in hell do you think you are? You're not a real de Bocarmé. You're no aristocrat. You just know how to imitate how real aristocrats behave. You're just another piece

176

of arse that's primarily good for one thing, and you turned out to be lousy at it. Mind you, if you ever warn your brother what's in store for him, you'll disappear and no one will ever find you. I told you that I'm good at hiding things.

"By the way, *if I am going to kill him in the house, I'll give you detailed instructions when we are alone in our bedroom on how to hide anyone who shouldn't be there, so there won't be no witnesses. I'll run over what I want you to do again and again, so you do it right.*"

***

Nauseated with fear, she quickly changed the subject. She turned to his mention of research, asking how he was going to go about it.

"I told you what to do, goddamn it! You write a letter for me. Send it to my father in Arkansas saying all the nice little things you're supposed to say first, and then tell him that I want to know if he's learned anything more about the poison in the arrow tips the Indians used to kill wolves. And I want seeds for three crops of Virginia tobacco.

"Tell him I'm happy growing tobacco and I want to know more about it. If there's anything written about this poison, I want him to tell me about something that's in a book. I can get it in a library in Brussels or in a big bookstore. Yeh, and don't forget that the main thing is to ask him to send me seeds of that strong Virginia tobacco he plants.

"While you're writing this letter, I'm going over to Ghent to see what poisonous plants, besides tobacco, are in the 'plant museum' or whatever the hell you call that place in Ghent. No harm in seeing."

CHAPTER 28

Gustave Plans to Marry

In July 1850, Gustave acquired Chateau de Grandmetz in the village of Grandmetz, four miles north of Peruwelz and about three miles from the Chateau de Bitremont.

Madame de Dudzcèle and her daughter, Antoinette, descendants of a count having the same name, had lived at the chateau for only a brief period. Mme de Dudzcèle's husband had been commissioner of the government's Geologic and Geodetic Survey Division for twenty-five years. He'd decided to sell their home in a suburb of Brussels and buy a comfortable countryside home in Grandmetz.

Being in perfect health, he had hoped to continue working in a consulting role offered by the government. He welcomed the opportunity because he'd spent more for the large home in Grandmetz than he had received from the sale of his smaller Brussels home. Income from the consulting job would help him to balance his loss and allow him to support his wife and daughter in Grandmetz.

Unfortunately, he'd died suddenly of a heart attack. The tragedy had left Mme de Dudzcèle in straitened circumstances; she had no choice but to advertise her lovely country home for sale.

Gustave bought the house. He found Antoinette de Dudzcèle attractive and feared that, when she and her mother left the home that he called "the Chateau," he would lose an opportunity to get to know her. For good and sufficient reason, then, he offered to let mother and daughter continue living in the chateau until January of the following year. His plan was to allow himself time to get to know the young lady, whom he found charming and who did not appear bothered by his physical handicap.

Gustave felt more ebullient than at any time in his life. He meditated as much as ever, but his mind now played with optimistic

178

thoughts. Remnants of anxiety and pessimism disappeared, and he looked forward to passing his days with renewed vigor and optimism. In spite of having to use crutches to move about, he displayed a lively spirit that was new to his friends and acquaintances. At times, his sense of humor left those in his company laughing uncontrollably.

He had the facility to be self-deprecating, using the subject of his disability to make his friends temporarily abandon the sympathy for his condition that they had grown predisposed to express. Sometimes, after drinking a moderate amount of beer, he would comically exaggerate his use of crutches to get around, doing so in a way that would make his friends laugh loudly and unreservedly. This facility endeared him to those around him because his humor was never at the expense of anyone but himself.

Gustave's new lease on life expressed itself in his paintings, which became more vibrant with color and movement. He painted colorful and lively pictures of horses, birds, and flowers, and after he had completed a portrait of Mlle de Dudzcèle in a rose garden and hung it on a prominent wall at his home, it became obvious to his friends that he had found someone special.

He frequently visited Antoinette and her mother, bringing flowers, wine, and special cheeses that he found in Peruwelz. He began to travel to Mons frequently to get freshly baked blueberry pastries that he knew Antoinette liked.

Both mother and daughter appeared fond of Gustave, and Gustave, in turn, found Antoinette de Dudzcèle charming, pretty, and endowed with a sense of humor. She was bright, and Gustave was smitten.

***

He had spent sad, lonesome evenings for so many years. His life could be magically changed if he had a close relationship with Antoinette. Gustave became preoccupied with thoughts of a life with her. He confided in his best friend, Arnaud Felicien, with whom he frequently shared, his concerns about marriage because of his physical condition. He wanted to have children but felt that no woman would relish the prospect of making love to a man with only one leg.

Arnaud discouraged this negative thinking and suggested that Gustave approach Antoinette honestly, if he were seriously interested in proposing marriage. He told Gustave that he could only settle his concerns and reservations if he had open and honest conversations with the woman he loved.

"Our society does not allow women to be aggressive in relationships," Arnaud counseled him, "so she will not display any outward signs of serious affection toward you. But you know in your heart that she is fond of you, so I urge you to have a serious talk with her."

"I have a problem, Arnaud. I have money and property, and she does not. How can I ever know that she wants me and not just the comforts of what I can provide? How will I ever know if she would marry me if I were poor? How can I know that she truly loves me?"

"You can't know for sure, Gustave. But if you spend time with her and share your dreams openly, I think you will be able to tell, from her reactions, if she would enjoy spending her life faithfully with you.

"If you conclude that she would not, well, I'm sure that would be disappointing to you, but at least you would know where you stand."

Like many with whom Gustave came in contact, Antoinette de Dudzcèle demonstrated concern for Gustave's condition, and was always prepared and willing to offer him physical support, when it seemed to her that it was needed. Gustave was initially irritated by this behavior but accepted her help after Antoinette made it obvious that her impulse to help was genuine and not just a cold social reflex.

Gustave learned the details of Antoinette and her mother's financial plight, and although he understood that his wealth would make him an attractive partner to many young women, he concluded that Antoinette could command the attention of other suitors, if she did not want to be married to him.

***

Although he felt that he had not discussed all he had intended with Antoinette (he omitted his anxiety that others might be attracted to her), one evening after Madame de Dudzcèle had retired, he lost all inhibitions and dared to ask Antoinette if she would marry him. She accepted his proposal without hesitation.

She admitted that she had thought about a life with him and had even discussed the possibility with her mother, who was supportive. Gustave surprised Antoinette by presenting her with a beautiful ring—a diamond surrounded by sapphires. He had purchased it in Mons the day before.

He quickly dismissed any presumptions and thoughts of inferiority that he might have held when she accepted the ring and kissed him gently on his lips as he hugged her.

Antoinette brought him to tears when she told him, as they held each other, "I know that you must wonder why I want to marry you. Please, do not ever wonder again. I want to marry you because I love you. I love your honesty. I love the way you treat everyone—even the poor people who can do nothing to help you. I love your decency, your values, and your kindness. I love your lively spirit, as well as the warmth and comfort I feel when I am with you. I love you because you make me laugh, and I love you because I miss you when we're apart. I will always love you, Gustave."

Gustave felt deep emotion. He felt truly happy for the first time in his life. He left the Chateau de Grandmetz at midnight and told Arnaud of his engagement the following evening, after which they both sat under the stars sipping Chateauneuf-du-Pape and rejoicing until daybreak.

Gustave had always believed that his father "loved" him, but he was now experiencing a different kind of love—an emotion that he had never known before. At long last, he was certain that life could be sweet and worth living.

He announced his engagement to Antoinette to his few close friends in Peruwelz and arranged to celebrate with a party at the Chateau de Grandmetz on the following Saturday. About thirty people, including some of Antoinette's family from Louvain and Brussels, ate, drank, sang, and danced until early Sunday morning.

Gustave announced to the revelers that he had invented what he called the "crutch dance" for the occasion; his demonstration of it resulted in howls of laughter and made even those who had met him for the first time that evening share warmly in celebrating his happiness.

***

Gustave's announcement of his intention to marry was a staggering blow to Hippolyte and an air of disappointment (probably self-defensively feigned) to his sister Lydie. They had not been aware that Gustave had returned to good health or that he was courting Mlle de Dudzcèle because they saw him too infrequently. They were unaware of the excitement he had found in his life.

Coincidentally, as happened to her partially after the long harangue from her husband, Lydie again felt healthier. Suddenly she felt very much less depressed and she could tell that her ability to think clearly was markedly improved.

She did not know why, but we know it was the typical course of neuroses to eventually heal, even the most serious of them. Probably, she was close to, or at, full recovery by now. It appears that she had suffered a whopping border neurosis.

***

Lydie had no opportunity to discuss her reaction to the "news" about Gustave and Antoinette. Her reaction was not joyful because she knew that her husband would be angry to hear of Gustave's plan to marry and would oppose it, if he could. She adopted a strategy that would not place her at odds with her husband. She decided, if asked, to say that she opposed the marriage because "it would probably not be good for Gustave" without any more explanation than that.

The count had been preoccupied with inheriting Gustave's money and property and shamelessly hoping for his early demise. He had been counting on Gustave's early death, which his doctors had incorrectly predicted, and on Lydie's inheritance, which would allow him to prolong his extravagant habits. The marriage would severely interrupt his plans.

Hippolyte had never hidden his impatience. He had visited Gustave's physician, Dr. Semel, in Peruwelz on at least three occasions (Dr. Semel is said to have told a detective that it was closer to ten) to ask how much time remained before Gustave met his death and whether it would be a slow death. He told the doctor that it would be helpful to know these things, so that he and his wife could plan their own lives accordingly.

On one occasion, giving the impression of deep concern for the welfare of a family member, Hippolyte visited Gustave's other physician, Dr. Lambris, in Tournai. Expressing interest in what he and his wife might do to improve Gustave's slowly worsening health, Hippolyte had asked for the doctor's prognosis for his "beloved" brother-in-law.

Naturally, he evoked sympathy, a response one would expect from a doctor told news that he still believed would eventually happen. Dr. Lambris told him that, unfortunately, the medical profession had no way to prognosticate how much longer his crippled brother-in-law was likely to live and lacked the means to treat him effectively. Fact was, Dr. Lambris had not seen or examined Gustave for two years since Hippolyte made his visit to him. It is unfortunate that neither Dr. Semel nor Dr. Lambris knew that the post-surgery redness and tenderness of Gustave's second surgical site had vanished spontaneously.

***

Gustave's marriage would presumably make his new wife, Antoinette de Dudzcèle, the sole beneficiary of his estate—his fortune. Hippolyte, expressed deep concern about this prospect, and Lydie had to act as though she was disappointed too. Hippolyte openly complained and threatened: "The little arsehole has lived too long," and, "I'm going to fix him once and for all."

Count de Bocarmé meant what he growled. He had hoped that his father-in-law was wealthy and, upon his death, would leave his daughter a generous inheritance. Even when it seemed unlikely that this hope would pan out, he'd forced his wife to be so recklessly extravagant that they had to resort to obtaining new large loans from notaries, to whom they eventually owed many hundreds of thousand francs.

To their chagrin, their financial condition had not improved upon Lydie's father's death in 1849. Among the junk fortune that he left for his daughter was a leftover sum of invested capital, which added an additional 5,000 francs to her annual income. This amount failed miserably to enable the count to pay their debts but made it possible to enjoy long weekends in Brussels.

Hippolyte ordered Lydie to sell more of the property she'd inherited from her mother to meet a small number of their many financial obligations. He also tried to sell some of her valuable jewelry. He took his wife's diamond-studded dress to a Brussels pawnbroker. Hippolyte told him the true value of the dress—namely, 9,900 francs that, truth be told, was among the bills he'd never originally paid. However, Hippolyte's prolonged haggling and his haughty, insulting manner made the exchange extremely counterproductive. The pawnbroker offered him only 400 francs for what he angrily and incorrectly insisted were paste, not real diamonds.

Hippolyte desperately needed the money to buy good wine to impress some guests who were arriving early the following day. It was near closing time, and no other pawnshops were available. He had to agree to the bad bargain. He also tried, injudiciously and fruitlessly, to borrow some small amounts of money from servants and simple daily workers at the chateau.

Utter ruin apparently faced the count and his oft-beaten wife if Gustave's death, on which he had long counted, did not occur soon. He was certain—although it is mysterious why he was so certain of it—that Lydie was the sole beneficiary of Gustave's wealth. While he did not know the extent of Gustave's wealth, he knew that his inheritance from his father was greater than Lydie's. Moreover, Gustave had lived conservatively, reinvesting his inheritance with advice from his notary and lawyer, Olivier Chercquefosse.

***

In June 1850, Mme de Dudzcèle and her daughter received two anonymous letters, mailed on the same day from a post office several miles from Bury. They caused concerns and reservations about the planned marriage. The first, addressed to Antoinette, referred to the bad reputation of Gustave's father as a womanizer. It stated that Gustave himself was neither noble nor worthy, as he had five or six children in the unregistered communes of Wiers, and his marriage would not prevent him from visiting his girlfriends.

A letter to Gustave also falsely accused Mlle de Dudzcèle of dark motives and of having lived a promiscuous past. It further stated, *"If you want to convince yourself that this is not slander, I can give you proof. If you go to Brussels, you will be able to 'see the document' with your own eyes, and you can meet the solicitor who prepared the civil document."* No address was provided for either the document or the alleged solicitor. Nor was the attorney identified.

Another letter to Gustave, written on the same day in the same penmanship and with the same ink, contained grave accusations. It told Gustave that, if he were desirous of having children, he should not be mistaken in his desire because Mlle de Dudzcèle had already provided proof of her fertility.

Next day, another letter, in Lydie's penmanship, came to Gustave. Written by the count's command, it feigned concern:

"I am interested in your predicament. I want to tell you that I have come to know everything. I know the whereabouts and name of the child his mother supports, which mean that he is a natural heir to part of the fortune of his mother.

"No one wants to cause problems, but according to what is being said everywhere, there are precautions you can take to avoid being duped. Confer with the priest in Grandmetz. If these accusations against Mlle de Dudzcèle are all slander and lies, go ahead and get married."

Lydie wrote all these letters in the course of two days because Hippolyte was barely capable of signing his name. She wrote the essence of what Hippolyte ordered her to write, as he threatened to beat her severely if she refused.

The letters, especially those to Antoinette, were so wild and bold, so disingenuous and daring, it is clear that Lydie made every effort to please the count. The count's vocabulary did not contain these words. He lacked the ability to write a grammatically correct letter, and he lacked the talent to write so fluently.

***

Actually, Lydie had written all these letters in the course of two earlier days. When she'd shown them to her husband and commented

186

that she could not send the anonymous letters in their present form, as everyone knew her handwriting, he'd slapped her face hard.

The next morning, Lydie had again shown Hippolyte all the letters she'd written at his request during the past two days and commented that she found it impossible to send the anonymous letters in their present form because everyone knew her handwriting. He immediately slapped her face hard again.

Trying to hold back tears of pain, Lydie told him, "I want those letters to be sent as much as you do. Striking me is not the answer."

"It's your responsibility, goddamn it. You find a way to get it done, or you'll regret it." When he used this expression, Lydie knew that he meant she would receive an exceptionally severe beating.

Through tears, Lydie replied that there was one nice man, in a little store in the village, where she had once looked at some merchandise. She said that he was friendly and perhaps all she had to do was approach him to see if he would be willing to help. "I might be able to pass off the letters as a joke or something."

"Then what in hell are you waiting for? Get your arse down there and don't dare to come back until you've settled it."

"I'll try," whispered Lydie solemnly.

***

This was the first opportunity Lydie had to be fully free to walk anywhere she wanted in the direction of the village without supervision. Ordinarily, Hippolyte would not allow her to leave the chateau without someone he trusted watching her, to be certain she did not try to run away. She had received a small bit of hope for her situation from an old associate of her husband's father and thought it might be useful.

CHAPTER 29

Secret Friends

Lydie hoped that Hippolyte was unaware that information had unexpectedly reached her from the oldest and most reliable of the chateau staff. Many years ago the count's father had hired Amand Wilbaut, a reliable man from Bury, to keep order in the use of the chateau property and oversee the behavior of employees. Later Wilbaut did his best to keep Hippolyte out of trouble but was not always successful. Wilbaut was a quiet, watchful man, who got along openly with the count but did not trust or like him. Hippolyte's treatment of his wife bothered him deeply, although she did not know it.

***

One day, when Lydie was alone in the dining room having a cup of coffee and no one was working in the kitchen, Wilbaut said he wanted to speak privately with her. He let her know that the wife of the tavern keeper had given Hippolyte a piece of her mind the last time he'd dropped in, with four unknown acquaintances, and left without paying the bill.

He had done this at least twice before, but the tavern keeper had been too timid to make an issue of Hippolyte's behavior. The straight-talking wife was angry with her husband for being afraid to speak up. She said she intended to "take on" the count, if he came again. A week later, Hippolyte returned. She went directly to his table as he was about to leave after he and his four unsavory acquaintances had spent nearly two hours drinking a total of fifteen large-sized mugs of her husband's beer.

The woman told the count sternly that he owed them money for the beer he'd drunk on two previous visits and on this third one. He pushed her aside rudely, saying, "The presence of a count does honor to your tavern," and brusquely left again, without leaving even a gratuity on the table or uttering a thank you.

The information, which in all likelihood was true, embarrassed Lydie, who gave Wilbaut fifteen francs to pay a part of Hippolyte's latest debt. She asked Wilbaut to beg the tavern keeper's wife to keep this matter to herself.

When he reported to the countess the following day, Wilbaut told her that he had completed the errand and had some information to relay. He'd arrived at the tavern in the early morning, before any of its clientele had come to drink, and he'd had a few pleasant words with the wife of the tavern keeper.

"She was grateful and asked me to thank you. She explained that her husband was not there. He needs sleep after an extended night of work behind the bar, and he has to find time to keep his barrels of beer, which he is always making, in proper order down in the cellar. He is a very hardworking man who is honest and, as she said, 'earned every franc for the fine quality of beer he sold.'"

Wilbaut said, "I found her to be a nice lady, and I asked if she had always lived in Bury. She said she had, which surprised me because I am also a native of Bury. Her mother is still living in an old house, set considerably back from the road up the hill across from the chateau. She said it is the house where she was born. "I was never aware of the house, as it's deep in the woods on a very narrow path, about a five- or six-minute walk from the road; most people don't know it exists. She described her mother as getting up in age but healthy and still energetic.

"The mother," Wilbaut continued, "keeps the old house in good order and gets exercise by taking care of a large vegetable garden during the growing season. The harvest keeps her in food in the cold seasons. However, she rarely leaves the house, preferring to occupy herself with reading. Apparently, she has a large library that she began when she was working and still adds to it by buying books and journals.

"Behind her house she maintains a barn where she keeps a single horse and an old cabriolet. Her daughter, the tavern keeper's wife, walks up the hill to visit her every afternoon. The path to the house is quite long and hidden by dense forest.

"The tavern keeper's wife was a little nosy about how the count and countess got along at the chateau, because she had heard so many rumors about you from the beer drinkers, especially on weekend evenings."

Wilbaut assured the countess that he had preferred not to try to answer such a wide-open question, so he'd answered only by raising his eyebrows in surprise, before taking his leave.

He did say to Lydie as he left, "I have a hunch that mother of hers could be a friend, if you needed one."

He knew well that his visit and the secret payment by the countess would quickly be related to the mother, who, in turn, would have reason to think well of the countess.

Lydie imagined that, if Wilbaut were correct, the elderly woman, whose nearness to the chateau was a great surprise to her, might be willing to give advice about how to handle the nasty, anonymous letters to Antoinette de Dudzcèle. If she'd read so many books, she was, perhaps, bright and might be able to provide advice.

***

Lydie hoped she could use this secret information to her advantage. She left through the front entrance of the chateau and made her way along the poplar-lined driveway leading to the road. She still felt the sting of her husband's slap in the face, along with a clear awareness that this was the first time he'd ever allowed her to leave without demanding to know "where in hell you think you're going alone."

Instead, he *had* ordered to her "get your goddamn arse out of here and get the letters written by someone other than you or you'll regret it."

She crossed the street and walked toward the village, looking carefully for a hard-to-see narrow path leading to a house hidden in the woods. She found it. The entrance to the path was halfway down the hill and out of the line of sight of the chateau. She found a small, white house about one-eighth of a mile down the path, which was narrower than she anticipated.

With a degree of apprehension, she knocked on the door and heard footsteps. An elderly woman opened the door. Lydie thought it prudent not to use "countess" in introducing herself. She said with a smile, "Good morning, I am your neighbor from up the road. My name is Lydie de Bocarmé."

The elderly woman, who seemed to be in sturdy health, greeted her pleasantly but not effusively and asked her please to come in; she did call Lydie "Countess." Lydie gave a half laugh; smiled graciously, which she knew how to do well; and said, "I'd prefer to be called Lydie. May I be?"

It was an opportunity for the responsive, rather charming woman to laugh as well and say, "Very well, and I am Anne Morceau; may I offer you a cup of tea?"

"I'd like that very much, thank you," replied Lydie.

They sat at a square table in the middle of the room and made small talk about the advantages and disadvantages of living in isolation. Mme Morceau remarked that the population of Bury had become smaller and the people older and older and fewer children were being born.

She commented that there used to be enough children for Bury to have its own grammar school, where she had been a teacher. "In recent years, though, Bury has been sending its handful of children to an adjacent village for their elementary education."

"What subjects did you teach?" asked Lydie.

"Oh, just about everything—reading, writing and arithmetic."

Lydie was close to certain she had found an trustworthy woman, but whether she could persuade her to help was another matter. Her expression became serious and Madame Morceau noticed it.

"Madame Morceau …" she began falteringly, only to hear, "No. I am Anne, and you are Lydie. I see you have something on your mind. Is there a way I can be helpful?"

"You are observant and kind. Yes, I do have a problem. I have numerous problems, in fact, but I have come to ask your help with just one—although it is a problem that relates to a larger one." Lydie's eyes welled with tears.

"Please, dear, tell me. I am, after all, an old, professional teacher trained in Tournai, and I know how to keep secrets about children's problems and those of their mothers and fathers—even from my own daughter."

"What school did you attend in Tournai?" asked Lydie.

"After elementary school, I matriculated at Belgium College."

"So did I," said Lydie. "I graduated only six years ago! It was a wonderful education!"

"Isn't that a remarkable coincidence!" said Anne Morceau. "I graduated fifty years ago. Undoubtedly, we speak pretty much the same language and have had similar educations."

They both laughed. Lydie became serious again. The elderly woman noticed it and asked not what she might do, but what she may do, for her.

She added, "Be assured that, especially in your case, where you are an important person in the community and we share a special background, whatever I hear of a personal matter will remain with me." As she spoke, she noted black and blue marks on Lydie's forearms almost to the wrists. She wondered if they were elsewhere on her torso.

Lydie, confident that she could trust this woman, knew she had little time to pour out her heart. "Time is very short. My husband is very strict with me." She was unable to hold back her tears. "Yes, too strict. He gets himself involved in matters that frighten me, especially because he demands that I be his accomplice and threatens me—I hate to say it—with doing to me what he intends to do with my brother, if I show any evidence of refusing.

"Right now, he is involved in trying to break up someone's marriage. It's complicated. He is clever, in certain ways, but I am ashamed to say, he cannot write a letter. He orders me to write letters for him.

"He doesn't dictate, just tells me in general what he wants me to write. With my education, I can tell what he wants to say and I get it into words he would never think of using.

"He demanded that I write anonymous hate letters. He did not understand, at first, that I am not a person who can write anonymous letters for him because everyone knows my handwriting.

"Yesterday I wrote a couple but only because, if I had refused, he would have beaten me again. This morning he told me to get these awful letters written by someone else. If I cannot do it, he will again beat me. He's completely unreasonable.

"Here are the letters to be sent anonymously. They are defamatory—not a word in them is true. I would go to the city police, but I have three small children in that isolated chateau, and I do not know how to get away cleanly. He keeps a very sharp eye on money and allows me to have little to spend.

"I'll be open with you. I dream that I could find a way to extricate the four of us, but it hardly seems possible now or in the immediate future. If I had very discreet, powerful outside help, I suppose I might be able to hide somewhere and wait patiently for a chance to sue for divorce. It's disgraceful that politicians have been able to forbid that right. It's a cold, cruel law. They have no business intruding in the personal lives of citizens."

Anne smiled and whispered, "I'm with you all the way about personal freedom. But you have to have a thick skin. There are a lot of ignorant people who would call you names or try to hurt you in other ways. Belgium has a lot to learn from the fifty-year-old US Constitution, which makes it illegal for clerics of whatever stripe to poke their noses in anyone's personal beliefs."

"It's a terrible thing to ask, but I have no choice. I hoped to find someone to copy these letters so they can be truly anonymous. It is a shameful thing to ask, but I have to because he brutalizes me so badly, especially when I'm alone with him in our bedroom, that I scream, shriek, and moan with pain.

"The domestics hear the screams, but they misconstrue their significance, and my husband encourages the staff in their ignorance. The word around the chateau is that the noise is related to—I don't know how to say it properly—marital lovemaking. In reality, the noise is my shrieking when he hits me with his fists. He's very strong and sadistic."

Anne then told her, "There are, of course, rumors about life in the chateau. I hear them. Among them is what you have just told me. I have always been suspicious of slanderous gossip, especially when it comes mainly out of a tavern filled with beer drinkers. Alcohol is a powerful drug that has filled the imaginations of more than a few, thankfully not all, novelists. I am certain that it has the same effect on a much larger population of foul-minded, ignorant blabbermouths.

"I appreciate your being so straightforward. Now I know that the unspeakable distortions broadcast about your personal behavior at the chateau are simply untrue. I suspect, though, that there is even more that you can tell me, at another time. You had better get back, my child, lest that oaf beats you. Yes, I do know that he is an oaf, but as I promised, I will not confirm that common piece of information or ever discuss it.

"Of course I'll take care of these letters; they are probably defamatory from what little I read by scanning them as you spoke. I will copy them and have them mailed, too. I suspect that they are illegal, but if traced to me, the justice department would be dizzy wondering why a seventy year-old woman would write such filth.

"It is unusual to meet a highly educated person like you in isolated Bury. *You've thus far not uttered a single word with which I disagree. That's unusual for me, but it's absolutely true.*

"I leave it to you to tell your husband a fable about an anonymous person who thought the foul letters were only good fun and was glad to copy and mail them.

"You had courage to let me know a part of your problems. Please, never hesitate to see me secretly, as you have done today, and you may be absolutely certain that I will do all I can to help."

Anne was motherly and held Lydie's hand. Rather than a tearful Lydie, it was Anne who came close to shedding tears. Lydie felt one as it trickled down her face after Anne kissed her cheek.

Anne had a stern parting suggestion: "Keep your visit to me a secret, *even from my daughter at the tavern.* She's a fine person, but she might be tempted to tell a so-called best friend, and you know what happens then."

As Anne opened the door to let Lydie take her leave, this treasure of a human being gave the young woman a strong hug and another kiss on the cheek. Lydie was emotionally touched. At last, she had a secret, dependable friend close to the chateau. She might need this lovely, insightful person one day in some other capacity in the future. We will discover that Anne would, *again, be* of vital help to Lydie.

CHAPTER 30

Lethal Seeds

Soon after his return to the chateau, Hippolyte received a letter that read as follows:

Julien de Bocarmé
13 November 1848
General Delivery, Arkansas County, DeWitt, Ark, USA

Dear Son,

Here's some information to let you be a little ahead of your friends. There is reliable evidence that nicotine was isolated in Heidelberg in 1826 and found to be very poisonous. Given into a vein or smaller blood vessels, dogs died very suddenly, a lot like the wolves.

The means of chemical isolation for molecular study is a complicated procedure, involving the use of dangerous, highly concentrated acetic acid. Don't you try to use concentrated acetic acid; it is very rough stuff. However, nicotine can be extracted in pure form from tobacco plants.

The only published book that has a chapter about nicotine poisoning is a big volume by a professor working in Paris. He is of Spanish origin but has spent most of his life in France. The book is the bible of toxicology for ordinary practicing doctors.

It was initially published in French, so it ought to be available in big bookstores in Brussels. The author's name is Mathieu Orfila, and the title has the word "Toxicology" in it.

Enclosed, in a separate envelope of thick paper, is a good supply of seeds. I think there are enough for at least three large crops.

Glad to hear you're keeping yourself busy. Please give my love to Lydie and those grandchildren I hope to see one day.

All the best,
Father

In March 1849, Hippolyte planted two-thirds of the seeds, and in November, he had grown a crop of at least ninety kilograms—more than two hundred pounds—of high-grade Virginia tobacco, whose nicotine content was 10 percent, more or less.[18]

***

Having acquired so much Virginia tobacco, as well as a way to search for the Orfila book, he made a trip to Brussels, accompanied by his wife; a child; and a new nursemaid, Louise Prevost. (He had already tried to persuade the new nursemaid to have sex with him, but she'd refused. Lydie may not yet have been aware of this.) Hippolyte visited a large bookstore owned by Monsieur Jean-Baptiste Tircher. The count was looking for the latest edition of Orfila's authoritative treatise on toxicology. Tircher had the latest edition, but the price was high. Although he did not buy it, he had no qualms about spending more than an hour keeping the book on the counter and leafing through the section on nicotine. Sales personnel asked if he

---

[18] Hippolyte never revealed how he'd come into possession of it. He always maintained that any tobacco he grew was the local species. He could have bought Virginia tobacco from a European tobacco wholesaler, but apparently, he did not. It was expensive. In court he insisted that he had only dealt with local tobacco. Lydie knew this was a lie.

needed any help, but he ignorantly paid little attention to them as he slowly read what Orfila had written about poisoning by nicotine. The salesmen and women may have cared but did not interfere with him.

The most important lines in the section clearly stated that, although nicotine was an extremely powerful poison, *there existed, as yet, no way to recover it from the tissues of animals cruelly sacrificed by putting a small quantity on their tongues.* Nicotine must be rapidly absorbed from mucous membrane because, given a few drops of pure nicotine, the animals have convulsions within a few seconds and are usually dead within a minute. It acts like no other known poison. Its effects on animals, as described, are the only means of determining whether a poison contains nicotine. In a summary, it was again noted that *nicotine is unable to be recovered from the tissues of these animals.*

Hippolyte explained to his wife that Orfila's work allowed him to learn that one can measure the strength, and therefore the relative value, of any tobacco by analyzing it for its nicotine content. He never bought the expensive book. The sales staff allowed him to keep it on the counter for an hour or more to read it and show selected sentences to his wife.

Hippolyte emphasized to Lydie that he'd now confirmed what he had previously suspected; *there is no known way to isolate nicotine from the tissues of anyone poisoned by it. He showed her the words,* to read herself and believed he was now in a stronger position to encourage his beaten wife to lessen her fear of obeying him in a premeditated murder plot.

$$***$$

Within a week of the visit to Tircher's bookstore, *Hippolyte, using the alias Berant, paid a visit to Monsieur Loppens, professor of chemistry at The Industrial School in Ghent.* He inquired of Professor Loppens what sorts of apparatus would be needed to extract essential oils of plants. It is extremely curious that the professor asked him no delving questions.

The count informed the professor that he had observed American savages poison their arrows with the juice of certain plants, and he wished to make a little of this poison to give to his parents as a present. He told him they lived in the southern United States, grew tobacco, and would appreciate a vial of it as a "conversation piece."[19]

Following this first meeting with Professor Loppens, *the count ordered a Monsieur Van den Bergh, a brazier in Brussels to whom he also introduced himself as Monsieur Berant, to make the apparatus.*

M. Van den Bergh began, without question or delay, to fashion a brass distillation apparatus according to the written instructions and drawings that Monsieur Berant had obtained from Professor Loppens. The brazier completed it by March 1, 1850, when Hippolyte, masquerading as Berant, came to fetch it.

Berant went to see Professor Loppens in May and, filled with excitement, handed the professor a vial with the first sample of nicotine he had endeavored to extract and then awaited his evaluation of it. Berant was disappointed. The professor thought the extraction could be done better—the nicotine was not sufficiently pure.

On his return to Bitremont, the count practiced more, obtained more oily material, and returned to Professor Loppens to ask him to grade the quality of the poison. Loppens found it as impure as the original sample but kindly *he offered the count two days of personal instruction*, which he readily accepted before returning to Bitremont to try his hand again.

---

[19] It is not fiction to say that Loppens' response contains no reported question or comment. He allegedly told the professor that, of all plant poisons, he was most interested in that of the tobacco plant nicotiana and in the methods used to extract it. Professor Loppens was happy to tell him how to proceed, even making detailed drawings of a bronze distillation apparatus he would need. (It is preposterous that Loppens failed to show a reasonable degree of curiosity.)

On the third visit to Professor Loppens, in October 1850, the enthusiastic Berant proudly announced, without waiting for a full analysis of his extract, that, this time, he must have been successful because whatever he was now distilling from his tobacco plants had *"striking effects on animals."*

Loppens gave him some pointers on how to increase his yield, with a larger distillatory and substitution of better reagents than he had been using. The count made a trip to Paris to pick up some of the new items.

Hippolyte worked secretly in the back of the laundry room, helped only by a gardener whom he considered feebleminded. (He arbitrarily classed all gardeners as "feebleminded.") He told the gardener that he was making eau de cologne.

One of the animals he killed, for test purposes, was the chateau's gray house cat, which he buried in a shallow grave in the front garden. For many days thereafter, he repeatedly asked the maids and cooks if they had seen the cat, expressing displeasure at losing the cat and disappointment at its failure to return. His wife happened to be changing sheets on a guest bed and the room's window provided her a view of what he was doing. He would have beaten her badly if she'd told her secret and given away his dishonesty.

He also killed two of the ducks that lived in and about his pond. He buried them near the cat but made no mention of them. The only thing now remaining was to procure the necessary chemical reagents and newer apparatus to allow him to continue on a larger scale.

As Loppens suggested, he would modify the procedure slightly by taking advantage of a technical refinement recently introduced by a French chemist. This required two lengthy visits to Brussels on the sixteenth and twenty-eighth of October, to complete the new purchases.

***

With his new equipment and modified method, Count Hippolyte de Bocarmé succeeded, by November 10, 1850, in obtaining two vials of pure nicotine. He had worked at it, nearly uninterruptedly, for ten days and nights. It was exhausting work that required very frequent observation of the temperature of a heated oil bath, within which the new distillatory stood.

Lydie said that she helped him by getting up at night to check the temperature, "to let my husband have some uninterrupted sleep." She claimed that she did him this favor, even though she did not know, at the time, what he was making and even though her attempts to find out were unsuccessful.

At first, the count told Lydie that he was making eau de cologne, but she did not believe him, and so she pressed him harder for the truth. Finally, he admitted he was extracting nicotine.

He said he was making it "to do Gustave in the very next time I see him. I won't let that little cripple get away alive."

Lydie said nothing to protect her brother from this evil scheme. She wanted badly to do it, but did not dare. If he were to kill her; what would happen to her three children, whom she loved?

Having successfully extracted the two vials of pure nicotine, Hippolyte sealed each with a cork stopper, placed them in an armoire where he kept wine, and then took ingenious steps to make the distillatory apparatus and the bottles of unused reagents disappear. Hippolyte had found his weapon; he needed a plan and an opportunity to use his poison.

CHAPTER 31

Felippe's Affair

Though Lydie may not have realized it, Felippe too had been devastated by his mother's actions outside the Mons Museum, and when he was first at the University of Zurich he was very unhappy. He had always been a good, responsible student, but now he found it difficult to concentrate on his academic work. He had become so preoccupied with his longing for Lydie that his grades were barely passing. He became a loner and did not socialize. He gave up all hope of having a professional career and considered returning to Belgium to ask Lydie to marry him.

However, the fact that he would have no career and would be unable to support himself and a wife were sufficiently sobering realizations to bring him to the conclusion that finishing his university degree was his better option.

It was after a morning session of a class in international law that he met Ula Frissen, a beautiful and outgoing young woman who approached him and introduced herself.

"You seem always so sad," she said with a look of concern on her face. "I have never seen you smile."

Felippe was surprised and, at the same time, flattered that someone had noticed him; he was also pleased that the person who'd noticed him was a very attractive young woman. "I'm sorry I have given that impression. I didn't realize that my mood was obvious, or that anyone was watching me."

"My name is Ula, and you have appeared very unhappy since you arrived at the university. I think it is obvious when people are sad, and I keep hoping that your demeanor will change. It is really none of my business, and I will leave you alone, if you think I am intruding.

"I thought, though, that perhaps meeting new people might be helpful. I remember that, when we all introduced ourselves to each other at a reception on the first day of the semester, you mentioned you are from Belgium. "I am studying music, and I have decided to write my class paper on the Belgian composer André-Ernest-Modeste Grétry, the most famous composer born in Belgium in the eighteenth century. I thought you might be able to give me some insight on where I might look for information. If you're not interested, that's all right; I will apologize and leave you alone."

"No, No, No! Please do not apologize. I didn't mean to appear unfriendly. Please stay. It is very thoughtful of you to talk to me. My name is Felippe Van Hendryk," he said, as he extended his hand to introduce himself. He realized that he was smiling for what he thought was the first time since he arrived in Zurich. "Will you join me for coffee?" he asked, exhilarated at the prospect of having the company of a female student, who was obviously interested in talking with him. "This will give us time to talk about how I might be able to help with your paper. Thank you very much for taking the initiative to talk to me, and I will try to get rid of my sad look when we are having coffee."

Felippe and Ula exchanged comments about their classes as they walked to a little café near the university campus.

***

"Do I still look sad?" Felippe asked, hoping that his mounting joy at having the attention of an attractive young woman was obvious. "To be very truthful, I never wanted to leave Belgium, and I think I have been irresponsible in not focusing on my studies as I should since the semester started."

"But you are here now. You never left to return to Belgium, so you had better make the most of your stay here and do what you must in order to graduate with honors. I am no psychologist, but I think

I have detected symptoms of heartache, and I bet you left someone special or someone special left you. I am not asking for an answer; nor am I prying. I'm only sharing a personal conclusion, and you should not feel obliged to tell me anything personal."

"You are very intuitive. I won't go into details, but suffice it to say, I enjoyed a wonderful relationship with someone, and it ended before I left Belgium. It is over forever; there's no chance of its being revived.

"I just need to face the facts and get on with my life. My behavior has been childish, I know; and you are correct that I need to focus on my life and my future, if I intend to graduate with honors. My parents would be extremely disappointed in me if I did not graduate and pursue a career in the diplomatic service. This has been my career dream, which they have encouraged.

"Again, I thank you for talking with me and waking me from my stupid and silly sleep. It's amazing how a few words from an objective source can quickly change a mood. Shouldn't you be studying psychology and not music?"

"I have indeed considered studying psychology, but my observations about you are purely those of an amateur," Ula offered. "My passion is music, but my parents have not encouraged my training in music, since this would break the tradition of generations of bankers in my family. I have always found a preoccupation with money boring, although I fully recognize that the option of poverty would make life extremely difficult.

"I feel fortunate to have parents who are able to make my education possible, but I want to succeed professionally, as a pianist, on my own. My father is in a position to help me get an apprenticeship with the Zürich Symphony, and I am lucky to have his help, but I want to be independent in my career."

Felippe felt as if he were hearing his favorite Mozart piano sonata as Ula spoke, and he held himself back from telling her that he felt precisely as she did about his own career and future. He felt a warm and special communion of spirit as they spoke about their dreams and the influence of their parents on their lives.

Felippe and Ula barely touched the coffee they had ordered, and after talking for about two hours, they agreed that they should have lunch together.

"I could ask my father to put you in contact with the royal historian and the archivist in the office of the king of Belgium," offered Felippe. "My father is an active patron of the Brussels symphony, and he could arrange for you to personally meet some well-known music historians at the University of Louvain.

"You would be able to get almost anything you needed for your paper. Perhaps you might be able to visit Brussels to meet them personally during an upcoming vacation."

"Could you really do that?"

"Certainly, I would be happy to do that as a down payment on my appreciation for your getting me out of my stupid mood."

As she acknowledged the attention that she received from a few young men who passed their table, it was obvious to Felippe that Ula was a popular young woman.

***

Although not aggressive, Ula was assertive, and while this did not trouble Felippe, he could not help comparing her personality with that of Lydie, who still occupied a very warm spot in his heart. He remembered Lydie's quiet sweetness, and he found himself contrasting her to Ula, whose worldliness, social ease, and quick wit spoke to her exposure to a world that seemed similar to that in which he had been raised in Belgium.

While he and Ula had met only that morning, Felippe was shocked at himself for feeling a tinge of jealousy when Ula excused herself and left their table to speak briefly with a young man who was also having lunch with some friends at the same restaurant. It felt, to Felippe, that Ula's brief departure to chat with the young man was impolite, but he convinced himself that he had no right to be bothered, since he did not know what they spoke about; nor did he know anything of their relationship. He had only just met her, he kept telling himself. He also felt that he liked his new friend and hoped they would see each other again.

Following lunch, they exchanged contact information before they parted. Felippe felt invigorated and had a bounce to his step as he went to his afternoon and evening classes. How quickly the attention of a woman with similar interests and an apparently similar background had changed his demeanor and removed a little of his memory of Lydie, which he had thought was indelible.

Not wanting to appear aggressive, Felippe resisted the urge to contact Ula. However, two days later, he returned to the same restaurant where he'd had lunch with her. He was disturbed to see Ula involved in an animated, and seemingly angry, conversation with the young man to whom she had spoken briefly two days earlier.

The pair could not see Felippe, who was able to observe them unnoticed. After about fifteen minutes, the man got up and left the restaurant, leaving Ula alone. She finished a glass of wine without showing any emotion, paid the waiter, calmly got up, and left the restaurant. Felippe decided that he would not follow her, and told himself that he would contact her that evening.

***

Felippe's visit to Ula's residence that evening was the first of many that followed, and it soon became obvious that Ula seemed to have replaced Lydie and had become a significant and positive influence in Felippe's life. He became more disciplined and focused and credited Ula with his new lease on life. Within a few months of their meeting, they became lovers and were involved in a committed relationship. Ula introduced Felippe to her parents, and she spent two weeks in

Brussels visiting Felippe's parents, who were overjoyed at their son's friendship with a young woman whose family met with their approval. Although their parents had never met, they were each aware of the other because of their connections and prominence in elevated social circles in their respective countries.

With the knowledge of both sets of parents, Felippe and Ula joined Felippe's widowed aunt on one of her frequent vacations. In August, during a break in their studies, they traveled with her to walk about and enjoy England's Cumbrian Mountains in the Lake District. For two weeks they observed, indigenous animals and birds in the wild, which both of them enjoyed. One evening, in a forest clearing overlooking Derwentwater, Felippe told Ula of his love for her and asked her to marry him. He promised that he would ask her father for her hand upon their return to Zürich. He knew that Ula's parents liked him, just as his parents liked and approved of Ula, and he had no doubt that Ula's parents would give their consent to their daughter's becoming Baroness Van Hendryk.

***

After returning to Zürich, Felippe soon began to harbor a haunting concern and reservation about Ula, in spite of her apparent love for him. Occasionally, he would observe her flirting with men, which bothered him. She often made herself obvious to other men by wearing clothing that revealed more of her attractive body than was necessary or acceptable. He hid his discomfort, although it continually troubled him. When awake at night, he felt a knot in his stomach when he thought about Ula and her flirtatious behavior and thought he should share his concern with her.

He decided not to do that. He wanted to avoid any discussion that he thought she might interpret as mistrust of her. He believed that marriage would curb his wife's inclination to be attractive to other men, and he convinced himself that he would be her sole focus after they were married.

Ula Frissen became Baroness Van Hendryk in a lavish wedding at the elegant Hotel Frissen, located on the River Limmat in Zurich. Over a thousand guests attended the wedding gala at the hotel owned by the Frissen family, and icons of Zurich and Brussels society enjoyed a wedding celebration unlike any seen in Zurich for a very long time.

After a month-long honeymoon on the French Riviera in a spectacular villa that Ula's parents owned, the happy couple settled in a lovely home on the shores of the River Limmat in Zürich—a wedding gift to Felippe from his parents.

Following his graduation, with a degree in law with emphasis in international affairs, Felippe and Ula moved to London, where Felippe began his diplomatic career as a Belgian legal attaché with responsibility for developing strategies to improve Belgium's position in international trade. Belgium, like other European countries, wanted to industrialize as England had, but no other European country had effectively combined commercial development with naval supremacy as England had.

England was significantly more involved in the operation of the entire world economy than were other European countries, and King Leopold of Belgium thought that having a diplomatic representative at the Court of St. James would likely help little Belgium to emulate England, where the industrial revolution began. Felippe set about to make a name for himself and worked tirelessly, studying England's mechanization of its textile industries, its development of iron-making techniques, and its increased use of refined coal.

He encouraged Ula to apply her training and proficiency as a musician to teaching; and he was prepared to invest in a large piano studio to facilitate this objective. She showed no interest in a professional career, preferring to spend her time shopping and preparing herself for participation in the very active diplomatic social scene in London.

Felippe worked long hours and frequently was away from his home on business trips throughout England. About two years following their arrival in London, it became clear to both Felippe and his wife that their frequent separations were increasingly affecting their marriage, and when Felippe occasionally took time away from his work for holidays, Ula always seemed to have a reason not to want to leave London. While he had no evidence of infidelity on her part, he suspected that she had met someone for whom she had developed a fondness. Unlike the outgoing, talkative, and adventurous person he had known before they moved to England, Ula had become somewhat withdrawn, and she became moody and easily annoyed at any suggestion from Felippe that they go away on a holiday together.

***

Ula had become cold; and as time passed, any intimacy between them disappeared. Because Felippe felt that the pressures of his job had interfered with his relationship with Ula, he decided that he would return to Brussels to request, in person, an appointment in Brussels.

He had been away specifically to inquire about a possible appointment to the Belgian Foreign Service in Brussels, a position that would not involve extensive travel. He had presented his thoughts about obtaining an appointment of the kind in a long letter to his father. He responded with the recommendation that he return to Brussels to meet with King Leopold, who would make the decision.

Felippe went to Brussels with a plan to be away from London for a week, but he was able to conclude his discussions and meeting with the king in three days and returned to London about four days earlier than he had planned.

He was surprised to find no one at his home when he returned, not even one of his servants. He was excited to share his news of a new job with Ula, but he did not know where she had gone. He found it odd that his home was empty and thought Ula must have given the servants time off while she was attending some social event. Felippe had poured himself a glass of cognac, lit a fire in his library, and sat down to read the newspaper when he heard the front door of the house open, followed by voices and laughter. One voice belonged to Ula, and another was a masculine voice.

"Let's have a lovely evening together, my love. You can leave early in the morning, before the servants arrive. I have asked them not to return until after ten o'clock in the morning. I am alone, and my idiot husband will not return from Brussels for a few days."

***

This was Ula's voice. Felippe sat stunned, as he listened to his wife's cruel, derisive description of him.

"When we left Zurich, I had given up on ever seeing you again," she said to her companion. "I am so happy that you now live in London. I have spent a lot of time wondering why I left you. Let us have a glass of wine."

Ula and her friend entered the library together laughing, but they simultaneously froze as they saw Felippe staring at them as he sat beside the fire.

Ula's companion was the man she had argued with at the restaurant near the university in Zürich several years earlier. He appeared as Felippe remembered him, with a few years added, and his presence explained to Felippe, one reason at least, why Ula's disposition had changed. The presence of another man in his home with his wife was sufficient explanation for Felippe, and he had no interest in hearing anything from her. No doubt, she had had other liaisons, which had interfered with their relationship, but he could deal only with the situation with which he was presently confronted.

***

Although filled with anger, Felippe calmly put his glass down, stood up, and walked over to his wife's evening companion, who had

210

turned white with fear. He did not bother to turn toward his wife. "My name is Felippe Van Hendryk, and this is my home. I do not recall having invited you here, and I have no interest in learning who you are. Frankly, I do not give a damn. Get out of my home immediately, or I will either throw you out or summon the police. Get outright now!"

Ula's companion left at once, without comment.

Felippe then turned to his wife and calmly said, "To bring another man into our home when you thought I was away is unacceptable and disgraceful. You have no explanation that I am willing to accept. I had hoped that if ever we had differences of any kind, we would be able to discuss them openly and try to resolve them. That is now impossibility.

He then calmly announced that he had made plans to return to Brussels to work and would be leaving London within a month. "I shall be going to Brussels alone," he told her.

"I suggest that you make arrangements, with your gentleman friend or with your parents, immediately, for a place to stay tonight. You will first remove your belongings from our suite this evening, since I intend to occupy the room alone until I depart for Brussels."

Felippe turned around and walked away, leaving his wife frightened, humiliated, humbled, ashamed, and speechless. He did not feel sorry for insolent Ula. He had no interest in speaking with her again. In the morning, he would begin proceedings for a divorce. It was legal in Switzerland.

CHAPTER 32

Reconnection

With his parents' understanding and support, Felippe was able to terminate his marriage easily, since neither he nor his wife made any claims on the other for property, they had no children, and both were residents in Switzerland.

Ula made feeble pleas and promises of future fidelity to Felippe, spurred mainly by a need to protect her image rather than any sincere wish for reconciliation. Felippe, however, was determined to put this chapter of his life behind him and make plans to occupy his time with work in the Belgian Foreign Service in Brussels.

He impressed King Leopold with his diligence in applying his knowledge of international law, and the king frequently sought Felippe's opinions on matters of international trade.

Felippe made no effort to find Lydie, fearing rejection, which would be too difficult to bear. He knew also that his parents would never accept Lydie, and he did not wish to expose her to further insults from them. He kept himself satisfied with memories of the person he once knew, having no knowledge of how she might have changed since he had last seen her or of the person she might have become. He assumed that she was now married.

***

On a rainy Brussels morning in spring, King Leopold's secretary summoned Felippe to his office.

A member of an important family based in Brussels had approached the king, proposing that he consider a foreign posting for a nephew currently living in Hainaut province. His reputation had become a serious embarrassment to him and his Brussels family. The nephew had become "renowned" around Hainaut province, as well as in Brussels, for purchasing goods on credit and defaulting in his payments. He was in serious debt to many vendors and was known to leave nonexistent addresses with creditors.

The king's initial impression was that it would be unwise to find an opportunity for his friend's nephew because it was reasonable to assume that a foreign posting would be tantamount to transferring the problem, with likely embarrassment to Belgium and with no conceivable solution. Nonetheless, his interest in wanting to help a friend led him to ask Felippe to look into the background of one "Count Hippolyte de Bocarmé," without telling Felippe any personal concerns that he held. It seemed to the king that Felippe would be an ideal person to conduct the investigation. The Van Hendryk family had strong historical contacts in Hainaut province, and he would not need the introductions to authorities that others might need to get information.

Since returning to Belgium, Felippe had avoided weekend visits to his parents' country home in Peruwelz, fearing an accidental meeting with Lydie, which would be difficult for them both. He fantasized about visiting the museum in Mons where he had initially met her, hoping that, perhaps, he would find her staring at the Bruegel painting that had initiated their first conversation. He replaced his dreaming with the conviction that Lydie was happily married, with a loving family, and he needed to forget the past. He would set about his investigative task and not preoccupy himself with the possibility of a chance meeting with the woman he almost certainly still loved.

The beauty of the surroundings and remembrance of his youthful days of horseback riding in the area pleased Felippe, as his carriage entered the poplar-lined road leading to the front entrance of the Chateau de Bitremont. He had never had reason to visit the chateau before and wondered about the occupants of this stately, well-kept residence. Whoever lived here now, he thought, must have the background, refinement, and knowledge of Belgium's history to make them acceptable representatives of the king.

He had purposely arranged for his arrival to be unannounced. He thought it best to meet first with the count, before interviewing residents in the community and shopkeepers in Peruwelz. His purpose was clear; he preferred that the count not receive information that a representative of the king was making inquiries about him.

***

A young servant opened the entrance door to the chateau, said that she would inform the count, and offered him a seat in the salon. Soon after he sat, he heard a coarse voice. "I don't think I know you, and if you're here to collect money from me, you'd better get the hell outa here."

Felippe, stunned, stood up at once.

The rude outburst had emanated from someone whom he had never met before and who made no attempt to introduce himself or ask Felippe his name. He had entered the salon silently, from a stairway that Felippe had not observed from where he sat. Felippe knew at once that no one as impolite and crude as this man could ever represent Belgium in any capacity. Although he had made his decision, he would try to pry more information from this ignorant man, to flesh out the reason for his quick decision for when he met with the king.

"I am not here to collect anything from you, sir. My name is Felippe Van Hendryk, and I am here as a representative of the king. I am here on official business, but your rudeness has convinced me that I should leave."

Felippe was about to leave when he heard a voice from the stairs leading to the floor above. The voice sounded distantly familiar. "Who is there with you, Hippolyte?"

"Some Flemish fool named Van Hendryk, who is trying to screw money out of me and says he represents the king. Nobody who represents the king drops in without telling people ahead of time, so he must be a faker. I've never before encountered this new trick … hah! I'm surprised it's not the king himself." He let out a short laugh.

"I guess I pulled off his mask because he looks like he's about to run away. Why don't you come downstairs and meet a representative of the king?" The rude count shouted upstairs sarcastically, while staring at Felippe with a smirk.

The name, Van Hendryk, made the countess come partway downstairs at once. But she was emotionally unprepared, after eight years, to see the Felippe she had known. She stopped midway on the stairs and stared at Felippe, speechless.

The surprised Felippe returned her stare. Hippolyte stood with a confused and suspicious look on his face. Lydie Fougnies was now the Countess de Bocarmé, and although the years had added maturity to her appearance, she still radiated the quiet beauty he remembered. Her red eyes made it obvious that she had been crying, and the surprise of seeing Felippe, whom she had not seen for nine years, added to the difficulty she had in saying anything.

"Who is this man, Lydie? Are you hiding something from me? Do you know him?"

"He is someone I met many years ago, long before I met and fell in love with you." Hippolyte was out of her line of sight but Felippe wasn't, so she winked as she said it, and Felippe got the point. Lydie continued, "I have not seen him for years. If he is truly the Van Hendryk I knew, I believe he is being truthful in saying that he represents the king and that he is not a collector."

"I don't believe you. We'll settle this later."

The sudden look of fright on Lydie's face made it clear to Felippe that she was in an unhappy, abusive marriage. He noticed a superficial redness near her temple, consistent with a recent slap on the face.

Felippe felt an impulse to protect Lydie, but he repressed it, recognizing that old emotions were motivating him. He thought it best to leave the chateau. He wanted to talk with Lydie, but this was an inappropriate time.

***

"I will be in the area for a few days, sir, caring for more of His Majesty's official business, and if we happen to meet again, accidentally, I will not be inclined to speak with you unless you offer an apology to me for your rude behavior today."

Felippe left the salon and walked, unaccompanied, toward his carriage, while Hippolyte tried, with feigned laughter, to camouflage his anger over his apparent loss of word battle. As Felippe had parked his cabriolet almost directly opposite the front entrance to the chateau, he turned briefly leftward to judge whether he might be too close to it. As he made this brief turn of his head, he could see directly into and through the open door to the inside staircase. Lydie was still sitting on a stair, and the count was peering directly at Felippe with his back to the entrance. She thought it safe to make a distinct kissing movement of her lips and a bit of a smile just after Felippe repeated that he would be in the area "for a few days." He passed a throwaway line to the count, "I *do* hope, sir, that you might come to your senses."

Felippe now felt certain that he would spend the following morning at the museum in Mons, and he felt intuitively that Lydie would be there also. He knew that he should not try to see her but could not help wanting to. He decided that if she were able to meet him in Mons, he would suggest that she follow him to his parents' estate, where they could be alone, away from the watchful eyes of locals and away from any possible hostile confrontation with Count Hippolyte de Bocarmé.

216

Felippe left the Chateau de Bitremont immediately, wondering to himself why anyone who knew the count would ever recommend him for a position of any kind in which he would have to interact with grace and dignity. Felippe would have no reservations in telling the king why he was convinced that Count Hippolyte de Bocarmé was unsuitable to represent Belgium, in *any* capacity.

He would avoid mentioning that he had once known the count's wife and, indeed, had been in love with her. He would also not tell the king that he'd left his brief meeting with Count de Bocarmé hoping to spend the following morning and possibly the following day with the count's wife.

CHAPTER 33

The Meeting

After leaving the Chateau de Bitremont, Felippe stopped at the tavern in Bury village. He was thirsty and wanted, for old-time's sake, to quaff a little local houblon.

A middle-aged woman brought his beer to him in a porcelain tankard emblazoned with a large crest and shield. He needed time to contemplate what he had just experienced and felt the need to sit and think, alone. Juxtaposed in his brain were the insulting welcome directed at him from an ignoramus, along with the startling surprise of seeing Lydie. It bothered, nearly sickened, him to see her so unhappy, living in what he gathered had to be an unhappy and abusive marriage.

***

It had been eight years, since 1841, when she'd swiveled too quickly and left him as he'd tried to extend their last, sad meeting in front of the Mons Museum. He recalled that she had turned too quickly, probably to hide her tears, and then he'd cried at his loss. He hadn't had time to finish what he wanted to say to her. He wanted to suggest that they remain in touch by mail, that Zürich was not the end of the world. Lydie was hardly poor; she could have taken the train to Zürich to visit him on weekends from time to time. It would be only a matter of four years before he had his degree, but they would still be young.

He would be able easily to find a good job as an international lawyer, and they could then marry, have children, and be happy ever afterward. He imagined that his mother would have had to accept Lydie, the mother of grandchildren she would, almost certainly, have adored. Once she knew Lydie, she would have accepted her, perhaps loved her. In a word, keeping family relationships civil would have become his mother's problem. However, his fidelity would be to his wife, the woman he loved.

Trouble was, as had been alluded to earlier, Lydie's quick swivel had unfortunate consequences. The disaster of the parting reminded him of lines from a children's story: "For lack of a nail, the horseshoe was lost / for lack of a rider, the battle was lost." He *did* have a good and workable suggestion to share with her. He still remembered it.

As he raised the container of houblon to his lips, he saw the name Bocarmé prominently engraved beneath the shield on the container. "Who is Bocarmé?" Felippe asked the elderly tavern keeper. "I see the name engraved on this jug from which I am drinking."

The old man remained silent, but his wife was not hesitant in saying, "I have pleaded with my husband to throw away the Bocarmé beer steins, but he fears the man who bears this name. I refer to Count de Bocarmé, who occasionally brings his roughneck friends from Brussels to drink our houblon.

"We brew the best in the province. My husband says, if he discards the steins, we will lose the Bocarmé business. How can we lose business that we don't have? That Bocarmé scum never pays for anything. We have attempted to get him to pay us, but his regular response is that he helps to bring us business, and that is sufficient pay. If we stopped serving him, we fear he would use his influence to close us down. We have tried to appeal to his wife, when he is not at the chateau, but we have found her to be cold and often rude. They deserve each other!"

***

What Felippe heard about Count Hippolyte de Bocarmé was not surprising, but he was troubled to think that Lydie could be cold or insensitive to anyone. He needed to talk to her. Felippe spent the

219

night at his parents' estate in Peruwelz. He slept fitfully, preoccupied with thoughts of possibly seeing Lydie in Mons the following morning. Although he still loved her, he thought that seeing her would accomplish little, and he did not want to interfere in her life. Too much time had passed since they were last together. She was now a married woman. Nevertheless, the urge to see Lydie was too strong for Felippe to overcome.

The following morning, Felippe arose early and drove his carriage to Mons. He parked it a short distance from the museum. He had no way of knowing if Lydie wanted to see him, or even if she could leave the Chateau de Bitremont to get to Mons. He could not bear the thought of not being in Mons to meet her, if she had been able to get there. He knew precisely where they would find each other in the museum.

He walked through a light rain from his carriage, not knowing if he were on a fool's mission, deluded and controlled by fantasy and unrealistic visions of something he thought he wanted, but was unsure. He found the Bruegel painting which he well remembered and stood before it, turning over in his mind the first time he'd met Lydie and their conversation about the painting. After standing there for what seemed a long time, without any sign of Lydie, he felt silly and disappointed.

"Are you Baron Van Hendryk?" a quiet voice asked.

Felippe quickly turned toward the source of the question and saw a woman who appeared to be about seventy years of age.

"Yes, Madame, my name is Van Hendryk. Why do you ask?"

"Please follow me, sir. Lydie, the Countess de Bocarmé, wants to see you, but she is afraid. I am her friend, and I will drop you off, close to my little house in the countryside near Bury, where she is waiting for you. We will have to hurry because she does not have much time.

"She is terrified of her husband being aware of her talking with you, and we must be extremely careful. You will not have much time, and the count cannot know! I honestly believe that he would beat her, without mercy, if he thought she showed interest in another man."

***

The woman touched Felippe's elbow, as if he were leading her on a casual day in the museum. She smiled, and said in a barely audible voice, "We must be careful. The count must not know."

Felippe set his jaw and tried to maintain his composure.

She gave him more explicit directions, telling him she would drop him off and then retrieve him and take him back to his carriage parked by the museum. She would return alone to her small house in Bury. It was a long trip she was undertaking for Lydie.

"Please be careful! Lydie is my friend, sir, and I revere that lovely, troubled woman. May God be with you both. From where I drop you off in Bury, simply follow the path I point to and slither through the trees to the small, white house. I will return for you in one hour."

The woman rode with him at a fast pace in her old, rusted carriage all the way to Bury. Felippe followed the path, as directed, to a small house about a hundred yards from the point in the road where she deposited him. He walked toward the house, feeling that its secluded location would allow privacy, but he worried that he might not be sufficiently far from the count and the Chateau de Bitremont to feel completely safe.

***

As he approached the house, its front door opened, and Lydie stood in the doorway staring at him. She was able to say, "Thank you for coming, Felippe," before she broke down, sobbing loudly.

Felippe put his arms around her in an attempt to console her, knowing that it was not an affectionate embrace of lovers; he was being supportive and a concerned and sympathetic friend.

221

"I never thought I would ever see you again, Felippe. Yesterday, when I saw you after so many years, I realized more than ever that I have been living in a hell that I have helped to create. I needed to talk with someone who would understand what has happened to me. My mind always turns to you.

"It is my life, and only I can control what I do, but I have not been able to do anything. You don't need to know my problems, and I don't want to burden you with them. I only wanted to see you again and talk to you.

"How are you? I read that you got married in Switzerland. How is your wife? Do you have a family?"

"I am divorced, Lydie, and I have no children. I now work in Brussels, in the Belgian Foreign Service. King Leopold asked me to investigate your husband for a position in our country's diplomatic service. A relative of your husband made this request of the king, and I'm here at the king's service. I knew nothing about your husband before I visited yesterday; nor did I know that he was your husband. I will be honest with you and tell you that, after yesterday, I will not recommend him for anything. I found his behavior insulting and disgraceful. Why would he have assumed that I wanted to see him to collect money? How could you be married to someone like that?"

"We have serious financial problems, Felippe; Hippolyte and I have not been honest with those from whom we have borrowed money. We are in deep debt, but we really don't know how to garner the funds we need to pay our creditors.

"I only want to see my children happy, and our financial problems have led to constant quarreling and physical abuse from him, which is bad for our children to see. I want to leave him, but I cannot until we solve our problem. If I left him, I wouldn't know where to go."

"You could live with your brother, couldn't you? Even temporarily, just to escape from your husband's abuse? How is Gustave, by the way?"

"Felippe, I don't want to talk about him," Lydie responded, with coldness that Felippe could not understand. He remembered that, although Lydie and her brother were *not* very close, at least there was a tolerable sibling relationship that should have allowed Lydie to turn to her brother, if she had the need. (She may have been anticipating his murder and did not wish any possibly subpoenaed witness to be able to testify that she had ever discussed Gustave with anyone beyond the walls of the chateau.)

"Gustave is talking about getting married, and we don't know why anyone would want to be married to that one-legged cripple. Can you imagine any sensible woman being in a bed with him?"

Felippe was appalled at Lydie's insensitive remarks about her brother and was filled with confusing emotions as he listened to Lydie tell him about her life at the Chateau de Bitremont. (She wanted no witness to be able to say she spoke derisively of Gustave.)[20]

Beneath her report of a way of living that she and her husband could not afford and the disrespectful, abusive behavior to which her husband subjected her, Felippe detected the love of a mother who wanted to remove her children from the unhealthy environment of the Chateau de Bitremont. He saw a frightened and obviously confused woman who needed help and whom he felt had led a life, in recent years, which had forced her to hide the warmth that he once knew and remembered. He learned of Hippolyte's infidelities, and without getting any details, he learned of a child that Hippolyte had fathered with a servant at the chateau.

***

Felippe's instincts were to help Lydie, but he did not know what he could possibly do, without inviting the wrath of her husband, whom he had no interest in ever seeing again.

Tears and uncontrolled sobbing made it difficult to understand all that she said. She mentioned a particular doctor, once or twice, but

---

[20] See later about defensive strategies of captive wives.

her sobbing prevented Felippe from making out his name. Without doubt, Felippe wanted fervently to enter Lydie's life once again, but Hippolyte, her husband, was an insurmountable obstacle about which he could do nothing. He knew that types like the count often belong to vicious street gangs. Felippe did not want his name to become public; the king would be bound to ask questions of a personal nature. Newspapers would get hold of the story.

"Monsieur, it is now time to go," announced the woman who had taken him to see Lydie less than an hour after she had left him at the side of the road near her little house.

"Please, sir, come quickly. We don't have much time, and the countess must return to the chateau before the count returns."

With a purposely platonic embrace and a gentle kiss on her forehead, Felippe left Lydie, without any plan for another meeting, although her situation seemed precarious. He could not help deploring the action of his mother; she had destroyed the life of the only woman he had ever truly loved. He knew he still loved her and would do anything he could to save her, if it were possible. It seemed impossible as long as she remained married to that repugnant husband.

CHAPTER 34

Emerance Talks with Gustave

Emerance Bricout became Lydie's chambermaid fourteen days before Gustave's murder. She had not worked there long enough to know all the ins and outs. Nor had she been there long enough to have been propositioned by the count.

She was a nursing assistant from Paris, with extensive experience caring for stroke victims. She had worked at the Fougnies' home in Peruwelz, where she cared for Lydie's father from the first day he had a mild stroke in 1841 until he died of a massive stroke in 1849. Monsieur Fougnies so liked her care and personality that Lydie offered her a permanent job as a member of the Fougnies family. She continued to oversee the other attendants at the Fougnies' home after M. Fougnies's death.

When it more recently became clear that Gustave would very soon be married and the home was about to be sold, Emerance turned to Lydie to ask if there were a job for her in the chateau. Emerance had always considered herself Lydie's employee because Lydie had personally taken responsibility for having her become one of the family, so to speak, in early November of 1850. Lydie's current chambermaid, Louise Prevost, happened to have given notice that she would be quitting shortly, within the week, and Lydie gladly gave the position to Emerance, who did have another small source of income as well. M. Fougnies so liked her that he'd left her a small pension. She preferred to stave off using it until she had no other income.

Emerance knew nothing about the internal politics of the house or Lydie's precarious life. She did not know that Lydie had inadvertently

225

married a brutal psychopath, who was cooking up a scheme to kill Gustave. Lydie was, of course, afraid to tell her.

***

In her fourteen days of service, where her sole job was to care for the countess's needs, Emerance did come to realize that the count was an ignorant brute. Like chambermaids before her, shedid not help the countess bathe because she would have noticed the multiple, serious bruises with which Hippolyte's fists had decorated Lydie's torso. Emerance had no time to discover that the count was a sexual deviant.

During Emerance's first week at the chateau, Gustave visited twice. These were short visits, which afforded them little opportunity to speak at any length. However, on the first of these visits, Emerance realized that Gustave disliked the count, which surprised her.

Emerance did not know that Gustave had called the count an "unsophisticated idiot" and that Lydie had repeated that sobriquet to the count after his second meeting with him. Sharing this information had been thoughtless of Lydie in any case. The personal slight was enough for the Count to swear that he would eventually kill Gustave, although he had another and greater reason. It is unlikely that Gustave would have confided anything so personal to Emerance, despite his admiration of her.

Emerance also did not know that Lydie had foolishly married the oaf of a count largely because she wanted so badly to be a countess. However, on Gustave's first visit, Emerance was among the domestic staff on hand to greet him warmly. After he had had a small breakfast with his sister, he asked Emerance to join him in a walk around the grounds of the chateau. They talked frankly for a full hour.

Knowing one another well, they spoke openly about the conditions within the chateau.

He said, "Disorder reigns in this house. There are very many domestics here, and I am astonished that the place is in this shape; if I were here for eight hours, order would be restored."

Emerance replied, "That would be hard to do; it would be a great service, though, if you could come for a day or two."

"I have three domestics, and all get along well with me. My house is in proper order."

"Of course," said she, "domestics have more respect for their employers when the home is orderly."

"Emerance, please explain to me why a house with such an abundance of domestics cannot have a little order."

"Many of the employees are not domestics whose job it is to keep the house clean. There are two nursemaids and a special one for the oldest child. There is insufficient discipline of the few domestics.

***

"In fact, there is only one domestic in that house who does everything, including the cooking. That person is your sister. However, her husband interferes with her. He wants her for other things. Besides, he wants the world to think that he's a very wealthy aristocrat, but wealthy people can afford to have cooks, good domestics, and so forth.

"The count orders her to pass down his commands to employees. She is so afraid of him that she carries out his orders with utmost alacrity. He invariably orders her in a menacing voice. It's unhealthy, and unnerving to observe."

CHAPTER 35

Inadvertent Setup

Lydie pondered what she might do to throw a wrench into her husband's plans or to dissuade Hippolyte, who was eaten up by ferocity and anxiously determined to murder Gustave. While Lydie was sorely disappointed at how things seemed to be turning out, and mildly resented Gustave's intended marriage, her main anguish was a mixture of regret and depression over the state of her life. She regretted that she had not paid more attention to her father's light-handed attempt to persuade her to consider the economic consequences of the marriage she chose to make.

She retained her strong moral sense; she knew that murder was evil. She contemplated how to make the best of a bad situation. Although the exact date of the Gustave-Antoinette marriage had not been set in stone, she knew it would happen soon, and she wanted a way to avoid attending it. To what extent her wish not to attend was a tit-for-tat reminder to Gustave that he purposely had not attended her wedding is hard to gauge. Lydie's ingrained civility was as strong as ever. More likely, she was looking for a way to divert Hippolyte's attention from the wedding and give time for his impulsive anger to weaken.

At breakfast, she simply told her husband that she wanted to be far away when the marriage took place; she maintained that distance would allow her to show her "disappointment" with Gustave.

"Hippolyte, I do not want to be in Belgium at the time of this marriage that you and I both abhor. We do have some money in the bank; it's not enough to pay what we owe so many notaries, but it is enough for us to go away for a few weeks.

"Perhaps, a vacation will help us withstand the expected blow and think up a new way to proceed with our lives. My suggestion is that we buy train tickets to Germany, not outrageously expensive ones, and find a small house to rent in a quiet but inexpensive part of that country.

"It would allow us to think things over, Hippolyte, and, perhaps best of all, give us a good excuse for not attending that awful wedding. I do not want to be there, do you?"

"I don't want to go, either. Maybe we can make some friends in Germany—some people with money. There may be opportunities to get our hands on some of it."

***

"All right, we seem to agree for once. However, we have to decide how to keep the chateau in running order so that we have a place to live when we return, whenever that happens to be. In any case, I would set a limit of no more than six months away from Bury."

"That's going to require a goddamn lot of planning. We've got this house in pretty fancy shape, and I don't want anything to happen to it. What the hell are we going to do with the domestic staff? Who's going to look after everything?"

"We will have to think long and hard about those matters and do so in an organized way."

"Have you made a plan yet?"

"It seems to me that the most valuable thing we have in our house is expensive furniture and carpets. Perhaps I am too optimistic, but if Gustave is going to be living in Grandmetz, he would be leaving an empty apartment in the building that my ailing Uncle Ferdinand owns.

"Uncle Ferdinand is sick, probably would be fussy, and would take some time to decide who ought to rent that space. He is, after all, a Fougnies, my uncle, and has no reason to dislike me, as far as I know. I hate to say it, but you're not his favorite person."

"No wonder he never spoke a word to me since our wedding," Hippolyte quickly replied, "To hell with him."

"Well, he's been friendly to me, and I would like to visit him to ask if we might store a few of our very expensive pieces of furniture in that empty apartment, for a limited period. I cannot see why he would not give us permission. I take it that you don't want to come with me when I speak to him?"

"Of course not. This is all your idea. If you want to make it work, goddamn it, you take care of all the details. I've got other things to do. In fact, I have some important business to take care of in Brussels this weekend. It's personal and none of your business."

***

Hippolyte's personal business was to meet with several of his rogue friends to do a lot of drinking and whoring. How Hippolyte had money for these weekend excursions to Brussels was mysterious. Lydie had heard rumors about his mini-vacations in Brussels but did not question him about them, fearing that she would receive a severe beating as an answer.

"Will you permit me to pay a short visit to my uncle to ask if he would allow me to use the empty apartment for a short period of time? If he agrees, we will have to decide how to handle the domestics."

"Yeh, it's all right with me, as long as you don't get my name involved in any legal agreements."

The following morning, on November 13, Lydie asked Gilles Van den Bergh to take her to Peruwelz. She told him she wanted to visit with her uncle and take her four-year old son, Gonzalès, with her.

She found Uncle Ferdinand in bed at midmorning. He was quite pleasant. His mind was clear, but he appeared to be frail and chronically ill. She shook his hand gently, leaned over, and kissed his cheek lightly.

She turned to Gonzalès, picked him up and told him, "Gonzalès, here is your grandfather's brother. Will you always remember meeting him?"

The little boy turned his head, shyly, from his Uncle Ferdinand and buried it in her shoulder but managed to say, "Yes."

Lydie set him down on his feet again and turned to her uncle, who said, "Pull that chair over here so that you can be comfortable and I can hear you better."

She did that, and as she sat by his side, he asked, "Why have you come?"

***

Lydie smiled and replied, "To be honest, I have come to ask a favor. My husband and I are planning to be away in Germany, for several months. Since Gustave has, for practical purposes, moved his belongings to Grandmetz, his apartment is, presumably, nearly empty. My husband and I happen to have some very beautiful and expensive furniture in our home, and I wondered if we might place the better pieces in a safe place while we are away. It occurred to me to ask if we might use this space in Gustave's old apartment to store them for the short time we will be away. I know that the apartment belongs to you, and I would need your permission."

"Lydie, I haven't yet made up my mind when I will advertise that apartment for rent. It could be soon, perhaps later. Really, I would not be comfortable with having your very beautiful and valuable furniture there, should I decide to rent. Frankly speaking, I am, as you can see, not in the best of health, and I honestly don't want to bear any responsibility for it."

"I understand very well, Uncle Ferdinand. I thought that there would be little harm in asking. Your reaction is fully understandable and makes sense to me."

"It is not my business to ask whether this furniture has yet been paid for, but whether or not it has been, it must be protected; you are right about that. What comes to my mind is the need to insure it

231

because legitimate ownership is not the issue. The furniture has great value and should be insured."

"Wise words, Uncle. Do you happen to know of someone who is in the business of insuring items like these?"

"No, I do not. However, I am expecting a visit from my lawyer, M. Chercquefosse, tomorrow, to take care of other matters. I will use the opportunity to ask him. One of us, most likely he, will get in touch with you."

"What you say makes good sense. I look forward to hearing from M. Chercquefosse.

"To change the subject, Uncle, I haven't asked whether you're comfortable and whether, during the day, you manage to get out of bed and exercise your legs."

"Oh, yes, I do get up with the help of a day nurse, who will be here soon. She takes good care of me, and I am doing as well as can be expected."

With a brief laugh, he remarked, "I have had a good life and have nothing to be unhappy about. I hope that, when this little boy of yours is my age and he realizes that the sun will soon set upon him, he is able to feel the same way I do. I am terribly sorry that I could not be more useful to you, but I think Chercquefosse probably will be."

"Thank you very much, Uncle Ferdinand. I hope that I have not interrupted a late morning sleep. If so, I am terribly sorry. It has been a pleasure to speak with you. Gonzalès and I will take our leave now and let you rest. Thank you again."

Lydie returned to the chateau, gave Gonzalès a quick kiss, and handed him over to his relatively new full-time nursemaid, Miss Pale.

Lydie was grateful to her uncle for his advice. She remembered him as an active man, in years past, when he was in the real estate business. It was then, she imagined, that he'd bought that fine house with three large apartments. His foresight worked out well for him and Gustave. She could not help imagining that, if she had not married, she might, one day, have occupied the third apartment.

232

While anticipating hearing from M. Chercquefosse, she turned her thoughts to the lives of the domestics. She wondered how many she might consider anchors whose loss would be considerable and how many of the part-time help Hippolyte and she could easily dispense with. As for the men who worked the fields, approximately fifteen in all, Hippolyte would have to make similar decisions; but if he placed one to be in charge during their absence, the cultivation of vegetables, plants, and tobacco could proceed as usual.

Of course, there would always be a need for Amand Wilbaut to oversee the care of the land— the many acres of cultivable land and the land on which the chateau stood.

A key question was how to pay the wages of those who continued to work in the chateau and in the fields. The count had always lacked the ability to keep the payroll. Because he'd known Lydie since her childhood and was a close friend of her father's, M. Chercquefosse had managed such affairs after Lydie and the count had married. She would discuss this with him later.

***

Uncle Ferdinand did see M. Chercquefosse on November 14; he took care of his personal business and mentioned Lydie's visit to him the day before. The lawyer agreed that the questions were reasonable, although he could not understand the necessity for spending so much time in Germany.

M. Chercquefosse expected to see Gustave, at his office in Tournai, the following day, Friday the fifteenth, and would mention his sister's visit.

On that that Friday, Gustave signed a final prenuptial agreement with Antoinette. He was so in love and the intended husband and wife were such reasonable people that Chercquefosse could hardly imagine its necessity.

At the conclusion of that piece of business, the good lawyer informed Gustave of the information he had received regarding Lydie and Hippolyte's projected six-month stay in Germany. Insurance on the furniture was her major problem.

However, Monsieur Chercquefosse had a few concerns: "Frankly, Gustave, I don't believe they have any money to buy that insurance; it would be very expensive for them. Also, Lydie failed to mention which employees would be retained to look after the chateau in their absence. They will obviously let the majority of the domestics go, leaving behind those who are key to the chateau's internal upkeep.

"I have been thinking about the fifteen field workers. As long as they continue to cultivate and sell the vegetables and tobacco, there ought to be enough income to pay their wages. It requires Wilbaut's placing the most reliable of them in charge, and that, unfortunately will necessitate Hippolyte's agreement, which will depend on his mood.

"If Hippolyte wants to go to Germany, he (technically) has to give his approval to Wilbaut. *He*, of course, must stay on because he knows more about that place—those few thousand acres—than anyone else."

***

"Do I have enough in my rainy-day fund to cover those expenses for them?" asked Gustave. "I would be glad to do it because I know how much disappointment my impending marriage must be to them, especially my sister. I suspect that she wants an excuse not to be there. As for him, he hopes eternally to find a rich, naive old German from whom he might extract some money."

Chercquefosse laughed, before replying, "Oh, you will not have to dig very deeply in your rainy-day fund to take care of a matter like that. Personally, I think it would be a kind gesture on your part.

"It won't take me long to draw up what we might call a family trust with the details, in print, and have you sign them. If you have some other business to take care of in Tournai, I can have my secretary type it up within the hour and suggest a reliable insurance company."

"Very good! Great advice! Is there anything they have to sign, too?"

"Yes. They will have to agree, in writing. I will put a copy of this in the mail to you, and you should have it by Monday or Tuesday, at the latest. When are you planning your next trip to Grandmetz?"

"Probably this coming Wednesday. Would you please send them a note advising that I will stop by early that morning so we could sign the trust? Then, I will continue on to Grandmetz to see my lovely Antoinette."

Little did Gustave know how many times Hippolyte had told Lydie, "The next time I get my hands on that mean, little son of a bitch, I am going to do him in."

Little could Hippolyte forecast that the weather, on Wednesday, November 20, would play into his hands.

CHAPTER 36

Aie Aie, Hippolyte

At six thirty in the morning of Wednesday, November 20, 1850, an ominously overcast day with a light drizzle of rain, a young woman on horseback unexpectedly arrived at the Chateau de Bitremont with a message. Hippolyte was an unusually early riser that day. He was outside when he received her confirmation that his brother-in-law Gustave, would arrive later in the morning to pay only a short visit. He was on his way to distant Grandmetz for two or three days.

Hippolyte told the young woman to carry word to Gustave that ten in the morning would be a good time to arrive because the Countess de Bocarmé liked to sleep late.

He paused to study the dark gray sky attentively for a full minute before reentering the Chateau, where he woke his sleeping wife, who rose from her bed at nine. He announced in a sinister tone of voice, "Be ready to greet your brother in an hour." He added menacingly, *"Obey me, if you care to live, because today is 'the day!' If you happen to walk into the kitchen with the single lit candle and leave us in the dark, your excuse is that you were absentminded. You were looking for some fruit for Gustave. There wasn't any on the table and you knew he liked it."*

***

Gustave's fashionably blue, two-wheeled cabriolet, a so-called Tilbury, arrived at exactly ten at the front entrance of the Chateau at the end of its long, imposing tree-lined driveway. After adeptly alighting, using his cane to navigate the step to the ground, Lydie hurried forth to greet him with a hug and a kiss.

In doing so, she noticed that the weather was unexpectedly cold and raw and that there was a slight drizzle of rain. Something about

236

these wintry elements caused her fertile mind to wonder if they were in some way related to a note she had recently received from Gustave's lawyer M. Chercquefosse and Hippolyte's threatening comments when he woke her up. It bothered her.

The note, on Chercquefosse's office stationery, was directed both to her and Hippolyte. It read:

Gustave's stop at your home on the morning of November 20 will, of necessity, be brief. He plans to make the grueling trip to Grandmetz, to visit Mlle de Dudzcèle. The trip over badly rutted roads might take him and his driver six or more hours to finish safely in his cabriolet. The purpose of his visit to you is to obtain the signature of either of you to what we have named the 'family trust.'

Best wishes,
Olivier C.

Lydie, more than a little upset by her detestable spouse, put two and two together. She knew that he had planted crops for years, and knew how to forecast weather. Perhaps he knew it was likely that Gustave wouldn't dare defy a violent, long storm. Lydie could read Hippolyte's twisted mind.

***

Lydie and Gustave had breakfast alone, for about an hour. She thanked him for his generosity in agreeing to draw up the trust to cover the cost of insuring the chateau's elegant furniture and rugs during the stay in Germany. However, she dared not let him know of lurking danger. Her children needed a mother.

Yet, Lydie wanted to test her hunch. She invited Gustave to join Hippolyte and herself in a noon luncheon, to see if he would accept.

He *did* accept. During lunch, rain turned to sleet. It loudly peppered window panes facing the wind. Lydie again tested her hunch; she off-handedly asked Gustave if he cared to stay for a late afternoon tea.

He replied, "I'd like to go back to Peruwelz while there's daylight; not later than three o'clock. The strong wind will blow the brunt of the storm well beyond us by then, and make the return easier."

Hippolyte, who wanted him to stay for a long evening dinner in his darkened dining room, was not disappointed. He was certain that *this* storm will worsen and last into late night. He slyly thought, "I'll let *him* watch the storm go from bad to worse. He won't make any freezing run to Peruwelz."

When he heard Gustave say that he was willing to stay until three, his animal instinct told him that this intention to go home while the sun still shone was useless, it'll never save his life. There'll be plenty chance to do the little bastard in.

Hippolyte slyly decided not to say anything to raise Gustave's suspicion. He was convinced that Gustave would have to remain in the chateau until late at night, possibly until morning for the storm to abate. In order to murder him, it was necessary only for him to accept an invitation to have a long, evening dinner with me and Lydie in our dining room and he'll be asleep-for-good long before morning.

Lydie quickly divined her husband's depraved design when he told her, after lunch, that he expected her brother to stay for a "long, relaxed evening dinner."[21]

---

[21] Gustave later explained. As he and his handyman, Tellier, drove slowly toward the chateau, he followed the changing patterns in the sky and realized that his itinerary would necessarily change. The weather looked too threatening.

"I told him that his services would no longer be needed for the day. He was free to return to Peruwelz, a distance of little more than a mile, on foot. He needed only to stable the horse and cab, and have some food in the kitchen, if he wanted more breakfast. The horse would know how to deliver me back to Peruwelz safely. He accepted, and left. Apologies for forgetting to tell you this earlier."

Lydie now realized that she could hardly urge Gustave to disregard the weather and go very soon either to Grandmetz or, more logically, to Peruwelz. Hippolyte would wonder why he had changed his mind. He would never believe that she had not warned him; she was certain he would murder her.

Hippolyte repaired to the Red Salon to waste time by slowly and carelessly reading the trust, presumably to argue about its contents later. It's probable that he thought, at first, that it might be necessary to use a cooked-up argument as means to delay any sudden impulse of Gustave's to depart prematurely for Peruwelz in the face of the storm. But he also wanted to sit by a window to observe the progress of the violent storm.

The conscienceless Count de Bocarmé was well prepared and looking forward to killing his brother-in-law when he willingly chooses to stay for a long, late dinner.

He had unmercifully and ruthlessly convinced his sister Lydie, the mother of three small children, that if she wished to remain alive, she must help him to kill her brother. Hippolyte had secretly prepared Lydie, again and again, how to assist him in carrying out a cruel post dinner murder of Gustave. He meant what he said.

***

Lydie painfully regretted how she spoke at the lunch with Gustave. She felt she made a serious mistake to have asked him, in the presence of her husband, if he would accept an invitation to a late tea. She had a hunch that his willingness to remain as late as three, in the belief that the weather would begin to abate by then, strengthened Hippolyte's belief that there was a good chance to kill him She was right about that.

While Lydie was unable to encourage Gustave to return to Peruwelz earlier than three o'clock, she took some naïve comfort in his forthright tone of voice when he said he would leave by three.

Surely she was not obligated to openly *encourage* him to change his mind and stay for a late protracted dinner.

As for Hippolyte, like Lydie he had been under the impression that Gustave had not originally intended to stay long at their home. But his knowledge of weather forecasting told him that Gustave 'would, without doubt, have to "pay the price" because the weather will be worse at three o'clock.

Hippolyte *did* now give thought to how best to persuade Gustave to stay for a long dinner in his darkened dining room. He shrewdly concluded that rather than try to encourage Gustave to remain for a long, relaxed evening dinner, it would be better to continue to leave the decision up to Gustave.

There was reason for him to take this tack. The count was a farmer. He understood winter storms. He was certain that the current storm would become worse with each passing hour over the course of the early afternoon and evening. He was certain that Gustave Fougnies was bound to notice it and would never dare return to Peruwelz at *any* time today. Gustave, unfortunately, held an errant, amateur opinion that the increasing wind would soon drive the storm into other parts of Belgium or France. He was dead wrong, and cunning Hippolyte knew it. He also knew, though he chose not to tell him, that the wind was *already* too strong for Gustave to make it to Peruwelz safely even as early as one or two o'clock, because the wind speed was so high that it would probably topple Gustave's very light cabriolet. He would be thrown from his seat to the ground. If not badly injured, he would have to make his way to Peruwelz on his crutches. He could easily freeze to death.

Furthermore, the clouds were becoming rapidly denser; visibility will be extremely poor by two or three o'clock. It will be difficult for both the horse and driver to see the edges of the roadbed.

***

Lydie felt in her bones that she was likely facing a dilemma she always feared. She did not dare urge Gustave to disregard the weather and return to Peruwelz. Despite rain and a strong wind, her naïve opinion was that at three o'clock his sturdy horse would still have the ability to return him to his home with reasonable safety. But Lydie could not hint, let alone prevail upon her brother to take that single step. In fact, even if he were to leave *voluntarily* for Peruwelz, her husband was more than likely to accuse *her* of betrayal. He would inevitably assume that she had "double crossed" him by spoiling his long awaited pleasure in killing her brother and would either beat her mercilessly or kill her. Her children needed her; she could take no chances.

While Lydie was agonizing, Hippolyte remained seated in an overstuffed chair by a window in the Red Salon, still feigning interest in the trust, for which he cared not a whit.

Hippolyte had informed Lydie again and again that the time and place he would most like to murder Gustave was during or after a protracted evening dinner in their darkened dining room. He never imagined that a violent winter storm and a so-called family trust, in which he had no interest, would coincidentally assist him.

***

While it is difficult for a sane person to imagine, Hippolyte had taken the trouble to prepare Lydie in exactly how to assist him in a post dinner murder and, if she wished to remain alive, carry out his orders meticulously. Nearly every night, at bedtime, he warned her that if she ever refused to obey his orders, he would kill her: "You'd be easy to kill." Immediately thereafter, he molested her sexually and then habitually beat her painfully with his big fists for fifteen minutes for no reason other than he enjoyed it. Any complaint on her part was considered disobedience. It called for a crueler beating the following night. There was no way to escape with her children from this dangerous, isolated Chateau.

***

Lydie was upset. She harshly blamed herself for impulsively offering Gustave an invitation, in the presence of Hippolyte, to stay for a late tea.[22] She was certain her crazed husband would turn it into a long, evening dinner.

She could see and hear the pitiless menace of the worsening storm as well as Hippolyte and Gustave could notice it. While one might briefly have hesitated to let his pet dog outside for a moment, to defecate, social pressure demanded that one never hesitate for a moment to invite a brother to stay for dinner while he was awaiting subsidence of a historically violent storm. The temperature fell and the wind-blown rain became a furious hailstorm. Dark clouds turned a dim daytime into an ominously premature dusk. As Hippolyte predicted, Gustave announced at two-thirty, that he did not now intend to leave the shelter of a home to make his way even to relatively nearby Peruwelz.

When Hippolyte heard of Gustave's change of mind, he ordered that he be invited to join himself and Lydie in an evening dinner, a prolonged, and presumably relaxed, multi-course dinner beginning approximately at dusk and often lasting until nine in the night. With the epitome of pitilessness, he ordered Lydie to offer the invitation to her brother. As matron of the house, the onus to extend the invitation

---

[22] Even if Gustave had decided *voluntarily* to leave prematurely for Peruwelz, Hippolyte would automatically have accused Lydie of having deliberately 'tipped him off.' Her denial of having 'double crossed' (betrayed) him would have been disbelieved. He well might have killed her for destroying a long awaited chance to murder her brother.

was Lydie's, who knew that following his order was the equivalent of luring her innocent brother to a rendezvous with certain death.

One can only imagine, because it is impossible to describe, the extraordinary psychological distress that accompanied Lydie's offer to her younger brother to join Hippolyte and herself at a dinner, which she knew full well would be his last supper.

Gustave innocently accepted the invitation but did set a condition: "Regardless of the weather, my sturdy horse and cabriolet must be readied no later than nine o'clock this evening, to allow me to return to Peruwelz regardless of the seeming danger."

***

Accordingly, once Gustave agreed to stay for a late dinner, Lydie became suddenly officious and took unusual actions. She told her eldest child's nursemaid, Miss Pale, to dine with Gonzalès upstairs in his room rather than in the dining room, where the nursemaid and child habitually joined his parents at dinner.

She ordered her two smaller children's nursemaids to prepare their meals in the kitchen, but they were to be eaten upstairs in the nursery. Before today, the children had always supped in the kitchen while the adults' dinner was served in the dining room. Lydie asked even Emerance Bricout, now her chambermaid, to wait on table through the dessert course and then go upstairs and remain there for the remainder of the evening and night.

The count waited until three-fifteen, to order Alex Vandenberg, his coachman, to ride on horseback to Grandmetz and deliver a letter, written for him by Lydie, to Mlle de Dudzcèle's mother. It was minutes before dinner had begun. The letter, it turned out, had no objective other than to ask Madame de Dudzcèle what price she would ask for some of her gardening implements. It was a strange letter because Hippolyte had never shown any interest in Madame de Dudzcèle's gardening tools.

Although the distance was short by modern standards, rural roads were poor in 1850. The round trip on horseback on the evening of November 20, 1850 was cold, slow and dangerous in the dark, on neglected rutted roads with patches of ice.

Alex Vandenberg customarily served two jobs at Bitremont. He took care of the horses, and he waited on table at dinner. In his absence this evening, Emerance would be the server. When Alex returned from Grandmetz, he was so tired and hungry that he ate a quick, small supper in the kitchen and went directly to bed, where he slept soundly through the night.

The countess told Emerance, who was helping set the table in the dining room, that she expected her legal advisor, Monsieur Chercquefosse, to appear sometime during dinner for a confidential matter. All of the regular staff knew that words spoken in the dining room were audible in the kitchen; any member of the staff who heard her words might have been duped into believing that orders to stay upstairs made sense because they knew that rare meetings with a lawyer were always strictly confidential.

However, Emerance Bricout, new on the job, did not yet know that it was possible to see into the dining room or hear speech within it from the kitchen. The reason for it was that s very small pantry separated the dining room from the kitchen. A light, swinging door between kitchen and pantry had a coin-sized hole in its panel, through which servants in the kitchen could actually look into the dining room. Provided candles or a fire in the fireplace dimly lit the dining room, servants could see all but its right corner close to the kitchen. However, a heavier door, which was usually open, could separate the pantry from the dining room. Regardless, even if both doors were closed, there was no perfect soundproofing between the two larger rooms. Members of the staff knew that, even when the heavier door was shut, they could still clearly hear voices and sounds in the dining room merely by pressing an ear against the frame of the lighter door. Lydie did not, at first, choose to shut the heavier door.

If Monsieur Chercquefosse's presence had been needed, Lydie would have been telling the truth and her strange orders to household help seem reasonable to any who might possibly have heard them. Members of the staff knew that rare meetings with the lawyer were always strictly confidential. (It is unlikely that any were listening with ear to the door as she spoke).

It is probable that Lydie did not intentionally tell Emerance an untruth. In fact there was no reason for M. Chercquefosse to visit the chateau that evening. It was not necessary for him to sign the so-called family trust even if it did give him legal authority to *arrange for the care* of all possessions of the count and countess while they were in Germany. It is entirely possible that a frightened, unnerved Lydie wanted so badly for him to come that she imagined he *would brave the storm* and be with them.

***

Preparations for dinner were well underway. Emerance lit wall candles in the dining room, where she had also prepared a warm blaze in the fireplace. The sun would soon set, but Lydie knew that, a mile away in Peruwelz, several places remained open for business after dark. There were potential customers who came home late from work or who had forgotten to store their houses with nighttime supplies.

Within a minute or two before sitting down for dinner at nearly three-thirty, Lydie followed Hippolyte's preset orders. She summoned her other coachman, Gilles Van den Bergh, and asked him to do an errand in Peruwelz. She told him she had forgotten to send him earlier for four dozen candles, two gallons of kerosene, and two large bags of Ceylon tea along with three pounds of coffee, and miscellaneous candies for the children. She reminded him of how dark and cold it would be by four and wanted him to "take a blanket and drive *slowly*, with your usual care." She even gave him money in excess of what he would need to pay for the items she wanted. Lydie was aware of how much she gave him and added, "If you'd like, please stop and use the extra francs to have an unhurried glass of beer and a decent dinner at the new restaurant they've built at the hotel."

Van den Bergh thanked her for her unusual generosity, dressed warmly, and hastened to the stable to hitch his favorite big, strong horse to a heavy, flat wagon.

***

Dinner began at a candlelit table at dusk, shortly before three thirty in the evening. Warmth and light emanated from the fireplace, and two candles in a wall holder shed more light in the smartly furnished dining room.

The count preferred red wine, the countess white. As was his habit, Gustave did not drink the chateau's wine. He drank from a bottle of red wine that he had been in the habit of carrying with him on rare occasions in the past when he had dined at the chateau, especially when he thought toasts might be drunk after dinner. This was such an occasion; he imagined that the signing of the trust might call for it.

Seated at the table, the three sipped their wines, chatted very little and ate dinner at a snail's pace. Gustave sipped his wine very slowly. Despite Lydie's explanation for it, the arrangement she ordered struck Emerance as unusual. It bothered her. She didn't feel right about doing Vandenberg's job or about being sent off in a hurry once she was done. Between serving dinner and dessert, she bided her time in the kitchen, helping the cook Louisa Maes wash dishes. Mme Maes spoke no French, only Flemish.

Meanwhile, in the dining room, the three sat in weird silence. Hippolyte said nothing. To break the strange silence, Gustave said that he would be able to leave immediately after dinner, needing him or Lydie to sign the family trust. Lydie said she understood and

246

thanked her brother again for making the trust possible. The count then stared severely and threateningly at Lydie but said nothing. Neither did she speak.

Emerance noticed how dark it had become at four. Official Belgian meteorological records show that the sun set at 3:38 p.m. on what was already a dark, overcast day. Freezing rain had begun to fall prior to an invisible sunset. A waxing gibbous moon was also invisible through the dense, dark clouds in the night sky.

***

Concerned that the candles had burned down during one of the darkest November days in her memory, Emerance made a brief appearance in the dining room to ask if the diners would like her to light fresh ones.

"No, no, not yet!" shouted the count's gravel voice, echoed after a brief pause, by the countess, whose tone was less demanding.

A small flame from a short wax candle on the dining table, and the glow of burning embers in the fireplace, meagerly lit the room.

Emerance was in the kitchen taking a few minutes to help Mme Maes finish washing pots. While there, she was surprised to see the second coachman, Gilles Van den Bergh, return from the errand to Peruwelz, He temporarily put the items that were in the wagon on the kitchen floor.

Lydie heard him arrive, entered the kitchen; and (prematurely) asked Emerance to go upstairs and stay with the nursemaids Justine Thibaut and Virginia Chevalier, and the two younger children. She then turned to Gilles, who had already eaten a good dinner in the hotel restaurant, and ordered him to give Mme Maes a ride back to her home in the village of Leuze about a mile distant.

Gilles Van den Bergh walked back to the stable in the dark and readied another horse and carriage. He drove down the driveway with Mme Maes and entered onto what was called the High Road but realized that it was too dark to continue on so poor a roadbed.

His carriage had insufficient lanterns to allow him to see the rough roadbed. Furthermore, had Gilles managed to make it safely to the periphery of Leuze, it would have been too dark for Mme Maes to walk a narrow path safely into the village to her home.

Gilles returned very slowly and carefully to the chateau, and entered the dining room briefly, to explain what he had done. He noticed that the count, the countess, and her brother sat in near darkness. The only light came from the sputtering flame of a wax candle stub on the table and the pitifully weak gleam of a single dying ember in the fireplace. Gilles then disappeared, probably to use the latrine.

Mme Maes returned to the kitchen to help Charlotte Monjardez, a scullery maid, wash cooking vessels by the light of two candles and Emerance was still there waiting to serve a dessert course and remove its dishes. It was nearing eight-thirty.

***

Gustave announced it was time to sign the trust; that he intended to return to Peruwelz, said he would like to borrow a blanket to keep him warm during the short ride and asked that his horse and cab be prepared.

Hippolyte again stared severely and threateningly at Lydie but, again, she said nothing.

Gustave mused silently that it might have warmed a little outside only because, as far as he could tell, the very worst of the storm had passed about five hours earlier. Whether it was in fact warmer at eight-thirty is not known. It was true that about when they began to dine, the cold outside *had* worsened when freezing rain began to fall more heavily.

As Gustave mused briefly, Lydie turned to him and said that she understood his wish to get home. She told him she had a blanket, then rose to her feet and peered into the kitchen. Gilles was not there but Emerance was still biding her time despite previous orders to go upstairs. Having served the main courses, she was awaiting the moment when she could pick up dessert plates.

***

To appear to accommodate Gustave, Lydie ordered Emerance, "Go fetch gardener Francis de Blicquy from his nearby cabin. Tell him to prepare my brother's horse and Tilbury, and then, *please go upstairs*!"

Francis returned minutes later to report that he could not enter the stable because it was locked; Gilles had obviously forgotten to replace the key to the stable when he made his attempt to return Mme Maes to Leuze.

***

About ten minutes later Gilles returned to the kitchen. The count heard his voice. He left the dining room, entered the kitchen and gave Gilles the same orders de Blicquy was given. Therefore, the count was out of the dining room for almost a minute, leaving Lydie and Gustave alone long enough for her to have quickly warned her brother of his peril before the count returned. Lydie did not dare warn him.

Moments after her husband seated himself, Lydie reached for the candle holder, stood and hastily mouthed, "Oh! We forgot the dessert fruit. May I interest you, Gustave?"

"Before he could respond, Lydie had taken the puny candle and its holder into the kitchen, leaving Gustave and Hippolyte in *complete* darkness.

***

249

Lantern in hand, Gilles was already walking to the stable with his key to ready Gustave's horse. He hitched him to the Tilbury and waited for Gustave to exit the back entrance to the chateau and walk the short distance around the garden and pond to the stable. He wondered what was taking Gustave so long.

***

By coincidence, at the very moment that Gilles left for the stable, one of the young nursemaids, Justine Thibaut, disobeyed the order to remain upstairs. The youngest child, Rose-Marie Eugènie, was hungry and fussy. Justine went to get some milk for her. Justine carried no lantern but was acquainted with the circular staircase. She wore no shoes as she held the banister and descended silently in the dark toward the vestibule. She knew the layout well enough. Her intention was to tiptoe soundlessly past the closed dining room door toward the back door of the kitchen. Candlelight would be visible beneath it.

She had no way to know that she would not find any milk in the kitchen. Lydie had removed and hidden it in the cellar. Hippolyte had given her this unusual order.

Justine was on the last stair, about to step onto the vestibule floor, when she heard what sounded like someone falling in the dining room and Gustave's voice hysterically crying out, "Aie! Aie! Forgive me, Hippolyte!" [23] It was Wednesday night, November 20, 1850, about ten minutes before nine o'clock.

The alarmed nursemaid hastened through the back door to the kitchen, to see or hear what was happening in the dining room. She was unable to see into the dining room through the coin-sized hole

---

[23] Why "forgive me?" Had the count accused Gustave of having called him an "unsophisticated idiot?" It seems unlikely that he was apologizing in response to "Why haven't you shared your money with us?"

in the lightweight, pantry door. It was clear to her why she could see nothing; she heard the sound of the pantry's heavy door being shut by someone entering the pantry from the dining room, and hiding there. It was quickly obvious to Justine that the person hiding in the pantry was the countess because of the unique rustle of her dress, presumably as her arm brushed her body. All of the domestics were aware of this elegant silk dress. No one else in the house had one like it.

Justine then held her ear against the doorframe of the swinging door and heard gagging sounds from the dining room, which she associated with attempts to vomit, and loud thumping noises that made her think someone was moving heavy furniture about or overturning it. Frightened though she was, Justine mustered sufficient composure to ask Charlotte Monjardez, who was now helping Mme Maes to wash pots, to listen at the doorframe. Charlotte agreed that whoever was in the pantry was moving about a little and the rustle sounded like the arm of a dress brushing against the chest or body. She, too, knew of the countess's dress and that no one else in the chateau had one made of material that could make a sound like that. Whether Charlotte also heard the thumping noises is not recorded. Presumably, she heard them.

Terrified by these observations, young Justine ran to reach the chateau's inner courtyard by a seldom-used passageway from the kitchen. Again, although she had no lantern, she knew the layout well. She had briefly to endure the cold wind as she passed by the windows of the dining room, from which she reported hearing "cries" that now had a muffled quality. Charlotte remained in the kitchen with Mme Maes.

***

Using back steps, Justine ran up to the children's apartment, where she found Emerance Bricout, and the other nursemaid, Virginia Chevalier. Justine was frightened and hardly able to talk. It took a minute or two for her to describe what she had heard.

Emerance, more mature than the others, picked up her lantern and immediately ran down the corridor toward the stairs, intending to reach the vestibule below and the dining room. However, at the top of the stairs, at the entrance to his and Lydie's bedroom, she ran into the count.

He carried no light and was having a hard time opening the bedroom door. She shone her lantern on him and saw that he was trembling; his forehead was covered with sweat; he was deathly pale; and, from the look on his face, he seemed ill. On his forehead was a laceration, from which blood was running down his nose. He was wearing a brown cardigan sweater.

Emerance's nearness bothered him. "No. Get away. Leave me alone!" he ordered in a weak voice.

She watched him and saw that he succeeded, with difficulty, in opening the door to his bedroom and closing it behind him. He left blood on the doorframe above the knob and on the door itself.

It did not occur, at first, to Emerance that, in addition to his laceration, he might also be acutely ill. She did not know that he had vomited downstairs in a corner of the colonnaded salon, before climbing the stairs to his room. She certainly could not have known that vomiting is one of the first symptoms of nicotine poisoning.[24]

***

Emerance continued down the staircase, and on reaching the entrance hall, she saw Lydie emerge from the door opening from the kitchen to the hall, carrying a jug of water.

---

[24] Nor did Hippolyte understand pure nicotine, beyond how to obtain it from tobacco leaves by distillation. He knew nothing of its high vapor pressure. Its fumes immediately fill a room and are extremely noxious to breathe. Its first effect is to cause vomiting. Sustained exposure to the vapor is lethal. He came close to killing himself along with Gustave.

Lydie had a frightened look, and again ordered Emerance to return upstairs at once to the children's room with light from Emerance's lamp. They mounted the circular staircase together as Lydie held Emerance's other arm.

"It seems something has gone wrong," said Emerance, who felt Lydie's arm shake ungovernably. Her response was, "No. It will all be settled."

The countess disappeared into her bedroom, while Emerance continued down the hall to the room from which she had come. Nevertheless, from the children's room, it was possible to hear the count and countess speaking loudly, although she could not make out the words.

The countess was with her husband for five or six minutes, after which she entered the children's room and blurted, "Quick. Get me a glass of water. I ate too much salt today, and I am very thirsty."

Emerance left at once and ran down the stairs to the kitchen to get the water for the countess. At the bottom of the staircase, Emerance once more bumped into the count. Sick as he was, he had forced himself to go down again to the vestibule to stand guard. He blocked her way and demanded, "Where is Madame?"

"She is in the children's room."

"Tell her to come down immediately! I want to talk to her!"

"But she sent me down for a glass of water. Let me get that first."

"No! Do as I say, and be quick about it! Go tell her to come down *now!*"

Emerance had no choice. She again ran up to the children's room, without the glass of water, and explained to Lydie that the count wanted her downstairs immediately.

The countess flew out the door and ran down the corridor to the staircase, with Emerance two steps behind holding her lantern.

At the base of the stairs, the sick count had managed still to be there, standing guard. He whispered something to Lydie while Emerance retreated upstairs once again.

Suddenly, the two in the vestibule began to cry out loudly. The count shouted, "Some vinegar! I want some vinegar!"[25]

And the countess, in a screeching voice, cried out "Help! Help! Gustave is sick!"

***

Gilles van den Bergh, who was in the new stable behind the chateau, had, long since, attached Gustave's horse to his Tilbury and was impatiently waiting for Gustave to appear. It dawned on Gilles, that perhaps no one had told Gustave where his Tilbury would be. Perhaps he thought it might be at the *front* entrance to the Chateau.

The coachman returned the horse and Tilbury to the stable and hastened with his lantern to the chateau, by way of the back entrance, to reach the vestibule and the door to the dining room.

He pushed lightly on the door to open it and peer into the room. To his surprise, he found Hippolyte, who pushed hard on the door from the inside, stopping Gilles in his tracks, and asking, "Who's there?" His voice gave away his identity.

Gilles began to ask, "Where do I—" only to be interrupted by a meaningless, repetitive, "Yes, yes, yes!"

"But where should I lead the horse—to the drawbridge?"

"Yes, yes, yes!"

Gilles returned to the stable and walked the horse a few feet to the drawbridge, where once again he waited. He frequently glanced toward the rear of the chateau to see if anyone was coming, but no one came. He noticed that no light was visible in the dining room windows, although there was light in the kitchen.

What he did not know was that, while he was waiting, the count had been frantically busy in the pitch-black dining room. He had

---

[25] Vinegar is very highly diluted acetic acid. Refer to the chapter entitled "Lethal Seeds."

dragged Gustave's nearly dead body from the corner of the table lying diagonally opposite to where he had been seated, to the other side of the room, where he imagined servants in the kitchen might not see it through the hole in the kitchen door. In the pitch-black, he'd overturned chairs and moved the dining table.

Hippolyte took so long that Van den Bergh's patience was wearing thin and he even became a little anxious. He tied the horse to a post by the drawbridge and walked again through the back entrance to the vestibule, where he called out, "Isn't anyone ready?" I've been out there in the cold for twenty minutes already."

He heard no response and started again for the drawbridge. Only then did he hear cries from the vestibule. The count was calling, "Help!" And the countess was crying, "My God! My God! What a tragedy!" He ran to them and noticed that, although she cried loudly, she shed no tears.

***

The only members of the staff who were downstairs at the time of the murder were Charlotte Monjardez, Mme Maes and Justine Thibaut. Charlotte Monjardez and Mme Maes remained in the kitchen out of fright, after Justine ran away a minute or two earlier.

After some minutes, the countess *allegedly* [26] entered the kitchen *again* from the pantry [sic], seeming so distraught and confused that she was walking into chairs and tables. She asked for hot water, and Charlotte gave her a jug of it. (During the pursuant trial, the jury was ordered not to consider this testimony by Charlotte Monjardez).

This was the same jug that Emerance had previously seen the countess carry upstairs.

"Emerance, please! I told you to go back to children's room."

---

[26] We will learn that when the count asked Emerance how Charlotte Monjardez will testify, her reply was, "With whatever you tell her to say, Monsieur."

They climbed the stairs together, walking toward the children's quarters, aided by the light from Emerance's lantern.

"Countess, it looks to me as though something has gone wrong." She held Lydie's arm as she opened and then closed the door to the children's room behind her as the countess answered "No, all will be straightened out." Emerance would later testify that she felt her arm trembling ungovernably.

***

Taking five minutes to settle down, Lydie at once took extraordinary steps, lasting through the night and well into the post-midnight hours of the next day (November 21). She aimed to destroy every last item of evidence. She knew that her husband had killed her brother with nicotine and was particularly intent on the indiscriminate destruction of any clothing that might be stained with nicotine, whether worn by her husband or her brother. She ordered domestics to burn shirts, ties, handkerchiefs, sweaters, and work pants. Nicotine stains on the oaken planks of the parquet dining room floor were a special problem. The servants diligently used scrubbing brushes with soap and water. As hard as they tried, they never succeeded in obliterating the stains, and the telltale discolorations remained.

In desperation, the countess ordered them to scrape the planks with knife-edged tools, which was all for naught because the stains were too embedded in the wood. In Lydie's final attempt to cover them or prevent their use as evidence, she ordered the servants to pour rapeseed oil on them.

Lydie also had a large amount of written and printed evidence to burn. Aside from Hippolyte's books or papers dealing in any way with chemistry, she had numerous letters she had written at Hippolyte's orders, including those she had also signed as countess. They ran the gamut, from letters addressed to persons like the chemist Loppens and the horticulturalist Vanhoutte to drafts of those she'd sent to Gustave libeling his prospective wife, Antoinette de Dudzcèle.

The list must have seemed endless to Lydie. She claimed, whether true or not, that it was she who, at the count's demands, had personally thrown the half-empty vials, once filled with nicotine, into the pond, although the police were unable find them.

***

Her motivation for all these actions was manifold. She felt she might rationalize that she had a duty to try to cover up for the father of her three children, regardless of his uncivilized brutality and use of "duress" to make her perform countless wicked acts. Far more importantly, she genuinely believed that had she done less or done a sloppy job, her uncivilized husband might beat or kill her for not doing all she could to cover up for him. Out of stark fear, she felt strongly that she should appear to defend him and attend a meeting with Emerance and him in her bedroom at three in the morning of what was now November 21. In fact she was not of much help to him at the meeting, where it became evident that the count wanted *Emerance* to help him by instructing all the other domestics how to answer questions the police might ask.

He had difficulty trying to manipulate Emerance, who despised him. The countess, despite her desire to defend her husband, said very little, except to interject a rare, hardly audible "that's right" when Emerance made a useful suggestion. She was, therefore, minimally complicit in suborning witnesses, a felonious crime.

***

The count began by asking Emerance what she would tell authorities.

She replied that she would tell them, "What I saw and heard. Would you have me tell them anything other than that?" The hostility Emerance felt for the count, and vice versa, came into the open.

The critical information, the count knew, was what Justine Thibaut had clearly heard, as she was about to place her foot on the vestibule floor at the moment when the murder was under way. All that she'd heard, in the vestibule or the kitchen, had come through the closed door of the dining room.

The count asked Emerance, "What did Justine say she heard?'

"She says she clearly remembers the words, "Aie! Aie, Hippolyte, Forgive me."

Hippolyte replied, "You are wrong. She must have told you, 'Aie, Aie, Hippolyte. Help me!'" Hippolyte argued this because the latter was consistent with *his* story of Gustave feeling suddenly ill and asking for his assistance.

He asked her four or five times to repeat what her testimony would be, and she continued to supply the same answer.

He exploded with anger, declaring, "Justine is a liar and a beast!"

Emerance, who was not afraid of the count, contradicted him, asserting that Justine was extremely honest and incapable of telling an untruth.

He asked Emerance what Charlotte Monjardez would say. She answered, "Monsieur, she will say whatever you tell her to say."

***

The count went down the list of every employee of the chateau, asking Emerance to tell them what to say. She told him it would be better if he spoke to them himself.

This was the one time when the countess said softly, "That's right," agreeing, therefore with Emerance.

The count grudgingly agreed. Later, he did ask practically every one of the domestics, as he met them in rooms and corridors throughout the house, what they would say they'd seen and heard and what they *should* say, if he heard anything that displeased him.

Before the small meeting ended, the count loudly declared, "Justine, or anyone else, should not discuss hearing opening and closing of doors. The less said the better. Even a single word can cause trouble."

***

Emerance deeply distrusted the count. She felt that he was trying to "corrupt" possible witnesses. She asked Lydie for permission to visit the curé of the church in Bury to seek his counsel, and Lydie promptly gave it. Emerance advised other servants to join her, but it was she alone who first met the curé.

In strong and specific terms, he told her, and then others, to tell the whole truth. "You must not withhold information to aid a criminal, if the justice department should question you." He did tell Emerance that other domestics had, in the past, come to discuss the issue of the count's 'apparent insanity.'

***

Immediately after Gustave's ghastly death just before nine o'clock in the evening of November 20, the count became quite ill. He had been poisoned by nicotine, although not fatally. The major symptom was intermittent vomiting, which afflicted him for nearly five hours after the murder.

Throughout the evening and after midnight, Lydie periodically supplied him with water so that, when he vomited, he would have something in his stomach to eject rather than suffer dry heaves. At times, through the first couple of early morning hours of November 21, Lydie commiserated with him, using such calculated endearing terms as "my poor darling."

She commiserated with him even though she had, at his command, patently pretended to be devastated over the death of her brother by

259

wailing without shedding a single tear. *Her "commiseration" was the insincere pity of a captive wife.* In 1851, practically nothing was known of captive wives and their survival tactics. In *Procès de Bocarmé* nuances of this sort are conspicuously missing.[27] One can easily conclude wrongly, that Lydie was lovingly sorry for Hippolyte. In fact, Lydie had learned to use endearing terms in communicating with this man she loathed and feared. She thought that her use of this language might lessen the brutality of his near-daily beatings, a common strategy of captive, abused women.

---

[27] Is this an indication that the trial may have been the first to involve a Captive Wife? Read Nurse deFrance's testimony in Chapter 44.

CHAPTER 37

Dawn

on the morning of November 21, the countess, acting on the count's orders, made an initial mistake. She overestimated her closeness to Dr. Semel, and that of others in the chateau who were his patients, assuming that he would be a lenient, protective, and sympathetic friend. Shortly after dawn She sent a housemaid to summon him. About the same rime, she sent Alex Vandenberg to a carpenter who made caskets, to get one and bring it back immediately.

On Dr. Semel's arrival, Lydie told him that Gustave had died of apoplexy during dinner the evening before, but he found a body with a wounded face—someone who had died a violent death. The law called for him to advise the Bury Alderman, Monsieur Xavier Laurent.

***

Although Laurent did not at first come to the chateau, he learned of Gustave's death (presumably from Dr. Semel) and sent a message by fast horse to the Justice of the Peace in Tournai, advising him of Gustave Fougnies' demise. At about same time. Laurent also advised the king's prosecutor in Tournai of Fougnies's death the evening before, adding, "Monsieur complained of violent headaches at dinner before he collapsed and died." He added, "The Count and Countess de Bocarmé are my informants. The Bocarmés are not surprised because doctors had predicted that he would die suddenly. Monsieur Fougnies had a very delicate constitution from a lingering bone illness. He had an aunt who died like that."

Laurent, also a member of the Bury City Council, let it be known to the count and countess that he had ruled that there was no need for

261

an investigation and gave his permission for a burial. Within minutes thereafter, Vandenberg, who had slept soundly and knew nothing of the commotion, set the casket on the floor of the Salon à Colonnes. Someone else carried Gustave's body from its station in Emerance's room and placed it in the casket.

Still, a burial was impossible, because Dr. Semel refused to sign a physician's death certificate, which required his stating a *probable* cause of death. He could not sign, he told the de Bocarmés, because "apoplexy is not a probable cause of death at Gustave Fougnies's age."

By nine in the morning, the slightly used casket was back in the possession of the carpenter and Gustave's body had been returned to the bed in the dark alcove upstairs in Emerance's room.

Just as the count suddenly appeared, the countess ordered Amand Wilbaut, "Ride with Emerance to Grandmetz to tell those two prostitutes that my brother died last night of apoplexy."

The count added, "Be sure to get a key to the place and bring back any silver service you can find. If there's any cash in his drawers, take it."

Wilbaut ignored the request, and Emerance's deep dislike for the count grew. How Emerance would explain to the de Dudzcèles what happened to Gustave is not in the trial notes, but one can be certain that she planned to handle the difficult responsibility with grace. She well knew how Antoinette's fiancé had died.

Prostitute was not a word common to Lydie's vocabulary. The count used the word frequently when he ranted to Lydie that only a prostitute would marry a one-legged man. Battered women are alert to little ways to ingratiate themselves with the monsters they have as husbands, using any device to lessen their beatings, even aping their language in their presence. Lydie knew full well that Antoinette de Dudzcèle and her mother must be refined people. Gustave would otherwise not have asked Antoinette to marry him.

***

It is remarkable that Monsieur Laurent's observations led him to conclude that further examination into the circumstances surrounding Gustave's death was not warranted. For very many it was not surprising because most people in Bury knew that Laurent and the count had a mutually beneficial compact of a vague sort. They were friends.

In spite of this back-scratching relationship with Hippolyte, Laurent finally did send a second message to Justice of the Peace Jacques Messine after noon. He probably did so grudgingly but knew that his job required it. Laurent informed the judge that rumors were circulating in Bury about there having been a murder at the chateau the previous evening. He believed that there was nothing behind the rumors but felt obliged to let the judge know of them.

Whether he knew it or not, Messine disliked Laurent. He didn't trust him.

CHAPTER 38

Rumor

Jacques Messine, justice of the peace for the region extending from Tournai to Peruwelz and Bury, was at his desk in midmorning of November 21. Once he had finished his routine paperwork, he read the alderman's second message that Bury was alive with murmurs and speculation about a murder that had occurred at the chateau.

Rumor had it that Gustave Fougnies, a friend of Messines's, was the victim. The justice of the peace (usually called judge) thought he ought to look at once into what might merely be a rumor; there were always rumors about life at the chateau.

He took a carriage with two fast horses and was soon at the chateau, ten miles distant. He entered the chateau, asked a few questions, and viewed the body of Gustave Fougnies. He had always admired Gustave and had heard that his friend was likely to marry soon. He realized that the sudden death was suspicious.

Messine rode back to Tournai, where he notified the police, along with Judge Ryckman, a substitute chief investigator. Ryckman was at first hesitant to believe that a murder was likely to have taken place at the home of a count and countess. He quickly changed his mind when he came face-to-face with Messine, who emphasized that he had seen the dead man and expressed his own suspicious opinions.

After a slight delay, Messine and three police officers rushed toward Bury. What Judge Ryckman observed convinced him that the cause of death required investigation.

By the time the group had returned to Tournai, it was mid-afternoon on a short winter day in November. It would soon be dusk, and the sun would set too early in the day. Investigative work required daylight, if possible. On November 21, the chateau depended on light only from kerosene lamps, so Ryckman decided to send his full team of experts to Bury very early the following morning.

Dr. Semel was firm in his belief that Gustave Fougnies was not of an age when apoplexy was a likely cause of death. He adamantly refused to sign a death certificate. No legal burial was possible without a medical doctor's diagnosis and his signature on a death certificate.

CHAPTER 39

Arrests

On November 22, Ryckman's team of experts gathered before dawn in Tournai. The team included Judge Ryckman and a young assistant; his top investigative detective, Constant Heughebart; a secretary; and three doctors, all specialists in performing autopsies.

Heughebart had no prior knowledge of the count or countess and, frankly, was hard-pressed to believe that a murder might have occurred in the home of such presumably high-minded personages. Ryckman was open to the possibility of wrongful activity and took detailed notes:

"Upon arriving at Bitremont, I entered with M. Heughebart and Messine, found the countess having breakfast in the dining room. She was alone. Because in all such cases, it is necessary to do an autopsy, I explained its purpose to her. There were some rumors circulating, and I wanted to see if they were ill-founded.

"She seemed slightly taken aback, but she recovered very quickly. She said her husband was outside and would soon be here. As we waited for him, we noticed a good deal of carbonized paper stuffed into the fireplace. Then we noticed that there was an outline of a book buried in the paper. She, and later her husband, told us that the book was a catalogue of flowers from Vanhoutte's horticultural institute in Ghent.

"The count appeared; I told him the purpose of my visit, asked him to show me the cadaver and find us a good locale in which to perform an autopsy. Drs. Zoude, Gosse, and Marousé needed a place with better light than there was in the alcove where someone had ordered the body be placed.

266

"As we left to look around for a better place, Dr. Zoude and I carried the light bed with the body next to a window where the light was better. I could not help noticing that there were deep gouges, almost certainly made by fingernails, on the dead man's left cheek—one of which had to have bled, because there was a wound within one gouge that had dried blood. Besides that, the lips and tongue were, veritably, almost black.

"Someone found us a coach house in the courtyard where the light was good. I told the doctors to go ahead with the autopsy, which they began at once. Messine asked Judge Ryckman's assistant to stay behind and watch the autopsy, and "to report to me anything of extreme interest."

Ryckman wanted to walk around the house and speak to people, especially the count and countess. He wanted them, under oath, to fill him in on what had happened.

"I wanted to know the circumstances that accompanied and followed the death of Gustave Fougnies, assuming that a verbal trial of sorts would give a lead to the truth.

"I found the count sitting in the Red Salon and had him take an oath, and very soon, it was easy to tell that he was having a hard time trying to tell a straight story. He was, so to say, beating around the bush. His speech and thoughts were not well organized. Here is a summary of his first statement: "The day before yesterday, me and my madam" (his grammar was poor) "was dining with Fougnies. It was a long dinner, which began around dusk."

"He could not say what they had for dinner, and he was not able to say who served the dinner. He averred that, as they sat there, his wife suddenly left the room and took the lamp with her but didn't know why she did this.

"He and Fougnies were suddenly in the dark. Fougnies was sitting at an angle from him,

across the table near windows facing the court. Suddenly, Gustave Fougnies cried out, "Quick! Quick! Aie, Aie, Hippolyte, help me!

"He rushed to help and wanted to hold him up, but both fell to the floor, he on me and me on him. In the fall, one of his crutches broke and when he saw[28] "what a mess we were in," he called for help.

"I asked who the first person was to come to help and he claimed, "It is impossible to know." I asked how the room looked when light arrived, and he said that was also impossible to know. All this seemed suspicious to me. I believed he was eluding questions; and since he spoke vulgarly, I thought he was not being square with me.

"The fingernail wound on the cheek of the corpse came to mind; my blood ran hotter in the face of all this indecisiveness, so I asked him to show me his right hand. I saw a trace of red under a nail; it looked like he had tried to wash something away but was unable to do it.

"This first observation startled the count. I saw that he had numerous small wounds and scratches on the rest of the hand. I told him that they looked to be not more than forty-eight hours old.

"Oh, they're nothing," he replied.

"In his left hand, one of the fingers appeared to have sustained a serious human bite. I asked how he accounted for this.

"He said, "I don't know. It might have come from our fight."

---

[28] If the Count de Bocarmé claimed that he saw something in a pitch-black room, either he loosely used the word or was mixed up in his account of events.

"Based on the nature of that response," I told him, "I want you to know that I am putting you under provisionary arrest immediately."

"Effectively, that preliminary interrogation ended, and I asked Judge Messine, Justice of the Peace, to keep a careful, close eye on him. I told the judge that I had interrogated him and he was under provisionary arrest. They were not to converse. They sat on adjacent seats in the colonnaded salon, near the entrance hall.

"I next went to interrogate the countess, who was lying on her bed upstairs. While she seemed to want to answer questions, I placed her under arrest, too."

***

Judge Messine knew the count all too well and vice versa. "Hippolyte was not Messine's favorite person in Peruwelz and Bury. The two were not supposed to communicate with each other, but according to Messine, "the count tried to initiate a little conversation by asking him pointed questions," as follows:

"Have they found anything in the cadaver?" he asked me.

"It's taking quite a long time," he remarked.

"The doctors do what they have to do."

"Will the doctors question the witnesses?"

"The doctors do what they have to do."

"But that's your responsibility; you should do that."

"The investigative judge knows what it is necessary to do, but if I were in his place, I would interrogate them," I admitted to him.

"Someone asked the countess, when she'd been arrested, if she would prefer to ride with me rather than with the gendarme, and she emphatically replied, Yes. Then she asked me if she would be in prison for a long time. If she might be there as long as eight hours."

"Oh, yes," I answered, "but if you tell the truth— you won't be there long."

"Oh, but I *have* told the truth," she replied.

***

They arrived at about two o'clock in the morning of November 23 at the Detention Center in Tournai, where jailers immediately placed count and countess in separate, distanced cells. "They underwent thorough entrance physical examinations and then we let them sleep."

According to Judge Heughebart's notes, "Lydie slept soundly until early morning when the sun came up. The prison nurse, Sister La France, reexamined her under sunlight."

***

Judge Heughebart, in Tournai, subjected the prisoners to intense interrogation, daily for five months, until the second week of May, in the following year. They were then transferred to Mons, where the trial would commence on May 27, 1851.

Although Heughebart spent more time interrogating the count, he found that the countess readily told the truth. "She seemed to involve herself either in murder or as an accomplice to murder. Nevertheless, neither would provide an outright confession of guilt."

Part Two

CHAPTER 40

The Trial Begins

Investigative Judge Ryckman organized essential, collected evidence. He made it available, together with additional background information, to Judge Lyon, president of the Court of Assizes.

Judge Lyon, an experienced judge, extracted information from selected witnesses during the trial, which was in session from May 27 to June 14, 1851. He questioned some singly and in several cases quizzed a few at one sitting. The two defendants were cross-examined as "witnesses."

Later in the trial, he heard the testimony of eighty-six other witnesses. He offered no reason for the order in which they testified. Note that, in an 1851 Belgian trial, the judge, who was technically president of the court, did most questioning of witnesses. Lawyers intervened far less than in modern trials in the United States. For this reason it was possible to begin and end the major portion of the trial, deliberations of the jury and sentencing of the accused by June 19, 1851. The sessions were many and long with few recesses.

The first witness was a coiffeuse from Peruwelz, who had been traipsing more than a mile to the chateau at Bury, regularly, for three years to set Lydie's hair. She took her seat in the witness chair, obviously angry and eager to tell her story.

The countess owed her only nineteen francs, but she'd avoided paying by repeatedly assuring the woman that she intended to pay in the future but had no cash on her person now.

One day, the two met in the public square in Peruwelz and the coiffeuse remarked, "It's strange. You owe me some money, but won't pay."

Lydie audibly snorted as she turned her back on the well-dressed woman and cautioned her, "Keep your distance from me."

The second witness, a shopkeeper and an elderly widow, cleared her throat and spoke hesitantly at first, saying that she thought the count was craftier than the blunt countess. She explained how the count had resorted to various ruses to avoid paying his debt, adding that his credit was so bad in Peruwelz that he had to avail himself of stores in Brussels.

"He bought groceries worth 367 francs at my small shop and asked me to send the bill to what he called 'my new address on rue de Coin, in Bruges.'

"I knew who he was and that he had been living in Bury but took him at his word.

"But when he didn't pay me, I wanted to be sure that I'd sent the bills to the correct address and found out, from the postmaster, that there is no rue de Coin in Bruges.

"I wrote the count at his address in Bury, demanding payment within ten days, informing him that I would report him to the police, if he didn't send the money. He ignored my letter and then he found out that I reported him to Judge Messine, Justice of the Peace in Peruwelz.

"News of what happened reached a Visart relation in Brussels. He sent me 380 francs, to make up for part of my trouble and to avoid public embarrassment to his family's name," she concluded.

The third witness was a cabinetmaker from Peruwelz who felt angry with himself as well as the count because he had done business with the count even after friends had told him not to have anything to do with the count, as he didn't pay bills, especially not from people in Peruwelz.

"I made two cabinets—good ones—for him. I sent him a fair bill for 216 francs, but he never paid me, even after I'd sent several bills. I even had to walk to Bury to try to collect.

"One day I somehow got inside his house, where I saw him with his wife. The count said he lost the bill and asked me to make out another. I wrote another one and then he ordered me to make out two bills—one for his wife and the other for him. Each was made out for 108 francs.

"One or the other handed me 160 francs, and the count said, 'All right, why don't you call it quits, now that you've been paid something?'

"I refused, and he told me the rest of the money would be sent to me in the afternoon. It never came, and so I called Justice of the Peace, Judge Messine, and he went with me to Bury to help me collect.

"They again promised to pay, but no one did. So I went back to the chateau the next day, but when they saw me coming, they raised the drawbridge over the pond."

"Ah," said Judge Lyon, "I gather that this is the new way to settle accounts."

This statement caused hilarity in the courtroom.

The fourth witness, Amand Wilbaut, the oldest employee of the Chateau de Bitremont, followed and gave a contemptuous account of Hippolyte, with whom he worked at the chateau. He testified that Hippolyte cheated individual people as much as he did merchants.

When Judge Lyon asked him if the count paid domestics their wages on time, Wilbaut testified, "Sometimes he paid them, and other times he did not. He found excuses to withhold their pay; he'd accuse them of stealing or of using household money to buy things for themselves."

The fifth witness, a butcher, testified that the de Bocarmé couple never paid him for sausages bought in 1847 and 1848. They owed him thirty francs.

"I went to the chateau to ask for his money. At first, someone told me that neither the count nor the countess was at home.

"After many useless attempts to collect, a servant told me she had been ordered never to pay the butcher because, when old man

Fougnies was alive, he'd let me grow some vegetables on his land. This angered Fougnies by my being so thoughtless as to grow beets, a vegetable the old man considered beneath the dignity of his land."

When the judge asked the butcher what he thought of Lydie's character, the butcher told the court that he had known her since childhood before her mother left her father. He added that she went to the expensive Belgium College in Tournai and that, when her mother had come to visit her, she'd become so snooty a girl that she'd refused to speak to her. "She snubbed her own mother," he said.

The stenographer reported that this testimony caused "a movement in the audience."

Judge Lyon, more interested in the count, asked the butcher how he got along with him and added a question, "How did Gustave Fougnies get along with the count?"

The butcher said, "Gustave disliked and feared the count. Gustave would never eat anything at the chateau until after he had satisfied himself that the count had eaten the same thing from the same platter. The butcher knew this because the count was in the habit of sending Gustave gifts of sausage meats, but he never ate them because he feared the count would poison him. Gustave always had his domestics burn these gifts."

Many others, in the course of the trial, also testified that Gustave invariably carried his own wine to dinner on occasions when he ate at the chateau and that he refused to drink anything Hippolyte offered him, out of fear that it might poison him.

The sixth witness was Justice of the Peace Judge Messine, favorite of nearly all the people. He was close to six feet tall; was clean shaven; and always wore neat clothes, even if they weren't the most fashionable. He had a pleasant voice and smiled a lot, but he could be tough on lawbreakers and men who were disrespectful or brutal to their wives. He was intelligent and competent.

Judge Messine was the first to testify about Gustave Fougnies's death. He was friendly with Gustave; he considered him a model citizen.

"Last November 21, while I was at my desk in Tournai at about ten in the morning, I received a note from an Alderman at Bury. He wrote that Gustave Fougnies died the day before at five in the evening and that this had caused rumors of murder to circulate in the community, although he, the Alderman, personally did not believe that any crime was involved.

"My paperwork was completed, so I decided to make my own visit to Bury. There, I found out that the townspeople claimed that M. Fougnies had been murdered. I then recalled that Gustave Fougnies had told me, many times, that he did not dare to eat at Bury because someone there might poison him, and that if he did eat there, he would only take what the others had eaten before him. Therefore, I decided to hasten to the chateau.

"On arriving at the Chateau de Bitremont, someone escorted me into the dining room, where I found the notary, M. Chercquefosse, who, at my request, called for Countess de Bocarmé.

"The moment the countess appeared, she said to me, 'What a tragedy! Yesterday at five, after we had had a good dinner, my brother suddenly, and surprisingly, dropped dead of apoplexy.'"

Judge Messine continued, "Count de Bocarmé arrived at that moment bearing a clearly apparent wound on his forehead, large enough to attract my attention. He seemed to want to hide his hands in his bathrobe pockets; he told me exactly what Countess de Bocarmé had told me.

"I asked to see the cadaver and was taken to it by Lydie's chambermaid, Emerance Bricout, who seemed disconsolate. I recognized M. Fougnies, my friend, and I noticed that he had four obvious scratches on his left cheek and a blue stain on the bridge of his nose.

"I ordered a man named Michel, who was standing guard over the body, not to allow it to be moved from where it was and not to allow anyone to touch it without my express order.

"I then returned to Tournai, where I saw both the royal prosecutor and the investigative judge, M. Ryckman, who at first, offered me a group of people to help, stating that, if it were necessary, I was to send them an express message. But having heard more of what I had already seen, and heard what was being said in Bury about conditions in the de Bocarmé household whenever the subject came up for conversation, it was decided that all of us should return together to Bury, along with three doctors and three gendarmes. And that was that.

"Someone led us into the dining room of the chateau, where the countess was having her lunch. She didn't seem the least bit ill at ease and beckoned to us to enter. We then returned to where the cadaver was. There, Dr. Zoude noted the traces of violence on the face, about which I have spoken. He opened the mouth and said, 'This is a very serious matter! The mouth has been cauterized.'"

The seventh witness was Investigative Judge Ryckman. He took the stand and said, "When we arrived, the countess seemed not in the least disturbed, but her husband was obviously self-conscious. I asked Judge Messine to keep an eye on things while I interrogated the couple separately."

Ryckman asked to see Gustave's body, which he examined carefully.

"I sought the count," he continued, "asked him in a friendly way to tell him what had happened on the evening of November 20, and requested that he take an oath to tell the truth. He rambled, could not say what they ate for dinner, or who served them.

"The count said that his wife suddenly left the dining room with the lantern, and he was alone in the dark with Gustave. Shortly thereafter, Gustave cried out, 'Hippolyte, help me.'

"The count described how he went to help him but both fell to the floor together in the dark. In the fall, one of Gustave's crutches broke and he fell on the count and vice versa. He could not say who came running with the lantern when he called for it; nor did he recall the condition of the room when it was light enough to look about.

"I found his jumbled story hard to believe. He was definitely beating around the bush. Suddenly, I recalled the gouges on Gustave's left cheek, a little dried blood still in the deepest of them.

"I asked the count to show me his right hand and saw what appeared to be blood under a nail bed. Perhaps he had not been able to wash it away. I asked to see the count's left hand and saw a severe bite on the middle finger. I asked how it happened. The answer was, 'I guess it was while we were fighting.'

"I said, 'Sorry, that answer alone is enough to put you under provisionary arrest.'

"I informed Judge Messine that I had examined the count and arrested him and requested that the judge keep a careful eye on him while the two sat on adjacent chairs in the colonnaded salon. Furthermore, the count was not to have communication with anyone.

"Messine reported, though, that some minor dialogue took place between himself and the count, the least likeable person he knew in all of Bury and Peruwelz. It started with the count asking, 'Have they found anything in the cadaver?' To which I answered, 'I don't know.'

"'It's taking quite a long time,' the count remarked.

"'The doctors do what they have to do.'

"'Will they be interrogating the domestics?'

"'I don't know.'

"'But that's your responsibility; you should do that.'

"'The investigative judge knows what is necessary to do, but if I were in his place, I would interrogate them,' I admitted to him."

The count did not tell Messine that he had already ordered all domestics to change what they originally were going to say they heard and saw if detectives questioned them.

The eighth witness was again Judge Messine. He replied to numerous questions put to him by Judge Lyon. The core of his testimony was as follows:

"In 1846, Count de Bocarmé asked me to dissuade Gustave Fougnies from marrying—something he was giving thought to at that time—arguing that Gustave was 'not capable of being married.' He added that M. Fougnies would die if he married; but I never mentioned a word of this to M. Fougnies.

"Later, when the question of marriage to Mlle de Dudzcèle came up, everyone said publicly that Count de Bocarmé was very strongly opposed to it, but he never spoke about it to me.

"M. Fougnies very rarely went to the Chateau de Bitremont. He often told me that both of the accused were always short of money and always touched him up for some.

"He told me that Count de Bocarmé and his sister were two extravagant people and that this would eventually cause them trouble. He also said that he (Gustave Fougnies) was afraid of being poisoned, but I did not believe him. I could not believe that a sister would poison her brother.

"I often had to go to the chateau to speak with the count and countess about paying the debts they owed. One day, as I approached, I could see the count in the dining room. He fled, to avoid my claims and demands."

At this point, Count de Bocarmé, from his seat on a courtroom bench, objected to the court that he had been in the garden and had left the chateau because he was not properly dressed.

Messine, speaking from the witness stand, declared that the count was not in the garden. "He was, without doubt, in the dining room." There is no recorded response by the count.

Judge[29] Messine then told the court that, with regard to one of the de Bocarmés' debts, he'd had to make as many as ten trips to the chateau and that, in this case, Madame had shown no better faith than her husband had.

---

[29] Messine was a Justice of the Peace, a busy, responsible job. People more often referred to him as "Judge" than "Justice."

Next, Judge Lyon asked the witness if he had any knowledge about the accused having once promised thirty francs to a witness if he would lie for him in court. Messine answered that he was well aware of the situation.

Judge Lyon then asked about the accused count's reputation for morality.

Judge Messine replied, "He is known as an immoral man in every sense of the word. He is known to have had a child with a domestic working at his chateau."

"Is there not a special name by which he is generally called?" asked Judge Lyon.

"They call him 'le bouquin.' It means 'buck rabbit.'"

This argot with obvious meaning, caused laughter that filled the courtroom.

Once the laughter had died down, Judge Lyon asked whether Messine was aware of circumstances surrounding the case of an illegitimate child fathered by Count de Bocarmé.

Justice Messine answered that he was aware of most of the details. "Countess de Bocarmé paid me a visit one day to tell me that her husband had an illegitimate child with one of the housemaids. He wanted her to take the child in with her three children and consider the child one of theirs in all respects, insisting that she give this illegitimate child the same care that she gave her own children. She told him she was unwilling to do that.

"I told her to wipe her hands of it, refuse to consider this child one of her own.

"She feared that her husband would then beat her. (I did not know at the time how brutal he could be with his wife.) Anyway, I told her to contact me if this happened. She was always close-mouthed about how she and her husband ordinarily got along.

"I heard, shortly afterward, that the infant had mysteriously vanished and was so alarmed that I was about to alert the Royal

280

Prosecutor, but stayed my hand when I learned that the countess and her brother had placed the child in a good orphanage in Brussels."

Judge Lyon asked Messine what he knew of the morality of the countess. Judge Messine replied, "During the long illness of her father, M. Joseph Fougnies, she took excellent care of him; I never heard an unkind word about her on this count. On the other hand, she was the subject of gossip about her morals as a young girl and even since her marriage. It was even rumored that she had an evil streak. I never believed a word of that and don't believe any of it now."

The ninth "witness" was a medley of young women who had been propositioned by the count. Also included is Mme Adelaide Chercquefosse, wife of Gustave's lawyer and old friend of the Fougnies family.

Among Hippolyte's worst derangement was utter disrespect for his marriage vows. He would attempt to fornicate with nearly any reasonably attractive young woman he laid eyes on. Those with dark eyes and an olive complexion were especially likely to be targets.

In questioning nearly twenty-five domestics and former domestics of the Chateau de Bitremont, Judge Lyon made it a practice to ask most of them if the count had tried to seduce them.

Most of them hung their heads, blushed, and admitted to having had *relations coupables* (illegal, extramarital sex) with him.

Judge Lyon confronted the seated count himself about his obsession early in the trial by asking, "Are you acquainted with Louise Prevost, who worked at the chateau?"

"Yeh, she was my wife's chambermaid."

"Didn't you try to have relations coupables with this woman?"

He raised one side of his upper lip and angrily grunted, "Never!"

(That was a lie. He had a key to her bedroom and forced himself on her at least four times. It was why she quit her job and left an opening for Lydie to hire Emerance Bricout.)

"Uh-huh. And weren't young Justine, who cared for the children, and several other quite young girls objects of your desire, and didn't you try to have criminal sex with them?"

He flared his nostrils contemptuously. "No! Never!"

Immediately thereafter, Françoise Éschofflaire, a young woman described by the stenographer as pretty, modest, and refined, took the witness stand and recounted that she had worked at the chateau for Count and Countess de Bocarmé for a three-week period as recently as 1850. "I quit because, Monsieur, the count, propositioned me."

"What kinds of propositions?" asked the judge.

She lowered her eyes and failed to respond.

"Were they meant to seduce you?"

"Yes, Monsieur le President," she said with much emotion.

"These propositions were attempts to establish relations coupables between him and you?"

"Yes, Monsieur le President."

"Did he offer you anything?"

"He said that there was nothing in the house that I couldn't have."

"Did he look for you in your room when you were alone?"

"Yes, many times."

"Is that when he propositioned you?"

"Yes."

"Didn't you write to your parents?"

"Only twice."

"Why?"

"Because he had made all these propositions and I was afraid my parents might not believe me."

Her response drew a loud response of amiable laughter from the audience.

"Wasn't one of these letters intercepted?"

"Yes, sir. The count took my letter from the postman to see what was in it."

"Accusé! What do you have to say about this testimony?"

The count had developed a way of elevating his upper lip and squinting his eyes into a facial expression of hatred when he answered Judge Lyon's questions. This time, he answered, "I have nothing to say."

"Well, is it the truth?"

"It was a letter that my wife asked me to intercept." He spoke angrily.

"I am asking you if what the witness has said is the truth or a lie."

"I don't care to make any comments."

"Lydie Fougnies, did you ever ask your husband to intercept this letter that this young woman wrote to her parents?"

"Certainly not, Monsieur le President!"

"Accusé! Tell us if you ever had illicit sex with domestics?"

"No! Never! All these women are angry because they were fired and now they're slandering me!"

The judge paused and said merely, "Hmm," before asking his next question, which was powerful. "And were you *ever* acquainted with a Celestine Legrain, who worked at the chateau?"

The count was waiting for this question and gave an evidently prepared series of answers. "Very well. She cared for one of my children. She was meticulous in her duties."

"Didn't you have illicit sex with this woman? And didn't that result in her giving birth to a child on September 13, 1847?"

Trying to avoid the essence of the question, he responded. "I haven't had any relations with her for a long time. But realizing later that I loved her, I told her, 'Celestine, you'll have to leave.' Sometime after that, she told me that she was pregnant. When she had her baby, I supplied everything she needed."

"You forced your wife to take this child, the product of your adultery, into the chateau and to care for him?"

"No, when he was weaned, I told my wife what had happened and asked if she would take him in. She agreed and even went with me to pick him up."

At this, Judge Lyon turned to Lydie and asked if this was really true.

"I had to, Your Honor. I was under severe duress. Hippolyte threatened me, 'If you don't, you know what means, don't you?' I knew that he meant that that he would beat me mercilessly if I didn't take the child in."

Changing the direction of the subject, the judge turned again to the count, whom he apparently refused to address by his noble title, preferring instead to bark, "Accusé!" at him. "Accusé! Your wife and her brother, Gustave Fougnies, did they secretly remove the child from the chateau one night?"

The count cleared his throat and went through the facial moves of someone trying to spit, before answering, "Yeh, later, my wife went back on her word. She consulted with her brother, Gustave, and he arranged to have the baby snatched away without my knowledge."

The imitation spitting caused much serious-sounding chatter in the audience. There was absolutely no laughter.

"Is this one of the reasons you never ceased to have it in for Gustave?"

"No, I never 'had it in' for Gustave because I didn't know until later, that he had anything to do with the baby's disappearance."

Low murmurs in the audience contained a few audible whispers of, "I don't believe him."

"Didn't you use that occasion to deal violently and brutally with your wife?"

"No I've never been brutal to my wife." This frequent denial would eventually cause him serious trouble.

"Isn't that the incident that Madame Chercquefosse told Investigative Judge Ryckman about? She was visiting at your chateau at that time. Wasn't it the act of a wild man when you tried to strangle your wife and beat her up that caused Madame Chercquefosse to tell you that, if you don't change your behavior, you'll die in a prison or perhaps on a scaffold!? Those are serious words."

"Madame Chercquefosse never said that."

"What did she say?"

"I don't remember it good. After my wife complained to her, she said that it's terrible to treat a wife that way."

***

Madame Chercquefosse, who was now in the witness chair, turned her head from side to side, as if to say, *"The man is one of the boldest liars I have ever heard."* She leaned over to the judge to whisper this to him.

To support the implied charge, the judge called a Fidelice Fournier to the stand. This woman had been a chambermaid at the chateau for the year 1848. She testified, "Here is a scene that I witnessed. I went to the kitchen to get some milk for the children. I heard Madame screaming, 'Help! Please!' I ran to the Salon à Colonnes; she was bleeding from her teeth, but I didn't actually see monsieur do it. I fled with Madame into the adjoining Red Salon. Madame Chercquefosse stopped monsieur in the corridor, but I don't know what she said to him."

When Judge Lyon reminded Mlle Fournier that she'd told Investigative Judge Ryckman that she had pulled the count from his wife, whom he had pinned on the floor, she apologized for an "oversight." She testified that she'd had to pull the count off his wife. He was slapping her face. She averred, too, that the count had chased his wife from the Salon à Colonnes into the Red Salon.

She also told of Celestine's baby's presence at the chateau and reported that, while she had never herself been propositioned, she had heard from others working at the chateau that several domestics had had affairs with the count. When Judge Lyon asked if the count had had sex with a Sylvie Dutrieux, Mlle Fournier said she had heard about it. (This hearsay evidence was admissible to the jury provided the judge permitted it.)

***

The principal witness to the count's brutality was Mme Adelaide Chercquefosse, the wife of Gustave Fougnies's lawyer, and also a friend of the de Bocarmé couple, especially Lydie. She had received an invitation from Lydie to visit her for a few days, although she did not know why.

"It was shortly after the secret removal of the Legrain child from the chateau, and Hippolyte was in an angry mood. After Mme Chercquefosse's arrival, Lydie told her that she and her husband had agreed to accept a young child named Paul, but his presence had caused unpleasant disagreement to the point where she and her brother Gustave arranged for his removal from the chateau without informing the count.

"Her brother had agreed to pay for the child's care at a good orphanage in Brussels. The count was very angry, and Lydie was afraid he would brutalize her with his fists.

"She informed me that the count had left the chateau three days earlier, probably trying to find the child. She had invited me to visit her at the chateau two or three times, but she now felt that the count was never aware of those invitations because, 'when he saw me on those previous visits, he always seemed surprised.'"

As Lydie and her houseguest conversed in the Salon à Colonnes, Lydie saw her husband approaching slowly on foot, from the village below, still a good distance away.

Mme Chercquefosse testified, "Lydie told me it would be better if I absented myself, and I returned to my room. About thirty minutes later, I heard a noise and her screaming, 'Mme Chercquefosse, help!'

"I ran to the Salon à Colonnes and pushed her behind me to block his way. She was disheveled and pale; she was also pregnant. Every ounce of indignation in me escaped my mouth. I cannot remember positively everything I said to him at the beginning but do distinctly remember how I ended. 'Monsieur count, if you do not change your behavior, you will finish your days in jail or on the scaffold.'

"When I said that, I really didn't believe that I would one day see him in the position he is in today. The count did not seem at all upset. He even acted at first as though he never heard me. He must have heard it because he proceeded to tell me that what I said was laughable—that he had only chased her."

Judge Lyon asked, "Was Madame bleeding?"

"I'm nearsighted, so I cannot say for sure, but she was sick, unnerved."

"What state was the count in? Was he furiously angry?"

"He was in his usual morbid state. He didn't seem angry; he acted as he always does naturally."

"Did the countess let you in on all that went on in their marriage?"

"No, she hid a part of the truth—somewhat out of good manners and somewhat because she did not care to let me know that the crown of a countess is a crown of thorns, of long thorns." Mme Chercquefosse cried as she spoke.

"When the count said 'that's laughable,' did the countess say anything?"

"Yes. She rebuked him, 'It's laughable for someone to strangle his wife and throw her to the floor?!'"

After having opined audibly to her that the count was mean, hypocritical, cruel, crafty, and a liar, Judge Lyon asked her what she thought of the countess. She cried profusely as she said, "Monsieur le president, I have known Mademoiselle Fougnies for eighteen years, and I have always considered her an angel of kindness, sweetness, and patience."

The audience remained very quiet. It is almost a certainty that most of the people in Peruwelz who had dealt with Lydie would have disagreed. It was easy to infer that Lydie Fougnies was a gifted, two-faced, and haughty actress. By general agreement, she was "very good-looking."

Some who dealt with her might have imagined that she ingratiated herself easily with those who were well positioned socially, whom she probably envied, but treated others like scum.

***

Sylvie Dutrieux came to the stand, admitted having had *relations coupables* with the count in 1845 or 1846, when his wife was pregnant, and having received two gifts. One was a handkerchief; the other was a one-time gift of money.

She very likely hoped to make up for her indiscretion by describing an incident when the count locked his wife in his office and was obviously beating her as she cried loudly for help.

Marchioness Ida Chasteler de Bocarmé, Hippolyte's mother, chanced to be staying at the chateau when this occurred, and Sylvie had taken it upon herself to call her to come. The count's mother had managed to stop the battering. When the count released his wife, her dress was in tatters, but he was furious with Sylvie because she had called his mother. Hippolyte usually fired those who dared call his mother at moments like this, and Sylvie claimed that he fired her, which contradicts testimony that the countess was the one who fired her.

In any event, we know from other witnesses that he continued to visit Sylvie afterward. Most domestics whom the count fired were never paid, but Sylvie Dutrieux received all of her wages.

Aside from demonstrating that the count's crude infidelity had begun several years before his affair with Celestine Legrain, the above also establishes beyond reasonable doubt that he was in the habit of beating his wife years before the illegitimate child incident.

The tenth witness was again Amand Wilbaut. Judge Lyon wanted to know more about the count's adulterous affair with Celestine Legrain, and Wilbaut knew how it had begun. He was the oldest employee of the chateau, hired by Count Julien, Hippolyte's father, many years before as an overseer of the chateau's acreage. He knew Hippolyte as well as anyone who worked about the chateau and was a useful prosecution witness, especially because he had also unknowingly helped Hippolyte in ways that could have implicated him as an accessory to murder. The prosecution dropped the weak charges before the trial began. He was forthcoming on the stand, as he would have been in any case.

Judge Lyon asked Amand Wilbaut, among other things, what he thought of the morality of the count.

Wilbaut, hesitating a moment, answered, "In the county and roundabout he's known as a 'filthy, rotten fish.'"

This caused loud laughter throughout the courtroom, and the count joined in.

The judge reprimanded him, "Accusé de Bocarmé! You have no reason to laugh. What they call you is not to your credit! You are in too serious trouble to be laughing."

The count stuffed his cravat into his mouth to stifle his continuing laughter.

Wilbaut continued, "They say he likes the girls. A year after his marriage, he hired a nursemaid for their first child, the infant who died. The nursemaid was Sylvie Dutrieux.

"The cook told me that she thought the count was fooling around with her, so I told his uncle-in-law, Ferdinand Fougnies, how he was behaving. Soon afterward, Madame caught him at it two or three times and fired the girl.

"One day, the count gave me a suitcase and a dress to take to her and gave me only a single franc for my expenses along the way, which was twenty miles from the chateau."

Mention of the single franc for expenses caused much noise in the audience.

Amand Wilbaut, dressed in clean working garments, continued to testify: "The count found me one morning and asked me to go along with him to Tournai. On the way, he told me that he wanted to find a new nursemaid for a child soon to be born and a new chambermaid for his wife. I told him, 'It's your business, but if you get involved in that, everyone is going to say that you're chasing after women for some other reason.'

"He told me not to call him by his real name in front of anyone and to head to the village of Antoing. He said that there was a village fair there and added, 'If ever anyone should ask why I had to stop there, I would blame it on the weather.'

"The count chatted with the daughter of the saddlemaker in Antoing, M. Legrain, after introducing himself as Treasurer to Countess de Bocarmé, and got his permission to hire his daughter as Nursemaid for an expected new child.

"When she had been at the chateau only about two weeks, I noticed that something was going on between Celestine and the count. When everyone was supposed to have gone to bed, the count was in his office with her. So I went and found his Uncle Ferdinand, again, and I told him that his nephew-in-law was playing around with a domestic at the chateau."

"'What can I do?' he said, 'That's disgusting!'"

Wilbaut continued, "At this time there was a laborer who was quitting his job at the chateau. So, I told him, 'Look, don't bring my name into this; but tell the saddlemaker at Antoing that his daughter is up to mischief with the count. I feel sure that Legrain will come up here right away. Otherwise, the countess will find out, and then there'll be a hell of a ruckus in the house.

"When M. Legrain came, I could see that he looked serious. He asked me what was going, on, and I told him that things had got out of hand at the chateau and he ought to take his daughter away from it."

Wilbaut, a man in his fifties, spoke well. He had a pleasant face and occasionally smiled or laughed briefly as he testified. He was the oldest employee of the chateau, hired by Count Julien well before he left for Java. Wilbaut's job was primarily to keep an eye out for any misuse of the chateau's many acres. He was Hippolyte's superior, and he did not trust Hippolyte's judgment or integrity. He was the single employee who observed and disliked the disrespect with which Hippolyte treated Lydie. Amand Wilbaut was married. He and his wife had no children.

The eleventh witness was Celestine Legrain. The prosecution had availed itself of both Celestine and her father. The courtroom crowd looked forward to her appearance. When she came to the stand, she impressed everyone with her austere beauty. She was tall, had perfect features and a complexion said to be of the "Spanish type." Her beauty caused a distinct ripple of sound in the audience.

Judge Lyon asked, "Do you know the accused Visart?"

"Yes, Monsieur le President—*intimately*."

Her unexpected boldness caused courtroom noise.

Celeste stated that she had worked for the de Bocarmés for ten months in 1846, had become pregnant, and had had a child in September 1847.

She reviewed the child's placement at the chateau; his removal to an orphanage in Brussels; his brief reinstatement at the chateau; and, finally, his placement with her parents in Antoing. She added new information about how the count had hired her.

"He came to the village looking for me, saying he was Treasurer to the Countess de Bocarmé and had been asked, by her, to hire me as a nursemaid for a child. He looked me over very, very closely just before that, and then offered me the job.

"I told him that I didn't know him and that he had to speak with my parents, which he did, always using the same title, Treasurer to the Countess de Bocarmé."

"Accusé! Is that true?" asked Judge Lyon of the count.

"I don't remember using that title, but everything else she said is true."

Questioning then revealed that the count had paid her rent, 200 francs per month, for a small, windowless basement room in a suburb of Brussels, where she stayed with her infant child for six months after its birth. On one occasion, Hippolyte had given her 1300 francs.

Hippolyte had visited her many times, and one day, he told her he was "broke" and asked if she had any money. On hearing that, by living as frugally as possible, she had saved 1,000 francs, he asked if he could borrow it, to repay it at 5 percent interest, but he had never paid it back.

"Did you ask him for a receipt for the money?"

"Yes, but monsieur said receipts are useless."

Judge Lyon turned to the count. "So, Accusé, you got this young woman pregnant, had her live in frugal hardship, and when she saved some money you took it!"

The count attempted to justify his action as reasonable because, he claimed, he had "every intention of repaying it"—this from a man several hundred thousand francs in debt. The audience laughed at his response.

The judge then addressed Celestine. "How often has the count visited you since you moved to the one-room apartment in the de Molenbek outskirt of Brussels?"

Celestine answered, "Several times."

"Can you be more specific than that? Would it be more likely a dozen times, fifteen times, or more?"

"I would say between twelve and fifteen times."

And hasn't he slept overnight there with you on most, if not all, of these visits?"

"Yes, he had no other place to sleep."

"On these visits, he slept in your bed and you had relations *coupables*?"

"Yes, *we did*!" she stated with defiance.

"Didn't you often meet him within the city to have lunch or dinner?"

"Yes."

"You visited some very nice places, didn't you?"

"I would say so. Yes."

"Well, we haven't the time to describe every one of them, so we'll take one in particular. Let us, for example, take the rue de Laeken in Brussels. Have you ever been on that street?"

"Probably."

"No, I would say with *certainty* that you have been there with Accusé Visart. It's a street with elegant boutiques. Does that description remind you of your having been there?"

"I cannot say for sure."

"If I mentioned a swanky boutique where you acquired three decorative pieces of jewelry, would that be enough to jog your memory?"

"Yes, Monsieur le President."

"Tell us fully and frankly how you happened to be there, with whom, about the jewelry and any conversation you recall. He added a stern warning: "Be *careful* to be *accurate* and *complete*, because a hired person was also there watching and listening closely. But you were apparently not aware of her."

Celestine paused, and then said reluctantly and slowly, "Monsieur was visiting Brussels for three or four days. He brought his wife, her chambermaid, and their child. He told me she was expecting another child.

"They were staying at the Hotel Regency, but Monsieur preferred to stay with *me* during the day. He *dined* with them at the hotel but told them that the hotel was too expensive—that he would save money by staying *elsewhere at night*.

"I told him that, if his wife occupied a room and he stayed *with her*, the hotel would *not* be any more expensive than it already was. [pause]. He said *he* knew that but didn't think his wife was *smart enough* to know that.

"I think it was on the *second* day of his visit that he took me to a boutique that sells fine jewelry. He bought me a *gold brooch* edged with small diamonds; *gold earrings*, each with a diamond; and a very *nice pearl necklace*."

"Was the person behind the counter a man or a woman?"

"A woman."

"How did Count de Bocarmé introduce himself to her?"

"By his name."

"Did he call himself Count de Bocarmé?

"*Yes.*"

"Did he introduce you as a countess or use the word in speaking to you? *Be truthful* about this!" There was a tone of warning in his voice.

"*Yes*. He used the word several times as the saleswoman showed pieces of jewelry to me. *He would ask, 'Do you like this, Countess?'* But he *never* introduced me to her as his wife."

"The saleswoman was in close hearing distance. She believed you were the countess. Did he pay for the jewelry or ask for credit?"

"He had a lot of ten- and twenty-franc bills in his wallet and paid in cash."

"Where did you go then?"

"We took a walk in a park and then all the way back to my room. We shopped for lamb and vegetables, and I made dinner."

"And then you had relations coupables?"

"Yes, Monsieur le president." (She avoided saying this boldly).

"Does your room have a bathtub?"

"I have a sink with cold running water."

Judge Lyon shook his head from side to side and stared at his desk as if deeply struck by the maelstrom of almost unbelievable social pathology he had just heard. It made for a long pause. He eventually responded to her almost pitifully and kindly with, "I see."

"Well, you've told what happened truthfully. Tell us, has the count ever let you know how wealthy he is?"

Count de Bocarmé shouted, "I object to that question. It's personal and unimportant."

Judge Lyon retorted, "You are overruled. The witness will answer the question. The stenographer will repeat it for you Mademoiselle Legrain."

"I remember it. He has never told me, but he's *obviously very wealthy* to live in a large home with such gorgeous furniture and expensive rugs."

"Young woman," Judge Lyon questioned, "are you unaware that a matter basic to this trial about *a murder* is the established fact that the count owes thousands of francs to notaries but hasn't enough to repay them. He has not enough to pay a butcher for sausages and many other small expenses. Yet, he finds enough to cheat on his wife, the true Countess de Bocarmé—to be extremely generous to and have illegal sexual relations with you."

The twelfth witness was defendant Count Hippolyte de Bocarmé. Since Celestine did not respond, the judge addressed the count. "Accusé, how do you defend behavior of the kind?"

"I don't think it's anybody's business how wealthy I am."

"Yet," persisted Judge Lyon, "you must not forget that you are on trial to determine if you cruelly murdered your wife's brother. The alleged motivation is that you believed that he named her as the sole beneficiary of his fortune, *unless* he recovered his health and should decide to marry."

"Talk like that can prejudice the jury!" the count said in a *bitter* response.

"I *was careful* not to say anything that the jury does not already know. *However*, I have a reminder for you. Remember that, whenever you speak, you speak under oath, and I assume that it would hurt your conscience and interfere with your ability to sleep if you did not tell the truth."

"I have not had a hard time sleeping from the time I was accused and arrested by Detective Judge Heughebart, nearly six months ago."

"If true, I envy you, but only in that single respect—because *you* are in *grave* trouble. Here is my question. Where did you get the money to buy Celestine Legrain expensive jewelry? From her description, you had a wad of francs in your wallet? Where did they come from?"

"I *don't care to say*. If I did, the court would probably want me to hand it over, like I have to give up the agreement my wife willingly signed within the first year we were married."

"The court does not need to know *where* you have hidden any money. Therefore, I am using my subpoena power to demand that *any and all* money belonging to you that has, to this moment, not been known to the court, be surrendered to the court within twenty-four hours, to be held *at least until* the outcome of this trial.

"You have lawyers; they have people who can run it down. You do, naturally, have to be honest with your lawyers and tell them where it is. Any defendant who is dishonest with his defending lawyer is playing a dangerous game.

"Now, I can ask you to tell the court the origin of the money. How did you obtain it?"

"The visit to Brussels was four years ago. I have none of it left and I forget now where it came from."

"Have you visited Celestine Legrain again since that occasion in 1848?"

"No, not that I can remember."

"You did tell your wife, not long before you were arrested in 1850, that you had to go to Brussels 'next weekend, but that's none of your business...' Tell *us* about *that* trip."

"My wife talks too much. But I'm beginning to learn that you don't ask questions if you don't already know the answer. So, yeh, I spent a weekend with a few friends there."

The audience remained very quiet.

"How did you meet these friends? As far as I know, you have never lived in Brussels, so how did you meet them?"

"I used to go there occasionally before I married, and I met them mainly in cabarets that make good drinks, we would have a few drinks and exchange names and addresses and talk about a lot of things you talk about over drinks."

Movement and a little hushed talk in the audience followed.

"I suppose you spoke about women?"

"Yeh, that's right."

The audience laughed.

"Were these friends married or single?"

"No one talked about that. It isn't something you ask in a cabaret."

Louder chatter and a little laughter ensued.

"Did you talk about the availability of loose women?"

A sudden quietness fell over the gathered crowd. People wanted to hear.

"I don't think you can call them 'loose.' It's how they make an honest living."

This was met with some laughter.

Judge Lyon tried not to laugh as he continued his questioning. "All right, you mean prostitutes, members of the world's oldest profession?"

Now the audience erupted in outright laughter.

"Yeh. I'm talking about high-class prostitutes—experienced ones from good families."

The loud laughter continued.

"I suppose that one arranges to meet one of these women to chat with them about affairs of the world in an intellectual way?"

This time, sustained loud laughter filled the room.

"Yeh. Then—"

"Excuse me for interrupting this romantic story, but I *do* wish to remind the witness that this is a court. One correctly addresses the presiding judge as 'Your Honor.' 'Yeh' alone is insufficient."

The audience met this with some clapping but little or no laughter.

"Please, I will go ahead to hear your depiction of a night on the town and what it entails. *I'll* know when I hear it, if it exceeds the bounds of courtroom propriety."

A few in the audience chattered.

"About the initial meeting—is that customarily in a given place, for example, the reading room of the public library? Or is it elsewhere?"

Again, the room was filled with very loud laughter and a few claps.

"Of course not, Monsieur le President. You have to meet in a high-class hotel, where there are not many people. It's almost always in a hotel where the lights are dim, and there'll be a piano player tapping out some music in the same room where they make drinks only with whisky. These dames are pretty polite; they don't usually have any use for beer drinkers."

Much chatter and talk followed, but words were unclear.

"They prefer that what they call their 'escort' drink things like whisky and water, but never more than two. Most of *them* drink lemon-flavored water with crushed ice in it. Sometimes, if they know the bartender pretty well, he puts a cherry on top."

The audience erupted into very loud, sustained laughter.

"After about forty-five minutes, she'll come right out with it and say, 'I can do with dinner, couldn't *you*?' Almost before you can answer, she's standing and leading you to the dining room."

Some movement could be detected among the crowd but not much chatter.

"During that apparently civilized forty-five-minute interlude, what do you talk about?"

"That's no problem. They have a way to get you to talk by asking questions, and the answers lead into more questions."

An ordinary level of chatter returned to the courtroom. Here and there one heard 'too stupid'. . .

"Excuse me, Monsieur le President. They time that conversation pretty close to around forty-five minutes, and then they always say, 'Go to the front desk, please, and tell them you want to have a room with a double bed, a pitcher of cold water, and a kettle of hot water. He'll know what room to give you. Pay for the room in full right then, and it's customary to leave *three* francs behind for him. If you don't have exactly three, give him a larger coin or bill and ask him to give you some change for it. He'll always give you five single francs. You leave three for him. Then, *please*, bring the key back to *me*.'"

The chatter in the room was broken by women talking in very loud voices, deep inhalations, and the occasional, "Ohhhh!" and "my God!."

"Anyway, as I was saying, the menu in the dining room is pretty fancy, but she seems to know what's best to eat. About the only time she'll give an escort hell by speaking sharply to him is, if he talks while he's still chewing a mouthful. I don't really know why it bothers them so, but if you don't finish chewing and swallowing before trying to speak, they have a fit."

The crowd didn't react. (Too few middle-class people thought it a significant point.)

"They are teaching you basic, good table manners."

The audience grew quiet. (A not unexpected response.)

"You can't live your life that strictly. No one I know eats that way at home."

No audible reaction followed. (Of course not. See above.)

At this statement, the judge turned to the seated countess and said, with a twinkle in his eye, "Lydie Fougnies, were you strictly taught not to speak with food in your mouth?"

A little laughter broke out among the crowd. (A few thought it was a strange, funny query.)

"Absolutely, Monsieur le President. I have practiced the same manners since I was a small child. My husband has so little interest in manners that he has never noticed how I eat. He does not seem to care how disgusting it can be to sit across the table from him when eating together."

Noises of disgust from a scattered few could be heard. (*Only* a scattered few cared.)

"It was one of the social graces I was going to try to teach him, but I delayed because he is so impulsive. If an idea comes into his head, he cannot finish chewing and swallowing before announcing it, spewing masticated food all about him."

The chatter picked up, but the crowd seemed to care not a whit about table manners.

"All right. Accusé Visart, from what you told me I gather that the delicate prostitute wants you to fill a bathtub about one-quarter full of tap water, warm it with the hot water in the kettle to cleanse your haunches, and then the act begins."

Now, the audience exploded in loud laughter.

"*Wait*, there's more to it."

The laughter continued, though it was now more moderate.

"I am certain of that, but I think we've heard enough about your dalliances with high-quality harlots, except for mentioning the total cost for the dubious privilege."

"Around 90 francs for the lady."

Many "Ohs" sounded from among the crowd.

"And what about the dinner and drinks?"

"It adds up in all to over 120 francs."

Many more "Ohs" and much chatter ensued.

"You have had things made for you that require as much work as the harlot does, but you refuse to pay for it. We have a deluge of letters from persons to whom you refused to pay for several days of hard work. I asked you this to get an idea of how you have wasted your thousands of borrowed francs."

The crowd apparently had much to say to each other, as chatter increased.

The thirteenth witness, was Leopold Boël.[30] Judge Lyon called him to the stand to flesh out an unintended oversight in "Judge" Messine's testimony.

Scholarly and aging, Leopold Boël was an honorable citizen of both Bury and Roucourt. He was elected to an unsalaried position as Secretary (mainly of historical events) in the two small communes. As a person, he was known to be faithfully motivated to deal with his fellow citizens tolerantly and sympathetically. His brief deposition revealed a profound sense of decency, which some might label naiveté. In fact, his intentions were those of a careful public servant with unusual respect for troubled citizens. First and foremost, he was the chronicler of notable events in the lives of ordinary citizens of Roucourt, which required tact and accuracy. Although known as Communal Secretary for both Roucourt and Bury, he was active in this respect only in Roucourt. Obviously, he would deal from time to time with the citizenry of Bury as well. It is why he agreed to try to help Lydie.

For a reason that one can only speculate about, he was the first elected notable to learn of Gustave Fougnies' death. He took the witness stand in the Mons courtroom in late morning of July 6, 1851. In his introduction to posterity, the public learned of his unsalaried

---

[30] When my wife, Mary, and I met Madame Boël in Roucourt eighteen years ago, she mentioned that her uncle had been a witness at the trial of the Count and Countess deBocarmé. Stenographic notes confirm that he *was* in fact a witness. They also reveal that he was initially considered to be a witness with the likelihood of being called to the stand near the end of the trial to do nothing more than cite his name, address, and occupation. Indication of his low initial priority, was his listing only as potential witness number seventy-three of one hundred and five available witnesses. Nonetheless, Judge Lyon called him to the stand on the eighth day of the trial as the thirteenth witness, to fill a hiatus in the stenographic record. Judge Lyon was concerned with the history of the trial.

elected office, and that his major 'occupation' was 'gentleman farmer.'

***

M. Boël told the assembled court how, on the morning of November 21, 1850, following the death of Gustave Fougnies, he was awakened before sunrise. A messenger informed him that his presence was requested by a resident of the Chateau Bitremont, in Bury. He promptly dressed and left in the messenger's carriage. As he put it, "I rendered myself to the chateau atop Bitremont."

"A polite young woman led me to a bedroom where I found Monsieur on a low bed and Madame on a high bed on which a child was amusing itself. Madame spoke to me, *not* her husband, 'My brother is dead. I'm calling on you to provide without delay any documents needed for his expeditious burial.' Lydie was verbally rich but legalistically impoverished.

"Madame," I said, "as an old Communal Secretary, I strongly advise you that in a case such as this, it is requisite that, *ahead of all else*, you must notify a member of the Third Estate (town government) who will perhaps notify a *Justice of the Peace.*" She beseeched me, '*You* do it.'

"So, *I* went to see M. Laurent, the elected Alderman of Bury, at his home. He asked if I had viewed the body and I answered in the negative. However, a messenger carried a note from him about my observation to Justice of the Peace Messine in Tournai."

***

The official record shows that Justice of the Peace Messine had testified as sixth witness that he received a 21 November morning message from M. Laurent reporting a death in Bury, specifically, the countess' brother. In the afternoon, a second note from Laurent

302

described rumors in Bury. The latter prompted Messine to take a horse to the village, visit the chateau, and view the body of his slain friend Gustave Fougnies.

Why Laurent made no mention of M. Boël's visit to his home was perhaps because M. Laurent wanted *his* message to imply that it was *he* who was first to discover that Gustave Fougnies had died. If so, he would have hidden an historical fact, namely, Leopold Boël was the first person to learn that the countess' younger brother was dead and that his body probably still lay in the Chateau Bitremont on November 21. Moreover, Laurent notified Messine of his death on the word of an honest man who, he knew, had not seen the body.

Messine, as well as Lyon, distrusted Laurent. They knew that he "enjoyed" a friendly relationship with the count. Police detectives learned, when questioning the countess, that Laurent did not visit the chateau until afternoon of November 21, when he first viewed the body. Judge Lyon wanted the trial record to contain as few unanswered questions as possible.

Therefore, Judge Lyon asked M. Boël, "When you arrived at the chateau, did you notice if the Bocarmé wife shed tears; if her facial expression was sorrowful?"

His answer was, "No, hers was a normal countenance."

Lyon asked with a smile, "Didn't that seem out of the ordinary to you?"

When he answered, "A little," some in the audience laughed.

Lyon then asked, "Did anyone tell you how Gustave died?"

The President of the Court also wanted to know if she or anyone else at the chateau told him the cause of death. M. Boël responded that no one had mentioned the reason for the man's demise.

The Attorney General, who was a rather elegantly and expensively dressed young man, asked Communal Secretary Boël, who seemed quite relaxed, if he could speak to what people in the community thought of the "the count's reputation."

There was a pause before M. Boël replied quite seriously, "I suppose that he's an individual who is uniquely unlike everyone else."

When the audience laughed loudly, the Attorney General asked in a somewhat annoyed, lofty tone of voice, "Well, did you not hear anyone remark that he's a bouquin, a veritable 'buck rabbit,' who chases women and girls?"

After a good pause, M. Boël, with a piercing stare, responded in a loud, precise declamatory voice, **"I don't know anything about that!"**

The young Attorney General, a veritable Beau Brummell, had no response.

Lawyer dePaepe, one of two lawyers defending the count, asked, "Do you mean to say then, that you heard *no* insinuation to the effect that the Count de Bocarmé is a *rotten count*?

M. Boël paused before replying, "Gentlemen, I have heard *only* that he's a rotten **rabbit!"**

Judge Lyon thought he ought to intercede in an exchange that was becoming somewhat heated. He knew that M. Leopold Boël had no reputation as a difficult man. Yet, he had himself, only yesterday, cross-examined the count and exposed him as a sexual malefactor; perhaps he could get the ageing *benefactor* to agree that the count *was* less than a model citizen.

In a respectful tone of voice, and with a smile, he asked the kind gentleman, "Isn't the Count de Bocarmé stuck with a deprecating label because he does, without any question, conduct himself immorally in public? He is known habitually to philander. Assuming that I am correct, isn't he, or other any other man who acts similarly, likely to become known publicly by a denigrating label?"

"His conduct is news to **me**."

Judge Lyon asked with deep concern, "Do *you, M. Boël,* live in **Bury**?"

"No. Indeed. I **dwell in Roucourt**."

If the courtroom audience thought M. Boël naive, they were wrong. Secretary Boël was **principled**. He ignored coarse slurs against a relatively unknown man from Bury. *He,* Boël, lived *in another town and didn't know enough about the count to ridicule him.* It finally took Judge Lyon to justify M. Boël's decorous deposition.

The fourteenth witness was Monsieur Chercquefosse, a notary from Tournai. After giving his oath, the notary discussed the opinions of legal authorities about the privileges enjoyed by attorneys when questioned in a deposition.

Judge Lyon, the president of the court, told him that, in becoming a notary, he had abdicated his capacity as a lawyer and must give evidence without any reservations.

M. Chercquefosse was a suave and politic witness. He stated that he now considered himself free of all legal responsibility if he mentioned any privileged information.

The audience was quiet and listened carefully.

"On November 21, I visited the Chateau de Bitremont. They didn't expect me. It was there that I heard that Gustave Fougnies was dead. I was taken aback when Hippolyte appeared and told me, 'I have a bite on my finger. Do you think that's important?'

"I told him that how he'd got the bite could be important, naturally.

"He then asked me if he should hide his hand in his pocket, and I refused to answer that question."

There were many "Ohs" and "Ahs" in the audience.

"Frankly, I thought he was stupid to ask me that question.

There was loud chatter among the spectators.

"I asked him and Countess Lydie how much time passed between the time when Gustave cried, 'Aie Aie, Hippolyte,' and when a domestic got to the scene."

"How did you know about the 'Aie Aie' cry?" asked Judge Lyon.

"Sorry. I got ahead of myself. I've been sitting through testimony of a lot of witnesses. I couldn't have asked that question. Is it possible to scrub it, Your Honor?"

"Yes. It will still be on the record, but it's shown as scrubbed."

Murmurs among the audience could be heard.

"I wanted to leave then and there. However, I *did* stay because I became convinced of the innocence of the Countess de Bocarmé because of her absolute calm."

This testimony caused a good deal of chatter in the courtroom.

Chercquefosse cleared his throat and continued. "Also, I recall the countess, whom I had known for twenty years, had four years before asked me to oversee the education of their children. I didn't want to give her an answer, so I said nothing.

"I stayed there even though the count said nothing more to me about how Gustave happened to die. It made me suspicious.

"I finally got an answer: 'All three of us were around the fire. All of a sudden, Gustave became sick and cried, "Aie, Aie, Hippolyte." I put my hand on his shoulder, and we fell; I injured myself on one of the crutches. He was still alive when he fell to the floor, but I was told by a domestic that he then died.'"

"Didn't he tell you that M. Fougnies had complained of a headache during dinner?" asked the judge.

"Possibly, but I'm not sure. A domestic did tell me that, on the morning of November 20, Gustave was in the kitchen not feeling well and was warming himself by the stove."

"When the accused spoke to you about his injury, didn't you ask him how it happened?"

"Yes, Monsieur le President, and he told me that he had put a finger in Fougnies's mouth as he fell down with him."

"Was the injury still bleeding when you saw it?"

"It was red."

"What did Lydie Fougnies say at that moment? Didn't she say anything about the death of her brother?"

"For goodness sake, *I* don't *recall* that."

M. Chercquefosse replied in an annoyed tone, as the audience, noticing it, laughed loudly.

Judge Lyon offered, "I would refresh your memory, but any facts that you did not declare to the investigating judge are unknown to me."

"Oh, well, I do remember, that the countess took part in the conversation in an insignificant way, which is to say that I don't remember a word she was able to say."

"Did Hippolyte de Bocarmé tell you that there was a fight between him and Gustave?"

"No, he told me that he went to help him and that they fell down together."

"Didn't he tell you that Gustave died of apoplexy or of congestion in the brain?"

"I don't think so." The witness yawned.

Through this series of questions, the audience was lost in serious contemplation and was quiet.

"But you were told you that Gustave had fallen, that someone had picked him up and had carried him to a room upstairs where he died? That's what you told Judge Ryckman."

"I'm not sure if that was what the count said, or the countess told me."

"When Hippolyte de Bocarmé wanted to find out from you if he ought to hide the injury on his left hand when the police came to the chateau … when he asked that, didn't you ask him why he would ask you such a question?

"If his injury had resulted from an involuntary act, there would be no need to take any precautions in front of the police. Wasn't that a question of a kind that would alert you and bring forth a comment of some sort on your part—isn't that right?"

"Monsieur le President, I understand your question." (He sounded tired) "The best way I can answer is that the count has come to me for advice many times over many years when he he's had judicial business. I have the honor to tell you that he doesn't follow the advice I've given him. "His behavior has so stretched my patience that I finished dealing with him by telling him, 'You've come to ask my advice and I've given it to you, and you change what I've told you to testify. From here on, I wish you would leave me *alone!*' (Your Honor, I *can* be impatient). I'll address Monsieur le president's comment or question this way: Since he refused to answer three or four questions, I didn't have the patience to try him out a fourth time and never got an answer to your *reasonable* question, Your Honor. I, therefore, spoke to the domestics. One of them told me that Gustave Fougnies did *not* die upstairs.

"I chatted a long time with Emerance Bricout. I can still see her holding a jug containing wine of such strength that I told this young woman, '*You* are going to be *indisposed.*'"

"When you arrived at the Chateau de Bitremont, didn't you notice some stains on the floor of the dining room?"

"After leaving the countess's bedroom, we went downstairs, all three of us, into the first of the sitting rooms, where there was a sofa. We sat ourselves down; I was between Count and Countess de Bocarmé.

"All of a sudden, they vanished and I found myself alone. I got up and walked about, and I eyed an enormous spot of oil on the dining room floor. I took my time looking about to see as much as possible. I tried to touch the greasy spot, believing there was some blood there. I did not find any. A short time after this, the countess reappeared. There was an area around the greasy spots where some oil had been extended, apparently with a broom."

A clerk showed the witness a small brush with a short handle decorated with flowers. The witness stated that he recognized it, and then yawned again.

Judge Lyon realized he was asking about events that occurred six months ago.

Judge Lyon continued, "You said, I believe, that you have not been the notary for the couple!"

"Yes, Monsieur le President. I do not believe that I have ever, a single time, received the signature of Count and Countess de Bocarmé in a notarial act."

"Have you dealt with him as a lawyer?"

"Yes. I have on several occasions. It was some time ago."

"You are free to inform the court if they were serious matters. Were they?"

"Yes, Your Honor, they were serious."

"Were the cases serious enough to be heard before this Court of Assizes in Mons?"

"Yes, Your Honor."

"If it were some time ago, he must have been considerably younger, isn't that so?"

"Yes, Your Honor."

"Did the presiding judge choose to incarcerate him?"

"Yes, Your Honor. On one occasion he was incarcerated for several months. In another, for a year or more." (This stimulated a good deal of chatter in the courtroom audience.)

"Well, perhaps that gives us a little more insight into the defendant's character.

***

"Let us return to November 21, 1850. What, actually, accounts for your being there? What were you doing at the Chateau de Bitremont?"

"Some weeks before, Gustave came to consult me about his wanting to marry. At the same time that he planned his marriage, there was a plan to move some furniture.

"The count and countess were hoping to live in the house where Gustave was then living with his Uncle Ferdinand, but Gustave was moving to his new chateau in Grandmetz.

"Were the Count and Countess de Bocarmé going to remain with M. Ferdinand, Gustave's uncle?"

"Yes, Monsieur le President."

"Wasn't that to get closer to him in the hope of inheriting from him?"

"I presumed so."

"And did M. Ferdinand refuse?"

"Yes."

"You were Gustave's attorney?"

"Yes, Monsieur le President."

"Didn't he speak to you of his marriage plans and ask you to draw up a contract?"

"Yes, Monsieur le president."

"When?"

"A few days before Gustave died: He executed the contract on Saturday, November 16."

"Were you asked by the de Bocarmé couple to discourage Gustave from this marriage?"

"Absolutely so! They habitually importuned me to help them obtain everything they wanted, but it is one thing to be *importuned* to carry out an act and another to *carry out* the act."

"Who importuned you to do this?"

"The solicitations were direct: 'What a God-awful thing this marriage is! We're counting on you to prevent it,' etc. The count was *much* exercised about the matter—a *whole* lot more than his wife."

"What do you suppose their motives were?"

"The countess's mild objection was that the marriage would turn out badly for Gustave. The count, he had no specific motive that he *spoke* of, but I *thought* he *somehow* had a financial interest."

Assuming that you, M. Chercquefosse, strictly followed *Joseph Fougnies's* orders, to the letter, when you and he discussed the change in his will, Lydie could *not* have been the recipient of Gustave's estate when he died, *unless* she left the count. It would be important to know what was actually in Gustave's will.

In a voice tinged with slight consternation, M. Chercquefosse replied retorted, "I *think* I know what the *public's impression* is!" (The meaning of this response is unclear.).

"What do you think of the character of Hippolyte de Bocarmé?"

"I have said, unconditionally, when I appeared before the investigational judge, that he is a man with qualities that provoke resentment in me at times but, at other times, pity.

"We have here a man and a savage. On the one hand, he commits a shameful act; on the other hand, some gentle act. If Count de Bocarmé is in proper society, he will use his handkerchief; otherwise he will blow his nose in his hat.

There were some laughs in the tired audience.

"How much is the de Bocarmé couple in debt to you?"

"About 12,000 francs."

"Is the couple able to repay that sum?"

"Yes, Monsieur le President. This money passed from my hands into those of the countess's brother, and it is guaranteed by some of the property that surrounds the chateau."

"The Countess de Bocarmé said in her interrogatory that, if she were opposed to the marriage of Gustave, it was because she had received, from Monsieur Chercquefosse, some foul information about Mademoiselle de Dudzcèle."

"That does not conform to the truth. That surprises me. I have had nothing but good things to say about Mademoiselle de Dudzcèle's character. Furthermore, I have never known the countess purposely to tell a lie of that sort about people."

The fifteenth witness was Professor Jean Servais Stas, the man who dealt the finishing blow to the count. If one individual stands out as a hero in this story of a murder, it is Professor Stas. He was Belgium's finest physicist-chemist. His major contribution to science came in 1840, when his studies made simple sense of reigning confusion over atomic weights. Citations of his name continue to be prominent today in the circles of professional physicists and chemists.

Stas's contribution to the historic de Bocarmé trial was his ingenious discovery of nicotine in the tissues of Gustave Fougnies.

The finding proved, beyond reasonable doubt, that his murderer was the infamous Count de Bocarmé.

In his life, Stas turned to laboratory research and served studentships with Louvain's distinguished faculty. By 1850, he was famous as professor of chemistry at Belgium's military academy (École Militaire). When the police faced the task of finding proof of the Count de Bocarmé's guilt, the director of Belgian police wanted none other than Stas to help them. The chemical problem was to discover the exact nature of the poison that killed Gustave Fougnies.

The necessary chemical work was of a kind that was new to Stas, to whom the police sent samples of all major organs taken from the murdered man's body. Stas received these samples in the third week of November 1850, soon after Gustave's death. He studied them alone in his laboratory. He did not show himself in the courtroom for any lengthy periods until June 9, 1851, when the trial was well under way.

The outlook for finding the poison in the tissues appeared gloomy. However, hard, persistent work and a stroke of serendipity—scientists' secret weapon—dissipated his gloom, and he informed the police of a discovery, which they brought to the attention of Judge Lyon.

The stenographic notes of the trial hearing on June 9, 1851, are brief but very interesting:

Monsieur le President, I do not know what saint to thank for turning my attention to the dregs in a retort I was about to wash out. I happened, though, to examine its contents again, and, lo and behold, I found tartaric acid in it—a highly reactive substance nearly universal in plant life.

The poison, then, might be a naturally occurring plant poison, what we call an alkaloid. Little is known [about] how to isolate plant poisons from tissues of animals, but tartaric acid was the key.

Standard pharmacologic tests [31] of the retort's fluid contents proved it to contain nicotine. They provided undeniable evidence that nicotine was the poison that killed Gustave Fougnies.

***

Immediately after Stas's testimony, *Lydie Fougnies was overcome with emotion.* So great was her emotion that her lawyer announced to the court that his client had taken ill. However, she quickly recovered because she returned to her seat on the prisoner's bench within ten minutes.

Although she did not yet know what her own fate would be at the hands of the jury, she now knew that nicotine was proved to be the cause of her brother's death. Her husband was the proven murderer. Would she, she wondered, be punished as an accessory to the crime for actions the demented count had forced her to carry out under the threat of death if she disobeyed him?

The sixteenth witness was a Secret Friend. Some of the testimony given to date had cast Countess Lydie in an unfavorable light, as a cold, uncivil individual. At the same time, testimony strongly suggested that her husband had seriously abused her. It seemed paradoxical that a severely abused wife would nonetheless treat

---

[31] To clarify: once Stas knew there might be a plant poison in Gustave's tissue juices, he made no attempt to isolate nicotine. Wisely, he turned to what pharmacologists had known for a long time, namely, nicotine in minute doses kills tiny birds. Nothing was known to be so effective. The juice itself acted exactly like nicotine. A reasonable assumption was that the juice contained a very small amount of nicotine. Given the count's interest in tobacco and that the victim was a non-smoker, made the count appear to be the killer that, in fact, he was. The tests provided undeniable evidence that nicotine was in Gustave's tissues.

people, especially those to whom they owed money, with almost the same cruel disdain as her husband, whom she despised.

Following a short delay in courtroom proceedings, Judge Lyon seemed to be reordering the papers on his desk or, more likely, searching for one in particular. He found what he wanted and then invited a new witness to take a seat and an oath to tell the whole truth.

Lydie was immensely surprised to see her secret friend, Anne Morceau, take the stand and promptly catch the attention and respect of the audience.

Anne was dressed in a well-fitting crimson wool suit with a white silken scarf. The suit's style smacked of yesteryear or earlier but was nevertheless eye-catching. She wore no jewelry except a thin wedding ring. She appeared to be in the mid to late sixties and was confidently poised. Her face wore a resolute expression, and her first words, addressed to Judge Lyon, signified that she was an educated person, possibly an experienced public speaker.

Without ceremony, he briefly invited Mme Morceau to tell the jury "the purpose of your presence as a witness."

Anne Morceau's clear, confident words created a stir in the audience when she declared, "Monsieur le President, I am here primarily to point to an error in the Act of Accusation, where it states that my friend, Lydie, sent vulgar letters anonymously to individuals her husband hated. She did not send those letters!

"It was I who sent those anonymous, filthy, and deceptive letters that the count ordered her to write. The Act of Accusation is simply wrong."

Anne explained that, when Lydie told her husband that the letters could not be "anonymous" because her handwriting was too well known, he instructed her to "fix them so the handwriting has been changed, 'or you'll regret it—his way of saying that he would beat her exceptionally hard with his bare fists."

Madame Morceau went on to explain, "Lydie's extreme fear of horrific beatings and credible threats of death compelled her to make

314

an unprecedented request of me. As the closest neighbor to the Chateau de Bitremont, I had become acquainted with the frightening tale of the horrible de Bocarmé marriage, in which Lydie was trapped. Among many foul tasks summarily forced upon her was his demand one afternoon to spend several hours writing infamous, untrue letters for him.

"The intended recipients were all family members for whom her uncivilized husband harbored malicious animosity. Since he can barely write his name, he did not consider that Lydie was the wrong person to write those anonymous letters and then be expected to mail them herself. Her handwriting was too well known to the addressees.

"When she informed him of this problem the next day, he blamed her for *his* lack of foresight and insisted that she either mask her handwriting or find someone to copy them, else he would subject her to another of his frequent and particularly painful beatings with his big, bare fists. Lydie secretly told me of her predicament and showed me the vile letters.

"I told Lydie that I would copy the letters in my handwriting on different stationery and arrange to have them mailed from a post office other than Bury."

Mme Morceau announced that she had purposely made duplicates of the letters she'd copied in *her* hand and mailed. She told the court that she had Lydie's originals and a copy of those she'd rewritten, adding, "They are on my person for presentation to the court as evidence." She handed the letters to the judge, who leafed through them and agreed to enter the documents as evidence.

Judge Lyon, speaking directly to the jury, said, "This explains what, until now, had been a mystery to us and, in this respect at least, renders one of the charges in the Act of Accusation worthless."

Anne Morceau continued, insisting now to speak to the jurymen directly. "Lydie once believed that Hippolyte, who was not afraid to dirty his hands, made a greater contribution to society as a farmer than ever she could by writing novels. She thought she could teach him social graces.

"After two years, and over the objections of her quite distinguished family, she took Hippolyte's offer of marriage seriously. So idealistic was she that she never inquired whether he had a regular and adequate income to support a wife. Her father gently told her to ask him about his ability to support a wife, and she returned with an answer that her father immediately noticed contained false information.

"Her father was a very bright, self-made man, who worked hard to establish what is now Mons' largest food store. He sold it to the present owners some years ago for a fair price and invested the sum wisely.

"He returned to Peruwelz, sent Lydie in the finest grammar schools and a first-rate college, from which I am also a graduate, but fifty years before she graduated. I was a good student, but never earned the honors *she* did.

"Monsieur Fougnies's old boyhood chums in Peruwelz, envious of his success, told untrue stories about him behind his back. In fact, he lived a solitary life with his two bright children and responded to rumors about him by ignoring them. He cultivated no friends in Peruwelz as an adult.

"Well, the innocent-appearing farmer whom she mentored two afternoons a week for two years expressed a wish to marry her, and eventually she accepted, although her father thought there was something strange about the count. Monsieur Fougnies did not trust him.

"M. Fougnies even changed his will, which would reinstate her initially intended, plentiful income after his death, only if she had permanently separated from an individual he took to be a crude, cunning man whose sincerity he profoundly doubted. His gut feeling was that he wanted to marry Lydie to gain access to her inheritance.

"Monsieur Fougnies was a very wise man. He hated to do what he did, because he loved Lydie very much; he was proud of her, but he was also a rational man. He wanted not a franc that he left to be available to that male defendant seated on the prisoner's bench.

"Lydie's father had his own means to check out Hippolyte and discovered that Lydie was simply wrong. The count was well known to police and legal authorities as 'bad news.' Trouble was, the moment after the marriage took place, he suddenly became the bad news person he is.

"As a retired schoolteacher, I read extensively. It's all I have to do, living alone. I love books of all kinds. Based on material I have run across, my guess is that the count acted like a nice boy, all the while wondering how he could know Lydie sexually. She is too idealistic ever to have thought of this. Being older and less idealistic, I am reasonably certain that he offered marriage only as a way to gratify his immediate sexual needs.

"This hypothesis *does* seem to make sense because, during the time he acted like an innocent boy, the rate of his extramarital fornication sessions with three young housemaids, who were known to be promiscuous, rose according to 'talk' at the Bury Tavern— information passed on by Bury-born housemaids working in the chateau is the source of this talk.

"In any case, *I* was the sender of the anonymous, egregiously threatening letters that the count ordered written because he cannot himself write literately. This, of course, is why the Act of Accusation is simply wrong.

"Mind you, members of the jury, had the letters not been sent, Lydie would have been beaten mercilessly by her thug-like husband, whom I know she hates passionately.

"What I did was undoubtedly illegal, but I had no compunction about doing it to save this young, frail woman from another battering. I could see the black and blue bruises on her forearms, when we spoke, and I assumed that her whole body was covered with similar bruises.

Judge Lyon turned to Lydie, "Is there truth to what this witness has just spoken?

"The court had not called Mme Morceau to the stand. She'd volunteered to be a witness as Lydie's "secret friend."

"She is a kind, intelligent, and good friend," Lydie responded. "I am surprised to see her as a witness. I did not ask for a subpoena to be sent to her because, if my husband were not jailed for life, he would find a way to seek revenge."

M. Lachaud objected to the inclusion of Madame Morceau's testimony into the trial record. "This is nothing more than a character assassination of my client.

Judge Lyon replied that her testimony about the origin of the letters sent to Mademoiselle de Dudzcèle was extremely important. It rendered one of the Accusations worthless. It is important enough to keep it in the record.

The seventeenth witness was Ida Chasteler de Bocarmé, mother of Hippolyte Visart de Bocarmé. (Two witnesses for Lydie divide her testimony.) Justification for this addition to the manuscript is attestation under oath by Olivier Chercquefosse, the count's former attorney. Specifically, the count had a record of criminal activity and imprisonment. It is reasonable to assume that his mother must have been aware of this before she introduced Lydie to him.

Judge Lyon asked the subpoenaed mother if she had taken the solemn oath to tell the whole truth to all questions, to which she answered in the affirmative. The judge questioned her thoroughly and at length.

Judge Lyon asked, "What is your full, official name?"

"Ida Chasteler."

"Are you married?"

"Not now."

"Were you ever married?"

"Yes, Monsieur le President."

"What was your name before you lost your husband?"

"Ida Chasteler de Bocarmé."

"I gather that you were divorced."

"No, Monsieur le President, my husband is dead."

"Is it usual for a widow not to continue to use her husband's family name?"

"No, but I prefer it that way."

"Then you did not tell us the official, the whole truth, which the oath requires."

"Excuse me. You may add de Bocarmé, if you wish."

"Ida Chasteler de Bocarmé, you are in his Majesty's Court of Assizes now. No one has the right to be sloppy under oath. What is your relationship to the accused, Count Alfred Hippolyte de Bocarmé?"

"I am his mother."

"Prior to this trial, you wrote an essay about your son. A prominent newspaper published it. What was your reason for doing that?"

"Because everyone was prejudiced against my son."

"*Everyone* is an inclusive word which implies that there is no one who wants to know *all* the facts. Did you really mean to say *everyone*, or would you like to modify that answer?"

"I meant the general public."

"Uh-huh. Even that is a too inclusive word. Did you mean to include the courts and the justice system of the nation?"

"I did not."

"Have you been following this trial, in the newspapers, or as an observer here in the courtroom?"

"From within the courtroom."

"Have you observed any evidence of prejudice or bias in the proceedings thus far?"

"I don't care to answer that question."

"That is an unsatisfactory response. I suggest that you provide the best truthful answer you can, or you may be found in contempt of court."

"I have a feeling that there is bias against my son."

"Please give me one specific event that causes you to have that feeling?

"The people in the audience are against him."

"I will allow that answer because it innocently demonstrates your lack of understanding of how the justice system works. But I *will* tag another question. Do you have any reason in the world to believe that the jury is prejudiced or biased?"

"I cannot tell."

"That is exactly how it should be. Would you have it any other way?"

"I guess not."

"Do *you* harbor any personal biases or prejudices?"

"Certainly not! I pride myself on having an open mind. One ought never to come to conclusions without examining all sides of an issue."

"The essay or editorial you wrote for a newspaper before this trial began—how many newspapers did you have to show it to before one agreed to publish it?"

"Several. I forget how many."

"Was it more than five?"

"About that."

"Did you have to pay to have it printed?"

"Why do you have to ask that question?"

"Should I gather that the evasiveness of your answer means that you did have to pay for it?"

"Yes, I had to."

"So, it was really a paid advertisement."

"Those are your words."

"Did the other four or so newspapers just turn you down flatly?"

"More or less."

"Why do you think they did that?"

"I wish I knew. I could never understand their behavior toward a prominent citizen."

"So, you believe that because you're prominent, you deserve special treatment?"

"I didn't say that."

"The newspaper record will show that you did. Do you happen to have a copy of your advertisement with you? If not, I have two copies; one for you and one for me.

"The clerk will place one of these in the evidence folder. Tell us the circumstances surrounding your introduction of Lydie Fougnies to your son, Count Hippolyte de Bocarmé."

"I don't know all the details. She visited him at the chateau. I suppose she wanted to meet him because he wasn't married, and neither was she."

"How did you know she wasn't married?"

"I had to assume it. If she were married, she would not be anxious to meet an eligible bachelor."

"And you played no part whatever in arranging their meeting?"

"My memory is getting a bit faulty. It would be impossible to say with any certainty."

"You remembered quite well the details of having your advertisement published."

"I told you that that description of it was yours, not mine."

"I'll ignore the irrelevance of that response. I prefer to ask if you attended a meeting of the Peruwelz Literary Society several years ago and listen to Miss Fougnies present a lecture on the talents needed to write a novel?"

"I have no such recollection."

"Did you not order tea to be brought to the table for Miss Fougnies and yourself?"

"I do not recall."

"Was it not you who introduced Miss Fougnies to your son?"

"I do not even know what you are talking about."

"I am not certain what your motivation is, but let me remind you that intentional avoidance to answer questions while under oath is a punishable crime."

"I don't like your attitude, young man."

"I am sorry. I shall have to order your arrest for what is unquestionably criminal contempt of court. May I quickly have two women bailiffs to lead Mme Ida Chasteler de Bocarmé, in handcuffs, to a seat in the back row.

"Sit on either side of her and keep an eye on her at all times. She is to have no small talk with anyone. If she asks questions, give no answers. If we break for lunch, please offer her the employee's lunch. The witness is allowed to know that I am by no means finished questioning her."

As the bailiffs led her away, a very angry Ida Chasteler de Bocarmé cried out, "That man is nothing more than an inquisitor!"

The judge called a two-hour recess for lunch.

The eighteenth witness was Mme Odile Levant.

"Is the former Mademoiselle Odile Robert in the courtroom yet?" asked President Lyon.

A hand rose, and a handsome young woman stood up. A clerk conducted her to the judge's stand.

"Thank you for appearing from so far away as Rheims in France. What is your name?"

"I am *now* Mme Odile Levant. My husband is Belgian, but he works in France."

"Do you have any children?"

"Yes, Monsieur le President. My son is now three years-old. I brought him with me. He is with my parents in Peruwelz."

"Please be seated; you may take the oath from the clerk. Do you have any idea why I asked you to be a witness in this trial?"

"I assumed that it was because I worked at the chateau, as a housemaid, during a summer vacation from school in Peruwelz. I was very young, sixteen, I think."

"Exactly. Do you happen to recall a day when a pretty young woman, a little older than you, entered the chateau, presumably to meet the Count de Bocarmé?"

Mme Levant's answer was clear: "Yes, it is stuck in my memory forever. It is not a nice story. The count had hired me no more than a week before an older woman brought that pretty, tastefully dressed, young woman to the chateau.

"I just had a chance to see that older woman again when she was on the stand. Her name was said to be Madame Ida Chasteler. She knocked on the front door, and I admitted her. I saw that she paid the cabbie, so it seemed that she was taking the younger woman to the chateau as a guest. They sat in the Salon à Colonnes.

"Mme Chasteler asked me if I would be kind enough to bring three cups of tea to them. I did not know why it was three cups she wanted until I returned with the tea and saw that the third person was the count, dressed in his work clothes.

"I have to confess to you that the mere sight of that man caused a mixture of anger and nausea. He had tried, desperately, the evening before to proposition me to have sexual intercourse with him. He came to my room and was quite persistent until I became angry; I told him that he had a filthy mind and that I resented his proposition. I never thought I would be asking a real count, 'Who do you think you are? Get out!'

"I would have kicked him in his 'you know whats' if I had had the chance. He was quite persistent, until I managed to get between him and the door to my room, pointed with my arm and finger, and used an expression that I *did* occasionally use. I said loudly and sternly, 'Get the hell out of here, you rotten bum. If you don't, I have every intention of reporting this to the police.'

"He seemed not to like that, so he gave me an angry look and slowly slinked away. There was no lock on that door, and I was afraid he might come back, but he didn't. I was so angry that I almost wanted a second chance to kick him hard with a leather boot where he would never forget it. I was one of the rare female athletes at the local high school, and I was in good shape. He was not going to fool around with me.

"When he sat down before the third cup of tea, he looked up at me with an angry scowl and yelled out, 'Bring us some food, too!' I do not think the word *please* was part of his vocabulary.

"I recall going back into the kitchen where there was a cook and a helper, another girl a little older, who asked why I looked so angry. I told her to make up at least three or four bread and butter sandwiches for some guests, and then I'd tell her.

"When I brought the sandwiches into the sitting room, the count looked daggers at me; a look so angry that I guessed then and there that he was sick in his head.

"When I went back to the kitchen and told the older girl what had happened the night before, she said that someone should have warned me. She said the count had propositioned every housemaid in the chateau and had been doing this for several years.

"She said, 'Don't be surprised if he suddenly fires you for no good reason without paying you any wages he owes.'

"I told her that, if he did that, I would tell the police what had happened.

"She said that was a good idea, that she was going to tell others, who might be fired for refusing him, to do the same. Word probably got back to him, and he became afraid to fire me.

"I was also made aware of the fact that there were some not-too-bright maids and a couple with higher positions who *did* satisfy his insane needs, but it was known that, if he were successful one time, he didn't have as much interest as at first. Eventually, he fired these, too.

"*I wondered whether his mother knew this about him and, if so, why she would introduce an apparently very pretty, refined young woman to him.*"

Judge Lyon said, "You tell a very intriguing and, as you say, not a pretty story, to this jury.

"Is there anyone, I am thinking specifically of the defendant's legal staff, who wishes to ask Mme Levant any questions? Rheims is quite distant. If there are questions, please ask them now."

No lawyers or jurymen asked questions, but the Count de Bocarmé rose from his bench seat and, without asking permission to speak, did so anyway. "There is absolutely no truth to this story. I would have remembered it if it happened. Perhaps one of the guests pestered her."

Mme Levant replied, "You're lying through your teeth, and you know it!"

He replied in an intimidating tone with an equally threatening facial expression, "You better watch out—*you* and *your kid*, too. I have friends in Rheims, and they won't take this crap."

One of his lawyers grabbed his prison uniform, pulled back and downward on it, and ordered him loudly, "Sit down! And shut up!"

He sat and became silent but persisted in staring daggers at the witness until Judge Lyon thanked and dismissed her. He asked if anyone cared to comment.

Lydie raised her hand and asked permission to comment. The judge gave his permission and Lydie said, "Mme Levant, I was the young woman whom Mme Chasteler de Bocarmé brought to the Chateau de Bitremont that summer afternoon, after asking me if I would like to see it. I didn't know her and took her offer even before she was able to say anything meaningful about, 'my son, who is so busy that he rarely leaves the chateau.' When we got there in a cab that she ordered and paid for, she introduced me to him and said, 'I have brought a young lady who asked to meet you.' That was a brazen lie on her part.

"She met with me after I had been guest speaker at the Literary Society meeting in Peruwelz and invited me to the chateau. I was idealistically foolish enough to feel sorry for the count—for the poor upbringing he had had. I offered to mentor him in how to read better; tried to teach him to write; and, by example, introduced a few social niceties.

"I recall exactly how he treated you. It was shocking. I foolishly rationalized that it was due to his ignorance of appropriate behavior.

I was actually foolish enough to agree to marry him two years later, and he immediately changed from a taciturn, obedient farmer to an aggressive, sadistic person with a severe sexual deviance.

"Thank you for coming so far to be a witness. You seem to be so happy. It's uplifting to see what's become of you; I have often wondered."

After Lydie's statement, the judge offered his sincerest gratitude to Mme Levant. "Thank you very much for coming all the way from Rheims to be an extremely useful witness. Is there a direct train from Rheims to Mons?"

"I am happy to help. There is just one brief stop between Rheims and Mons, Monsieur le president. Since I told my husband the story about the count, he has been following the case closely. Thank you for inviting me."

"You're free to return to your child and parents in Peruwelz."

The nineteenth witness was Mme Pauline Cloude.

After Mme Odile Levant had left the stand, the judge surveyed the courtroom, looking for the next witness. "Has the court been able to find and rush Mme Pauline Cloude of Peruwelz to Mons?" he inquired. "Has Mme Pauline Cloude arrived yet?"

A voice, from someone seated close to the witness stand beside the judge's dais, called out, "Here I am."

"How nice to see you. How did you manage to get here so soon?"

"I was at home. Someone telegraphed the police, and they put me onto a train that was just coming into the station, headed for Mons."

"Please have a seat in the witness chair and take the oath to tell the truth and the whole of it.

The judge then asked, "Mme Cloude, at one time, you were the secretary or, whatever the title, you ran the Peruwelz Literary Society. Is that correct?"

"Yes, Monsieur le President. In fact, I am still its presiding officer."

"Good. We have asked you to testify, to clarify for us, if you can, a day several years ago, when you invited Lydie Fougnies to speak; it was an afternoon meeting."

"Oh, yes, yes. I remember it very well. There were a goodly number of people, mainly women but a fair sampling of men. I knew that Lydie, whom we all well remember as the most scholarly young woman in Peruwelz, spoke to us, fascinatingly, about the qualities that a person must have or develop to write novels. I had never thought of the subject and found it especially edifying. I made that known when I said a few words to thank her."

"How long did Lydie speak?"

"Pretty close to an hour, as I recall. She was enthusiastic, but aware of time. She knew how to hold the attention of an audience."

"Did she speak grammatically?"

"Of course! Many members were impressed by her eloquence. It was a professional presentation. We've had good ones since, but none quite as good as hers."

"You had tea afterward?"

"Yes. It was a chance for old friends to get together."

"Do you happen to recall if a woman named Chasteler or Chasteler de Bocarmé was there?"

"Yes, Monsieur le President, I can say that I do remember because she came as a guest, after asking *my* permission, which of course I gave her."

"Did you chat with her during the teatime?"

"Yes, I did," the head of Peruwelz's Literary Society replied and continued to give a rather lengthy account during the teatime on that fateful day when Lydie first met her mother-in-law-to-be. "She thanked me for the pleasure of attending and told me how much she enjoyed Lydie's lecture. I recall that she quickly turned around, which made our conversation brief. She very much wanted to meet with Lydie. In fact, she asked me if Lydie was married.

"I told her that she was not, and I laughed when I said that there were no local young men who could keep up with her, intellectually.

"I could hear Mme Chasteler introducing herself to Lydie and repeating the question she asked me. It was, 'Are you married?'

"Others heard that, too, and we all laughed a little because Ida had a reputation for looking for someone to marry her son. She even sent him to meet girls she found in Germany and elsewhere, but no one would agree to marry him.

"This problem distressed her because, between you and me and the lamppost, Ida thinks she's someone special. To be spurned is an experience she doesn't think should ever happen to her because her father or great-grandfather was considered a military hero. The usual reason the refusing girls gave her was 'He's too bizarre. I couldn't marry him!' This is common knowledge. All of us who knew Lydie were astounded when we learned she had agreed to marry this bizarre son.

"I think Lydie thought she could change his personality by having regular teaching sessions with him. It's like Lydie to do that. She's pleasantly pedantic, always wanting to educate the less educated. She is, if anything, too good a human being.

"There has to be more than meets the eye here, because Lydie is not capable of doing the awful things she is accused of doing. That is the opinion of, shall I say, the intelligentsia of Peruwelz.

"*The people who never knew her believe everything they read in the newspapers,* and a lot of them are convinced that she became a fiendish killer when suddenly occupied by the devil. There has to be a wrinkle here that has eluded realization."

"You have been a very important witness, Mme Cloude. Thank you *very* much for answering my call."

"Thank *you*, Monsieur le President."

***

328

The twentieth witness was, again, Ida Chasteler de Bocarmé.

At this point, the judge redirected his focus to the count's mother. "The bailiffs will please remove Mme Chasteler de Bocarmé's handcuffs and return her to the witness stand."

Turning to Mme Chasteler, he reminded her, "You are still under oath, Madame. In a neutral tone, he said, "I have a duty, as one human being to another, to let you know that any continuation of your previous behavior might be punished more severely than before. Judges are neither unfriendly nor friendly. They are unprejudiced umpires."

After a pause, he continued, "You heard testimony today that related to your son's pathological behavior. Did it surprise you?"

Mme Chasteler replied quickly "Yes it did. It has made me feel worse. Those things happen. Lydie couldn't tell either."

"I'm sorry," the judge said, "I didn't understand what you meant by that comment about Lydie Fougnies."

"Lydie didn't know any more than I did about his problem with women," Hippolyte's mother, Marchioness Ida Chasteler de Bocarmé, explained.

"I take it from that comment that *you* had no idea that he had what you call his 'bizarre problem' and no knowledge of *any* premarital history of sexual misbehavior?" The judge peered at the witness. "Is that correct?"

"Yes, Your Honor."

"That answer implies that you *do* agree that, although he gained a reputation as 'bizarre,' sexual problems were not apparent to *you* until he married Lydie," the judge pressed.

"Yes, you've expressed what I wanted to say."

"When he was a young man, was he not schooled in Lille among other places?

"Yes, Your Honor

"He was nineteen and not long after this you began to seek a wife for him, is that correct?"

329

"Yes, I did. I wanted to see him married and settled"

"As I understand your published 'essay' (let us call it that for the moment), you went so far as to seek a wife for him in countries beyond France?"

"I did do that, yes, Your Honor."

"You went to Germany with him, I believe"

"Indeed, I did.

"Where in Germany did you go?"

"We went to several cities, mainly Berlin. I wanted to introduce Hippolyte to German culture and language before introducing him to a young woman whose parents I knew. Two of them were my classmates in finishing school. They spoke French."

"I see. Were you, personally, able to speak German when in Germany?"

"Well, I picked up a little. Enough to get around. But that was a long time ago. I've forgotten all of it. I found it a difficult language, Your Honor."

"And what about Hippolyte? Was he able to learn enough to make conversation with German people?"

"I must admit that he found it difficult. Progress was slow for him. I had to stay there for a much longer time than I had intended before he could get the hang of it."

"That is quite understandable. Especially because your intention was to have him meet young German women who might find him attractive enough to marry. They would have to converse. In fact, how long did you have to stay there?"

"Well, had it not been for two or three German women with whom I became acquainted during my schooldays, it would never have been possible to stay as long as we did. They had friends in various suburbs, who were gracious enough to allow us to live in a variety of homes."

"While there, did you manage to correspond with your family and friends in Belgium?"

"Your Honor, I was concerned mainly with my three younger daughters. They moved into a cousin's home in Tournai. I wrote now and then to her to be reassured that my daughters did not forget me and their brother. We were away for two years or more. My cousin has since passed on.

"Sorry to hear that. That was quite a long time away from home. How old was Hippolyte?"

"*I think he was about nineteen or twenty.* It was so many years ago that I'm not able to recall exactly.

"In your essay, you gave his age as nineteen when he finished at Lille. Did he meet many attractive young German women?"

"Your Honor, I confess that he disappointed me. He never got a good enough handle on the language to meet and converse with any more than one. She was from Berlin and spoke French. He liked her very much but she was unwilling to consider marrying him.

"Did she give a reason for her reluctance?

"Yes, she did. She said he was bizarre." But she was a bashful young woman and did not elaborate.

"Is it possible that he made sexual advances that she cared not to mention?

"I have no reason to think so."

"Uh-huh. I can imagine your disappointment. You returned then to Belgium after two—or was it three years ?"

"Closer to three, I would say, Your Honor."

"And he soon began to live with his grandfather, is that correct?"

"Yes it is, Your Honor.

"To return to the issue that we face now, have you given any thought to why this unusual sexual behavior has persisted through his marital years?"

"Yes," Mme Chasteler replied without hesitation, "I thought it might be that Lydie was what they call a 'frigid' woman."

"Had you given thought to suggesting they seek psychological advice?" the judge inquired.

"It crossed my mind several times, but I never took the actions I should have. It's not a subject that I find proper to think or speak about. Perhaps this why I prevaricated."

"Have you no reason at all to think that extramarital sex and its complications were ever on his mind *before* he married?"

Mme Chasteler shook her head. "I have no reason to think so. Well, of course, a mother doesn't know *everything* about what her son does." She smiled.

"No," he answered, peering quietly at the ceiling. He paused, seemed to be thinking, and remarked, "Unless he had ever been involved previously in sexual offenses." He added this offhandedly with a smile and a yawn. (He was a good actor)

"Well, of *course* not, Your Honor," Mme Chasteler replied in a friendly, agreeable voice.

"Hmm. Tell the court again about when you rode with Lydie that first time to the Chateau in Bury. You *will* agree that you told Hippolyte, 'I have a young lady here who wants to meet you'? You don't deny that, do you?"

"I admit that I *did* say something *like* that. It happened to come out of my mouth that way, Sir."

"Aside from then, after introducing them and having a tour of the chateau's upstairs, did you encourage their relationship in any *other* way?"

"I did not, Your Honor. Absolutely not." Her speech was flat— without intonation.

"Are you aware that, at that time, Lydie had no personal interest in your son and attempted to let you know that in a subtle note to you? Do you recall it?

(Pause) "Your expression leads me to believe that you may not wish to recall it. Lydie Fougnies, do you have either the original or a copy of that note?"

"Yes. M. Harmignies has just handed me the original. It is mine, and the handwriting is mine…"

"Please read it loudly and clearly to the court."

"My dear Ida,

I hasten to write you briefly to thank you for your interesting tour of the Chateau de Bitremont. It is doubtless of architectural and archeological interest.

Perhaps we will meet again at a future meeting of the Peruwelz Literary Society.

Again, thank you for your kindness,
Lydie Fougnies.

"Lydie, you also wrote a memo that you put in your desk drawer. Our detectives found it. What was it for?"

"My purpose in writing that memo was to shore up my own confidence that my note to Madame Chasteler de Bocarmé, in which I addressed only the chateau and omitted any mention of her son, would make it clear that I had joined Ida primarily to see the chateau, not to meet her son. It was subtle, but I hoped she would get the point. For her to have invited me to see the chateau and, on meeting her son, to twist words and say, 'I brought a young woman who wanted to meet you' struck me as flagrantly false. Besides, her loud, imperious manner of speaking bothered me. She sounded unrefined."

"Madame Chasteler de Bocarmé, when you received the above note and got the point that Lydie was not at the moment interested in anything more than the architecture of the château, did you ever take action to light a fire under Lydie and induce her to change her mind and take an interest in your son?"

"Certainly not."

"I take it for the record that that is the absolute truth, Madame?"

"Yes, of course."

333

"How then do you explain another note that Lydie received *from* you five days after she wrote the earlier note *to* you?

"Lydie, do you have that note? If so, please read it to the court." Lydie complied:

Dear Lydie,

I must tell you that Hippolyte so enjoyed meeting you that he would like to see you again. Apparently, he found you interesting and attractive. He insists that, if you visited him with some regularity, he could form an affectionate relationship with you.

Ida

"Madame Chasteler de Bocarmé, that note is in your handwriting, is it not?"

"I must have written it hurriedly if it was dictated to me by Hippolyte. He doesn't write well, you know. And then I guess I forgot about it."

"The court has a hard time believing that. The vocabulary, grammar, and fluency of language are not those of your son. The answer is artificial enough to make *me* suspicious about your *overall* veracity."

The judge cleared his throat. "I have a hypothetical question for you. Please listen closely.

"If you were someone else, and had an only beloved daughter who—for whatever reason—had trouble finding a suitable husband, would you be tempted to introduce her to your son Hippolyte, knowing what you now know of his history of propositioning young women to have illegal sex? Did you understand the question? Would you readily introduce a beloved daughter to a man who, from what you *now* know, has had difficulty gaining the interest of young women and has now been described as treating them *disrespectfully*, including propositioning them for illegal sexual relations?"

"I don't know how to answer that question," Mme Chasteler replied. "It isn't *fair.*"

"The *court* deems it a fair question, and expects a thoughtful answer to it," the judge insisted.

Mme Chasteler persisted in avoiding the question. "I don't know if all the testimony I've heard describes my son correctly."

"Are you responding by saying that you do *not believe* the testimony by the witness from Rheims, not to mention the 'medley' of young women who *worked* at the chateau?" the judge asked.

"None of them can *prove* what happened," Mme Chasteler insisted. "It's their word against his."

"I'll ask the question again. On the basis of what you *now* know of your son's sexual proclivities, *would* you introduce your beloved, unmarried daughter to your son?"

"It's an *unfair* question because it boxes me in."

"You've boxed *yourself* in. Unless you know more about his sex life than we heard today."

"Whether I answer that question yes or no, it makes *me* look bad."

"All right," the judge asked, now taking the initiative more firmly. Tell me, is this the first time you have ever been in this Court of Assizes in Mons?"

"I'm not sure. I don't remember," she replied too irritably, raised both shoulders and furrowed her brow, as if the question were needlessly bothersome. (She too was a good thespian.)

The judge peered at her for a few moments and asked, "Madame. Is it likely that, at your age and experience, you have *never* been in Mons? It would be *strange* if an aristocratic woman from Tournai had never visited the larger, more *cosmopolitan* city of Mons."

Mme. Chasteler de Bocarmé hesitated before replying, "Oh ! I'm *sorry*. I was confused. I have, *of course,* visited Mons."

Informed that the travel to Mons before the railroads was "not easy," she responded, "I have *always*, like my *great-great-grandfather*, never relied on 'easy travel.'"

"I admire that," said the judge, adding that "as recently as *five years* ago, it wasn't easy to get here from Tournai." He asked, "How *did* you come?"

"We had horse-drawn carriages."

"Of course you did. But they could be *freezing cold* in winter."

"*I* came in warm weather, *never* in the winter. Summer months were easier travel."

"*So* you came in months like *June and July*?

"Of course."

Was there a particular reason you liked to visit Mons?"

"Oh! For *shopping*. Compared to Tournai, shopping in Mons is *heaven*."

"Did you ever have any reason *othe*r than shopping to visit Mons in July?"

"I don't remember any."

"I don't believe you are being truthful." Judge Lyon's voice was suddenly very serious.

Marchioness Chasteler de Bocarmé adopted a frightened countenance.

"Your son was arrested, in Peruwelz in July 1837, when he was nineteen. The Peruwelz police arrested him on a charge of raping a young woman, also nineteen years old, and of trying then to choke her to death. She screamed for the police; they got there fast and arrested him. Considering the seriousness of the charge, they sent him to Mons, where he was imprisoned. He gave you, his mother, as his closest relative, and you were *soon* up here. A judge ordered him kept in a prison cell. A week later, he sentenced 'the Count de Bocarmé, of Bury' to imprisonment for six months. You were at his side in this very courtroom when he was found guilty and imprisoned for only six months with a severe warning that a repeat would bring

336

a longer prison sentence. Also, the judge spoke to you and warned *you* to keep a close eye on him. Do you remember that?"

"Yes, Your Honor."

"Why, then, did you tell the court moments ago that you had been here in Mons *only* for shopping? Do you care to see the arrest record from the justice department files? Here it is; I'll *show* it to you." Wherewith, he handed to her the record.

"I don't care to see it, Your Honor. Those things *do* happen." She was expressionless.

"It happened again the following year—*again* in Peruwelz. By then he had turned *twenty-one*. He was *imprisoned here* for 24 months. *You* were with him and were accompanied by a prominent Tournai attorney. Lucky you hired him. Had *he* not been there, your son might have been imprisoned for *five* years instead of only two. Here is the justice department record and report, again."

The judge handed her the report, but she refused to read it, handing it immediately back to him.

"I know about it and *don't* want to be reminded."

"That is *your* decision. But *why did you lie under oath* and say that you had been in Mons only for shopping?"

"I didn't know you had those records."

The astonished judge caught his breath. He purposely showed no special change in emotion but asked plainly, "Do you realize the magnitude of the crime you have just admitted to committing? You lied under oath because you guessed you might get away with it. (pause) *That* is an egregious crime. Madame, you are in *grave trouble*—you must expect to be duly punished for it.

Another pause before, "*Now*, let us go back to your earlier testimonial response in which you said, with respect to your son's sexual proclivities: 'Those things *happen*. Not even *Lydie* could tell.' You were not telling the truth, were you?"

Ida squirmed in the witness chair, lowered her eyes and raised them to say, "No, Your Honor."

337

"And your story of being with Hippolyte in Germany was fictitious, too, was it not? It was a way to keep neighbors and friends from learning the real reason for Hippolyte's disappearance.

"Yes. It was *effective*. But *you've ruined* not only *Hippolyte's* reputation. You've ruined *mine* too!

"Madame Marchioness, the fact is that you told a fictitious story *under oath*. That is criminal behavior. How do you *justify* this flagrant criminality?"

After a considerable pause, Ida replied, "I was trying to protect his public image."

"I understand your embarrassment, but telling untruthful stories to the public in an advertisement is one thing. Telling them *under oath in a courtroom* is a violation of law.

"Let me ask you again if you would drive your innocent, unmarried daughter to the chateau to meet your son?"

"The question isn't fair, as I said."

"Why is it not fair?"

"Because you've boxed me in. Whether I answer yes or no, I'll look bad in the eyes of the public."

"You've boxed yourself in by not telling the truth in the first place."

Ida was overtly angrier than was the judge. "I refuse to answer that question because it is an inherently unfair trap!"

"You *do* recall how serious a criminal act it is to refuse to answer questions under oath? You are not a stupid woman. I think you know perfectly well that you would *not* introduce your beloved daughter to a man who sounds not only immoral; he's perhaps *amoral*. Do you know the difference between the two?"

"Yes. I am a learned person."

"Well, is my hypothesis 'commonsensical'? Would your behavior be the one I suggested?"

She paused before remarking, "It *seems* like common sense." Her tone was acid.

338

"Yet you introduced the attractive, beloved—and idealistic to the point of naiveté—daughter of another person to have a *marital relationship* with your son. Did you feel *no* responsibility to inform Lydie Fougnies that your son had spent two prison terms for rape and attempted murder, even as you acted to encourage her relationship with him?"

"No, I did not."

"I take it that you *really* meant *that* to be your answer. "If no one else except Lydie, her family, and you had been present, would you not have expected that the prospective spouse ought to have been told?"

"I cannot answer for them."

"There is something unsatisfactory about that answer. Were you so anxious for your son to have a wife that you decided *not* to tell her?"

Beads of sweat were now visible on the witness's forehead. The subject made her uncomfortable but Judge Lyon would not yet let her go. "You have daughters. Had they been Lydie, would you have wanted to know if they were intending to marry a man you knew had been imprisoned for sexual crimes?"

Tears were now flowing but she gave no direct answer. "I made a mess of things. I am sorry for what I did and hope and pray that Lydie and her family will forgive me."

"When you wrote her that your son found her 'interesting and attractive,' you also insisted in the note that, if Lydie were to visit your son with some regularity, he could form an affectionate relationship with her. Did it cross your mind that you were being dishonest with her?"

"I don't know what you're talking about."

"You *did* overtly encourage the relationship—is that not the case?"

"I have *no recollection* of having encouraged it."

"Do you mean over and above the invitational note that you sent to her for him?"

"You've put me through the 'third degree.' Please, I want to beg Almighty *God's forgiveness* and be let alone and out of here."

"Madame, this is not a church. It is a courtroom. Have you ever had conscience pangs over the degree of brutality and suffering that your uncivilized dishonesty has caused Lydie Fougnies, a beloved daughter, to have to undergo? *Have* you? Your intentionally denying information expected of a civil, unselfish person was reprehensible. *Instead*, you led her on with 'he insists that, if you visited him with some regularity, he could form an affectionate relationship with you.'

Ida Chasteler de Bocarmé stared at the floor.

"I know that you feel ashamed now, though I'm not sure whether some of what you call 'shame' is merely embarrassment over what your neighbors will know tomorrow when they read the newspapers. Because you are in very serious trouble.

"Did you not think you owed it to Lydie Fougnies to inform her about your son's criminal history? You are a mature, knowledgeable person, who takes pride in being a 'prominent' citizen. Did you think that much of the testimony about his sick, sexual dalliances was unknown to the police and the justice department?"

"I beg your pardon! I had *no* such knowledge. What I heard today made me feel *as though someone hit me over the head* with a cudgel."

"I asked, 'Was it not you who introduced Miss Fougnies to your son? Your answer was, 'I *do not even know* what you are talking about."

"You earlier informed the court that you would lie if you thought you could get away with it, specifically, 'if there were no records' to disprove your testimony. You admitted that you did so *'because I didn't think you had records [of my son's arrests for rape and attempted murder].'"

"You are crucifying me!" Her voice was an angry one.

"You uttered a miscellany of other lies and made attempts to avoid answering straightforward questions."

"You, sir, have *too much power*. If *you* were *upper class*, you would *never* speak to *me* as you have!"

"That does it. You have had the temerity to hold the president of this court in contempt. Behavior of that sort demonstrates your *utter contempt* for law and justice. You are *not* the high-minded citizen you would like others to think you are.

"My dear Marchioness, you must obey the laws, as must everyone. For insulting the president of the court, as you just did, I have added to the punishment for an astonishing degree of criminal contempt of court that I have *never before* encountered. I have never heard a burglar— or an embezzler— act as contemptuously. ***The questions I asked you were related, not as distantly as it might seem***: **1. to the cause of a murder; 2. to numerous illegal sexual incidents; 3. to the brutal treatment of a young wife**; and **4. to the need for an expensive trial**.

"<u>**You** are going nowhere but to prison</u>."

"But I admitted to guilt as a sinner and have begged the forgiveness of God and of Countess Lydie Fougnies. What *more* can I do?"

"This is a courtroom, *not* a church."

"Like any other criminal, you will be imprisoned as an example to others as to the importance of honesty and respect for the justice system. Bear in mind that every word you uttered has been copied by stenographers and collected, *for posterity,* in hundreds of witnesses and the newspapers of Western Europe. The consequence of your refusal to answer questions, unless you knew it was safe to lie, will *forever* be loud and clear.

"For your squalid, selfish, and contemptible attitude toward this court and its president, I am sentencing you to twenty-four months— *two years*—in this prison in Mons. During the first month, you will be alone in a cell. It will give you time to lighten the burden of the conscience pangs you must feel—*if you are a normal person*. During the remainder of your incarceration, you will share a large cell with various other women from all classes and walks of life, who have also violated laws. One is never too old to learn.

"You will have the right to have your criminal record and sentence reviewed. If you do, I suggest you employ a good lawyer. You will be questioned frequently by a court alienist to discover if you know right from wrong. His findings and impressions will ultimately be reviewed by a no-nonsense trio of judges. They will determine whether you are capable of distinguishing right from wrong and complete your sentence, or whether you ought to spend your remaining years in an institution for the mentally sick. Take them seriously; they do no favors for aristocrats or anyone else.

"Would the female court police take Mme Chasteler de Bocarmé to her cell? Treat her *no differently* than you would treat any other incarcerated female criminal. Thank you."

Madame Chasteler de Bocarmé was afraid to say anything more. Judge Lyon's friendly initial tone of voice had possibly led her to believe that she could pull the wool over his eyes.

She *had* played a pernicious role in a tragedy. Many alert citizens who followed the trial closely thought she deserved to be severely punished. Her selfish promotion of a marriage linking an unknowing, trusting, young woman to her son, a person with a history of imprisonment for sex crimes, was secretively, deceitfully, and destructively antisocial. Judge Lyon's only means to chastise her was to punish her for a perverse inclination to act contemptuously on the witness stand. In 1851, it was unusual to be sentenced to prison for contempt of court. Judge Lyon punished her to the limit of the law for her pathologic ruthlessness.

CHAPTER 41

Judge Lyon's Concern

Having listened to testimony by both Lydie and Hippolyte de Bocarmé on the first day of the trial, the obvious difference in the education of the two defendants struck Judge Lyon as strange. He wondered how and why an obviously educated, refined Lydie Fougnies stooped to marry so ignorant an individual.

The judge, who meticulously followed every aspect of the case, knew that Lydie underwent a thorough physical examination at the prison in Tournai soon after her arrest. There was evidence that someone had been wickedly brutalizing her. An original report of the examination remained in Tournai and he acquired it.

Having read it carefully, he submitted it two days after the trial began as potential evidence in an Evidence File located in the courtroom in Mons. Lyon waited for the prosecutor or his staff to find the evidence he had filed, but they apparently did not use it, perhaps had not read the contents of the File.

He supposed that the king's prosecutor had not periodically combed the file for additions to it or to refresh his memory about details within older reported evidence.

Review of older reports might reveal previously unrecognized significant information. Failing to remain abreast of old and new evidence in a murder trial, where the death penalty is a possibility, is tantamount to heinous dereliction of duty. Judge Lyon asked no questions about it, deciding to wait and see if one or the other side entered the report as evidence.

If Lydie's defending lawyers failed to enter it, he would suppose that they were unaware of its existence. In any event, he would himself enter the report as evidence before the trial ended, to be thorough and fair. His hunch was that it might be vital evidence.

When it seems to be nearly time for each of the jurors to have digested enough evidence and to have begun, personally, to decide guilt or innocence of the accused and to determine their fates, prosecutors and defense lawyers struggle with whether every juror knows what they want them to know.

The individual who was most concerned about fairness in this competitive game was Judge Lyon. He noticed that, when Lydie, the Countess de Bocarmé, spoke, whether he personally believed she was telling the truth, her diction and grammatical speech differed in the extreme from that of her husband, the Count de Bocarmé.

She was, without doubt, a well-spoken, polite, person, whereas her husband was a crude loudmouth. He spoke and behaved as though he had had little education and lacked the gentility that was always a part of his wife's behavior.

The judge was unable to erase his inquisitiveness about how and why Lydie Fougnies had married a man whom he considered to be an ignoramus. Lydie had often referred in open courtroom to her having to take an action "under duress," a nonspecific expression. The judge now wanted to know from Lydie exactly what she meant by "duress."

She had earlier referred to the count's having threatened to beat her on one occasion early in her marriage, when he demanded that she make him the sole beneficiary of her estate or would beat her when she left the hospital. She was pregnant and hospitalized in difficult labor. Recollection of earlier beatings by her husband caused her to sign his prepared document. Lyon wanted to know more about it, especially because he had a vitally important medical report of November 23, 1850.

Lyon was a man of immense integrity. He was a no-nonsense judge, but he was also compassionate. He was able to sleep very little throughout the trial because of its international notoriety and his concern that no stone be unturned and the jury's verdicts fair. His conduct of this trial would be his legacy to the legal world.

He wanted every juryman to know all the truth and was not certain that all of the truth about Lydie had been unearthed. He was, to be frank, anxious about her fate and the fates of her three children.

The judge did not feel that anyone had delved deeply enough into how an apparently decent person like Lydie Fougnies had become involved in an infamous murder. She had never had any trouble with the law before now.

The evidence the jury had already heard, if the trial should end very soon, would steer them inevitably to the conclusion that she was, at the least, guilty of aiding and abetting the murder of a young man described by all witnesses as a decent and likeable person with no record of having committed as much as a misdemeanor.

Judge Lyon knew much of Lydie's educational background and academic achievements because of assiduous sleuthing by detectives. He knew that the faculty of the fine college she attended respected her, that she was an honor student, and that her classmates universally looked up to her. He had a hunch that he had not yet looked carefully under enough rocks.

***

Early in the trial, he had chosen not to call to the attention of the jury the report of a medical examination that all prisoners must undergo upon their arrival at a prison. He thought that Lydie would, herself, bring up certain striking findings of the examination but she did not, even on the first day of questioning when Judge Lyon asked her if her marriage with Visart de Bocarmé was a happy one.

Lydie's hesitation before answering was noticeable enough that the stenographer made mention of it before recording her single word, "No."

***

The prisons had no full-time women doctors. Instead, they had nurses trained to make careful examinations of all new female prisoners and to report their findings.

The nurse in Tournai examined Lydie in a moderately well-illuminated room within ten minutes of her arrival at two in the morning on November 23, 1850, and again a few hours later, in sunlight. She wrote a comprehensive report of her observations that intrigued Judge Lyon immensely.

She found an extraordinarily large number of black and blue bruises on Lydie's ribs, breasts, back, and buttocks; on her arms and forearms; and also on the fronts and backs of her thighs and the calves of both legs. The nurse wrote that she was unable to recall having previously seen such extensive evidence of brutality during her ten years of service at the prison. She included a statement that blows with fists had caused all of the individual bruises, noting that the linearly arranged darker spots within the bruises were consistent with damage to flesh and overlying skin by knuckles. The bruises were in various degrees of discoloration, indicating that the trauma had not occurred on a single day, more likely continuously day after day.

The face alone had no bruise, and the teeth were intact. The bruises on the calves were so numerous that she asked the prisoner if it was painful, to which the countess replied, "Yes, especially in the mornings."

When she was questioned about the person who struck her, the prisoner answered, without hesitation, "my husband." To the query of whether he used his fists, she said, "Always."

The report added that the ankle-length dresses the countess wore hid practically all of these marks, except those on her forearms near the wrists.

The nurse's conclusion was that the prisoner known to her as Lydie de Bocarmé "appears to be a severely and chronically battered woman, whose face has been spared, at least recently. When asked if

346

her face had been slapped at any time, she answered, 'Yes, hard, but not in the past several days.'"

***

Judge Lyon expected that, at some point in the proceedings, Lydie would volunteer, for the record, that she was a victim of chronic physical abuse, but she did not. He wondered why. He strongly suspected that it was her half-civilized husband who had been beating her with his fists.

There were questions regarding the circumstances of the brutality, as well as the effect that chronic trauma might have on the mental state of an young woman. Perhaps, a psychological effect of some kind was a reason for concealing the degree of her victimization.

His imagination led him to think that such trauma—continuing and severe for several years—might have affected her mind and influenced her ability to know right from wrong. Judge Lyon was a man capable of creative thought.

Lydie had shown spunk when sparring with her husband, when he'd slyly implied to Investigator Heughebart that *she* was the murderer. She refuted his design with hard rhetorical questions such as, "If it were I who was murdering Gustave, why did he cry, 'Pardon, Hippolyte,' not 'Pardon, Lydie? Why is it that *your* finger was bitten, not *mine*?'"[32]

Her answer impressed the judge but certainly did not clear the thought that she'd aided and abetted the count by not warning her brother of her husband's murderous intentions.

In addition, this cultivated woman had attempted to hide evidence of death by poisoning and had made no effort beforehand to ask strong coachmen, such as Alex Vandenberg or Gilles Van den Bergh,

---

[32] This bite almost certainly added to the count's temporary poisoning by nicotine at the time of the murder.

347

to restrain her husband and protect her brother. She could have asked either of the coachmen to ride quickly to Peruwelz early in the morning to ask for police intervention.

A common question was why did Lydie not destroy the equipment Hippolyte was using to gather nicotine from tobacco?

Once more, it crossed the judge's mind that nearly daily beatings and meaningful threats to kill her might have been the reason for her obedience, although he had never read nor heard of recent studies of exactly these effects at the Salpetrière Hospital (a major neuropsychiatry research institution in Paris).

Nothing in Lydie's history suggested a criminal streak. Her obviously close involvement in the premeditation of a murder, aiding and abetting murder, and trying to hide it was, Judge Lyon thought, so highly irregular that it required investigation. Why, he pondered, would *this* young woman act this way?

He knew that she and her husband were in debt and wanted to prevent Gustave's marriage. He could understand that her husband was crude, mean, and avaricious enough to murder her brother but could not understand what had motivated her to join him in a cruel assassination.

The morning after her brother's death, the countess had calmly told several people that he'd died of apoplexy, a cover-up for her husband. She had tried, with great effort, to destroy evidence that would show poisoning as the cause of her brother's death.

CHAPTER 42

Lydie's Dignity

When the court began its session on the following morning, Judge Lyon called Lydie to the stand. and asked her to pull back her veil, which she had customarily worn in the courtroom until now, There was no reason to hide what he thought was the face of an attractive, intelligent woman. The jury ought to see her face and her expressions as she answered questions.

Judge Lyon began with a warm greeting and was answered with a modest smile along with her salutation.

"Lydie," he said, "early in the trial, why did you hesitate when I asked you if your marriage was a happy one? There had to be a deep-seated reason for the pause. Frankly, I would not have believed you if you had said your marriage was a happy one."

Lydie replied, "Monsieur le President, I remember that occasion. If you were to ask that same question now, there would be no hesitation. A trial was new to me. I had no idea how one is conducted or how it would turn out because I had never seen a trial or even imagined how carefully prepared they are.

"I was, I can tell you now, somewhat afraid that the court would not be able to bring out such strong evidence as it has against him. I was afraid that there was a possibility he might not be found guilty and, since there would be no chance of a safe separation from him, I would again have to live with him and his animal-like brutality. I was still extremely fearful of him."

"Lydie, what made you believe that there would be no evidence to incriminate him?"

"He insisted that he had read in books that it is impossible for any chemist to find a trace of nicotine in the body and showed me a statement in *The Textbook of Toxicology*, which said the same

349

thing. Still, I told him that the police were clever. He insisted that he intended to commit the murder because it was impossible to find the nicotine.

"I told him that I did not like the idea of killing anyone. He told me that, now that I knew his intention, he would kill me if I double-crossed him. I think he meant 'betrayed,' but I did not want to correct him. He doesn't like to be corrected since we married—but not before we were married, when I felt sorry for him and tried to teach him to read and speak more effectively."

She then told the judge all of the events that had occurred and had culminated in her eventual marriage to the count—nearly five years spent in hell. She bared her soul, instinctively knowing that this was her last chance to describe to the jury in clear, fluent language the Lydie she had been—so full of hope, dreams, and trust; willing and eager to share the knowledge she had gleaned—before Hippolyte. He had systematically and malevolently erased almost all of the early Lydie through threats, beatings, and humiliation.

She continued, "I completely missed, or ignored, all the signs showing what kind of man Hippolyte is and I scorned all the attempts of my friends, my father, and my brother to get me away from a relationship which was bad for me and was doomed to end painfully.

"Several doctors had told my brother, Gustave, that due to his chronic bone illness he would die early, so he had written his will in such a way that when he died his considerable fortune would presumably go to me, if he remained a bachelor. However, I have a deep-down feeling that I might not be mentioned in Gustave's will at all, although I dared not mention it for a long time, fearing it would anger my husband. Anyway, the doctors were wrong. Gustave did seemingly recover and planned to be married.

"My husband became very angry because he had always coveted Gustave's money and that's why he decided to kill him. I believe that he might even have planned that once I had inherited Gustave's fortune, he might kill me, too."

Judge Lyon said sternly, "That is a very serious remark. I am glad you said 'might.' But what made you say that?"

"Because when Hippolyte talked about Gustave's money, he talked about its coming to *us*. Another time, I think twice, he reminded me that he had a written agreement, signed by me, that said that all of my estate would pass to him, when I died.

"I was in labor delivering my first child and was very sick. Even so, he insisted that I sign the agreement or he would later beat me. So, I signed it under duress because he had beaten me many times before I became pregnant, and I knew how hurtful his beatings are.

"He had a long after-dinner session with me, telling of his plans to kill Gustave. He demanded that I not only help him, but threatened me with death if ever 'in the slightest way' I should warn my brother of his intention. He was already counting the money. 'Don't be stingy with that money when you get it. Anyone can have an accidental death, as you know, and it would all become mine.'

"Just before he murdered Gustave, he reminded me again of the note that I had signed and said, 'I've got it and have hidden it, and I know how to hide things well. So do not ever ask to see it again.'"

M. dePaepe, one of the count's lawyers, objected. "Monsieur le President, this is a very serious, damaging charge. The Count de Bocarmé has the right to defend himself on the record."

"What observations do *you* have to make, Accusé de Bocarmé?" questioned Judge Lyon.

The count replied indignantly, "I never beat my wife. Never! That's an outright lie. She signed the note, voluntarily. My wife keeps saying that I murdered her brother. It's an absolute lie. This trial is not over. Words like that can sway the jury. I have nothing more to say. This woman can make up lies easier than anyone."

The judge said, "Thank you, Accusé. We have your remarks on the record. I should like to ask you a separate question unrelated to what has just been discussed. In the days when you were busy preparing nicotine, hiding it and meditating what you might do with it, is it not true that your wife was home with you in the chateau, doing all she could to oversee the maids and the cook, who prepared your dinners?"

"As far as I know, that's right."

"And you and your wife got along in your usual peaceful way?"

"Yes, as far as I remember."

"Did you have any arguments?"

"It's possible, but I don't remember any."

"Were you questioning how she should handle affairs to keep people away from the dining room in the event her brother should visit and decide to have dinner with the two of you?"

"No!"

"I have a personal question that you may, or may not, wish to answer. In the few days before the day of Gustave's last visit, did you have intimate relations with your wife?"

(The count's sexual mania was so often mentioned that the question seemed reasonable and was not at once objected to by his lawyers.)

"It's possible."

"Is that a yes?"

At this point, M. dePaepe said, "Monsieur le President, this is a very personal question."

Judge Lyon replied, "I made it clear that it is a personal question that he might not wish to answer."

After consulting with his lawyer, the count sheepishly said, "The answer is, I don't remember, but it's possible."

The judge then turned to the countess, "Lydie, do you care to answer?"

Lydie thought carefully before answering, "It is an extremely personal matter. It is so personal that I hesitate to speak of it in detail before such a large, public audience. There are newspaper reporters in the courtroom.

"What I want you and the jurors to know is confidential. Newspapers in all of Europe would make headlines of it. I would be too embarrassed to continue to live."

"Well," said Judge Lyon, "I believe we can do something about that. Would you tell a limited number of persons—me, in the presence of your lawyers—about these personal matters, in a session held under oath? A senior stenographer will record all testimony and will have an assistant or two. The courtroom will be cleared of everyone else, including even the bailiffs."

"I object!" cried the count.

"Your objection is overruled, Accusé Visart."

M. Harmignies, Lydie's chief lawyer, stood and said, "I fully agree, Monsieur le President."

Messieurs Lachaud and dePaepe, the count's lawyers, asked to be included, and the judge granted them permission. The count refused to attend what he referred to as an "absolutely illegal session."

Judge Lyon then said, "It is within the rules of this jurisdiction to hear nonpublic testimony whose minutes a stenographer copies, to allow distribution to jurors alone. The prosecutor may have a copy to read but none to keep.

"They are, to my knowledge, honest men, who will never speak publicly about the testimony in any part of this trial now, or once the trial is at an end. Nor will anyone remove written or printed material from the court."

He addressed the head juror. "I ask you to repeat this order of the court to the jurymen. Violation will be a punishable offense."

Judge Lyon then turned to Lydie and asked, "Will you agree to this degree of confidentiality? It will allow you to let the jury know your testimony confidentially. Whether you want your lawyers, and your husband, to be present will also be your choice. However, if your husband is present, I shall have to order bailiffs to remain in the courtroom for your protection and mine."

Lydie asked, "Monsieur le President, would the bailiffs also be under an oath of absolute confidentiality?"

The judge informed her, "Bailiffs are already under strict oaths of confidentiality, and know that it is a punishable crime to speak about, let alone take copies of any testimony from the courtroom."

Lydie agreed to testify during such confidential conditions.

The count reiterated his refusal to attend on the basis that a secret session is illegal. But if his lawyers wished to attend, "it's up to them."

CHAPTER 43

Lydie Tells Her Story

The courtroom was emptied; two bailiffs handcuffed the count, removed him through a rear door of the courtroom, and took a flight of steps to the floor above. A solid floor and door prevented any ability to hear speech within the courtroom.

Judge Lyon now asked Lydie, "Do you feel comfortable about the arrangement for this special session?"

Lydie responded, "Yes, Monsieur le President, I will answer any questions you ask."

The judge looked at the lawyers and reminded them of the oaths of confidentiality they had taken when they received licenses to practice law in Belgium. Then, he asked Lydie to relax, and she replied that she was at ease and composed.

Lydie began her testimony with an accusation, "My husband's response to your question about frequency of intimacy during the week before he murdered Gustave was incomplete and an evasion.

"He demanded sexual intercourse not just every night before the day of the murder but also every afternoon before the day of the murder. These less-than-joyful couplings were each followed by seriously concentrated beatings with his fists and my customary crying out with pain, because he has big fists and punches very hard."

"How long has he been dealing so brutally with you?" asked the judge.

"Since the first week of our marriage."

The judge then announced, "I would like to enter into the record, a report of the examination of the countess by the examining nurse at the prison in Tournai, when she carefully evaluated the physical condition of the countess at the time of her imprisonment.

355

"Lydie, we know from your examination by the nurse at Tournai that black and blue bruises covered practically all of your body. They were in various stages of discoloration, indicating that many were remnants of a continuum of beatings. It seemed to the experienced nurse that a fist made those bruises. Am I correct if I infer that the fists were those of your husband?"

"You are entirely correct, Monsieur le President. All of them were."

"Tell us what you can about the reasons for these terrible beatings."

Without hesitation, she said, "My husband beat me very frequently for a variety of reasons."

"Would you please testify what some of the reasons were?"

"Perhaps your question is best answered if I start at the beginning. Is that all right?"

"That will be acceptable. If I have additional questions, I will append them or interrupt, as needed, to clarify or dig more deeply into what you have related."

"The first time he slapped my face and beat me was on our wedding night. For the preceding two years, he had acted as though he enjoyed my visits, where we read a daily newspaper and I explained how to pronounce words he did not know and explained their meanings by using synonyms.

"He was a mediocre student but was always well behaved, although his social graces were badly in need of improvement. I had no idea, at the time, that he was a sex maniac.

"On our marriage night, he acted like someone I had never before seen or known. When I entered the bedroom, he slapped my face hard. No one in my life had ever used physical force on me.

"It is not exaggeration to say that whatever intimate relations took place were animal-like. For all intents, he raped me after *literally* ripping my clothes off as he berated me in foul language, claiming that I was not *immediately* accessible to him.

356

"He was drunk, with a repulsive odor on his breath, and struck my head with a fist to force me to breathe his foul breath. I kept my eyes closed. He very slowly undressed, although I do not know why he took such pains to go about it.

"I closed my eyes and refused to watch the perverted act. Without a sound, he then jumped on me and forced himself into me. I cried out with pain. I was a virgin. He cared only for his own carnal pleasure. He fell deeply asleep immediately seconds after he had had a quick orgasm.

"I gave serious thought to quietly dressing myself and waking Vandenberg to take me from the isolated chateau in Bury to my father and brother in Peruwelz. Foolishly, I did not, because I had made Hippolyte a promise that I would educate him and teach him social graces becoming a count. My *extreme* idealism, which I was once warned about by a doctor, got me into long-term trouble.

"I had taken him to be a hardworking farmer who, because of a faulty upbringing as a small child in Java and for three years as an adolescent in the wilds of Arkansas, had never learned social graces. I admired him when I met him. He appeared manly and productive for himself and society.

"No sooner were we married, than he became an entirely different person with no more interest in learning to be sociable. Obviously, it was a serious error not to have acted on the thought of fleeing that night as he slept.

"He drank so much, actually, that he fell asleep; he passed out on a downstairs sofa for an hour before waking and then stumbling up the stairs to the bedroom. Stupidly, I sat beside him in a chair during that hour. That would have been the ideal time to have left him. Consummation of the marriage would not have taken place, and there could have been an annulment.

"Late in the morning, when we were awake but still in the bed, I distanced myself from him and told him sternly that his behavior the previous night was appalling.

"Merely having to be near him frightened me and would even have inhibited what I might say, in strict confidence, about him. I have no such inhibitions now. I believe he should have a copy of what I testify to here. He ought to have a chance to answer anything I say."

Judge Lyon thought for a moment and said, "He was given his chance; expressed belief that this session is illegal, and yet let his lawyers attend. They will obtain copies of your testimony and prompt him how to reply, if he can logically do so."

Lydie thanked him and remarked that his response was fair.

Even so, the judge wrote and signed a brief note guaranteeing that every word the countess uttered under oath, as she was, would be available for the count's study and reply despite his having voluntarily absented himself from this *in camera* session.

Once Lydie felt there was adequate confidentiality and that her husband *would* have access to her testimony, she repeated that she'd sternly told Hippolyte the morning after the marriage night, "You were not the person I married when you acted like an animal last night, when you brutally raped me."

Lydie held her head high as she continued. "I told him, 'Hippolyte, if we are to live under the same roof, we must respect one another.'

"He never offered an apologetic word. Instead, he became extremely angry and said, 'No goddamn woman is going to talk that way to *me*.

"From that point, he treated me as though I were a special sort of domestic. He could use me as a sexual object whenever he wanted, but he also reserved the right to beat me whenever he wanted. It's important to know that he is a perverted sadist. I'll repeat it below, so that's very clear.

"As I wanted to begin to say, he's a sex maniac who is constantly propositioning the young maids, and it's common for him to fire one on the spot, if she turns him down. It's both a way of getting revenge but also saving money—he refuses to pay whatever wages he owes the young girl.

"Frankly, I have made no comment at all about these almost innumerable sexual affairs and trysts he's had because, if his prurience can be satisfied for a few hours, he doesn't bother me."

"Now, Lydie," said the judge, "will you respond again to your husband's answer that he may have been intimate with you in the week before Gustave died."

"Yes, I will. Every night before the day of the murder is only partially correct. He also insisted on sexual intercourse with me on each of those afternoons, and he beat me after each of them. He has an insatiable appetite for what I call 'quick sex.'"

"How long did each beating take?"

"Fifteen minutes."

"And how long does the sexual performance last?"

"From ten to fifteen seconds, rarely a few seconds longer. He suffers from premature ejaculation. As I understand it from the cognoscenti, assuredly not from my own experience, he would be a very poor lover."

"What then, does he give as the reason for beating you each time this happens?"

"He says that I failed to act as a true lover, which I think are words to cover his embarrassment over his premature ejaculation. I have a feeling that he wants to blame his problem on me. He claims that I have not maximized the exquisite pleasure he anticipated from the coupling. Frankly, Monsieur le President, I believe he enjoys beating me more than coupling with me.

"A particularly disgusting accompaniment to these beatings is hard to talk about but necessary to give a full description of the scenario. He struck so hard with his fists that he frequently and loudly passed particularly foul gas per rectum. By the time he had concluded the punching, the room had an obnoxious odor that was nearly nauseating. Although it was painful to move quickly, the minute he left the room I always have had to open the windows to allow fresh air in, to diminish the odor. Come to think of it, I have never known of his taking a bath, and for some unknown reason, he has never left it to me to pick up his dirty underwear to remove it to the laundry. His body is probably as filthy as his mind."

"I see why you wanted this to be confidential."

"Yes, imagine the off-color jokes that this would spawn all over the world. However, the worst beatings come after he demands that I have sexual intercourse with him during the daytime. It is not a pleasurable experience because I so despise him that I cannot respond as a true lover could.

"Once he has had his orgasm, which takes about fifteen seconds— he screams at me venomously, 'You're no good at it. You don't respond!' Of course not. I wouldn't respond warmly to that lunatic in ten seconds, ten hours, or ten days. What never made sense to me was that, when he had his orgasm in seconds, his organ shriveled and tumbled out of me, so how could I continue to be a copulating lover?? If I had ever posed that question to him, he would probably have choked me to death for excessive disobedience.

"While he screams, 'You're no good at it,' he's already at work beating me up, hard, with his fists as I lie on the bed and cry and scream with pain. Sometimes I lie prone, otherwise on my back as he beats me. Despite the quick orgasm, he apparently does squirt enough semen into me to have made me pregnant four times in a little less than four and a half years. When my pregnancies began to show, I would lie on one or other side, trying to protect the fetus. Many of the household staff misconstrue my painful screaming. They think I am screaming with orgasmic joy. Believe me, I am not. How can a woman respond lovingly to a man she despises?"

"Are there other times when he beats you?"

Lydie said, "Yes. Actually, there were two occasions I cannot forget—when he forced me into the garden outside where there was recently dug-up dirt for seeding. He forced my face into it and rocked my head in it back and forth, using my long hair as a handle. I remember the reasons for them. The first time he did that was an afternoon when he began his daily round of sadism by ordering me to take off all my clothes and position myself on my hands and knees on the bed. I didn't realize why he wanted me to do this until he took the same position above me and then tried to insert his organ, which was turgid, into my anus. The moment I realized that, I fell prone and prevented this disgusting perversion. He became blisteringly angry, mumbling something about wanting "to do it like the animals do their sex." I distinctly remember that he repeated this and that he also used the word "fornicate." This surprised me because he had never used that word before and it wasn't one I'd ever taught him. He was, of course, misusing the word and confusing the functions of pelvic orifices. What he wanted to accomplish was not what he had seen animals do. They don't mix up their protrusions and orifices and *do* have a coital experience. He wanted to masturbate *and use my anus* as a receptacle. I saw a little humor in this sex maniac's confusion; he's less smart than squirrels and chipmunks. But he would have killed me if I had tried to educate him on the distinction between orifices."

Judge Lyon smiled to the point of laughter and asked Lydie how she managed to maintain a sense of humor through all the brutality.

Lydie managed a brief laugh. "An ingrained habit to look for humor even in the worst possible situations is probably why I'm still alive.

He made me put a thin housecoat over my naked body and marched me into the backyard, where there was a recently dug hole in wet soil. He pushed my face into the mud at the bottom and rubbed my face in it by pulling my hair this way and that. I thought I might die from asphyxia because my nose was blocked with mud and it was entering my mouth. I feared smothering, but he enjoyed the spectacle. He laughed and laughed, loudly. He enjoys his sadism. One of his farmers—the ones he calls feebleminded —approached to see what was going on, and he let me loose. That experience was too frightening to contain humor. (I never taught him the word 'feebleminded.' When I first met him, I found that he called all of his fifteen farmers feebleminded.)

"He beat me with special force when we got back to the room.

"The other time when he put my face in a mud hole was when it suddenly entered his head that he wanted to lie down late one morning but was unable to sleep because the maids were allegedly making noise in the corridor. He accused me of having purposely told them to work outside his bedroom door to keep him awake. Housemaids do talk loudly and make noise with pots of water and dustpans. On that occasion he beat me with special force.

"Frankly, I think that his main pleasure is not the intimacy with me. That provides him only with the quick orgasm he apparently needs, but I think he's a sadist who gets more prolonged sexual pleasure out of beating me. I am amazed that he has no sense of shame about his behavior.

"I don't know how he can look me straight in the face at the breakfast table without bursting into tears and asking me to forgive him. I'm sure he's not all there in his head. If I treated someone the way he treats me, my conscience would hurt me. Of course, if he should ever say, 'I am sorry. Please forgive me,' I would never trust him. It's too late to forgive him."

Judge Lyon, President of the Court of Assizes in Mons, now spoke. "I can see with more certainty than ever why this testimony has had to be given in confidence and kept secret, except for the jury and very few others, and never allowed to be public. My judgment is that we've properly made use of the *in camera* allowance in this jurisdiction. The jury needed its testimony, but the public lost nothing of redeeming value by the blind."

Having divulged what she had, Lydie began to cry.

M. Harmignies handed her the clean handkerchief he carried in his breast pocket.

Once she had regained control, Lydie continued to paint the story of her life as the countess.

"Also, he forbade me ever to say 'thank you' to a domestic or ever to have pleasant conversations with any of them. Of course, I do chat normally with them, but if he notices it, he uses it as an excuse to beat me when we go to bed.

"He also refuses, whenever he can, to pay bills to those who have done work around the house or have provided services. He allows me very little money and counts what is there when I return to the house. If there is less money than I had when I left, and I tell him that I paid a bill we've owed, he swears at me, tells me I'm a fool for paying anything to anyone, if I don't have to. That offense is another excuse for a beating. People in Peruwelz hate me, but I behave as I do because I so excessively fear him while despising him."

Judge Lyon asked, "Do you have more testimony that the wide world might find salacious?"

Lydie paused, considered the question, and said, "I could add things, but it's probably enough to have testified about what I think is especially personal. It allowed me to retain my sense of dignity. Thank you, Judge Lyon.

"There *is* more that I can tell you about his character in the open session.

"I do want to make it clear, both in this session and in those that are public, that I have genuinely feared for my life in the five years since our marriage, and it has begun to have strange mental effects on me that I find hard to describe. I feel as though I'm not the same person I always have been.

"To try to lessen his capricious and sadistic beatings, I knowingly *do* act uncivilly to people and have begun to do it without conscience qualms. He has a way of doing what he threatens. You have to be someone stronger than I am to try to call his bluff when he says—I have no doubt that he means it —'If you ever even *hint* to your brother that I'm going to kill him or if you ever tell him, I'll kill the *both* of you!'

"I have to be devious; I tell him occasionally, 'How handsome you are!' He likes that and acts slightly more civilly for a day or two, but it does not affect the rigor of his beatings or the frequency with which he noisily passes foul gas.

"I will add that, if I had a sharp, hidden knife, I'd have been tempted to slice off his turgid organ at its base, but I suspected that this would be an arrestable offense. It is an especially horrible thought, but it comes to mind often. The housemaids would consider me a hero, and I'm curious to know what effect the loss would have on his already morbid personality. Would it affect his recurrent prurience? Where does the seat of this insane prurience lie?"

Lydie took a deep breath before she continued.

"Another thing that's happened is, I so fear the beatings, that I will purposely praise him, even throw in a loving word now and then, hoping to assuage whatever motive he has for beating me.

"I also say things to others that make him appear to be a wealthy man who practices noblesse oblige, when the truth is that he has no money and, if he did, he wouldn't have an ounce of generosity in him. He doesn't care about anyone but himself.

"On that terrible day of November 20, he followed me extremely and unusually closely. That is what *I* noticed. It indicated that he did not trust me and *would* kill both of us. He is insanely impulsive and does not bother to think of the consequences of what he does or the harm that he is carelessly willing to cause others.

"I know that people have asked why I didn't destroy his distillatory once I knew he was making nicotine. Do you think I would dare? He would have killed me and hidden my body. There was another time when he threatened to do this, but I have forgotten the details. He is a very dangerous animal."

A moment of silence hung in the room before Judge Lyon responded.

"Thank you, Lydie," said the judge. "The jury will receive this testimony as a transcript.

"One last thing: You undertook so many actions on the count's behalf that public opinion is running strongly against you, but whether that's true of the jury is not something I know or am supposed to know.

"A majority of the public, who have been following this trial closely, is convinced that you willingly did aid and abet a premeditated murder. You understand that in my position I merely organize the trial.

"It would be wrong for me to prepare you with questions that still have to be answered. I certainly am not able to answer the questions that lawyers put to you in cross-examination, although I think, now that we have had this session, there probably are rational replies to most of them.

"I am now announcing to the stenographic crew that none of this material must *ever* be discussed with *anyone*. As of this moment, we are still *in camera*. Our talk is being recorded and will be strictly confidential until I open the court."

Here, the judge cleared his throat.

"Before the opening, I want to ask Messieurs Harmignies and Toussaint, Lachaud and dePaepe, if they have any comments or questions. These must be in writing and addressed to the jury and to me. The lawyers are *not* to respond in open court. At the moment, they are entitled to make any comments they wish with respect to testimony they have heard."

Lydie asked permission to add comments, and the judge agreed to it.

She reminded him that: "M. Chercquefosse has not been clear about legal responsibility to ensure that funds be available to educate my children. I wonder if he has taken any steps with respect to that issue. For all I know, it's entirely possible that I will end up in prison for years. The children's futures are a matter of deep concern."

She also expressed her doubt that she was mentioned in Gustave's will, noting that she'd mentioned this to the count when he'd unveiled his plan to kill Gustave, "practically smacking his lips over *our* receiving all of his money." Her husband, she said, became extremely angry, slapped her face three times, and said he had inside information that she wasn't privy to. "He uses these words when he's lying," she explained.

"Might we follow it up?" she suggested, pointing out that M. Chercquefosse was probably in possession of Gustave's will. If my hunch that the will is *not* to me is correct, "he might have killed Gustave for no good reason."

"That is a *very* good point, Lydie," the judge replied. "We'll open that discussion after the very next witness I've scheduled. Thank you."

M. Lachaud thanked the countess for her "mind-clearing" testimony and wished her well.

M. Toussaint declared his gratitude for her "powerful testimony" for the jury.

M. dePaepe expressed his gratitude to her for her testimony and said that, although she had provided food for thought, "grave questions remained."

M. Harmignies, who was visibly moved by what he had heard, also thanked her and, to the surprise of all present, announced that he "would like to hug and kiss her cheek, if the judge would allow it."

Judge Lyon gave his permission and then called an end to the session and opened the courtroom.

CHAPTER 44

Nurse deFrance Testifies

All the people returned to their places and the judge called the court to order. He asked the clerk in a whisper to hunt down M. Chercquefosse by his personal telegraph number: "He will be needed to testify. Tell his secretary that the court wants Gustave's will without delay."

He then spoke directly to the count, who was seated on the prisoners' bench. "Accusé de Bocarmé, in a previous open session, we had before us the issue of whether you used duress to force your wife to put her name to a document that assigned all of her present and future money and valuables to you. She was hospitalized, at the time, with a complicated terminal pregnancy. Did she sign that document?"

"Yes, willingly," said the count.

"Where is that document now?" asked the judge.

"It is hidden in a safe place."

"The court orders that you show us the document. We find it relevant to the case. You have twenty-four hours to deliver it."

"That's *my* property," argued the count sullenly.

"It is, as of the moment, but there is a charge that you obtained the signature under duress. Specifically, that you had beaten your wife previously and she feared that once discharged from the hospital, if she asked to see it, she either would be beaten or told that it is hidden."

"I *have* hidden it, and it has nothing to do with being beaten. *I have never beaten my wife. The charge is hearsay. Damn it! I demand, and should have demanded a long time ago, that the court provide proof in the form of reliable evidence that I have ever beaten my wife!*"

Judge Lyon replied, "Well, it is a remarkable coincidence, but the court does intend to examine that very issue right now.

367

Will Nurse Ida deFrance please come to the witness stand?"

A matronly woman, dressed as a nurse, approached the stand. She spoke well and showed no evidence of nervousness. She had pleasant features but was not smiling. She did not in any way seem bewildered by her presence as a witness.

"What is your name?" asked the judge.

"Mme Ida deFrance. I am a registered nurse, and I took the oath a moment ago in the presence of the clerk of court."

"Sister,[33] have you any idea why you were contacted yesterday and asked to be in Mons by noon today?" continued Judge Lyon.

"I do not, Your Honor."

"Please sit and relax. I want to show you a document signed by you early in the morning of November 23, 1850. Would you kindly examine the document and describe it any way you will?"

The sister read the document carefully and then answered in a factual, unemotional way. She spoke well, an obviously serious and responsible person.

"Indeed, sir. I remember this case very well. This woman had been arrested and detained. I recall her as a refined person, and I was surprised to discover that her entire body and her legs showed indubitable evidence of what were continuing long-term fist bruises. The newer, the more black and blue, were the recent ones. The older ones changed color. Without doubt, this was a case of long-term continuing brutality by fist punching. I saw where the knuckles of someone with a big fist had struck her.

"I had seen many battered women before, but this was about the worst I could remember. I felt so sorry for this quiet young woman. I recall asking if her husband had done this. She said he had.

"It fit the distinct pattern of what has, in recent years, become known as the battering of so-called 'captive wives,' who have

---

[33] In Europe, it is common to call nurses Sister.

368

unknowingly married insane men. Often these men have what is termed Moral Insanity.

"I am not an expert on the battered wives of men who are morally insane, but I do know that this degree of beating is often deleterious to psychological as well as physical health.

"Some of these poor women become ambivalent about whether they should put themselves into positions where they refuse to assist their insane husbands in criminal activity or pay the price of continuing beatings."

Judge Lyon admitted that this was the first time he had heard of this kind of insanity.

Sister deFrance replied, "There are still too few experts on this. However, we do have one in Belgium who is in the forefront teaching and writing about it."

The judge remarked, "What you have just said could explain a great deal. Better not to make this expert's name public without our having contacted him. Would you kindly write his name on this sheet of paper? Sister, you seem to have clarified an important matter that was bothering many of us here, myself included."

At this point, the count jumped in, "I don't know what this nurse is all about. All I know is that I have never beaten my wife. The nurse must have my wife confused with someone else."

Judge Lyon asked Nurse deFrance if there were any likelihood of mixing up records. She responded without equivocation that she had *always* made it a practice to file away any papers relating to cases other than the one she works on. Stating that she knew that she was always working on a case for which the record might be of utmost importance, the likelihood of her confusing records was, and always had been, essentially impossible.

Ignoring the count, Judge Lyon asked Lydie her reaction to Ida deFrance's testimony. "Do you have any comment on what you have just heard from Sister deFrance?"

"Yes, Monsieur le President. I am overwhelmed by so much that she said in so few words, that I find it difficult to know how to present my reaction in an orderly way. I do want to discuss this vital topic with my lawyers before speaking further. Naturally, I wish to express my deep gratitude to Sister deFrance for her perfectly reliable evidence."

"For **Crissake!**" screamed the count, without asking permission to address the court. "Suddenly, a *woman*, who's not even a doctor—a *woman*, mind you—a nurse, has come out of nowhere, has undoubtedly mixed up her records, and now, because of a *woman*, I have to prove that *I'm* not *insane*. This is a hell of a goddamn thing. This judge has all sorts of tricks up his sleeve. I'm getting goddamn sick and tired of his picking on me. To tell the truth, I'd like to punch him in his face until his teeth and nose bleed."

The president of the court, Judge Lyon, maintained his composure. In accordance with the rules of the jurisdiction, it was his right to express his opinion about the quality and content of testimony. He stated for the record, "*I have never before observed the reaction of a pathological liar when reliable evidence has unexpectedly exposed him as what he is.* The reaction is of unusual psychological interest. It appears that the exposure is a complete surprise with a short period of confusion followed by a change of the subject to *ad hominem* argument. There is no substantial denial of lying, although the subject becomes extremely angry and threatens the individual responsible for the exposure with bodily harm.

"I see that in this case the central issue, namely, pathological lying, is not a front and center subject for discussion. Instead there is threatening of bodily harm to whoever has provided the proof. If one of the people who provides evidence happens to be a professional woman, the liar, who in this case is a misogynist, responds with special wrath.

"I do believe it reasonable to posit that one *must* be a misogynist to take pleasure in beating his wife and treating women generally with little or no respect.

"As for the threat to establish truth with fists, the lowest type of reaction, I have the power to order severe disciplinary measures, but will not. It is enough that the defendant's outbursts are being copied for posterity. Also, it enhances the power of justice when the jury is able to hear how the accused has responded. Jurymen are, naturally, free to draw their own conclusions. The accused has my permission, therefore, remain on his bench, provided he behaves himself."

Evidently attempting to keep attention focused on himself, the count declaimed, "I'm not afraid of you, you helpless, weak-kneed bastard. My mother was right; you enjoy the role of a mean inquisitor." The count's voice was gravelly as he screamed at the president of the court, who wisely chose not to satisfy him with any response.

Chapter 45

Gustave's Will

"Well, well, Monsieur Chercquefosse," said Judge Lyon, with a short laugh. "I found that you were already in the courtroom; and what I requested of your secretary has just arrived. Without mentioning its title or contents yet, please check that it is accurate. Have a seat. I'll call you very soon."

The judge turned his attention to the count.

"Accusé Visart, it has come to our attention that you have inside information regarding the contents of the deceased Gustave Fougnies's will. The wills of the deceased are public documents. Perhaps you knew that."

"I got my information from reliable sources."

"I am sure. What specifically did you find out?"

"That he has more money than he needs."

"I take it that that is your decision to make?

"Yes."

"In a democracy, no one can decide that someone else has too much money."

"Get off your high horse, Judge. You know some people have more than they need."

"But no law allows me to take any from him. Now, you apparently know who Gustave's main inheritor was or is to be?

"My sources told me that it's my wife."

"Do you know of anyone else who would inherit part of it?"

"No. It is primarily my wife to the best of my information."

"Are you so certain of this that any finding to the contrary might disturb you?"

"No, It wouldn't make no difference to me. I didn't kill him." Accusé was unnerved by the question.

372

"Lydie Fougnies, do you have any comments?"

"Yes. His answer has changed. He emotionally outlined his plan to kill Gustave, threatening me with death and 'disappearance of my body' if I should ever, under *any* circumstances, warn my brother of his intention to 'do him in.' Then he fantasized, 'How great it will be to have all that money.' He turned to warn me, 'Don't be stingy with it. Your accidental death would make it all mine because you signed away all your valuables to me, as you know.

"Amid all of this celebratory talk, I told him that I had doubt that my brother's will mentions me. He immediately got up from his seat, walked to me, and slapped my face hard three times. He told me, 'I don't want any remarks to question my plans to do the little bastard in!'

"He added, 'I have better information than you through private sources about what's in that will. The money is going to *you* when he's dead.' He added, 'Don't ever ask who my private sources are.' It's another line he uses when he's lying. Frankly, I don't know who my brother named as his inheritor."

Judge Lyon asked Monsieur Chercquefosse if he had an official copy of Gustave's will. He added, "Everything I hear from you will be headline news to *me.*"

"M. Chercquefosse, would you hit the *highlights* of the will? It looks long."

"It *is* long because the *official* will is hidden securely in a New York bank vault. Gustave regularly modified his financial data and high points of his will, put them together, and allowed me to hold it, although it requires a court order to see it. He took legal steps to nullify the simple original will."

(Hippolyte was noted to blush at the last sentence. Perhaps he *was* using the obsolete will, which is a public document.)

"His official will is intact in New York, but, as I said, he stayed abreast of the values of his holdings because he imagined that, one day, there might be reason for someone to read it. Also, he explained to me that, if he were threatened with poison, kidnapped, or had his life threatened in any fashion, he could offer to give a written promise to turn all his assets to the criminal, adding, 'I'll give you a letter to allow you to deal with my bankers.' With the will in New York City, are orders to ignore such a request and notify the police. Gustave was *especially* afraid of poisoning, Your Honor.

"The value of several complicated trusts within trusts is presently in excess of three and a half million dollars and a small number of francs and presently enjoys healthy sources of new income. When the sum reached a million francs, Gustave wisely began to invest income elsewhere than continental Europe, buying high rental apartment and commercial buildings. He always followed international politics closely. He had a dread of warfare because it could ruin those invested solely in Europe.

"He traveled several times, therefore, to the United States, where he consulted officers of investment banks. He chose one to invest his growing savings, and he bought undervalued buildings that would soon be replaced. Until then, its renters pay for its use by the square foot of floor space used.

He also visited Fifth Avenue, where New York's wealthy people want to live and pay very high rents. He scouted adjacent blocks where additional high-priced rental apartments were going to be built. Several of these have already been built and are adding dollars to the trust he has in New York's largest bank. The money, of course, is in dollars. He allows enough to trickle back into his main European bank to provide him with a modest but adequate standard of living here at home.

"Lydie will not receive any money unless her husband, the count, is dead. All funds that she would have received on his father's death were put into a special Lydie Trust. It's located within the larger, but separate, Gustave Fougnies 1849 Trust, from which he drew the money for his personal living expenses.

"Since Lydie has no power to tap the content of her trusts within a trust while she's married to the count, their values have grown significantly during that marriage.

"Another Trust is an important 'Educational Trust.' The funds are sufficient to guarantee an education to Lydie's three children in private schools of *her* choice. The transfer of funds from trusts to educational institutions will rigidly bypass Lydie and go directly to the institutions involved, to avoid any possibility that her husband, if alive, might find a means to appropriate any of it.

"It ends with a few lines that Gustave adamantly insisted be included: 'There shall be no amendment that would allow even one franc to become the property of Hippolyte Visart, Count de Bocarmé, or the upkeep of his Chateau de Bitremont or any successors of it regardless of its name(s).' In the event of Gustave's death, a special section guarantees a luxurious life to Lydie, regardless where in the world she happens to be living, provided her husband, Count de Bocarmé, is no longer living or she has successfully left him with her children, preferably to another nation.

"The answer to 'who is the inheritor' is written with latitude within the individual trusts. Technically, the anonymous trustees of each trust are 'limited inheritors'; there's a nominal payment for their making investment decisions with income from previous investments. He's had a great deal of discussion with them about his choices. Initially, he tended toward philanthropic organizations here at home, but the recent national election in Belgium caused an immediate change. He ruled out anyone with government oversight or a connection with charities which enable such persons to inherit from them. Also, he cancelled all his pending voluntary promises of funds to them, and also ruled out any and all religious organizations or their members.

"There are philanthropic groups in the USA that he has already helped to fund. He fears a population explosion will eventually cause widespread poverty and job scarcity. As a worldly man, he took a long-term view on this. The trustees, I know, have a parenthood education organization high on their list, but there are others that he considered socially progressive. All political contributions are off the table."

The judge thanked M. Chercquefosse. He added, "I see you were right, Lydie. Your husband was dead wrong." He then asked the count what he had to say about his mention in the will.

The angry count replied, "don't know any more than you. This is just another way to rub my nose in the dirt. You like doing that, you son of a bitch. When are we going to meet outside, use our fists, and see who's the better man?"

The judge sternly replied, "Shut up, Accusé! I had never before this moment been privy to Gustave's complicated will. I guess that he sized *you* up as someone who is 'no good.' Getting a view of the will was Lydie's idea, not mine."

"Thank you, Lydie. As you suggested, we have possibly had a murder for no reason whatever since the will contains nothing like your husband insisted it contained. His slapping your face about the will's content may very well have been his major undoing."

Lydie thanked him.

Her husband was evidently so angry with himself that he foolishly decided again to verbally attack the judge:

"You get a lot of pleasure from this little will story, don't you Mister Judge," he snarled. "First, you believed my wife's lie that the she told me she was not in the will and also that I slapped her face. She made that up out of thin air. You're feeling pretty good since you got that nurse either to lie or to repeat a medical report on another woman. I let some of that go because the jury can see both sides of the picture. But, in a way, you've stupidly cast doubt on the abilities of my friends in Brussels, the ones I drink beer and pal around with. Mister, they won't put up with anyone painting them as bunglers.

"We have oaths, too. And now I'm speaking in public to set them free to go, as our oath calls, for *you personally*—preferably on a dark street at night not far from where you live. They punch hard, and one of their favorites, after you're down, is to rib kick you for half an hour so every last rib is broken. Then they leave you to die in the worst kind of agony as they quietly disappear in the dark. You've set up your own death sentence, you arsehole."

The judge replied with vigor, "Accusé! You are under arrest on a second charge! Court police, seize him, strip him, put him in solitary in irons, and feed him only hardtack and water. He's to have no communication with anyone. Go ahead, lock his arms *and* legs and let him try to walk or crawl the entire distance by himself.

"The charge is extremely serious, namely, 'Threatening the life of a justice department official.' It is not very bright to do that in public. Give him a single thin blanket and leave him there to sleep on the concrete floor. A guilty verdict is, at a minimum, life in solitary. If death enters the picture, the main guilt is considered the instigator's. That means you, Accusé. As certain as the sun rises and sets, you can expect life imprisonment or a date with the guillotine if one of your 'friends in Brussels' even *threatens*, whether or not he kills me. Think that one over next time you impulsively open your mouth to speak. If, for any reason, you manage to avoid a death sentence with the present charge, you would have to face it again with another judge and jury. You could not have chosen a worse place to threaten me than here in my courtroom. Imagine how many witnesses there are to your threat.

"I declare a three-day recess, starting this moment."

CHAPTER 46

Felippe and Eugène

Having recalled Lydie's mention of a doctor she had met, who appeared to understand her psychological condition and behavior, Felippe felt compelled to speak with Lydie's lawyer, to tell him of his recollection of his secret visit with her. Perhaps, Lydie would remember and disclose the doctor's name and he could be persuaded to be an expert witness in Lydie's defense. Before he left the courtroom, Felippe jumped from his seat to the floor of the courtroom and introduced himself briefly to Lydie's lawyer, M. Harmignies. He introduced himself quickly to him and, taking as little time as necessary, told him briefly about Lydie's once-upon-a-time doctor.

The evidence presented to the court thus far did not support Lydie's innocence on every count, and Monsieur Harmignies seemed immediately interested. He expressed his belief that any *medical* evidence suggesting that her husband's cruelty caused Lydie's strange behavior leading up to, during and following the murder, would be useful. It might help convince the jury to be lenient.

He politely asked Felippe to please repeat his name—he had hurriedly introduced himself in a noisy location filled with conversation by others, and truly had not properly heard his name.

Felippe excused himself for not speaking clearly. "My name is Felippe Van Hendryk."

M. Harmignies immediately replied, "I'm very pleased to meet you, sir. I imagine that every lawyer in Belgium knows who you are; I'm honored to know that you're on our side. Be assured that your advice will be appreciated, sir."

Felippe blushed a bit and asked if they might deal with one another on a first-name basis.

The answer was, "I would be honored. I am Eugène. What do you prefer to be called?"

Felippe laughed a little and smiled warmly. "I'm Felippe." He asked, 'Is it possible to meet at my place early this evening for a quiet, private chat about your hard task, so I could pass onto you a little more about Lydie. You might find it informative."

***

"Perhaps you've noticed that there are five of us who sit together at every session and observe the proceedings closely?" asked Felippe as he poured two glasses of brandy.

Lydie's lawyer had come to the private meeting Felippe had suggested and now smiled warmly at his new friend. "Yes, I have noticed the group and have wondered who you are and your purpose. Frankly, I imagined that you were members of the press."

"I ought to let you know that King Leopold is aware of the case because the little he's heard made him think it might be about captive wives, a subject in which he's interested, and wanted his legal staff to attend. However, although I agreed to attend, I informed him, without supplying any personal details, that I would appreciate his considering my presence here as a simple, temporary leave from my position on his legal staff. I had already done some groundwork on the count for him on another pretrial matter, and he knows that I trashed the count harder than I have ever in my career denigrated anyone. The king was generously accommodating. I'm telling you this to let you know that my interest is purely personal and is in no way related to my occupation."

Eugène seemed to understand, although he was not sure what Felippe's "purely personal" interest was.

Felippe continued, I have, myself, been impressed by your attempt to defend Countess Lydie, and I share your obvious frustration and difficulty in finding credible arguments to prove her innocence. It saddens me even to consider the likelihood that the jury may find her an accomplice and send that lovely woman to prison. I believe her to be completely innocent. On the other hand, the testimony that seems to incriminate her is disheartening."

"I share your sentiment entirely," answered Eugène.

"Obviously, you do. You wouldn't be defending her if you thought otherwise."

As Felippe spoke, it was evident to Eugène that the downhearted fellow was convinced that she was unlikely to be found entirely innocent. It was, therefore, evident that he was unaware of the immensely important *in camera* session that Eugène had attended but was under oath not to share with anyone. He wished that he could relieve Felippe's fear by informing him of the session, during which Lydie presented testimony that was strongly persuasive in her favor. Her characterization of her husband's brutal behavior and threats to kill her if she did not cooperate with him in his personal plot to kill her brother were quite successful. Eugène's belief was that the jury was now tending toward broad lenience.

This confidential session was so secret that its contents were not printed in the official trial transcript; Eugène simply could not apprise Felippe of the confidential information he now knew practically by heart. The details of Lydie's personal life with the count were so salacious that it was thought best, for Lydie's dignity, to share it in detail only with the judge and jury.

Felippe continued, "So, I wanted you to be aware of information I have that you might find interesting, useful, and worth exploring.

"Many years ago, before Count de Bocarmé and the countess met, Lydie and I had a close friendship," Felippe confided. "The fact is, we were deeply in love. However, circumstances pulled us apart; I left Brussels, attended university in Zürich, was married and divorced, and then returned to Brussels to assume a position on King Leopold's legal staff.

"Lydie felt as sick about our severance as I did. It was when I was carrying out the king's investigation of Count Hippolyte de Bocarmé that I was shocked to learn that Lydie had become his wife and even more shocked to observe how she had changed since I last saw her years earlier. She appeared frightened, and I recall thinking that her behavior was that of a captured animal.

"At considerable danger for my life, I arranged for Lydie and me to meet secretly and all too briefly. We had an hour together on the day following my meeting with her husband, and it became clear to me that she was living in an extremely abusive relationship.

"Before we parted, she referred to a doctor who, she said, understood her problems well. She never mentioned the doctor's name clearly, but I have concluded that, if this doctor could be located, he might be willing to provide testimony on Lydie's behalf, and the jury might be sympathetic. It struck me that there would be nothing to lose if you could get the name of this doctor from Lydie and try to find him.

"I did learn, about five years ago, that Lydie had a serious nervous breakdown over the forced breakup of our love affair and that the doctor she saw is a famous psychiatrist, an expert on sexually demented psychopaths and how they treat their captive wives. I'm merely guessing, but it may be the same doctor to whom Nurse deFrance made reference when she testified.

"Problem is, during my meeting with Lydie, she cried so hard that I couldn't catch the doctor's name. I'd be willing to wager, though, that Lydie remembers his name. He was the father of one of her college classmates, and I think I was told that her name is Rose. There is a young neurologist in Bruges who is friendly with Rose and she may have let a very personal 'cat' out of the bag. This is possibly how I learned that Lydie visited her professor father to seek psychiatric counseling. His home and office were in Bruges."

Eugène was strongly impressed by Felippe's information. He was a wise man, who realized the potentially consolidating effect of an effective lecture by a medical authority who is an expert on the trauma and troubles of captive wives. Lydie was a textbook example of a captive wife. If the doctor is a good teacher, he ought to be able to glue together the multiple types of mental and physical injuries, whose continuation was bound to cause her death in a very few years.

Lawyer Harmignies opined that, if a bright, persuasive doctor could use lay language to paint an authoritative description of the lives of captive wives, Lydie might well be found not guilty on all counts.

"Felippe, I am most grateful to you. I will speak to 'Lydie,' as you so casually refer to the countess. I shall go visit her immediately and will tell her of our conversation. We must do everything possible and within our power to try to convince the court that her behavior was involuntarily contorted by duress. If she remembers the Bruges doctor's name, I will head for Bruges tonight."

"I know you'll do all you can to keep her spirits high. I leave it to you whether to whisper in her ear that, if she's found not guilty, I will be waiting for her in a cab in the exit road just outside the courtroom. If, by any chance, she does not exit, I will be the first to visit her in prison, as soon as that is possible."

"I'll take care of it, Felippe," promised Eugène, shaking Felippe's hand firmly. Then he ran off.

***

Although it was close to 8:00 in the evening, Monsieur Harmignies visited Lydie at the jail and excitedly reported on his conversation with Felippe regarding a doctor with whom Lydie had a meeting some years ago.

"Yes, yes, yes, Monsieur Harmignies. A classmate of mine introduced me to her father, Dr. André LeBrun, during the intermission at a play that I attended in Bruges long before I was married. I spent the night at their home, and Dr. LeBrun expressed concern over what he interpreted to be the cause of my sadness and lack of joie de vivre. He warned me about my excessive trusting idealism, which he found unusually strong and potentially dangerous. He urged me to be more careful with respect to whom I am willing to trust.

"If I had followed his advice more closely, I would never have ended up marrying a psychopath. He did warn me never to try to take on the burden of helping a socially backward man. The last words he said were, 'Always leave that to another man.'

"I spent some time telling him of the loss that had occurred in my life and the hatred that I bore for the mother of the person I loved. I recall his telling me that he trained as a medical doctor in Paris and that his postgraduate research was psychiatry, neuropsychiatry, or something like that.

"He has probably written books on the subject; I think he was a recognized authority on human behavior. He took time to tell me that I needed a more optimistic outlook on life and that I should travel and meet new people and make new friends, in order to forget the man with whom I had fallen in love.

"I remember his warning me to avoid men whom he described as being morally insane. He talked about men who appeared normal but who have severe personality disorders. In retrospect, his words now seem prophetic, since they describe Hippolyte. This conversation took place so many years ago that I had forgotten about it. Dr. LeBrun was living in Bruges. I remember his giving me a card with his contact information, but I would not know where to find it."

"Thank you, thank you, thank you, Countess Lydie," was all that Monsieur Harmignies said as he hurriedly left Lydie's quarters at the jail.

Fortunately, the trial was in recess for three days. Lydie's lawyer left Mons immediately for Bruges to find Dr. LeBrun.

Upon his arrival in Bruges, Monsieur Harmignies at once took a cab to the police station, hoping that Dr. LeBrun's name would be recognized and get directions to his home or office.

CHAPTER 47

Dr. LeBrun

"Dr. LeBrun is very well known in Mons," an officer responded to Monsieur Harmignies inquiry. "His office is at Trente Rue de la Paix, which can be easily found as it is the street which borders the gardens beside the museum. Dr. LeBrun is a very busy man."

"Merci, Monsieur," was M. Harmignies' hurried response as he rushed from the police station to his carriage.

He found LeBrun's office easily and concluded that the doctor might be available because a few people sat in a reception area apparently waiting to see him.

"May I help you?" a middle-aged lady who appeared to be a receptionist asked, as M. Harmignies entered the room.

"I have an urgent need to see Dr. LeBrun, Madame."

"*So*, you have an appointment, monsieur?"

"I am sorry to say that I do not, but I have just arrived from Mons, and my need to see him is urgent. In fact, it relates to a matter of life or death. It is not my intention to interfere with his schedule, but my need to see Dr. LeBrun relates to a matter of great importance."

"What is your name, monsieur?"

"My name is Eugène Harmignies. I am a lawyer representing someone in Mons who is known to the doctor, and I believe he will have an interest in speaking with me."

"Please have a seat, monsieur, and I will tell Dr. LeBrun that you are here. He has a full schedule today, but he might find it possible to see you after he learns of your reasons for wanting to see him."

Moments later, the receptionist emerged from the doctor's office and announced, "Dr. LeBrun will see you as soon as his current patient leaves, Monsieur Harmignies."

384

In about twenty minutes, Harmignies was ushered into Dr. LeBrun's office and faced a well-dressed man in his fifties, who seemed to be curious about the reason for meeting him "about a matter of life or death."

"I beg your forgiveness, Doctor, for attempting to speak with you without an appointment, but my mission is an urgent one; it involves someone whom you met years ago, who was a friend of your daughter Rose. When you met her, she was Lydie Fougnies. Today she is Countess Lydie de Bocarmé, and she is being tried for murder."

"Oh, my God!" exclaimed the doctor. I have been following the proceedings of the trial in the newspapers without any knowledge of who the countess was. It appears that she has committed a serious crime with her husband. This is difficult for me to learn, and even more difficult to believe.

"I need more details from you, but I have patients that I must see today. Can you join me for lunch? This will allow us more time to discuss details related to the case as well as your interest in my involvement."

"Yes, Dr. LeBrun, I will be pleased to join you for lunch, and I will wait for you outside your office."

***

Shortly after one o'clock, Dr. LeBrun and Monsieur Harmignies walked a few minutes to a small restaurant where LeBrun was apparently known to the maître d' and the staff, and the two men were escorted to what appeared to be Dr. LeBrun's regular table.

The two men placed their orders, and as each sipped wine, M. Harmignies recounted his meeting last evening with Lydie. It became obvious that Dr. LeBrun remembered his meeting with Lydie, as well as the advice he had given her.

Like most Belgians, he had followed newspaper reports of the trial carefully and was aware of some of the alleged cruelty that

Lydie had endured in her marriage. Without hesitation, he said he would need all available details related to Lydie's marriage to Count de Bocarmé, much of which had been reported in the newspapers.

"I remember Lydie Fougnies well, but the Countess de Bocarmé, who is on trial for murder, is definitely not the person I remember. There is much that I do not know, but I have no reservations in telling you that I will serve as a witness in her defense, if I am confident that she is not guilty.

"There is little doubt in my mind, even with limited information, that you are dealing with a classic case in which a woman has been under the total control of a man who has exhibited the symptoms of someone who is morally insane.

"Unfortunately, this syndrome is not well known or understood in the medical community, but I will do whatever I can to try to convince the jury that Lydie did not willingly commit a crime.

"Lydie Fougnies somehow became the captive of a cruel husband. Her behavior, which unfortunately included participation in the death of her brother, was not of her own volition but resulted from fear of death at the hands of her husband. Although not widely understood by medical professionals, it is a real syndrome, which I would explain in court.

"From what I have read in the newspapers, it is my professional opinion that Lydie exhibits symptoms typical of victimization and deserves leniency. I will cancel my appointments for the balance of this week and will return with you to Mons."

For the first time since Monsieur Harmignies began his defense of Countess Lydie de Bocarmé, he believed deeply in his client's innocence in the death of her brother. His challenge now was to prove this in court, with Dr. LeBrun providing important testimony.

He made available to Dr. LeBrun the printed notes to date of the trial, including the all-important testimony of the secret session where Lydie was able to communicate so openly and confidentially with the judge, her lawyers, and the jury. The contents of that session moved emotions even in Dr. LeBrun. It lent him a high degree of confidence that he could successfully influence the jury toward lenience, perhaps to a full not-guilty verdict. The doctor was a very bright student; no nuance slipped past him. He wrote well, and when he spoke, he demonstrated a fitting degree of oratory aimed exclusively at the jury.

He kept entirely to himself the information that he had twice previously spoken to the chief juryman, Dr. Gauthier, at medical society meetings here in Mons. He had reason to believe that his presentations had twice found Gauthier interested and sympathetic to his views. Nothing was to be gained by informing even Monsieur Harmignies.

Judge Lyon's obvious sympathy for Lydie was a favorable indicator, to say the least.

CHAPTER 48

A Defense Strategy

In anticipation of the announcement of a verdict on the day when the court reconvened, the crowd outside the courthouse was especially large, many having arrived at the courthouse early in the morning hoping to get a glimpse of the accused count and his wife as they entered and left the courthouse. Most observers had little doubt that the count and countess would be found guilty and sentenced to death by guillotine.

The packed courtroom fell silent as members of the jury entered and took their seats. Hushed whispers filled the courtroom as the count and the countess were escorted, separately, to their bench seats accompanied by their defense attorneys. Everyone rose from his or her seat as Judge Lyon entered the courtroom.

Judge Lyon spoke, "We have heard testimony from those representing the accused, and it is my duty to instruct the jury regarding their obligations.

"Because of the severity of the crime with which the defendants are charged, it is my responsibility to assure the king that they have been granted *every* opportunity to defend themselves against the charges brought against them."

Addressing the lawyers representing the accused, Judge Lyon continued, "Is there anything that remains to be shared with this court prior to the members of the jury deliberating and arriving at a judgment?"

Monsieur Harmignies immediately stood. Looking first at the judge and then at the jury, he made the following statement. "Two people, the Count and the Countess de Bocarmé, have been charged with the serious crime of murder.

"You have heard testimony from many witnesses. It would not be correct if testimony of *any kind* were left unheard, and it is my duty to report this morning that information has been brought to my attention that I am *obliged* to share with this court."

Judge Lyon was taken by surprise.

***

Lydie's lawyer continued, "There is no question that Countess Lydie was involved in the murder of her brother, but was her involvement voluntary? Were Countess Lydie's actions the result of a damaged mind, a mind that had been molded to follow the commands of someone, her husband, who controlled her actions with death as the penalty for her disobedience?"

"Goddamned nonsense. Damned lies!" shouted Hippolyte, who stood up in anger. (After three days in solitary confinement, he was allowed to leave his cold, concrete-floored cell to be present at meetings of the court. He looked no worse for his time in solitary confinement.)

"Another outburst from you, monsieur, and I will have you removed from my courtroom. You insult me and my court, and I will not tolerate another similar outburst," Judge Lyon reprimanded Hippolyte.

Monsieur Harmignies continued, "I am no expert on human behavior. Few in the medical profession have studied the behavior of severely abused individuals and would be able to speak with authority about the subject. We have an exceptional witness with us today—a medical authority who *can* speak and *is* one of Europe's most authoritative sources of information about the effects of abuse on human beings.

"I beg the court's attention to testimony of Dr. André LeBrun, a distinguished neurologist. He has spent his professional life studying the behavior of people held in captivity, an issue of the first order in

389

this trial. This case is destined to rank high in legal history. Our guest witness has studied and analyzed its recorded trial records closely. I have no doubt, Your Honor and members of the jury, that we are mandated to assure posterity that we sought an expert to share with us what the trial record can tell us about the defendants' behavior before, during, and after a particularly notorious murder.

"It is my opinion that this new witness's testimony must be taken into account in considering innocence or guilt of either defendant. To dismiss his information about abused captive wives would be regrettable. I ask the court to listen to Dr. André LeBrun."

"This *is* highly unusual, Monsieur Harmignies, but unless Messieurs Lachaud and dePaepe have objections, I invite Dr. André LeBrun to address this court after being sworn to tell the full truth."

No one expected to hear so eloquent a lecture. LeBrun's well-tempered lines struck and stuck in the minds of every juryman. Had they been allowed to clap their hands, they would have. He held their riveted attention, especially after he explained some simple but needed vocabulary. The especially poignant lines and paragraphs have been emphasized.

CHAPTER 49

Dr. LeBrun's Testimony

Dr. LeBrun walked slowly to the witness stand, where he swore that he would tell the entire truth and nothing else. His expression; bearing; and immaculately pressed, dark blue suit marked him as a professional of some importance. He carried with him some papers, and with a short, slight smile, he pulled out a page that he reviewed for a few seconds before looking around the crowded and silent courtroom.

He looked pleasantly at the members of the jury, who stared back at him as they anticipated hearing what he might contribute to what they had already learned. Dr. LeBrun addressed only the judge and jurymen, not the courtroom voyeurs.

"I am honored to be invited to share my analysis of this complicated trial, and the conclusions I have drawn from them. I beg your patience when I repeat some of what you have already heard. Perhaps the redundancy will strengthen my conclusions. Like you, I seek the truth, and I believe that we must consider every ounce of available evidence before we reach a verdict." His diction was that of a professional person without a trace of affectation. He had a friendly, authoritative voice of midrange frequency.

He could be deadly serious, and he *was* as he said, "My role today is not to blindly support Countess Lydie. My purpose is to present my opinion on how Countess Lydie became involved, to any degree, in the worst of all crimes.

"To understand what I have to say requires simply knowing the difference in meaning between two phrases. They are '*willing only for a personally compelling reason*'"—he paused—"and '*willing because the end serves a useful purpose.*' It is essential to understand the difference between the two, if we are to pass fair judgment on the countess's innocence or guilt. We must know if Lydie was an

391

enthusiastic helper who shared the motivations of the murderer as he conceived and prepared to carry out his dastardly act. Or might she have *perfunctorily* facilitated the murderer's project knowing that it was obscene, because refusal to do it would probably cost her life and leave three small children motherless. In deciding whether Lydie Fougnies planned the murder, we must consider the evidence we now have of *her* truthfulness, against the truthfulness of the man who *did* commit the murder.

"The jury now possesses *inarguable evidence* that the murderer is a *pathological liar*."

The line affected every member of the jury. Each of them nodded.

You, members of the jury, now know that he did beat his wife cruelly with regularity. You now know the sick reasons that led him to beat her nearly daily, almost from the day they married. You know the severity of those beatings from Sister deFrance's records. You know, as well, the testimony of the good Anne Morceau, the only secret friend Lydie had while she suffered as a *captive wife* in a sixteenth-century, isolated chateau.

"*Captive wife!* This term is the heart of my testimony.

"Having beaten her with his fists and slapped her face, he ordered her to write threatening letters to Antoinette de Dudzcèle (he cannot write literately) and then made Lydie figure out a way to hide her handwriting or suffer another excruciating beating. Yet he had the audacity to demand 'proof that I have ever beaten my wife.' When he got it, he wanted to have a fistfight with Judge Lyon, 'to see who's the better man.'

"Actually, the difference between the two attitudes, *willing* and not *really* willing, will automatically come clear to you in colors, gentlemen, if you allow me to insert *one* medical term. I want you to know: the term *Moral Insanity*."

He paused and looked into each of the twelve jurymen's faces, paying no additional time when he caught the eye of Dr. François Gauthier, who practiced in Hyon, a village near Mons.

392

Dr. LeBrun did not know this chairman of the jury well, but he remembered that Dr. Gauthier had attended the two lectures he had given, in past years, to members of the Medical Society of Mons. Most of those who attended had listened with congenial interest to those two lectures about Moral Insanity. They knew that Dr. LeBrun was dedicated to educating his fellow physicians about its social significance.

The doctor now provided the same, presumably new, information to the judge and jury. "Moral Insanity is a term for a serious disease. Doctors working in research hospitals understand its manifestations but not its cause. Regrettably, the majority of practicing medical doctors—*certainly not all*—are unaware of it.

"Moral Insanity is primarily a disease of men. They lack a normal conscience, and so they are unable to understand the emotional trauma, pain, and distress that they inflict on others because it provides them with a near-sexual delight. Morally insane men can be fairly intelligent; they can cleverly hide evidence of their disorder. Since they like attractive women, they are motivated to play this game. This is why good-looking women can mistakenly marry morally insane men without knowing it.

"These poor women learn, too late, about the sadistic side of their husbands, who feel no shame in beating them. Morally insane husbands can threaten their wives into doing what they command even when the wives know these actions are wrong. There are cases—the law courts have the records—of men threatening their wives with torture or death if they disobey their commands, even if it involves killing someone."

The jurymen sat up a bit straighter, faced one another, and furrowed their brows. Dr. LeBrun had awakened them from any inclination they may have felt that this was just another plea from a sociology professor.

"Wives whose insane husbands do not allow them to leave the house have developed a variety of survival strategies," Dr.

LeBrun continued. "Some, who have suffered brutal dominance and captivity for a long time, will simply give up. They learn to *protect* their savage husbands when they are in financial or other trouble by lying for them. The act of self-preservation has become a powerful psychological survival strategy. Another survival strategy trick that captive wives use is to do more than simply protect their husbands. A captive wife will *regularly display positive feelings* for her husband. By positive feelings, we mean extending unusual displays of kindness and generosity, even to the extent of acquiring useful gifts for these often pitiless men, in an effort to avoid beatings or diminish the frequency with which they are beaten.

"*Of special concern are captive wives like Lydie, who feel they no longer have control over their personal fates.* They suffer intense fear of physical harm because they know implicitly that their domination lies in arbitrary whims of tormentors who are crazy men like Hippolyte de Bocarmé.

"These women comprise a category of captive wives whose members may add *very* desperate tactics to their survival strategies. They are known to resort to a *nearly unspeakable strategy*—they will treat their contemptible husbands affectionately and flirtatiously, hoping to save their lives. However, it is fortunate that this abnormal survival mechanism is not fixed in perpetuity. If it were, they could never recover, and most of them *can* recover."

The members of the jury raised their heads and exchanged words. They were pleased.

"When children are involved, the problem becomes much more complex. The tormented wife will frequently bear torture and brutality in order not to lose her children. Wives who have gone so far as to avail themselves for sexual intercourse, with feigned declarations of love before, during, and after the performances, usually exhibit deep embarrassment and *feel deep guilt* even in the face of clear innocence.

394

"Typically, these women thoroughly despise their husbands and wish they could hurt them even as they display romantic love and attachment. If freed, *even these women will recover*, although they usually need professional counseling."

Again the jurymen raised their heads and exchanged words.

"There is no doubt whatsoever in *my* mind that what Countess Lydie has experienced fits the characterization of a victimized wife who was convinced that her husband, Count Hippolyte de Bocarmé, would severely beat her or, in the case of her brother, kill her, if she did not cooperate with his demands.

"The count made it clear to her that she would suffer his revenge, including death, if she betrayed him, and he frequently reminded Lydie of his power over her. His history of violence toward her convinced her that her obedience and allegiance were her *only* survival options. The count knew that he was dealing with a straight-speaking woman, one who understood reality. In the case of the Countess Lydie, we see one of the worst possible examples of an ill-treated captive wife. The jury must find a way to relieve her of the ghastly threat she has bravely faced for four and a half years. You are capable men who have the power to invent your *own* strategies.

"I challenge this court to find anyone who knew Lydie Fougnies before she became Countess Lydie de Bocarmé who will confirm under oath that both are the same person. Personally, I am of the opinion that she is a recoverable individual.

"This woman has been the victim of a sadistic and evil husband, who beat and raped her on their wedding night. Hippolyte used his power over his wife to force her to help him in a murder. Lydie is still alive only because she *steeled herself* to tolerate his abuse to preserve *her* life and the lives of her three children."

Dr. LeBrun had not quite finished. He now orated, "In my hand is written testimony presented earlier by Sister Ida deFrance, a medical professional, who provided sworn evidence to this court that she had examined Countess Lydie de Bocarmé immediately after her arrest."

(His words reminded jurors of the exposure of the count as a pathological liar, which nearly all of them suspected but wondered how it could ever be proved)

His next words were powerfully effective. "We must all force ourselves to answer the following question: Is it likely that Countess de Bocarmé's bruises, observed over her entire body, were self-inflicted? Would anyone, particularly someone with the countess's intelligence, display such brutality to herself? She was not crazy. She had no known psychiatric maladies. She had children she loved and beautifully cared for. Obviously, someone else had to have inflicted this punishment."

Dr. LeBrun thereby cut off the only remaining counterargument that Hippolyte's lawyers might use, although it would have been a very weak counterargument.

The courtroom became silent—stunned—and remained that way for a minute or more. It was a dramatic reaction to a dramatic address. The jurymen were especially affected and influenced even more than were the seated ticket holders. They used animated talk to relieve the ferment of emotions that LeBrun stirred up in them!

Members of the audience seated close to the small area the jury occupied reported hearing Dr. Gauthier remark, "This professor doesn't fool around."

Another juryman spoke loudly enough to be heard saying, "That man hit the nail on the head."

Without question, the men of the jury remained spellbound longer than the crowd that attended the trial only as voyeurs.

Lydie's highly confidential *in camera* testimony had only recently been shown to the jurymen. The jury seemed to be a strongly pro-Lydie group.

***

"Is Sister Ida deFrance present in the courtroom?" asked the judge. Sister Ida deFrance, dressed in her white uniform, stood up.

"Please remember that you remain under oath to speak only the truth. I ask the following question: Do you know Dr. LeBrun?"

"No, Monsieur le President, but I am aware of his reputation. I am a registered nurse, and I am familiar with his work. He is considered the foremost authority on the psychology of captive women."

The jurymen would remember the exchange that followed.

"Will you confirm that what Dr. LeBrun read is an accurate transcript of your testimony?" the judge asked.

"Yes, Monsieur le President," the nurse replied, adding "This type of behavioral strategy is quite common knowledge to those who explore how the brain reacts to stress, but there is also a growing number of practicing medical doctors who know about it. A few are considered authorities on this subject, and Dr. LeBrun is probably the best known of them; his work is now appearing in educational nursing mail."

"Thank you, Sister, you may be seated," the judge said.

Turning to the witness stand, he added, "Please continue, Dr. LeBrun."

"Monsieur le President and members of the jury, I thank you for having given me the opportunity to share a medical opinion which, I hope, explains Countess Lydie's involvement in the murder of her brother. Your understanding of her suffering and fear should contribute to a fair judgment.

"I have nothing more to say."

Turning to the count's lawyer, Monsieur Lachaud, Judge Lyon asked, "Do you have any questions for this witness, sir?"

"Dr. LeBrun," asked Monsieur Lachaud, "Why is it that the insanity you have described is not known in the medical profession?"

"It *is* known, sir, but only by those doctors who have studied the condition. Unfortunately, most medical schools emphasize the human body in their training and neglect problems of the human mind.

"Human behavior is affected by *many* causes, but because *physical* problems are more easily observed and detected, emphasis has been placed on studying these, and *mental* problems have been largely ignored."

"What confidences can this court and the jury place in your opinions, Dr. LeBrun?" Lachaud pressed.

"Only the confidence that over thirty years of investigation in human psychological problems deserve, sir. Neuropsychiatrists throughout Europe are increasingly recognizing the affliction I described for Count Hippolyte de Bocarmé, and they have concluded that treatment of mental problems deserves attention.

"Count de Bocarmé's condition has been observed on numerous occasions, but premeditated murder has not yet been the crime in cases with which *I* happen to be familiar. However, several other neuropsychiatrists have encountered it."

"I have no further questions for this witness, Monsieur le President."

***

To more than a few, however, pretty Lydie still appeared to be a good actress. Testimony about her angelic character by two upper-class women with whom she had ingratiated herself was a mild advantage for her.

However, affirmations by the plain folk of Peruwelz, those who thought they knew her best because they had had to deal directly with her, were compelling. For them, Lydie left the impression, understandably, of an overt liar, a cunning cheat, and a snob with a cruel, selfish streak.

None had even an intimation of the cloud of fear under which she lived in her marriage or why she'd adopted a haughty, sometimes fierce, demeanor. These folks tended to be skeptical of Dr. LeBrun's testimony.

On the other hand, only the jury had the testimony Lydie supplied in the all-important closed session. The public did not know about that all-important, informative testimony. It was kept confidential to protect Lydie's dignity.

CHAPTER 50

Closing Argument of the Prosecuting Attorney

The president of the court seemed to be in a cheerful mood when he addressed the audience and asked their cooperation in the final moments of the trial. This was, he made clear, a time for lawyers of the prosecution and defense to make their final pleas to the jury. He asked for silence in the courtroom out of respect for the speakers.

The king's prosecutor, de Maubant, rose to his feet. Maubant was expensively dressed and spoke with an unusually strong accent of an aristocrat. He read his speech from behind a lectern.

"Gentlemen of the jury," he began his closing arguments, "I believe that we have satisfied the Act of Accusation. From the moment of their marriage, two ambitious individuals each committed a serious crime.

"The little, middle-class girl wanted to be a countess; the count with no fortune wanted to be rich. Their common inclination and ambition was to own the fortune of the unfortunate Gustave Fougnies.

"With one accord, they worked together to prepare the means to steal it from him. They used underhanded and murderous means to gain their ends, but neither of them should be able to benefit from these actions. All of their work was carried on in secret and with malice.

"Gustave had regained his health and was able to marry. This is the reason that led them to decide to kill him. We know that they bought instruments to prepare a particularly nasty poison.

"The count used an alias, Monsieur Berant, to hide his true identity from a chemistry professor and a manufacturer of a distillatory. By November 10, 1850, they had the poison ready to be used. She sent various messages to her brother, Gustave, to attract him to the Chateau de Bitremont.

"On November 20, at 5:00 p.m., there was a meeting between the Bocarmés and Gustave. It was in a dining room that seemed perfectly secure. The coachmen and maids were scattered from the scene. At the instance of the assassination, the victim's cries signaled the attack on his life.

"Inspection of the cadaver was consistent with murder; the state of the clothing and the wounds of the assassin are proof of foul play. The wife admits it, and the investigation has established it, without question.

"There was a second person present during the perpetration of the crime. It was the countess, who shared the interests of her husband, and she did everything she could to facilitate and assure the execution of her brother. There is no doubt that the husband was the perpetrator, no doubt that the wife was either perpetrator or was sympathetically complicit.

"In her interrogation, she contradicted herself about important circumstances or avoided answering by testifying, 'I don't remember.' She never narrated the facts in the same way when she testified. As for her husband, he was not able to avoid mistakes in answering questions.

"He is a rogue, a hypocrite, and a miserable imposter, which he proved one hundred percent of the time during the trial. He had the audacity to say that the role he played for his wife was perfect—that, as far as he was concerned, he did not accuse this woman, that in fact he was her protector. He protected her even while *she* denounced him.

"There is no doubt of his culpability, but there has been an attempt to argue about the capacity of the instruments he owned, to make pure nicotine. That is an absurdity because, Professor Stas in his report, which for me is the written truth, has said that there is not, in this whole country, an equal quantity of nicotine which would cost less than eight or ten thousand francs to purchase. Neither he nor she had that kind of money.

"The accused count, after declaring that there was no fight possible, was contradicted by Emerance Bricout. She described the remarkable degree of disorder in the dining room after the event. The derangement of furniture was quite like what Justine Thibaut and Charlotte Monjardez heard when they put their ears to the frame of the kitchen door.

"Gentlemen, you have had more than enough opportunity to hear a special portion of the testimony, and most recently, you have been exposed to information which casts serious doubt on whether the count tells the truth.

"The extensive detective work we have carried out and presented to you is sufficient to consider the accused Visart an instigator of murder. As for his wife, if she is not a co-instigator, and we believe she is, at the very least, she is an accomplice to a vicious crime, the murder of her own brother—all for the sake of stealing his money."

CHAPTER 51

A Plea in Defense of the Count

Monsieur Lachaud rose from his seat and began his closing argument by standing directly in front of the short, wooden panel that separated the jury from the courtroom. He was about sixty-five years old, was clean-shaven, and wore a standard blue business suit. He appeared healthy. He gesticulated only moderately as he tried to appeal to sentimentality, although his tone of voice was oratorical, not conversational.

"Gentlemen of the jury, as the defending attorney of the accused Visart de Bocarmé, I ask you not to be taken in by the emotion of the moment. You have sat through long and lamentable arguments that sadden me, which I am going to speak briefly to you about.

"When I sat on the prisoners' 'bench of ignominy,' I was filled with a sense of sadness to see the beautiful names of our most beloved citizens, names respected and esteemed up to this moment, but now associated with depravity. It bothers me more than I can describe to anticipate that the honorable, unbroken line of the nobles named de Bocarmé, who fought gallantly for Belgium's freedom and independence, may be broken irrevocably if it is *your* wish to carry out this destruction.

"I cried for *them*. I cried for the de Bocarmé family of all Belgium and specifically of Bury. I cried *particularly* for the three children, poor little creatures born for disgrace, who do not know, lucky children, that at this supreme moment, their honor, their lives could perhaps be fractured forever. But only if this is your will. I know that you tremble with fear in drawing up the verdict. You have the right to tremble with fear because the accusations have not been enlightening.

403

"It honors me to know that I have before me at the moment men of intelligence and character. I have in this court a magistrate who listens only to his conscience, who deals only with reason, who does not allow the clamor of the crowd to influence his views.

"Monsieur de Maubant, the King's prosecutor, thinks it unnecessary to occupy himself, or take into consideration, a complete résumé of the case. As far as I am concerned, I wish to take a different track. I wish to examine this affair *as a whole*. It is time to set aside miserable petty details. It is time for us to discuss all the serious arguments.

"Thank you and God Bless you, especially your children and their futures."

(Note that Lachaud made no direct mention of the count.)

CHAPTER 52

Lawyer de Paepe's Insertion

Of special interest is an intriguing half column of stenographically recorded conversation in *Procès de Bocarmé* (p. 277, 14 June 1851). This was the final day of the trial, and the half column is the last printed material in the book.

At the rare *in camera* session (Chapter 43) Judge Lyon had reminded those who attended—only the count's lawyers, Lydie's lawyers, and two stenographers—of their solemn oaths to keep all that they heard strictly confidential. He added. "Violation of the oath will be a punishable breach of law."

Regardless, Attorney dePaepe, representing the count, did less than his best to let posterity know of the secret session by an extralegal means. He inserted into the record the following three sentences dated "Audience de 14 June, 1851,[34] asserting "…my client, Hippolyte de Bocarmé, wished to insert it." (Obviously, Hippolyte was unable to have written what follows):

> *"1. The accused Lydie Fougnies was interrogated on May 27, by the president in the absence of the accused Visart de Bocarmé;*
>
> *2. The audience was emptied without M. le President giving any account of what transpired in their absence;*
>
> *3. When M. the President interrogated the accused Hippolyte de Bocarmé the following day, May 28, he was not*

---

[34] May 27 was the date of the trial's first session. The entirety was devoted to a cross-examination of Lydie. Judge Lyon examined her in open court before a full audience. It was not a secret session!

informed, either before or after his interrogation, of his wife's responses to questions asked of her in secret."

Interestingly, lawyer dePaepe used a grossly incorrect date for the only secret session held during the trial. Secret sessions are always marked by an emptying of the courtroom. The May 27 session was open to a public audience! Judge Lyon must have noticed dePaepe's mistaken dating but wisely assumed that the question was directed to Lydie's answers to his questions in the June *in camera* session. He did not correct the falsified date for the official trial record. His response:

"To set things straight regarding the question put by the counsel for Visart de Bocarmé (after having reviewed the question by repeating its essence) is: "On May 28, Visart de Bocarmé was interrogated in his turn after Lydie Fougnies had undergone her interrogation. During and immediately after his interrogation and before attending to any of their court business, the president reminded the accused Visart that his lawyer had a copy of everything said and done in Visart's (voluntary) absence from the preceding session of May 27."

DePaepe's client, the count, chose not to rebut any of Lydie's secret testimony (in the closed June session) about daily sexual molestation, brutal fist beatings and credible death threats she suffered for 4½ years. Her *testimony* plus the court's proof that the count was a pathological liar almost certainly convinced his senior lawyer Lachaud that his client was guilty. Junior counsel dePaepe's sneaky insertion into the official record is, ironically, proof to posterity that *one* secret session *was* held in the first week of June, 1851. It allowed Lydie to answer Judge Lyon's queries persuasively and makes her secret testimony a warranted insertion. Jurors had to weigh a jolting tale of Lydie's life at a chateau when they convened to decide if she willingly encouraged and assisted in the murder of her brother, to inherit his wealth, as the Prosecutor charged in his summation to the jury. The penalty of a guilty verdict would, categorically, have been an ignominious beheading by guillotine, if dePaepe had swayed the jurors.

CHAPTER 53

June 14, 1851

Every layperson in the courtroom was anxious to know the jury's verdicts. Practically everyone imagined that the count was guilty. The air was tense. Might there be more evidence introduced? Judge Lyon was chatting with several people gathered about his dais having an unanimated conversation. Its meaning was unknown. At last, the chatter around the judge ended, and he struck the gavel strongly.

"It is agreed, by attorneys for the defense and the prosecutors, that the case may now be heard by the jury of twelve men who have impressed all of us with the attention they have shown and the illuminating questions they have asked.

"M. Adrien Gauthier, Chairman of the Jury, is your body of twelve persons ready and able to begin to study the testimony and deliver individual verdicts?"

"Yes, Monsieur le President, we are."

The president remained standing

Then, without reading, he announced, "I declare the debates closed. Gentlemen of the jury, you have attended a long and contentious investigation to which you have paid close and careful attention. Here are the questions to which you have to respond He read what follows:

"**One**. Alfred-Julien-Gabriel-Gérard-Hippolyte-Visart, Count de Bocarmé, here accused, is he guilty of voluntarily committing a criminal attempt at Bury, on November 20, 1851, on the life of Gustave Fougnies, his brother-in-law, with a substance able to cause death more or less quickly?

"**Two**. Alfred-Julien-Gabriel-Gérard-Hippolyte-Visart, Count de Bocarmé, here accused, is he, in the slightest way, complicit in the

408

criminal act referenced in question one, for having given instructions for its commission?

"**Three**. Alfred-Julien-Gabriel-Gérard-Hippolyte-Visart, Count de Bocarmé, here accused, is he guilty for having procured any substance all, or in part, to abet the act cited in question one?

"**Four**. Is Alfred-Julien-Gabriel-Gérard-Hippolyte-Visart, Count de Bocarmé, here accused, in the slightest way guilty of knowingly aiding the perpetrator of the crime described in question one?

"**Five**. Lydie Victoire-Joseph-Fougnies, wife of the Count de Bocarmé, here accused, is she guilty of voluntarily committing a criminal attempt at Bury, November 20, 1850, on the life of Gustave Fougnies, her brother, with a substance able to cause death more or less quickly?

"**Six**. Lydie Victoire-Joseph-Fougnies, wife of the Count de Bocarmé, here accused, is she, in the slightest way, complicit in the criminal act referenced in question one, for having given instructions for its commission?

"**Seven**. Lydie Victoire-Joseph-Fougnies, wife of the Count de Bocarmé, here accused, is she guilty for having procured any substance all, or in part, to abet the act cited in question one?

"**Eight**. Is Lydie Victoire-Joseph-Fougnies, wife of the Count de Bocarmé, here accused, in the slightest way guilty of knowingly aiding the perpetrator(s) of the crime described in question one?"

After listing all the questions, the judge said, "Now, I shall call a recess within the courtroom, and, in the meantime, I patiently await your decisions."

CHAPTER 54

The Crowd within the Courtroom

The jurymen retired to the comfortable jury room at the rear of the court as most of the audience stood, stretched, and turned its eyes to the benches where the accused and their lawyers sat. Bailiffs quickly removed the accused to cells, where they individually awaited their fates.

The crowd became impatient, and everyone who'd gathered chatted not only among themselves but with people they had not previously known. The conversation naturally centered on guessing what the jury might decide. A few were alert. They saw M. Lachaud, the well-known Paris lawyer, who had offered to defend the count because he believed that all persons accused of a crime deserve a lawyer, pack his papers into a briefcase. He was putting on his topcoat and leaving the courtroom.

The inference spread through the crowd that Lachaud must have concluded that the jury would find the count guilty—that he might think the count deserved to be found guilty and did not care to be at his client's side when the jury declared its verdict. He left that sad responsibility to his other lawyer, dePaepe of Ghent, who obviated need to abide by an oath. His insertion into the last page of the trial record contains an obvious reference to a session that required emptying the courtroom of all except the jury. His trick was to change the date of the session. Paradoxically, his deed tells posterity that there had indeed been only one closed session for Countess Lydie to testify secretly. An account of the trial 164 years later, in 2015, may justifiably include it in a description of the trial and imagine its likely testimony.

Expectation was that the accused would be executed by a guillotine, the *inflictive and ignominious* way the king's Act of

410

Accusation actually meant in citing Belgium's mid-19th century legal statutes defining capital punishment for premeditated murder.

The populace of Bury and Peruwelz were generally of the opinion that Lydie was, at the very least, an accomplice to a heinous crime. Dr. LeBrun's testimony did not persuade many that Lydie was not knowingly involved either in the murder itself or as a close accomplice to its realization.

Baron Felippe van Hendryk was optimistic that the countess, the woman he still loved, would be acquitted. He was grateful to Judge Lyon's scholarship in bringing up, in detail, the extensive beatings she was exposed to and to the testimony of a caring nurse, who recorded it.

Felippe believed that Dr. LeBrun had presented his lecture brilliantly to the laypersons on the jury. Although he lacked knowledge of the secret exculpatory testimony, Felippe still felt optimistic because the chairman of the jury, Adrien Gauthier, was a practicing physician. Felippe knew that the doctor had attended two of Dr. LeBrun's seminars on captive women and Moral Insanity, which were presented at meetings of the Mons Medical Society and that the attending doctors had received his messages well.

CHAPTER 55

Deliberation

Within the jury room, Dr. Gauthier, the chairman, asked each man, in turn, to provide his general impression of the trial and of the accused. He had a hard time persuading the group to express its feeling about Lydie's possible guilt or innocence due to its strong desire to discuss the count's guilt. Each juryman spoke negatively about the count. Only a minority spoke briefly. They disliked Hippolyte intensely and without equivocation let known their belief that he was, without question, the murderer. None of this denigrating attitude required a single question from Gauthier.

Several cited, among the evidence, the human bite on his finger, and others emphasized that they had carefully listened to and read the testimony of Detective Judge Heughebart. Of the detective's nearly daily interrogations of the count, the jury was primarily impressed by the count's "pleading" behavior, namely, the day the count pointed to a thick folder containing incriminating information about his use of an assumed name in dealing with Professor Loppens and the brazier Van den Bergh of Ghent. Without them, murder with nicotine would not have been possible. He begged Heughebart to "throw that stuff out."

Another asked his colleagues not to overlook cross-examiner Heughebart's testimony that the count was cunning and mean. He tried to slip a forbidden outward-bound letter into an envelope addressed to a Paris lawyer his wife had permission to contact. His purpose was to destroy her relationship with the lawyer and a defense strategy planned for her because it did not include him.

The banker, Orichaud of Chareloi, returned to the issue of the thick folder to remind the group of the count's pleading as he eyed the folder. He recalled to his fellow jurors how the count had literally thrown himself on one knee and begged his interrogator not only to destroy the folder and its contents but to open the cell door and let him escape. He promised, "My family would be so grateful to you for all time to come." To this, Heughebart had replied pointedly, "I am not authorized to do that, and, even if I were, I would not do it." Orichaud proposed that this episode was tantamount to a confession of guilt.

Baron de Secus, landholder from Bauffe, spoke at length. He remarked that he had never in his life heard anyone use the foul and ignorant language of the sort the count used in a court of law. He added that he had met a pitifully small number of pathological liars in his lifetime and always wondered how they would behave, if they were publicly exposed.

"The judge knew at once that we had seen something rare," he declared. "With essentially no way to deny that he had been lying pathologically all his life, he had no recourse except to do something as irrational as challenge the judge to a public fistfight! What an ignoramus!

"The nurse's notes and the care with which she keeps her records are, in themselves, enough to put him in jail for as long as lying in grand fashion under oath will allow. However, I strongly believe that so callous a murderer deserves the death penalty.

"It's too bad that the royal language in the penal code calls for an 'inflictive and ignominious' public execution. I know that means the guillotine, which is almost too kind a method for him. We have no place in our society for criminals like that man, but they ought to know they're being punished.

"I know that it would be categorized as a cruel and unusual way to do away with him, but I dislike him so that I can imagine forcing him to swallow some nicotine in public. I have asked a doctor or two about nicotine. It causes a horrific death—about the worst imaginable.

"After immediate vomiting and while the victim is conscious, there is great activity, by all muscles, that go into spasm which is the cause for the convulsions. Then all the same muscles become paralyzed, so you cannot even struggle to take a breath. You die of asphyxia. As you die, you lose control of your bowels."

Dr. Gauthier, who was good-natured chairman, had a gavel. He tapped it and said, "Thank you, Baron. That was a straightforward and medically correct description of how nicotine acts.

Gauthier continued, "Gentlemen, we have a duty to reach our verdicts in an organized way. So, the first question I am putting to you is this: Does anyone feel confused about some aspects of the testimony regarding Lydie Fougnies?" (He no longer called her "the countess.")

M. Derbaix, a gentleman farmer, replied, "Yes. I do, but I don't think any aspects are so important that they're going to change my mind."

Messieurs Orichaud, a banker, and Daubresse, a town supervisor, spontaneously spouted, "He's right," and, "I agree."

"Is there anyone who feels confused enough by the totality of what we have heard who wants to disagree with these colleagues?" asked Dr. Gauthier.

He heard a "No" from everyone except M. Griez, an overseer of mortgage agreements.

"To tell the truth," said Griez, "I found it hard to believe the medical professor's description of battered wives fooling around in bed with the same men who beat the daylights out of them."

M. Hezapfée, a wine merchant in Mons, asked M. Griez, "Have you ever studied psychology?"

"I have not."

"If you had, even though you might not be able to believe something like that could happen, you would open your mind to the possibility of it happening, if it would result in the saving of a life."

"People will do pretty crazy things to save their lives." M. Griez replied. "I guess you could be right; it's just that I had never thought about having to resort to something as nearly unbelievable as that."

Dr. Gauthier assured M. Griez, "It is rare, but medical journals and books have described this ugly phenomenon, although I have not encountered it in my practice."

"All right, all right, I'm now reassured that the professor wasn't exaggerating."

Gauthier asked each juryman, individually, if he had read the printed stenographic notes of testimony given under oath by Lydie Fougnies in the confidential session that Judge Lyon held with her in the presence of the lawyers. All hands rose to signal the affirmative. Nearly every juryman had a comment.

M. Demescemackers, a grain merchant, declared, "As far as I'm concerned, that was the most readable testimony in the trial. It definitely convinced me of the innocence of this young woman. It's now obvious that, if she had tried to destroy his distillatory, he would have killed her. Same goes for warning her brother.

"She was caught in a terrible dilemma. With three small children, she had to obey that insane man. Until I read that gripping testimony, I was somewhat ambivalent about the young woman's complete innocence. It should now be obvious to everyone with sense that, as long as that sadist dominated this frail, pretty woman, she was innocent across the board. If that damned fool count hadn't been so anxious to kill her brother—and hadn't been so impulsively dumb to believe that her brother hadn't changed his will after his father's death—that innocent, idealistic, young woman would have died within another year or two of his brutality. In a way, she was lucky he was so insanely impulsive. Imagine her having to put up with that filthy, brutal animal for five years!"

M. Spacy, an elderly man and a pensioner from Tournai, chimed in. "And when the judge reopened the session, we got to hear the nurse and had proof that the count is a pathological liar and . . ." M. Spacy suddenly had to adjust the uppers of his false teeth, and his colleagues politely remained silent until the elderly man finished.

"Sorry about that, gentlemen. I wanted to say that I always thought that the count's declarations that he never beat his wife were too frequent. That son of a bitch—excuse my language, gentlemen—thought that, if he repeated it often enough, everyone would believe him."

M. Duvieusart, a farmer, put a question to Dr. Gauthier. "The count's such frequent need to satisfy his sexual urge interests me in a few ways. What would happen if that sweet wife of his did get angry enough to slice off his pecker? He would still have his urge, wouldn't he, because he'd have his testicles? Do the doctors have an answer as to whether he'd have any personality change?"

All the jurymen, including Dr. Gauthier broke out in laughter, but not M. Duvieusart; he'd meant it as a serious question.

Dr. Gauthier answered him seriously, "That is, in fact, an interesting question. It's too bad we couldn't ask Dr. LeBrun. He's a medical doctor and might be able to answer you. I've wondered myself what would happen if Hippolyte suddenly lost his penis.

"My guess is that he would be a very, very angry man; perhaps he would have to be caged. I have also given thought to what would happen if the law demanded that his testicles be removed.

"We know that, not so long ago, they used men without testicles as guards in harems, because they were big and strong but they had no desire to be intimate with the women. *They* were the king's possessions.

"I have a hunch that there is some place in the brain that controls testicular function, but we are a long way from knowing if that's true. Another center might even control personality. If so, even if there were no testicular function, his aggressive, hostile nature might persist.

"I know that doesn't answer your interesting questions, but it's the best this doctor, who is certainly not a trained neurologist, can speculate about. Do you or someone else have any more comments or questions?"

M. Gardon, director of health and sanitation in a small city, said, "I think that M. Duvieusart questions are truly thought-provoking. I have to inspect the cleanliness of farms and have farmer friends who are involved in raising horses.

"I could be wrong about this, but I think that the stallions are not expected to mate every day. It seems to me that they need a rest, to restore their supply of semen, which is something else that testicular cells generate. If this is true of horses or any other animals, it also ought to be true of humans. But perhaps it isn't. I was thinking, when I heard about the legendary sexual activity of the accused count that, considering his promiscuity, he may have caused more pregnancies than we know about.

"According to the record, he did get his wife pregnant four times plus the illegitimate one with the not-too-bright Legrain girl. There's an obvious question here. We've heard no mention of pregnancies among the many other young women with whom he fornicated. It's hard to believe that he didn't get a few of those pregnant.

"I'm inquisitive, too. If his craziness produces so frequent urgent sexual desire, what in hell did he do to take care of it while he was in the jail for months?"

"To use an old expression," said Baron Secus, "he had to 'jerk off.' What did you think?"

"But what about those hours sitting in the courtroom?"

"By God, you *do* have something there," replied Baron Secus.

Dr. Gauthier interrupted. "Yes, you may well have something there to speculate about. Short of asking him, I have no idea. However, again, we are speculating when we ought to be working toward the extremely serious matter of the fates of two human beings. But for the hands of the Fates, *we* might be the ones being judged.

"I don't know about you, but this has been a long day. Frankly, I'm hungry and tired and would appreciate a night's sleep. How many of you would vote with me to tell Monsieur le President that we have decided not to continue our conclave and sober consideration of evidence until tomorrow?

"When nearly every head nodded approvingly, he responded with, "I move that we reassemble tomorrow morning at nine thirty with the confident expectation that we will arrive at unanimous verdicts by eleven in the morning, perhaps even a little earlier. Will someone second this motion?"

"Yes, by all means," said M. Orichaud.

The vote was unanimous, and Dr. Gauthier gaveled the session to a close, to meet at nine thirty the next morning.

Dr. Gauthier rang the bell to alert the clerk, who carried a short note signed by the chairman of the jury describing the jury's intentions.

Judge Lyon accepted it with relief because, truth be told, he was hoping that the jury would take just such action. He gaveled at his desk and told all who were still present that court would be in session at nine thirty in the morning.

CHAPTER 56
Considering the Verdicts

Strong emotions affected the twelve men, to a person, with respect to Lydie. First, it would be hard in any case for any one of them to vote to execute or jail the mother of three small children. Second, if, in fact, they believed she *was* guilty without question, they would have to agree on a mitigating factor or factors to justify their decision to release her. It took time for each of the twelve men to express the same opinion, in different words, but the solid basis of their opinion was the confidential oral testimony submitted in the *in camera* session.

In further discussion, there was general agreement that, even if she had had *no* children, the secret session alone would have freed her.

Dr. Gauthier then asked if the evidence that her husband had maltreated her was convincing. All agreed. The sum of their various comments was unquestioned agreement that the count was unconscionably cruel. Lydie's testimony alone was all they needed.

After this relatively short exchange, several declared, offhand, that the way "that almost unbelievably cruel count treated her, as she described it in her testimony—to which he did not even *try* to respond—is an absolute reason for lenience for her."

When Dr. Gauthier asked how Dr. LeBrun's testimony affected them, all but one had, at first. caught the gist of what the doctor was saying. That one then caught on. Nine called his testimony "convincing." The other three called it "educational" or words with a similar meaning. Gauthier asked if there might be a unanimous vote of *not guilty* for Lydie Fougnies.

All twelve voices called, "Aye," and the twelve raised their hands. A controlled outburst of joy filled the room. Jurymen slapped one another on the back.

419

Dr. Gauthier asked each, in turn, what they felt about the count. Twelve consecutive "He's no good," comments, not all of them as brief as that, followed. The chairman insisted, "Do I hear twelve unanimous votes that he is guilty of premeditated murder?"

All hands rose, in unison.

Each of the jurymen then had to carefully reread all the questions, One through Four, taking as long as needed to understand them. If there were confusion, anyone was free to ask Dr. Gauthier for help.

After reminding the jury that each man's vote had grave consequences, the chairman asked each to take a piece of notepaper from the supply on the table and write on one side at the top "Count Verdict." Then, without writing their names, the men were to write below the number of the question that best described the Count de Bocarmé's role. All numbers had to be filled in, even if it didn't seem necessary if they voted guilty on question one. One was what counted. If they voted guilty, they were instructed, "Vote as you will on questions two, three, and four as well.

No juryman hesitated. All twelve pieces of paper, including Dr. Gauthier's, were in his hand in a few seconds. He counted them. They comprised twelve votes. Dr. Gauthier called out the question number on each. Twelve voted yes for question one.

"Does anyone wish to change his vote? If so, raise your hand."

No hands were raised.

"Gentlemen," he said soberly, "we have sentenced the count to death. Shall we now consider the fate of Lydie Fougnies?"

Before they took their vote on Lydie, Baron de Secus inserted a comment, "I wonder how bravely that vicious bully is going to take this verdict. It wouldn't surprise me if they'll have to drag him kicking and screaming to the guillotine."

"Interesting," said M. Orichaud, the banker, "I was wondering whether, beneath it all, he's a coward."

Dr. Gauthier repeated, "Shall we now consider the fate of Lydie Fougnies?"

There were "Ayes" around the table.

"All right, gentlemen, in determining a verdict for her, do exactly the same as you did for the count. This time, you *must* again answer each of the questions Five through Eight either Yes or No. Is that clear? Does everyone understand?"

It took a little longer for all votes to be cast but not as long as Dr. Gauthier thought might be the case. When all of the twelve ballots were in his hand, he counted them out loud, examined each carefully, and was not surprised to find that the voting was unanimously No on questions Five, Six, Seven, and Eight.

"Gentlemen, does anyone wish to change a vote?"

He waited fifteen seconds by his railroad watch, and no hands rose.

"All right. We have voted to acquit Lydie Fougnies of all charges."

Every juryman clapped, expressed satisfaction, smiled, laughed, and slapped one another gently on their backs.

This time it was M. Hezapfée's opportunity to comment. "Great minds run in the same channel. My wine store is just around the corner in the Grande Place. I'd like to invite all of you to stop in for a little *vin* after our work is finished. Dr. Gauthier, is that allowed?"

"I see nothing wrong with it as long as the store contains only us. We know that we'll discuss the case, so there can be no eavesdroppers."

A lot of smiling "ayes" were directed at M. Hezapfée.

(One wishes that Felippe could have witnessed the scene. Lydie would have shed tears of joy.)

$$***$$

Dr. Gauthier rang the bell at 10:35 a.m., to tell the judge that they had reached their verdicts. He wrote them on a piece of stationery, which was sealed in an envelope. A clerk carried it from the jury room to Judge Lyon.

CHAPTER 57

Felippe Anxiously Awaits the Verdicts

After he heard Dr. LeBrun's testimony in the courtroom, Felippe maintained hope that Lydie would not be found guilty on all possible levels of guilt, even if a lot of bad evidence pointed to some degree of shared guilt in the murder of Gustave Fougnies. He had the distinct impression that everyone with inside knowledge of *all* the testimony seemed to know the 'bad" evidence was not compelling.

Dr. LeBrun's clear explanation of the behavior of individuals in captivity had shed new light on the probability that Lydie's involvement in her brother's murder was not of her own volition but was out of fear of her husband, who had physically abused her nearly daily and threatened her with death if she did not comply with his intention to murder her brother.

It seemed to Felippe that jurymen, who obviously listened carefully to Dr. LeBrun's testimony, may very well have been influenced to show lenience toward Lydie. Felippe was, therefore, cautiously optimistic that Lydie might even be allowed to go free.

If Lydie were to be released, after a *not-guilty* verdict, where in the world would she go? Felippe wondered. Would she *really* return to the Chateau de Bitremont? Could she bear to be reminded of her suffering at the hands of her husband and of the death of her brother? Could she handle suspicion of her guilt, which servants at the chateau no doubt still felt? Where, then, could she go with her children?

He decided to handle that *possible* problem his own way. Although he had no way to tell Lydie directly, he prepared for her possible exoneration by finding a veteran cab driver he had known for years, a man who was burly and tough. Handed a wad of cash well in excess of his usual weekly income, the driver agreed to arise early, plant himself and his horse first in a waiting line of cabs at the side exit of the courtroom, and hold it. He would insist that those behind him exit by the other, narrower exit lane. No other cabbie would have the audacity to try to move *that thoroughly respected tough guy* from his first-in-line position.

If Lydie were *not* set free, she would not exit by the side door of the courtroom, and the old cabbie would be free to relinquish his place in line.

Felippe had asked Eugène, Lydie's lawyer, to tip her off where to find a cab, if she were set free. He hoped he had done this as a favor. He could find out only if she were found not guilty.

CHAPTER 58

Announcing the Verdicts

At 10:39 a.m., the court came to order. Everyone could see that M. Lachaud was no longer on the defense bench. Judge Lyon asked Dr. Gauthier about the verdicts, and then he did something unusual. He asked all of the bailiffs to assemble with him.

"I want you bailiffs to recall, if you were on duty during the end of the session when we found the count to be a pathological liar. Right afterward we found out that he got the name on Gustave's will completely wrong, Whether or not you were there, he threatened that his bums in Brussels might kill me. I think he was faking it, but just in case he was not, I'll not announce verdicts before you see to it that every possible entry to the courtroom is locked tightly. Try not to miss any. As for the count, I'd like for four of you to be closer to my dais just in case he becomes belligerent or acts stupidly in some other way. So go about locking those doors while I speak to the audience."

When the bailiffs had dispersed, the judge turned to the audience. "Ladies and gentlemen, we will be announcing the verdicts shortly. If there is anyone there who feels a need, for any reason, to leave the room within the next fifteen minutes, I ask you to leave right now. The bailiffs will let you out by the only exit now open. Thank you.

The president of the court ordered the stenographer not to begin to record anything that follows, unless asked to record by a court officer. He had a hunch that the count might act in a way that would embarrass his distinguished relatives.

"Gentlemen of the jury, what is the result of your deliberations on the count's guilt or innocence?"

Dr. Gauthier, the chairman of the jury, spoke with a moving voice, his hand over his heart. "On my honor and my conscience, before God and mankind, the verdict of the jury is, guilty on all charges."

424

The judge then ordered the bailiffs, "Have the accused Visart brought to the courtroom and seated on the prisoner's bench, to be followed by Lydie Fougnies. Seat them both on the prisoner's bench. Their lawyers will sit between them."

The bailiffs led the accused count into the courtroom. It took two or three minutes for Lydie to appear. When she entered, the count threw her a slight smile. Lydie remained unmoved and expressionless. She totally ignored him.

The court secretary read the verdict of the jury: "With respect to the conclusion of the jury, Alfred-Julien-Gabriel-Gérard-Hippolyte Visart, Count de Bocarmé, *is guilty* as the perpetrator of the crime for which he was charged.

"Hear ye. Re Articles 302 and 303 of the Penal Code."

The royal prosecutor, M. de Maubant, read the Penal Code: "**We require that it please the court to condemn guilt with the penalty of death in an inflictive and ignominious manner, demanding that the execution take place in any of the public places in the city of Mons.**"

The count jumped up and yelled, "*What*!? They wanna chop my head off!?"

Judge Lyon ordered the count to be quiet and approach his dais. He spoke slowly, solemnly but kindly to him.

"The appropriate court officer has read the sentence of the court that has condemned you to death and holds you responsible for the payment of the expenses of the trial. It orders that your execution be in a public place in the city of Mons and that billboards in Mons and Bury carry news of the sentence. The sentence allows three days for application for clemency from His Royal Highness."

The judge asked Hippolyte, "What comments do you have?

"I don't like it. It's not fair! I'm afraid of being dead." The count suddenly lost control of his emotions and began to cry and shout his disapproval as copious tears and voluminous nasal secretions ran down his face. He shouted, "Please? Your Honor, even if I was guilty,

I'd be willing to stay in a prison all my life in solitary! But I don't want nobody choppin' off my head! *Please*?! *You* can get the king to make a change. I *know* you can explain it."

Hippolyte fell to his knees before the dais and loudly begged the judge, "*Save* my life—*please*, sir." The volume of his nasal secretions did not prevent his whining through them. "I don't *wanna die*! Nobody's gonna hold *me* down and chop off my head! I'm *afraid*! Some *son of a bitch* will hack on my neck, and another will *pull* my head off. For Crissake, *that's* no way to get revenge because they think I got a *wrong name* for a *will*. Please? Your Honor, I *never* did *nothin'* to hurt *you*. I *don't wanna die*! I'm *afraid*. Please Sir, Your Honor, *please* ask the king to *forever let me be in jail* and not be dead. Somethin' else, they got *no good proof* I murdered nobody." His tears were copious and his gravel voice unpleasantly loud.

Two strong bailiffs tried to raise the count to his feet, but he made their job difficult by throwing punches at them. A third bailiff managed to strap his arms to his body and pulled him erect.

He continued to cry profusely and blurted in the direction of the president of the court, "*If* I wanted *money*, I woulda *known the will better*. That's proof *I could'na been the killer*. I done stupid things *but nothin' as stupid* as that. I want the *king to know* the *jury was lousy. An innocent man shouldn'ave his head chopped off.*

"Your Honor, how would *you* like to have *your* head chopped off? The king should gimme a **break**."

Judge Lyon decided there was nothing to be gained by allowing the count to carry on. He was aware that some of the cruelest of murderers are afraid to die. When he glanced down and to his left, he saw Lydie waiting to hear *her* verdict. She was hiding her head in Eugène Harmignies's coat lapel and a blanket. Lyon could not know what thoughts ran through her mind, but at some point during this breakdown of Hippolyte's, it occurred to him that life imprisonment for her husband would make it impossible for Lydie to divorce him. It would ruin her life forever. For the first time, he realized the cruelty

426

of an anti-divorce law. He composed himself and demanded that the count get on his feet. The less said the better was what he said to himself as he gave orders to three bailiffs. He purposely spoke gently.

"Thank you, Count. Your entire statement and request for clemency will be sent in minutes to His Majesty. In the meantime, I order the bailiffs to pat this prisoner down, to remove anything on him or in his pockets that are sharp-edged, and then to conduct him to his cell on death row.

"Check that cell again for anything that he might use to harm himself or anyone else. Strip search him thoroughly and give him a clean set of clothing without belts of any kind. Feed him whatever he wishes. Let him have a heavy blanket. He is to have three eight-hour jail watches and will have no communication with anyone unless officially ordered by the prison's director."

The bailiffs "patted down" the prisoner and, to their surprise, removed several large, apparently used handkerchiefs from all six pockets of his prison uniform. The dried stains were nearly colorless but starch-like when dry. They looked up to Judge Lyon as if to ask, "What in the world are all these needed for; he's not had a runny nose during the trial."

Judge Lyon thought for a few moments, seemed as though he was about to address a bailiff, but hesitated, and said he would speak to the prison director himself. He ordered the bailiffs to carry on but put the "used handkerchiefs" in a clean bag because he had a use for them.

"All right. Take the prisoner to his cell," he concluded.

No sooner had the judge said that than *the prisoner again fell to the floor* and yelled that he refused to go "*to any goddamn death cell.*"

Judge Lyon would have no more of this. With a soft, gentle voice he asked the bailiffs, five in number now, "Use leg irons, and drag the prisoner to his cell, if necessary."

The judge then shook his head in thought with his eyes closed. He raised his head, smiled a *big* smile and rendered the following decree in a very kind voice. "Hear ye. The verdict of the jury is that Lydie Fougnies is *not* guilty.

"Hear ye. Article 350 of the Code of Official Directions: We, President of the Court of Assizes, declare that Lydie Fougnies is *acquitted* of the charges brought against her. We order that she be *set free*, for she faces no other charges. *Please*, set Lydie Fougnies free!"

Lydie, free at last, could have rushed at once to the locked side doors, but she wanted to thank Judge Lyon. At the same moment, he wanted to shake *her* hand, congratulate her, and wish her well. M. Harmignies interceded briefly to give her a warm, well-deserved hug and kissed her cheek.

The judge voiced concern whether she had enough money to get about and to eat. He asked if she knew where to go and where she would seek comfortable shelter. (That would have been Eugène Harmignies job, but, apparently, he knew he wasn't needed).

Lydie's reply to His Honor was that she had thought about all that, but unless she was grossly mistaken, she believed that "a dear friend is probably waiting for me in a cab outside the courtroom."

"A long lane of cabs *is* just outside the exit door. If, for *any* reason, your friend does not appear, I have already spoken to Mme Lyon, who would be pleased to provide you with a place to stay until you get matters worked out with M. Harmignies. That will of your brother's was *very* generous to you, but it *will* be a while before it passes through the special courts we have for matters of that kind. While waiting on those courts*, my suggestion is that it might be unpleasant, **possibly harmful***, to try to go back and live in the chateau. A lot of employees there still think you're guilty because they don't know the whole story. Perhaps you and my daughter could do some shopping together."*

Lydie thanked him deeply and meaningfully for all the kindness he had showered on her. *She dared to hug him.* "And, please, *extend my deep appreciation to the jury. They made no mistake*, and I will always be grateful to them."

"Why don't I stand outside to be certain that your friend *is* there? Otherwise, I'll simply *not* let you go free with no place to go, not even a small suitcase of extra clothing and pretty much a stranger to most of this city. Let us go see if your friend is there."

The judge had the key to an inside corridor and another to a windowless door. When he opened it, there was indeed a lane that held a long train of horses and cabs.

While Judge Lyon watched, Lydie followed her inclination to run toward the head of the line, which was about ten feet to her left and work her way back along the line. Her intuition that Felippe might be close to the front of the line was correct. He saw her before she saw him, and she fell into his gently hugging arms.

"Kiss me, darling, *please*," she said.

He did, and she asked, "*Darling, kiss me again!*"

Judge Lyon heard and observed it from a few feet away with wet eyes and a broad smile, and he waved to her as she threw a kiss to him.

Judge Lyon, who could be so tough when he wanted to be, knew intuitively that she was innocent of purposeful wrongdoing. He had treated her almost like a daughter after the *in camera* hearing and treated her warmly.

He treated Dr. LeBrun in a friendly way, remarking that he had taught him something he had not known before, namely, "captive wives." He had been imaginative enough to consider possible effects of incessant brutality on how and why a defendant might be reluctant to describe the brutality but, regardless, he recognized that Lydie was innocent before he heard the professor's lecture.

It was he who'd entered as evidence the examining nurse's careful notes that recorded the nearly infinite number of fist-induced bruises on Lydie's body. That record permitted him to prove, most inventively, that the count was a pathological liar. He *had* beaten Lydie cruelly.

Judge Lyon still had serious tasks to undertake and finish before finishing his day's work.

CHAPTER 59

M. de Maubant Is Severely Reprimanded

After the bailiffs had dragged the condemned count to his cell on death row, Judge Lyon asked Monsieur de Maubant, the prosecutor, to join him in his office. Lyon's face was stern, and so was his voice, as he put hard questions to de Maubant, who had no premonition that Judge Lyon would subject him to an ordeal.

"Tell me, de Maubant, when you first knew of the medical evidence that Lydie Fougnies had been beaten so badly."

"Not until it was presented as evidence."

"Did you not recurrently inspect the evidence file in the course of the trial?"

"A few times but not regularly."

"When you looked during those 'few times,' did you not see the nurse's report? It was I who obtained that evidence about her daily beatings—the evidence of black and blue marks of various ages, unquestioned evidence of continual daily beatings with fists. His knuckle marks, old and new, indicated that he used his fists. It was I who put a copy of her report in the evidence folder within three days of the start of the trial."

"I didn't *regularly* examine that file, Your Honor."

"Did it ever occur to you to wonder how a so well-spoken, educated woman married that piece of trash?"

Beads of sweat were now evident on de Maubant's forehead. "Women do a lot of harmful things to themselves," he replied.

"I'm going to put you under oath. The clerk is still outside. Go call him in."

430

The king's prosecutor de Maubant took the oath in the presence of Judge Lyon, who immediately asked him again, "Did you, *at any time* during the trial, inspect the evidence file for the insertion of new evidence?"

"I don't remember, sir." He was now sweating profusely.

"That's exactly how you deprecated Lydie's 'I don't remember' answers before Professor Stas successfully showed the presence of nicotine in her brother's tissues.

"Did Nurse deFrance's testimony support Lydie Fougnies's testimony about the beastliness of her insane, perverted husband?"

"Yes, Monsieur le President." De Maubant declined to reply further.

"What did you learn from Dr. LeBrun's testimony?"

"A great deal, Monsieur le President."

"You can be more specific than that, can you not?" Judge Lyon's voice rose in anger.

"I had not previously known about the lives of captive women."

"Did you believe him?"

"Yes, Monsieur le President."

"If so, why did you not raise the issue of captive wives in your speech to the jury?"

Monsieur le President, I assumed that my role as a prosecutor was to make the charges in the act of accusation stick."

"That is a stupid answer. The act of accusation does not convict! It does only what its name says it does! It accuses. The court has the *duty* to weigh those accusations. The rule of law demands that those accused have a fair trial, which includes the consideration of extenuating circumstances. Even pity! Did you hear my remarks about the need to lean over backward to give defendants a fair trial?"

De Maubant turned white, and his eyes began to tear. He was frightened to death by Judge Lyon, who, he had to admit to himself, was correct. He knew exactly what he had done, that he had enjoyed giving, within hearing of a large crowd, what seemed to him to be a very well-articulated and intonated speech. He had given little thought to the fine points that could have influenced the verdicts. He felt that his career was at a high point; even the King would read his words as well as the leading lawyers of the nation. Newspapers would mention his name. But he feared to confess this to Judge Lyon.

"Was this a death case where a guilty verdict might lead to a death sentence?"

"Yes, Your Honor."

"If you were a defendant and believed you were not guilty, would you want exculpatory evidence opened up?

"De Maubant, you have a degree in law?"

"Yes, Your Honor."

"Were you not taught, or wasn't it self-evident to you, that withholding evidence, especially in a murder case, is heinous dereliction of duty? Go back and read how you asked the jury to call Lydie Fougnies guilty, when there was evidence in a file that was essentially exculpatory. You would have liked them to consider *her* guilty of murder as well as the count, when the evidence showed that she acted as she *had* to, *under threat of death* at the hands of that crazy husband.

"As the supervising judge in this trial, I consider you to have violated a basic rule. I must and I will report you for serious dereliction of duty. I would be derelict in *my* duty if I did not report *your* derelict behavior to the authorities in Brussels.

De Maubant broke into a torrent of tears

"I don't feel at all sorry for you. Either you're stupid, or you have a mean and dishonest streak in you," the judge continued. "You are dismissed."

As the deeply disturbed man got up to leave, Lyon barked, "Get rid of the fake accent that a few of the aristocracy use. You're as much an aristocrat as I am. You're a rotten actor; you put it on too thick."

The sobbing man disappeared from the office hastily.

We have no knowledge of de Maubant's life after the second week of June 1851.

CHAPTER 60

Judge Lyon Visits the Prison Director

It was a long walk to the prison director's office. The director was in, and Judge Lyon handed him the closed bag, warning him not to open it.

"These are large handkerchiefs found in the pockets of the count's prison uniform. I suspect that he's had to masturbate frequently to relieve himself of his insane, frequent sexual urge.

"He's going to be your prisoner until he's guillotined. Do you have half a dozen heavy handkerchiefs to give him to use until he loses his head. It's pitiful that he has this illness, but he does need these or something like them. While he's rotten to his core, he *is* a sick man and is still a sentient human being."

"Your Honor, I have plenty of those large, heavy kerchiefs," replied the director.

"Good. I'd like to offer two suggestions. First, let the pitiful fellow out of solitary. Give him clean, heavy blankets and a mattress. He has three days to live. Second, arrange, if possible, *leaving my name unmentioned*, for the 'old jailer' who's so good at soothing the dying and the condemned to be on duty the night of the twentieth. He has a knack for dealing with frightened inmates. The prisoner has no compunction murdering others, but he is terrified of death for himself."

"No, problem, Judge. The old jailer is a nice man and very, very smart."

"Thank you. I've got to get back to my desk, to be sure my tasks are finished. It's been a long day."

433

Part Three

CHAPTER 61

Paradise

With no premonition whatever, Felippe's protective arms surrounded Lydie gently. He helped her into the seat for two behind the driver. She waved to Judge Lyon whose eyes became teary when he saw that the man he presumed was her early lover hugged and kissed her. As she leaned against Felippe, a guard opened the gate and the driver, whom Felippe had paid well to hold the head of the line, exited the lane hurriedly.

He made a right turn into the Grande Place of Mons, nearly circled it and stopped before Mons' most fashionable and largest women's clothing store. The director warmly greeted Baron Van Hendryk, whom he had known for years and with whom he had had a detailed meeting the day before.

Without another question, he escorted Lydie upstairs to a comfortable salon, where a handsome woman about fifty years of age met her. Mme Deloitte was the store's fashion director. She introduced herself warmly and said she was expecting Lydie, whom she addressed as Mlle Fougnies.

Mlle Fougnies had not lost her ability to bend her head, smile, and ask in a suppliant way, "Please call me Lydie?"

Mme Deloitte decided right away that she liked this pretty, young woman; offered her a comfortable seat at a small table; and joined her.

"Lydie," she said laughingly, "I used to dress Baron Van Hendryk's mother when she was alive, but you and she, I can tell, are very different people. You're younger, prettier, and have a more feminine figure.

"Baron Van Hendryk and I had a chat about you yesterday. He told me that he expected that you might be coming for a very short visit and asked me to help you begin to restore a wardrobe, once filled with tasteful clothing, that needs replenishing.

"He asked me to show you dresses and suits already on our racks, to try on and take with you; he set no limit on the number. He also mentioned accessories such as blouses, sweaters, robes, hose, shoes, and undergarments. Men, of course, are men. They think the task will be simple and relatively quick.

"I pointed out that you may be attracted only to four or five dresses on our racks. Being a reasonable man, he suggested that we take all your measurements, find out if there are particular fabrics, colors, or color combinations that you like—and that he likes to see on you—and to order them made here by our dressmaking department. They would be one of a kind for you."

"How very kind of him. I'm overwhelmed. When it comes to clothing, I admit that I enjoy having a variety of dresses. If I were to leave here this afternoon with only one, though, I would like a tailored, navy blue dress with a simple white collar. The weather is warm, so the material cannot be heavy.

"I like variety, but, really, I am not a *clothes horse*. If he is still downstairs, may I suggest that he find a way to kill not more than ninety minutes, and I'll have enough to start." Lydie had a hard time holding back tears.

Felippe got the message. There were things he did want to buy in other stores, and ninety minutes was a perfect interval.

Lydie suggested that, as a start she would like to choose five dresses from the rack and spend the remainder of her time, with help, acquiring the other items she needed. Mme Deloitte agreed.

Lydie found five tasteful summer dresses that appealed to her and Mme Deloitte found a sixth, which was the tailored blue dress with a simple white collar. A dressmaker took all measurements that she needed for making dresses in the future. Mme Deloitte advised that she might want to pick up a skirt or two, some blouses, and a couple of light wool sweaters.

She arranged for the other miscellany that she thought should be included in her wardrobe and four pairs of shoes—two for dress and two for lounging about. All was neatly packed, and Felippe could easily handle it; he would find a place for it on the seat of the cab next to or under Lydie's extended legs.

While Lydie was shopping, Felippe found a telegraph office and messaged his butler at the estate house in Peruwelz:

TAKING THREE O'CLOCK TRAIN MONS TO PERUWELZ, ARRIVING 3:45 WITH WOMAN FRIEND. PLEASE ASK FRANÇOIS TO COOK IMAGINATIVELY FOR CELEBRATORY DINNER, FIND FLOWERS FOR VASES IN SITTING AND DINING ROOMS, HAVE ONE ROSE IN NARROW VASE ON DINING TABLE, PREPARE BEDROOM FOR A LADY (MY LATE MOTHER'S WOULD DO), PREPARE ENOUGH HOT WATER TO ENABLE LADY TO BATHE COMFORTABLY, CHECK SHERRY AND WINE SUPPLIES; IF POSSIBLE, FIND YOUNG VIOLINIST TO PLAY SONATAS SOFTLY DURING DINNER. I HAVE CONFIDENCE IN YOU FOR SPECIAL OCCASION. COOL THE CHAMPAGNE.

Having completed that, Felippe visited Mons's best-known jewelers and bought a handsome diamond engagement ring and guard. As he looked about, he could not resist purchasing a simple but elegant pearl necklace. Imagining the blue dress he remembered and thought was the prettiest of those she wore, he felt that a perfectly circular, gold brooch would enhance the solid blue. Believing that nothing that he bought was ostentatious, he had each piece properly boxed and cheerfully paid for them.

It was time to return to the clothing store to meet his love again. She was waiting downstairs for him; she threw her arms about him, and they kissed.

Having thanked Mme Deloitte and the director, he and Lydie took a cab to the train station and easily caught the three o'clock to Peruwelz, with time enough to have tea and cake. They held hands on the train, which arrived in Peruwelz at quarter to four and then took a cab to the Van Hendryk estate, a ten-minute drive.

I think you'll feel at home in my place near Peruwelz. My father left it to me when he died two years ago. I keep it because it's convenient and cozy. And it provides jobs for kind people whom I have known from childhood.

He enjoyed introducing Lydie to his employees and was able to overhear complimentary remarks about her beauty. An elated Felippe could not have agreed more.

A young maid politely showed Lydie to her room, where, after resting for about fifteen minutes, she had a warm bath and dressed to meet Felippe in the sitting room.

Another young girl, who played the violin well, sat in an adjacent room and lightly played sonatas, each of which Lydie knew well.

CHAPTER 62

A Romantic Interlude

Felippe tied hard to avoid saying anything weighty that might remind Lydie of the last seven years of her life. He did suggest that they try, as soon as was feasible, to get the children from the foster home where they were presently residing. It happened to be a very good foster home, which was professionally run.

However, Felippe thought it essential to have at least two, possibly three, full-time nannies to look after Gonzalès and his sisters, Mathilde and Eugènie, before they moved the children.

"However, in the world did you know their names, darling?"

"It wasn't hard. I was concerned about them, so I asked M. Harmignies. He's a helpful fellow. There is a large playroom at my house, but it needs toys for children of various ages"—he leaned over, kissed her lips, and completed his sentence—"plenty and plenty of toys. I'll see to it tomorrow that the room is properly equipped for them because I know how much you want to see them. Of course, I badly want to meet them also, as I am going to become a father! That should be a new experience."

Lydie could not help herself—tears welled up in her eyes; she hugged Felippe and kissed him.

"Wait a minute," said Felippe, "wait; I was thinking that we are at the family home in Brussels. I'm mixed up, perhaps because being with you again is a dizzying experience. Let's get it straight, sweetheart; the children are in Brussels, not Peruwelz. You can thank Monsieur Chercquefosse for taking that initiative very quickly after the November 1850 crisis."

"How protective and thoughtful of him! I had no idea he did that. Did *you* have any hand in it?

439

"Minimally only; I suggested the place. I was very surprised that he contacted me; he must have a sixth sense." He was close to your father, who never ceased loving you. Neither of them ever lost faith in you. M. Chercquefosse and his wife did everything within their power to help you. His friendship with Judge Lyon couldn't have hurt you. Possibly, it was he who alerted Lyon to the count's criminal past and his mother's character flaws.

"Thank you very much, darling. I'll write to him and Madame Chercquefosse forthwith. She hugged and kissed him with teary eyes and muttered, "So much there was that I didn't know."

"It's done no harm to let you know that those who admired you always stood with you. I shall make every effort, tomorrow, to have the even larger playroom in Brussels equipped for the childrens' play. It will be easier to find trained nannies there than in Peruwelz. Besides, just between you and me, I don't *ever* want to make Peruwelz my *permanent* home, and I don't think you do either. Tell me if I'm wrong."

"Not if we can help it, thank you," agreed Lydie. "Outside of the children's playroom, there is little to attract or educate the little ones. Certainly, there are many kind and considerate people in Peruwelz but, on the whole, I'd choose Brussels for the children's sake."

***

Felippe took her hand and kissed it. "We have nearly an hour before dinner is served. It's fun being here with you in the sitting room, and I think it is time for an aperitif. What would you like?"

"Do you have any sherry that won't make my nose numb?"

"I'll have to ask, but I suppose we do."

"And what are you going to have?"

"Either champagne or some good Madeira. You're closer to the bell on the table beside you. Tinkle it once or twice, and someone will come to help us.

440

Felippe announced, "We have to make an important decision, and a very pleasant one. This is not something we have to decide immediately, but let us give some thought to our taking a trip to Switzerland. Frankly, I was thinking of the French-speaking side of the country. Here, you pull the globe over to us and see if the region of Lake Neuchatel might interest you. It's within your reach. I was examining it while you were resting."

Lydie easily found it and pulled it toward them.

"Can you find Lake Neuchatel in western Switzerland?"

"Uh-huh. It's a long, narrow lake."

Felippe explained, "The mountains on the west coast of it rise rather precipitously. They afford a magnificent view. There are some lovely small hotels above the lake. If the weather remains good, it will be an ideal place to visit, perhaps to walk some not too difficult paths or trails. What do you think of that?"

Lydie smiled coyly. "You know perfectly well that 'whither thou goest I shall follow.' It's a lovely idea sight-unseen, and it's worth a kiss."

Felippe did not get that kiss right away because a maid suddenly appeared and took orders for aperitifs. Lydie was soon sipping apple sherry, and Felippe was sipping his favorite Malmsey Madeira. Between sips, Felippe received a tender kiss on the cheek, and Lydie continued her questioning.

"Are you free to tell me exactly what your position is in the government? I did see you sitting with a group that I recognized as government officials during that awful trial, a memory I intend to shake from my mind as quickly as possible. What was your purpose in being there?"

Lydie gave him a very good kiss and a hug. Then she asked again, "Why were you at the trial?"

"The king took great interest in this affair. He sent a group of us who are his legal counselors to report back to him about its progress. I detached myself from the group and added nothing to the expected weekly report. Besides, I had already sent him a thoroughly devastating report about the character of your unattractive husband. But all that is in the past. It does us no good to regurgitate it. Anyone can make a mistake and marry the wrong person; that's all there is to it. The judge knew it, and the jury knew, too. Sweetheart, let's talk about *us* and forget that episode."

She placed her head on his shoulder, held his hand, and said, "You are very wise, gentle, and perceptive. Naturally, the trial experience had its peaks of trauma that I imagined I would never forget, but here we are, less than a day later, and they *are* beginning to fade. You're some kind of a magician." She kissed his cheek. "As long as I have you, they will continue to fade, and the old Lydie will blossom in full again. That's bound to happen, dearest, as long as I have you," she said as she smiled gently.

"But you never did tell me exactly what you do as a member of the king's advisory staff."

"You guessed it. I am his official magician."

"Please, *don't tease me*. What things does he ask your opinions about?"

"My specialty is international law, especially as it applies to international business. He is interested in knowing as much as he can about the factors responsible for the sprouting of the industrial revolution in England. He is a nice man, highly intelligent and curious about matters large and small. You'll meet him. I imagine he's interested enough in your case to want to meet you. You are something of a hero to a lot of people.

"To return to your question, he would like Belgium to emulate England, although he realizes that we do not have as large a technically educated population. For the time being, he is trying to attract entrepreneurs in the manufacture of simple tools needed to manufacture larger things like steam-driven boats and using steam power to generate electricity.

442

"It's a pretty easy and open game right now. If a person has a technical education and a good idea, he can borrow some money from a bank. They cannot be careless, though. Belgian entrepreneurs have to be careful not to infringe on someone else's inventions, and that's where I give advice."

"How do you know about inventions? They must fill encyclopedias."

"Nearly all countries keep track of inventions and make their details available; at least, that's what international law asks of them. If a man has a useful invention, he is supposed to inform his government.

"I keep an eye on that Belgian list to see if there's anything resembling it on any other country's list. If there is, notification goes to both parties, and they generally work things out themselves. There is only rarely a suit.

"Well, I enjoy what I'm doing, in large part because I enjoy the people I work with. I've met some clever inventors, too. They're generally very bright people, as you can imagine. Probably I'll stay on with the king for a few more years, if he wants me around. I'm getting a valuable education from this kind of work, but whether I'll do it for my entire life is something I simply do not know. There is a strain of the adventure in me that might lead me into another occupation or, at some point, into another part of the world.

"And you, my lovely, what do you intend to do when *you* grow up?"

"All I want to be is a mother to my children and be your wife, *if* you still want me."

"That's a very sensible, and agreeable, answer. I plan to raise these issues during dinner." He kissed her cheek.

The butler entered the adjoining dining room to decorate the table from which all leaves had been removed, leaving only two places. Felippe realized that his dinner with Lydie would be more intimate and romantic than he had previously imagined.

The butler appeared again, covered it with a starched linen tablecloth, and lit a single large candle in the center of the now small table, He arranged his parents' best china and silverware in the opposite places. Beside the table was a wine cooler in which he could not yet see the neck of a champagne bottle.

Four or five minutes later, the cook appeared from the kitchen in clean white garments, toque and all, to welcome Felippe, who clearly enjoyed getting up and introducing his Mademoiselle Lydie Fougnies to François. He was very pleasant, took her hand gently when she offered it, and expressed his pleasure that she was visiting. He added that he enjoyed cooking for two rather than one and added, "I do hope you enjoy your lemon sole.

"Why don't you take your seats at the table now? Would you like me to ask the young woman with the violin to play from this room instead of the dining room?"

Felippe replied, "Thank you, François."

From the way they addressed one another, it was apparent to Lydie that François had known Felippe for a long time.

CHAPTER 63

Proposal

Once seated, Felippe suggested that they sip some champagne to celebrate their togetherness. Lydie cheerily agreed.

"Will you stand a moment, my love," asked Felippe as he reached for his half-full glass of champagne. He looked lovingly at her as they touched glasses and locked their eyes into one another's.

In a manner neither solemn nor whimsical, they touched glasses and toasted one another saying, "avec amour," before they tipped a little of the gold, tingly liquid onto their tongues.

When they sat, Lydie was trying to hold back tears. Felippe did not notice it because he had diverted his thought into what he wanted to do or say next and how to say it. He became more serious and forgot any other way to ask.

"Lydie, will you marry me?"

Lydie, taken completely by surprise, replied in an almost matter-of-fact tone, "Of course I'll marry you. I love you."

Thereupon, Felippe put his hand in his coat pocket; opened a small, purple velvet box; removed a silver ring with six small but prominent diamonds; and slipped it on the fourth finger of her left hand, while asking again, this time with a broad smile, "Will you marry me?"

She glanced at her finger and could say nothing more than, "Oh, Felippe, I'm astounded. My tears will have to take the place of my words. I love you, I love you, I love you, and I always will. You are so kind, so thoughtful. I am the most fortunate woman in the world. It's a lovely engagement ring. Thank you.

***

445

"It was an old wide table of polished mahogany. She could not reach across it to kiss him. She shed tears and sobbed slightly for a few seconds before she raised her head to say again, "Thank you," and, "I love you, darling."

He reached, barely took her right hand, and kissed its fingers gently. He felt that he had a responsibility to speak kindly, off the cuff and unambiguously. He came around to her side of the table and held both her hands in his. He looked into her eyes kindly and opened his heart slowly with words he had certainly thought about but had never before spoken or rehearsed.

***

"I have loved you deeply, Lydie—from the moment we met in the museum in Mons, over the Bruegel—and as we then walked together in the garden. I have wanted ever since—and have waited for the appropriate time and place, to ask you to be my wife—to let you know, in a way that you can construe as a lifetime pledge—that I not only love you, I respect you as deeply. I wanted the perfect time to open my heart to you—and I believe that *this is* that perfect time—to tell you that this is as tender a moment of my love for you as I have *ever* confessed."

He put his arms around her and wanted to kiss her but laughed gently when she became temporarily unkissable because of her emotional response.

"Please excuse me, darling. I am so overjoyed that I cannot speak or even kiss you as much as I want to kiss you," was Lydie's reaction to Felippe's avowal of his love.

Once she regained her self-control, she threw her arms around his neck and kissed him repeatedly. Felippe then took *her* unaware, threw his arms around her, and found her deliciously osculant.

***

446

For the first time, she looked carefully at her ring and admired it as one that sent a message without being ostentatious. She was curious, "The size is perfect. How did you know?"

"I didn't. I guessed and depended on chance. I made sure that there's a guard ring. It may still be in the little box. We agreed that if the size were not right, they would fix it."

"Where did you buy this jewelry, if it isn't impolite to ask?"

"In Mons."

"But that was when—so much was still unsettled, if I may speak euphemistically."

"You mustn't forget that I'm a fairly well-trained lawyer. I never doubted the outcome." Although this was not true, he thought it useful not to say otherwise. He gave her a very warm, reassuring smile.

"Sweetheart, you're going to lose so much salt in those tears that you'd better add a little to your sole. I don't want a desalinated fiancée any more than I want an oversized one with swollen ankles. I don't mean to say that twenty or thirty years from now I'll not love you just as much as I do right now, even if your ankles *do* swell."

"That's all part of the bargain, isn't it?" Lydie answered. "If your waist or ankles swell, I'll still love you and your sense of humor. I promise that I will love everything about you. Darling, please let us not be too serious tonight. When they clear the table, may we repair to the couch? It's been a long wait for me to lie snugly and reassuringly in your arms again."

"I'm as much in need of tender love as you," he remarked as he raised his champagne glass and said, "Let's arrange a simple marriage soon. I remember how responsible you were when we hugged and kissed on the sitting room lounge. You seemed to know exactly when it was time to kiss me on the middle of my forehead as you moved away, stood, and said, "Darling, it's late. Time for you to take me home to Peruwelz. You always did that."

"Those were *exactly* my actions and words," she nodded, remembering. "It wasn't easy. I trusted your responsibility. I just wanted to guarantee it."

"Incidentally, I love that navy blue dress you're wearing tonight; you seem to have remembered that I always liked that color and that particular dress on you."

"Of course, I remembered. I wanted to tease you tonight. Didn't you realize that?"

"I confess, Lydie darling, that I've remembered it through thick and thin—since that worst of all bad days on the steps of the Mons Museum in 1841. Just to prove it, I have a little something here in my pocket." He opened the lid of a black, velvet jewel case and handed it to her.

She held her breath as she removed its content. It was a perfectly simple, three-dimensional ring of gold, a little less than half an inch in internal diameter.

Through a waterfall of new tears, Lydie held it to the left, upper part of the navy blue dress with its simple white collar. Felippe attached it there.

"It was selfish of me to give it to you because you can't see it. It's a feast for *my* eyes. That being the case, perhaps *I* should shed a few spirited tears."

"Darling, have you never shed tears?"

"Sure. When I was a child and wanted something that I couldn't have, or when I fell and hurt myself. As an adult, yes; I cried at my parents' funerals. If you promise never to tell anyone, I cried myself to sleep thinking of you when I suddenly found myself in Zürich, without you, in 1841. That was a cruel thing my parents did to both of us.

"No, I could be wrong but I do not recall ever crying tears of *joy*. I have friends who say they cry when they see a parade and patriotic flags. I've heard that it's common in the young United States, where they have frequent national holidays and marching bands.

"Thank you, thank you for that brooch just there; it is slightly above your heart."

Lydie touched the brooch with trembling fingers and quietly remarked, "Darling, you have excellent taste." She felt that she could not cry any more. She was too happy to cry. He raised his champagne glass, she reflexively did the same, and again they drank to one another.

"Thank you for wearing it. Yes, I admit that it *is* a handsome, simple piece. I love to see it on you.

Lydie again could not hold back her tears. She reached for his left hand and kissed it gently. He gave her his handkerchief because her nose was running too.

"I think I know how you feel," he said. "I feel the same way, but tears just don't come as easily to men. We suffer the same emotions. Romantic love is the best of them. I'll never be able to explain how deeply your loving tears affect me, but please, sweetheart, blow your nose." (He smiled as he said it.)

She did as he wished and then advised that they had better enjoy some of François's artistry because it would be bad manners not to. She added, "Besides, I'm hungry. It would be gauche of us not to enjoy what François has evidently taken pains to please us. It was an unforeseen kindness."

***

François' dinner was eminently fitting for what had now become a balmy evening in mid-June 1851. It was designed for two lovers, to be consumed slowly by the light of s single candle.

The starter was very cold, creamy vichyssoise that had the inimitable flavor of leeks. There were other seasonings as well but the residual taste of leeks was predominant. While the residual taste was tolerable, a cool, slightly syrupy white wine, a rare Montrachet, coveted by connoisseurs, cleansed the tongue and prepared an appetite for a bowl of cool, crisp leaves of lettuce. Chewed well, the cool water they held was liberal in quantity and readily quenched thirst.

Lydie was relaxed and good-humored. She frequently answered in kind to affectionate facial gestures by her devoted Felippe. Unable to speak and chew at the same time, he communicated with amorous gazes. Lydie could not recall ever before dining in so salubrious an atmosphere. She was exceptionally content, and pleasantly surprised when she again heard Mozart and Schubert melodies in the distance. (François had retained the young violinist. Her mission was to play in the background from a location farther than the sitting room)

The generous, tender steak of sole was delicious and satisfying. It required little or no seasoning. It was eaten slowly with more sips of the chilled, interesting white wine. A. piquant butter sauce on briefly-boiled string beans made a crunchy delicacy. And small scooped balls of potato, oven-browned, were consumed with a full-bodied red wine. A goblet of a Mèdoc filled the bill well.

Dessert was a plentiful and colorful selection of fresh fruits, almonds, unshelled walnuts and a hug and a kiss from Felippe.

It was a simple, yet exceptionally elegant, dinner that neither would forget for as long as they lived. It was a major early experience in a long and wonderful life together.

***

I'm still waiting to be held in your arms," said Lydie somewhat bashfully. Felippe picked her up and dropped her gently on the couch in the adjacent sitting room, where there was a large, soft pillow at one end. He lay down and snuggled closely to her.

It had been a long, tiring day for Lydie. She fell asleep in his arms. He carried her to her bedroom and let her sleep soundly until morning. There was hot water for a tepid bath, and at about ten, they enjoyed strong black coffee and delicious croissants.

***

They then sought out François, to express their appreciation for his kind, well-planned, unforgettable dinner. In few words, François surprised them by speaking first. He spoke heartfelt words before they could utter a sound. He wanted *them* to know that *his* pleasure was as full as theirs. He addressed Felippe warmly and very frankly, describing his lifelong admiration of him from boyhood and as a wise, kind and successful man. He then dared to commend "your choice of a charming, intelligent wife. May God bless the both of you."

Felippe was nonplussed and speechless. Lydie spoke for him. She thanked François amicably and very convincingly. She dared take the hand and kiss the cheek of the astonished, elderly man and told him that he now had two admiring friends.

A recovered Felippe shook his hand warmly, hugged him and expressed his appreciation for what he called "a lifetime of mutual devotion." Rest assured, kind François, that Lydie and I will *never* forget your kind friendship."

On the verge of tears, François was able to say, "Thank you, Felippe," then excused himself with, "I believe I'm needed in the kitchen."

It was appropriate for Felippe and Lydie to silently hug one another for a moment and exchange a kiss.

"Would you like me to send him a brief note with our more specific appreciation for his gracious dinner? He had obviously put a lot of thought into it.

Thank you, sweetheart. You're better at that sort of thing than I am. That kind, ageing man has been part of this household for as long as I can remember. He was middle-aged thirty years ago—must now be three years younger than God. He must have dipped into retirement funds in planning that dinner. The smooth white, syrupy wine is a rare, *very* costly product of fewer than two acres of grapes in Burgundy. So-called oenophiles will pay fortunes for a bottle of it. It's not one we carry in this house. Frankly, I know of no way to reciprocate that isn't impolite or crass. I'm surprised he found it; the vineyard is said to be suffering from a recent nasty infection. Perhaps he had to buy an older vintage, which would have added immensely to its cost. Frankly, I don't know how to make it up to him.

***

"I'm still waiting to be held in your arms," said Lydie somewhat bashfully. He picked her up and dropped her gently on the couch, where there was a large, soft pillow at one end. He lay down and snuggled closely to her.

It had been a long, tiring day for Lydie. She fell asleep in his arms. He carried her to her bed and let her sleep soundly until morning. There was hot water for a tepid bath, and at about ten, they enjoyed strong black coffee and delicious croissants.

CHAPTER 64

The Wedding

The LeBruns' presence on the evening before the wedding was the result of slight persuasion. Dr. and Mme LeBrun had arranged to have a soirée for Lydie without knowing that she and Felippe had chosen the same day, August 21, for a simple morning wedding. The LeBruns' messages to Lydie about their intention were misaddressed because she received none of them. (How were the LeBruns to know that she and her three children were living as guests on Felippe Van Hendryk's estate close to Brussels?)

By the third week in August, the LeBruns, at wits end, had invited thirty happily married, couples who wanted to meet the famous lady. It did not occur to Dr. LeBrun that Lydie would recover quickly from her imprisonment or that she would soon marry. Independently, Lydie, who had been drawing up a very short list of those she chose to invite to her small wedding, had wondered about the propriety of inviting Dr. LeBrun. Every newspaper, every day, featured articles about captive wives, her trial, and Dr. LeBrun's awakening testimony. He had become a widely invited speaker to all sorts of organizations throughout Holland, Belgium, France, and Germany. Lydie chose not to "bother" so famous and apparently frequent speaker to attend her little marriage, although, in truth, it would have added to the dignity of the occasion.

Felippe noticed that she had not invited the LeBrun family, surmised why, and invited them himself in a breakfast-time telegraphed message on August 20. A return message informed him that the LeBruns had planned a catered party for Lydie on the evening of the same day. Felippe coaxed them to finish their early breakfast and then take the 9:30 a.m. nonstop train from Bruges to Mons, because Lydie and he would enjoy having dinner with him and Mme

Lebrun that very evening before the wedding. He added, reassuringly, that it would be easy to take a "special train" from Mons to Bruges in plenty of time to have their soirée in Bruges with time to spare.

Dr. and Mme LeBrun and daughter Rose readily took his advice and accepted the invitation. They took the nonstop train from Bruges to Mons the morning of the day before the small morning wedding and easily joined the engaged couple for dinner at seven o'clock.

"Darling," said Lydie to Felippe immediately after the LeBruns agreed, there is one other person—and his wife if there is one, but I was too shy to ask; I think he lives right here in Mons. I thought about M. Harmignies."

"Good idea, sweetheart, I have Eugène's number in my wallet. I'll message him immediately with an invitation to the wedding. His message went through quickly.

Eugène replied that he would be delighted to attend, but he had to be in court all day on August 21 and the session would begin at 9:00 am. He expressed warm wishes and so on, and thanked Felippe.

Lydie wondered if she ought to invite Anne Morceau, Emerance Bricout, and Amand Wilbaut to join them at the table in the evening, but Anne and Emerance considered it inappropriate to accept any such invitation, which they were astute enough to foresee.

They knew what important role Dr. LeBrun had played in freeing Lydie, how famous he had since become, and that Amand would be uncomfortable. Dr. and Mme LeBrun with Lydie and Felippe, ought to have an intimate foursome at dinner. They arranged an earlier dinner for themselves and the children. Rose joined Anne and company for this earlier dinner.

Felippe had not previously met Dr. LeBrun and his kind, thoughtful wife. Lydie, as we know, had met both of them almost ten years ago in 1842. She'd stayed overnight at their home. She had since been at their home again when they were on vacation. It was when Rose had a party that lasted too long. The Houck medical student, a favorite of Dr. LeBrun's, was supposed to meet Lydie there, but Rose thought it would be less awkward if she just let them find one another. Without this foreknowledge, he chose to experiment by taking laboratory alcohol for sleep. Lydie was attracted to the young man; they had many interests in common. Ignorant of Dr. LeBrun's plan, he chose that evening and night as a medical student's chance to self-experiment soon in the evening. Had they hit it off, as Lydie thought they well might have, Lydie's and his lives would have turned out very differently. It was not long thereafter that she met the Count de Bocarmé.

An invitation to M. and Mme Chercquefosse, for whom Lydie felt not only indebtedness—she now felt love—filled her with disappointment and not a little anxiety. M. Chercquefosse confessed that he would love to be present but, unfortunately, could not be there. "Mme Chercquefosse has been ill in recent months and is housebound. I am unable to care for all her needs; we have professional caretakers with hospital experience looking after her. Mme is comfortable, remembers you well and announced her satisfaction when I told her of your coming marriage and who the groom will be. She was obviously pleased. As am I. I wish you many years of happiness. All of our best wishes to you and Felippe. Your father would be delighted. He was very fond of Felippe.

If you can, please stay in touch. Should you ever be near Peruwelz, please let us know.

Our love,

Olivier Chercquefosse

Lydie was disappointed but enjoyed his message.

To sum it up, Dr. and Mme LeBrun and Felippe and Lydie fit together well. Mme LeBrun had a warm place in her heart for Lydie, whose intelligence, natural beauty, and lack of pretentiousness deeply impressed her. She noticed, too, that Lydie was relaxed and more sure of herself than she remembered. Mme LeBrun knew only that she had been through a "rough spot" and survived, but knew nothing of the ugly, personal details.[35] Lydie perceived her warmth and motherliness. Their talk was about raising children, how housewives can arrange to have "a life of their own," and a little about Rose's new job as a librarian.

Mme LeBrun knew very little about Felippe but found him an unaffected, friendly man. She heard only bits of his conversation with her husband and noticed that they were very quickly into talk that sounded a little intellectual at times and was interrupted by quiet laughter at others. Each had wine, a good Burgundy, while she and Lydie sipped slowly of their glasses of something sweet and yellow.

As friendly a meeting as they were enjoying, all knew that tomorrow would be a busy, long day. As soon as Felippe and Dr. LeBrun had had their dinners and cognacs, they bid one another good night; next day would be a busy one.

The LeBruns went to their room, but Lydie and Felippe still occupied separate bedrooms.

***

Felippe had deep respect for Lydie. He kissed her twice. As she unlocked the door to her room, Lydie thanked him for his continual and unabated consideration for her self-esteem in the eyes of whoever may be observing them.

"Some people do like to gossip," she added.

"Let them," answered Felippe, with a reassuring gaze."

She then looked at Felippe quizzically and asked if they'd ever obtained a proper marriage license. Felippe laughed softly and reassured her that one was on file in an appropriate government bureau.

---

[35] Neither had Dr. LeBrun but he didn't know that the Countess was the former Lydie Fougnies. Her maiden name was poorly covered. Later, professional that he was, he did not inform his wife about details of Lydie's life as a countess.

"How did you manage it, darling? I thought it might be a problem with the new government."

"I met a kind gentleman at a meeting of new department directors in the king's office library. He was a clerically dressed, elderly monsignor, who seemed ill at ease in a large group. Until recently, he lived at the Vatican and customarily converses in Latin. His French needs improvement. I fetched him a cup of tea and tried to set him at ease with simple French conversation, and we hit it off. He asked if I were an Established Church member, and we somehow got into the Latin word *saeculum*, which means the same as the Greek 'aeons and aeons'—a very, very long time.

"Agreeing that an imbued will to do *humanitarian* works, and teaching its importance for generations to come is a religious concept, he gave a name to what you and I consider to be a civic duty. By ignoring the diphthong in *saeculum*, he modified it to 'secular humanism,' a term I've never heard before. Perhaps we're the first. He arranged for us to have our wedding as we want it. He has the place, date, and time. All we have to do is say 'Yes' to a simple question put to us by an assistant."

He added, "Being respectful can get you a long way in this world. He paused briefly; he had something to add: "If *you* hadn't brought up the matter of the license, *I* intended to bring it up and celebrate it by decorating a finger on your *right* hand to accompany the simple, forever meaningful, band you'll receive tomorrow morning and wear for many, many years on the fourth finger of your *left* hand. But we cannot leave your *right* hand envious of the left!"

Wherewith, Felippe reached into a pocket, retrieved another small, violet velvet box, opened it for her, plucked a diamond ring from it and slipped it onto the fourth finger of her right hand. Lydie was far too surprised to say anything more than "Thank you very much, darling."

Felippe replied merely with his inimitable broad smile, kissed her cheek, opened her door for her and said, "Sleep well. We'll meet in the morning." He turned and headed for his room.

***

On the morning of August 21, Lydie and Felippe married in a simple, catered wedding in the Mons Museum, which had since built a pleasant hotel with a connecting lounge and dining room. Felippe and Lydie's guests were few. They were Amand Wilbaut, Mme Anne Morceau, Mlle Emerance Bricout, and the LeBrun family of three. At the instant Felippe married Lydie, her three small children fathered by her late first husband, would be instantaneously adopted. Their family name would change from de Bocarmé to Van Hendryk.

The wedding went well. Dr. LeBrun asked Felippe's permission to give his bride away to him at an altar of comely flowers and, of course, received permission.

All were on time at 9:00 a.m., including a polite government agent dressed in black. He made no speeches. The functionary of the Church Party simply asked, "Do the bride and groom choose to be married?" Felippe and Lydie answered, "Yes," and the man vanished to enter into a logbook the marriage of Secular Humanists.

The kisses were sweet, and somewhere in the quick procedure, Felippe slipped a wedding ring onto the fourth finger of his wife's left hand. She looked at it briefly, gave him a sweet smile and a kiss on the cheek. In the moments before the ceremony, a violin had softly played wedding music, but now it was silent.

Felippe had arranged for a catered "brunch" of hors d'oeuvres, but no one partook of any until they had shaken Felippe's hand and hugged, sometimes pecked, the cheek of the remarkably relaxed and very happy bride.

Amand, a bit self-conscious in his new suit of blue, heavy cotton fabric, was eyeing the hors d'oeuvres, and Anne Morceau came at once to help him. She fixed up a sandwich of sorts for him and decided to give him a cup of black coffee. She was reluctant to introduce him, a known teetotaler, to champagne, which others were now sipping. She had some for herself, though, and so did Rose LeBrun.

Emerance took over the care of the children, for whom Felippe had ordered small, sweet jelly sandwiches, cookies, and sweet juices. Having now gone through the legalities to make him the father of Robert-Gonzalès, Mathilde-Blanche and Rose-Marie Eugènie Van Hendryk, Felippe took his responsibilities with humorous sincerity. Gonzalès, age four, took to him easily and was already calling him Daddy.

All was warm and friendly. While there was no jubilance, the atmosphere was cheerful. Even the children seemed to have fun as they played on the carpet. Lydie moved about more than Felippe, who chatted a good deal with Dr. LeBrun and was pleased to shake hands and express his sincere thanks to those who offered congratulations.

The guest who seemed closest to restrained jubilation was Anne Morceau. She wore a bright green dress, still walked like a woman twenty years her junior, and carried herself with dignity. She gave Lydie a hug that lasted a little longer than anyone else's did, pecked her cheek a little more forcefully, and held her hand longer than anyone else did.

She continued to keep an eye on Amand, at one point calling him over and telling him, in front of Lydie, that he had saved her life and that Lydie (all of the reference to her as countess had completely disappeared) was extremely grateful—that he ought to be proud of himself.

***

Lydie shook Amand's hand warmly, thanked him, and called him "My brave savior. What you did, Amand, saved my life. I cannot ever forget it."

She asked him what his plans were, and he told her that Felippe had offered him a job keeping an eye on the chateau's land and keeping him informed of offers to buy any of it or requests to take any land in lieu of debt.

Felippe, he reported, reminded him that the chateau and its acreage were now the possession of Mme Lydie Van Hendryk and that all questions about the land were to be directed to her. He gave Amand their address in Brussels and asked him to stay in close touch because he should know that a new "land manager" would be needed soon up there in Brussels. And the job was his, including a cottage for him to reside in with his wife. (For whatever reason, she was not at the wedding).

It was understandable that a land manager was needed there. The estate that Felippe had inherited from his parents was close enough to Brussels to say it was part of the capital city. It was, in fact, private land comprising thirty acres. On it were spacious quarters for the staff, and stables for horses and carriages of various types.

Since the death of his parents, Felippe had not had the time or help to care for the various features that accounted for its being one of the most beautiful of the estates in the Brussels region. Especially important were its gardens, which were rich in colorful, ornamental plants, some of them rare. Many unusual trees had evidently been planted years ago; they needed care and pruning. He would have to hire men competent to fix up the flower gardens and the trees.

Amand certainly deserved a bonus for what he had done for Lydie, and Felippe could not find an "older man" (actually, Amand was fifty-five years old) who was better suited for the job. The children might learn about gardening from him. Felippe had to choose where to build a small, comfortable house for Amand and his wife. They had no children.

CHAPTER 65

Post-wedding Train

Lydie moved about the lounge in good humor after her brief morning wedding, receiving best wishes from guests. She used a few seconds of the opportunity to chat, reminding people to take whatever belongings were in their rooms and to set them near the entrance to the lounge. Bellhops would transfer all of it to a train with a 2L painted on its side. It was the small wedding party's own car, to provide a relaxed but fast way to get to a catered party at the LeBrun's home in Bruges that same late afternoon. (Felippe chartered two cars and a locomotive. One car, immediately behind the locomotive, remained empty to provide some protection of the wedding party in the second car, from much of the exhalations of the coal-powered steam locomotive.) Lydie was astounded that he could afford such luxury but knew that talk, even hints, about money or wealth are vulgar.

Felippe had not yet spoken to her about their financial situation, but when he raised the subject, he discovered that the fine points of mannered conversation and inference had already been deeply imbued in Lydie in her earlier years. He gave her a hug and a kiss.

***

All managed to board train 2L (the designation had significance only to the railroad) on time. It was very roomy for so few people, who settled themselves spontaneously. Felippe and Dr. LeBrun occupied opposite seats alone; Mme LeBrun, Lydie, and Anne sat together, across the aisle by the windows, closer to the passing landscapes; and the children were on the same side in the care of Amand, who held Gonzalès on his lap much of the time. Nearby were Emerance

461

and Rose, who kept the two little girls entertained. Amand enjoyed pointing out horses, young colts playing with one another, and other grazing animals, mainly sheep. Although the children's foster home did what it could to keep the children interested, they used only books with colored pictures of animals. Hence, the sights of living creatures were an educational revelation to Gonzalès.

Dr. LeBrun now had an André-Felippe relationship, in which they conversed about much more than the trial. They had already, during dinner, wrung as much as they could about the pluses and minuses of André's sudden fame. André now wanted speak about the king and his relations with Felippe but chose to begin by telling about his own relationship with him.

He confessed to Felippe that, after the trial, the king, having heard about his testimony, invited him to his office. They sat in his library where the easygoing monarch offered him tea and informed him that an unexpectedly large number of citizens wanted a national program to stamp out the practice of men holding captive wives. Most of them mentioned "my testimony" in the trial. Most suggested that Dr. André LeBrun be asked to help organize the program.

How best to establish and organize such an idealistic program were hard problems, according to King Leopold. There would be political-religious implications in any organized campaign to encourage battered wives to leave their husbands and virulent opposition to making any opportunity for divorce easier.

André agreed with the king and told him he was well aware of possible sources of antagonism to his talks at medical societies and had purposely stayed away from the explosive divorce issue. He personally felt that the furthest he could go was to let the public know of the existence of battered wives. It was probably more of a problem than most of the population realized, although obtaining statistical information was difficult; captive wives were afraid to talk and most had no opportunity to do so even if they could work up the courage.

André's personal opinion was that mistreated wives having the volition to leave their husbands (and any program she did not care to join) seemed to him a matter of legally enforceable personal freedom. He chose not to express it, though. It sounded vapid, as captive wives had no personal freedom to enforce.

Leopold agreed that trying to set up marriage counseling offices was unlikely to work because religious officials would insist that their operation was within the scope of Church oversight. Moreover, abusive husbands with captive wives would discourage or prevent the intervention of such clinics. The captive wife who visited one would doubtless be beaten for such "disobedience."

Dr. LeBrun asked the king whether laws forbidding abuse of people under any circumstances might be legal. The king answered that such laws would be legal, but he doubted if they would amount to much more than words.

At the end of the conversation, both men had agreed to the importance of widely broadcasting the bitter fact that abuse exists in numerous marriages. As the realization dawned on enough of the population, people would themselves find a solution, one that might sound radical at the moment.

***

Conversation between Lydie, Mme LeBrun, and Anne Morceau did not touch on the trial. Mme Lebrun remained Mme LeBrun, although her first name was Marie. All three called Anne Morceau by her first name because she asked them to do that. It is difficult to cover the range of their conversations.

Mme LeBrun asked if she might see the ring on Lydie's right hand. She admired it for its sparkle and declared that it was beautiful. She could see that a very sparkly diamond was set among small rubies but would not ask about the diamond's size. She remarked only on its unusual reflection of light. She was impressed that the stone had been cut and set in a way that its sparkle caught the eye but was by no means too much for the eye. Anne saw it for the first time and remarked on its good taste. She recognized at once, from its sparkle, that it was a large diamond and hoped that Lydie would have the good sense to wear a guard ring beyond it. Perhaps she would whisper the suggestion to her later.

Lydie smiled and commented, "Thank you. The band on my left hand is, of course, more important."

In some way, discussion of the rings led to how pleasant it was not to be packed fully abreast with strangers in a train car. Mme LeBrun asked how that had been arranged, and Lydie casually answered, "It's better this way, don't you think?"

Mme LeBrun seemed satisfied with the response.

Anne, ever alert, had sensed when she'd met Felippe in the museum at Mons and arranged his personal meeting with his old love that he came from a privileged background. From the way he expressed himself and from what she learned in later meetings with Lydie about his working relationship with the king and how his parents had broken the relationship because she was "middle class," Anne knew that he must be an open-minded son of "bigoted parents of means." She was delighted at his interest in finding her. Anne was an optimist. She had always thought that, at some point, the count would do something stupidly wicked, which would lead to Lydie's freedom from him.

CHAPTER 66
The LeBruns' Party

The wedding party arrived in Bruges with plenty of time to spare for the members of the small party to get some rest. A large upstairs bedroom (with two double beds) was assigned to Lydie and Felippe. Another children's playroom with cribs and a bed for Emerance was available. Hired help had already heated water enough to let several ladies have a warm bath. Good friends, who lived next door, occupied a large domicile that had once been an upper class boarding house. It had five bathrooms; two were available for ladies to have warm baths. Three were available for men who wanted to wash up, though the water was less than tepid. There were individual bedrooms available to accommodate Anne and Amand.

It was a warm evening. The sun would be up for another two hours after the first guests arrived.

Lydie chose to wear the prettiest of the dresses she had chosen off the rack. It was pink sateen with small colored flowers. For the first time, she wore the pearl necklace that Felippe had given her the evening they'd become engaged. She discretely removed her diamond ring. She was relaxed, exceptionally attractive, and friendly. In a word, she was charming.

***

The LeBruns stood at the opening to the living room from the entrance hall to greet couples as they arrived and to introduce these friends to Lydie and Felippe Van Hendryk, who stood closely behind them. Courtesy and smiles abounded.

The first couple to arrive had come a good distance—from Ostend. The husband was a lawyer, who had heard of Felippe. As

465

would be true of all couples who would attend the party, the couple was surprised to find that Lydie Fougnies was now married—and to Felippe Van Hendryk, a well-known lawyer who (it was no secret) was one of several advisors to the king.

After the Van Hendryks had shaken the hands of the Ostend couple, the two early birds made their way into the large, living room with its attractive plum-colored carpet. One of the catering crew at once offered them champagne in half-filled glasses arrayed on a platter. As they helped themselves, two or three more couples arrived. The new arrivals were greeted and introduced to Lydie and her husband, joined the Ostend couple and were offered champagne. It did not take long for the guest couples to number approximately twenty-five. A few invitees were still expected. All were in some way connected with Dr. LeBrun and his work and had come to meet Lydie. Nearly all expressed surprise to learn that she had a husband, one whose name was familiar to many of them. The living room crowd spilled into the adjacent dining room. A constant buzz of conversation filled both rooms. A majority of the guests held a glass of champagne from which they sipped occasionally.

***

By the time all invitees had entered, most of whom seemed to know one another, the newly married couple had met other couples who lived in a variety of cities and towns. A slight majority came from places clustered within a few miles of Brussels. Louvain was prominent among them, as were Jette and Waterloo. Flanders was well represented, as were Roeselare, Mouscron, Anderlecht, and others. Two couples came from distant Charleroi, located in Hainaut Province. None came from as far as Liège, but two couples came all the way from Antwerp.

The last arrival—he came alone—was Dr. Gilles Houck of Bruges, the once young medical student Rose had invited to a party not long after Lydie had returned from Genoa. Lydie found him quite attractive. He was still unmarried, had put on considerable weight and spoke as interestingly as ever. He and Lydie shook hands. The thought of their almost having had a chance to learn about one another, to date together, must have passed their minds. Lydie thought he was brave to come to see her. She wondered why he had not married Rose. As far as she could tell, which was really very little, they might have a good life together. It was not to be.

Lydie introduced Dr. Houck to Felippe, to whom she had already told the story of what might have happened but for the laboratory alcohol episode. Felippe shook his hand with special warmth, as though he were meeting an old friend he had not seen in years. Dr. Houck was now a practicing neurologist in Bruges. He disappeared into a cluster of people in the dining room. Lydie sized him up as an unhappy man; she was sentimental and felt sorry for him. She wished she knew of an attractive woman to introduce to him.

All of the couples at this gathering were married and, in one way or other, were known to Dr. LeBrun. All had read the newspapers, were acquainted with his effective testimony, and knew very well about the problem of captive wives. They knew that the primary purpose of the LeBruns' party was to allow them to meet the famous woman who had managed to extricate herself from the clutches of a psychopath by convincing a jury, with help from Dr. LeBrun, that she was innocent of willful wrongdoing. They admired her and eagerly anticipated meeting her.

As Lydie, at last, had the freedom to join their clusters in the living and dining rooms—the rooms were large, as it was a large home—all seemed charmed to meet her. Felippe accompanied her, of course, and both of them questioned nearly all the guests about where they lived, their occupations, and their children. Here and there, one heard women remark that Lydie was "surprisingly beautiful," comments that pleased Felippe.

The majority were professional people. A few lawyers who knew Felippe's name and position were in the gathering, but there were many other interesting people too. Among them were scientists—two or three physicists on the faculty at Louvain. Here were medical faculty members at the same large institution. And close by were a couple of bankers. Over there was a good number of small and large business owners. An interesting, modest couple played in the National Symphony Orchestra.

After everyone had had an opportunity to meet or observe Lydie, it became general knowledge that she and Felippe had married this very morning, and many shook Felippe's hand.

***

The diversity of Dr. LeBrun's friends was remarkable. Felippe and Lydie used the generous get-together to meet warm, friendly people who might form a nucleus of simpatico acquaintances and friends. The newlyweds obtained the names and addresses of nearly everyone they met. As they moved through the small multitude, one could often hear miscellaneous remarks about one or the other, or both. The words, usually in women's voices, expressed surprise: "She is a beautiful woman!" "What remarkable poise she has." "They're a charming couple!" "I had no idea she was married to such a prominent man."

It surprised almost everyone that Lydie was more "charming" than anyone, including Dr. André and Madame LeBrun, expected. She had gentility but was by no means timid. She made conversation easily but never talked about herself. Every man she met considered her attractive, with a touch of sophistication. Her healthy good looks, quick smile; and cultured speech made her attractive to men. Her poise, pleasant eye-contact, and down-to-earth conversation made her attractive to women. Her handsome husband also caught their eyes.

***

It is not improbable that her marriage to a Van Hendryk, one with education, social station, and wealth, supplied Lydie with a degree of self-assurance that she had never before known. In no way, however, did it cross her mind that she was now superior to others. Her well-intentioned self was now *personally* free of an unfair, oppressive indignity. The ignorant sorting of persons by class had been the unpardonable reason for her recent, incalculable grief. Its disappearance had a deep, automatic effect: Lydie became an outspoken critic of intolerance and social classification based on birth or a parent's occupation.

Most of the guests had cards, which Lydie or Felippe gladly received either from wives or husbands, with names, addresses, and telegraph numbers. Lydie wore a white pocketbook strapped over a shoulder and collected cards primarily from women, while Felippe took cards offered him by men. He thanked them and put them in his pocket. Lydie had no cards, but Felippe did, and he saw to it that he had given one to at least one member of each couple.

Given how many of the guests lived at considerable distance from Bruges, a large number expected to remain overnight in hotels, where they intended to have dinner. The gathering broke up at dusk and early evening with much shaking of hands and pervasive parting remarks such as, "Let's try to meet again soon."

***

Dr. LeBrun took all of it in with delight. His soirée was a success, and so was Lydie. He had not realized until he watched her "in action" how naturally captivating and alluring a woman Lydie had become. He liked what he saw. The Lydie-Felippe marriage seemed to have been made in Elysian Fields. His hunch was that Felippe might become his close friend. He admired his broadly educated, wide open mind. His common sense was salted with judicious effectiveness. And he had a hell of a good sense of humor.

Naturally, both LeBruns, both Van Hendryks, Rose, Emerance, Anne, and Amand were tired and hungry. Amand reported that he had explained, to those who asked, that he was an "inside friend of Lydie's" when she'd been a "captured, beaten woman," and Anne explained that, when she circulated, she'd told people that she was Lydie's "secret friend," who had come to know of her problems and had tried to help her when she could. Anne impressed nearly everyone she met. She had firmness, dignity, and grace.

A small group, all attendees of the early morning wedding, really had not helped themselves to many of the hors d'oeuvres or any of the champagne. All, including the three LeBruns, were tired but hungry. They sat down to a dinner that the caterer had prepared for them—seafood bisque followed by green vegetables and excellent steaks of Atlantic cod. The champagne and wines were plentiful.

André again toasted the newly married couple, wished them well, and discovered that their plans were to return to Mons the next day. From there, they would go to Strasbourg by train and, by transport yet to be determined, find a chalet that Felippe had rented in Swiss mountains near the French border. They expected to return to Brussels in about three weeks.

Felippe spoke after raising his glass, to congratulate André for his well-thought-out soirée to introduce Lydie. "Personally, I felt like someone crashing a party." He felt he had to comment on his wife's "smashing" introduction to Belgian society. "I have loved Lydie for many a year but was, frankly, awed by a presence and poise I had never before seen.

"There's a lot that my bride and I still have to iron out about our long, long future together. Emerance has kindly offered to keep an eye on our children at home in Brussels. She'll have a way to reach us in case it's necessary.

"It will never, of course, be possible for us to do for you, André and Madame LeBrun, what you have done for Lydie. That, of course, means that you have been kind and generous friends to *me*, too. We are, both of us, endowed with long memories, and it is impossible to forget the extraordinary well of goodness that lies in your hearts. Neither of us can find words to tell you how appreciative we are.

"Mme LeBrun, I must tell you that Lydie remembers vividly the evening she met you in a theater lobby. You and André were sipping champagne and offered her some. To make a good impression on Rose's parents, she forced herself to say, 'No, thank you.'"

A few laughs ensued.

"Lydie told me you asked how she would get back to pitiful Peruwelz that night. She would stay at a hotel and return next day, she told you. Something about this sounded threatening to you. You told her in a stern, motherly way, 'I'll not have that!' and either invited or commanded her to stay at *your* home. André then explained to her next morning the threats facing pretty young women staying alone at hotels. That was a pretty important point in Lydie's and my life. She was so trusting back then that she could easily have disappeared and never been found. At any rate, *I personally thank you* for your protecting Lydie for me.

"Dr. André LeBrun, the Western world now knows what you did for Lydie and thousands of women like her. No need to repeat it. You deserve a special medal.

"When we get back from our trip, we'll arrange to see you and your kind spouse soon thereafter at *our* place." He raised his glass and toasted, "All the LeBruns."

A slightly tearful Lydie stood and briefly thanked the couple who had played such an important role in her life. "Dr. and Mme LeBrun, with all my heart, I love you both. Thank you, Amand, Anne, and Rose." She was purposely brief, lest she shed the tears in her eyes.

Anne asked if she, too, could extend her profound appreciation to Dr. and Mme LeBrun for their "selfless, civilized action that rescued a lovely woman from what might have been her death. One sees too little of that virtue today.

"I thought the group ought to know about Felippe's kindness." With a smile directed to Lydie, she said to her, "That charming husband of yours, with whom I too have fallen in love, has seen to it that Amand and I have comfortable transportation back to little Bury tomorrow. We intend to clarify your role in this drama to newspaper reporters and to people with credibility." She smiled very warmly as she threw a kiss, this one directed toward Felippe.

"I *do so much hope* that there will be opportunities, from time to time, to meet with you kind, hospitable people again. Thank you very much."

It was ten before they had finished dinner and were tired. Rose surprised them and kept them up another minute. She rose and smiled at her parents. "I want to thank my mother and father for showing me how civilized and kind they are, and, of course, I wish the newly married couple all best wishes and congratulations. And I would not be truthful if I failed to add that, naturally, I am envious of you two, but in no way does that diminish my very best wishes for your long, happy lives together."

Rose then shed a few tears accompanied by a broad smile.

Her mother smiled, but she also cried. She had been hesitating about asking Amand if he had anything to add.

Amand rose to his feet and soberly summed things up, "Thank ye all. It's been a very good story."

CHAPTER 67

Love's Power to Heal

Lydie's host of Friends from Tournai was concerned with her fate. All of them had feared that, if or when a jury freed her, Lydie would be very ill, requiring prolonged psychological intervention. They'd agreed, unanimously, that the most efficacious medicine for her would be love.

Lydie's miraculous and quick recovery is a tribute to the integrity of her personal strength. Still, it may not have happened so quickly had she not been supported by the man she had always loved and who had always loved her. Felippe's warm and keen insight and his deep respect, protectiveness, and unselfishness had to have girded her self-confidence and courage. So did his good humor and high intelligence. Felippe did more for her quick recovery than a battery of psychologists and counselors. Less than two months after she regained her freedom, she rarely thought of Bury, the chateau, or her once-cruel and crazy husband. All she knew of him was that he no longer existed. Now and again, she thought of kind Judge Lyon and had in the past sent him short letters. She quickly received warm responses.

Eventually, he wrote that age was catching up with him, and he made mention of illness. That brief note was the last she heard of him.

CHAPTER 68

Eighty Years

In 1866, King Leopold died. Felippe resigned his government job and gave careful consideration to a very hard decision, namely, how best to devote his time beneficially for his country. He met and spoke at length with people from every cultural level. In the course of it he learned that, long after the murder trial, a vast number of people still hated Lydie. Judge Lyon's decision to take evidence in a highly confidential way saved Lydie's life and dignity but left very many Belgian citizens suspicious that she got away with murder.

Felippe was concerned for Lydie's safety. As a busy housewife managing the estate in Brussels, she was unaware of the widespread antipathy for her. Felippe decided "on a dime" to prevent any possible tragedy He bought one way tickets to the United States without disclosing his reason. He aimed to leave unsafe Belgium and immigrate to safer America. He never, then or thereafter, spelled out to Lydie the main reason for his stunning decision.

***

At ages forty-nine and fifty, in 1868, he and the wife he dearly loved, came to America, where they lived for short periods in two small New England towns and became citizens of the United States. Felippe transferred his substantial inheritance to a New York bank just as Gustave had done.

In 1870 both decided to enjoy their remaining years in a countryside home. Felippe bought fifty-acres of land in both their names in upper New York State. The nearest village was Ghent. They built an ample, comfortable home and a second house with large quarters to keep a full-time staff of help, similar to the staff Felippe was used to when he grew up on the estate adjacent to Brussels.

They kept riding horses for exercise and traveled nearly every spring to Europe for a month, except when they traveled westward to see the remarkable features of the Rockies. Lydie's enthusiasm for life never faltered. She enjoyed all of every day but never forgot that she was fortunate to be secure and loved by a wise, gentle and generous husband. She never forgot the less fortunate of her new fellow citizens. She gave most substantially to several United States charities of her choice and always anonymously.

The three children, who were Lydie's by her first marriage, were healthy and successful. They had emigrated from Belgium when young and became Canadian citizens. They chose Canada because the Civil War raged in the United States at that time. Felippe loved those children as though they were biologically his own.

Lydie remarked to Felippe at dinner about a year after arriving in this country, "Your decision to remain in the United States was wise. I sincerely thank you for it, darling. I would never leave this country; I love it and admire the wisdom of its founding fathers." Felippe's response was simply a broad, loving smile.

Their alacrity in applying for citizenship, was fortunate. They were unaware that they were avoiding personal exposure to World War I, which decimated more of Belgium than other nations.

*** *** ***

Felippe handled his considerable inheritance with farsighted acumen. He sensibly invested in several countries, especially the United States, and amassed comfortable assets. His lengthy experience studying inventions and inventors during the sixteen years he'd worked as a legal advisor to Belgium's king was of great use to him as a professional investor.

Felippe and Lydie remained deeply in love with one another, addressing and treating each other endearingly and considerately every day. They lived reasonably disciplined lives, following a flexible schedule:

Rise at 7:00 o'clock, bathe, dress informally, and breakfast from 7:30 to 8:00. Both had ample time to talk with employees including Amand Wilbaut,[36] about *their* health, any personal problems in which either of them might be helpful, and to ask their suggestions for the day's working agenda. Lydie often had a suggestion or question for the gardener. Felippe, for example, wanted to hear their advice on possibly impending new projects such as raising prize cattle and building stables for them. He certainly had lots of hay to feed them. They were mainly young, creative men and women who had been raised on farms. Their suggestions were useful.

At two minutes before nine Felippe opened the telegraph line from his office to the Stock Market in New York City and worked assiduously but carefully until eleven. He scrupulously devoted his investment business only to two hours. He was determined not to become a slave to financial gambling. He was knowingly conservative and patient. In the period before lunch, he wrote miscellaneous

---

[36] Felippe had a proper small home built for Amand and his wife. It was fully furnished, including a modern kitchen and bathroom plumbing. The home had its own well. His position as Chief Land Manager was a sinecure that earned a salary and an annual bonus. He 'oversaw' long grass-cutting by men with scythes. During cold months he used the resulting hay to shelter a few flower gardens he created. Amand also watched snow shoveling of foot paths by strong young men. Lydie often invited him and his wife to join Felippe and her at lunch. He had done so much for Lydie that Felippe left out nothing to make life comfortable for both of them. They always invited them to join celebrations of any kind. Amand died at about age seventy-five and his wife followed him in death two years afterward.

personal notes (mainly to his children) and brief notes to business contacts.

***

Felippe used whatever spare time he had, to read books, which he took to be an essential part of a cultured life. He sometimes chose books recommended by the literary editor of what he considered New York's best newspaper, but his years as one of a group of advisors to King Leopold taught him about authors and he kept a list of books that were worth reading. In truth, he was inclined to read informative histories of any epoch and any novel that two or three colleagues insisted were "a hell of a good read."

As a schoolboy of affluent parents, Felippe, it was assumed, would eventually enter a university where he would master his lifetime profession. Prior to entering the university in Zürich, he had had a standard six-year education, which began by memorizing Latin declensions and conjugations. This made it possible to stumble through Caesar's memoirs of his Gallic Wars, Cicero's orations, and sections of Sallust's history of Rome, topped by Virgil's *Aeneid*. He translated them fairly well, and got a passing grade even with a few poems by Ovid added to them. He felt that most of it was pure drudgery. It *was* pure drudgery, but essential, he later discovered, to reading law books easily.

He made it through advanced algebra and trigonometry, ancient history (primarily of Greece) and had an excellent exposure to conversational English. Probably, his homework included summertime reading of assigned material. His language master had a deep interest in the origins of modern French as well as a sense of humor. Probably he admired Felippe; one summer he assigned excerpts of François Rabelais' Pantagruel. Since Felippe's native language was French, he understood and enjoyed Rabelais' new words that enlivened French, as well as his racy diversions and dissents from orthodoxy. His assignment in the summer before senior class began was Jonathan Swift's Gulliver's Travels, an ideal assignment for a young man who read English fluently and had a fine sense of humor,

Once settled in Ghent, Felippe read for entertainment or education. He heard that Stendhal was a first-rate author. Someone suggested his The Red and the Black. It surely caught his attention, but the characters' motivations and behavior evoked less than clean satisfaction. Thomas Hardy's Far from the Madding Crowd was readable but Hardy was too amateurishly inventive in devising ways to wriggle out of critical situations. And what in the world was the "Madding Crowd?" Hardy never used the term in the story! So it went. A biography of Catherine the Great so held his attention, he was sorry when it ended. Oliver Twist surprised him; he was unaware of such poverty in wealthy England. Fascinated by Charles Darwin's Origin of Species, he became a believer in Evolution by Natural Selection. Felippe was always grateful to whoever acquainted him with a good book.

***

Lydie was largely occupied writing letters to old friends from college, especially Angelica Bregosi. Felippe and she traveled to Genoa to meet her. Lydie loved to write—she always had—and she tried to stay in touch with the few people who'd played a significant role in her life. Of them, some were obviously closer than others. She sent invitations to a small number to visit the United States as their guests. She would ask guests-to-be to let her know when they would like to visit. If it was a convenient time for Felippe and Lydie, she sent them round-trip tickets on a steamship to New York City. It was easy to find carriage drivers who would take them to the Van Hendryk home near Ghent.

The LeBruns, including Rose, were obviously on the guest list, as was Anne Morceau. Shortly after Felippe and Lydie moved into their newly built house and, as they were looking for reliable full-time help, Felippe and Lydie thought of offering Emerance Bricout a permanent position overseeing the kitchen crew of what they hoped could become a bistro kitchen. She came, as a guest, to look at the home, including the purposely unfinished kitchen waiting to be fitted the way she would choose to complete it and hire the employees she would supervise. She had had Parisian restaurant experience; her father owned and ran a small restaurant.

Felippe had earlier sent her a personal letter letting her know that he wanted their kitchen to resemble a small, happy bistro in Paris and could think of no one better equipped than she was to get it off the ground and run it. He wrote, "Within reason, you may set your salary. We hope you will, at least, visit us and look the facility over. I am enclosing a ticket of first-class passage to New York."

Emerance remembered how charming Felippe had been at his wedding to Lydie in August 1851. She was thirty years old, and he was thirty-one. Emerance was Lydie's age. She had been hoping to work at most another ten years as a poorly-paid dressmaker in Brussels.

In answer to Felippe, she explained that her health was still good, but in the decade to come, it would be impossible to promise any given number of years. If she could take the position with him and Lydie despite her reluctance to promise ten years (and possibly as few as five), she would be happy to come. Her agreement must be one that recognizes that, while she is well at present, she is anxious about her financial security in the event she should become chronically ill. Should that happen, might she expect that they would bear the costs of private medical and nursing care?

To her surprise, Felippe replied almost immediately. He telegraphed a confidential message to her: "Answer to your important query is Yes. More explicit letter follows. Best wishes, Felippe and Lydie."

In the follow-up letter, he wrote that, in case of any illness, even if minor, Emerance would have access to the best private doctors and consulting specialists; nurses; hospitals; and, if needed, first-class, long-term care "at our expense." He explained that the letter serves as a written, contractual agreement to that end, adding that, if Emerance should fall ill on the first day of employment, he and Lydie would provide this best available private medical care and any needed follow-up care or consultation.

About three weeks later, Emerance was with them. She had aged, but normally so. She looked well. She thought that Felippe and Lydie had built a wonderful home in an almost unbelievably gorgeous location. After letting her recover her land legs with three nights of sleep, Felippe and Lydie took her to dinner at a small French restaurant reputed to be one of New York's favorites.

Emerance was impressed. "I certainly cannot reproduce this restaurant in your home," she told them. "I would introduce a few French cooking tools and make additions to the menu. We would need to work with an open-minded American cook and an assistant willing to learn a few techniques. We can add a French flavor to American staples by shopping in food stores that attract the immigrant population in New York City."

Within six weeks, Emerance had added an intriguing European atmosphere to the dining room and dinner meals. Felippe was forever renaming the room, tongue-in-cheek, after famous Parisian restaurants. Lydie so enjoyed observing Felippe's newfound delight in savoring Emerance's varieties of soups and stews: *vichyssoise* and various *ragouts*, that she thought it appropriate to add something more than a single guarantee of medical care by using her Lydie Trust.

After consulting a lawyer, she established a formal Emerance Bricout Medical Care and Nursing Fund[37] and continued to support

---

[37] One surmises that those Belgians on public assistance who needed nursing home care found themselves in poorly equipped or otherwise undesirable caretaking places. Desirable caretaking facilities must have been available to the well-to-do and wealthy populace. A good source of social inequities in mid-nineteenth century Belgium is in the Encyclopedia Britannica, ninth edition. Emerance now had means to avoid poor-quality care.

philanthropic organizations. By establishing a medical fund for Emerance, she strengthened the earlier agreement she'd signed with Felippe alone; it had not been witnessed by a third disinterested party. Another amendment to the Lydie Trust added a generous, annual bonus to Emerance's salary. She deserved it; her accomplishment had begun to give special joy to Felippe. It soon became apparent that dinner guests also relished invitations more than ever. Those who knew a little French dared to try speaking it. Lydie, still a pedant, encouraged them by supplying the missing phrases and words they had forgotten. (Most guests thought Lydie was English because she spoke it so apparently naturally. Discovering that her native language was French surprised them).

Emerance mentioned to Lydie, in French, that it was common to overhear talk mixed with fun and laughter at tables in her father's Paris bistro, a hangout for American visitors with French friends. Usually there were four Americans trying to use their forgotten French and a native French couple helping, as Lydie was doing. Small parties composed of six people seemed to her and to her father to produce more frivolity and greater interest in language than parties of four.

Felippe overheard Emerance's French and asked, after dinner while having a brandy, to have their handyman add a plank to lengthen the dining table. Lydie therefore invited two neighbor couples to dinner the following week. It allowed Felippe to have more stimulating dinner conversation.

***

The reader will recall that Lydie's murdered brother Gustave, set up a very generous trust for Lydie's use, to support her, but only if her first husband (her brother's murderer) should die. The guillotine settled that potential obstacle. The site of the trust was a New York City bank (see "Gustave's Will.") Trustees with a mandate to be generous managed reinvestment of its income. As Gustave's sister, she had been forced, in an awful dilemma, to choose life for herself and three children but sacrificed her brother. She had no way to imagine that her heartrending but logical choice was destined to provide her with a very large trust that her late brother had intended for her. She was uncomfortable about using any of it for herself. She chose to give its dividends generously (and anonymously) to charitable organizations.

She did not need the money—she was married to a very wealthy man. (She never asked her husband his total worth). He hugged and kissed her when he learned that her trust money was all going to charity. She took this to mean that he agreed with her that she didn't need it and with her own feeling that to use it luxuriantly on herself was extremely poor taste. Deep down, she knew well that she neither deserved nor needed that large sum of money. Her suspicion was that, if Gustave still lived, he would agree that her trust not be used selfishly.

She asked the trustees to add a salary bonus at Christmas for Emerance. The trustees thought that a bonus should be equivalent to a month's salary, but she wanted to discuss this matter with her husband. Felippe was proud of his wife; he agreed that Emerance's bonus should be equal to her monthly salary, which was well deserved. At Felippe's request, there ought also be a gift in the form of, say, a good wool sweater under the tree for Emerance. Felippe felt strongly that it was appropriate for any bonus money to be disbursed personally and confidentially in sealed envelopes well before the holiday, so that recipients might use some of it to buy gifts for friends, or family overseas, if he or she wished.

Because Lydie's major philanthropic giving was anonymous, we can only speculate what organizations received her help. These organizations received the bulk of annual income from her trust.

Felippe felt adamantly that there be no mention of money at any time in the presence of children, guests, or Emerance. Felippe asked Lydie to keep the subject off limits even to their children. Children, teenagers, and even immature people in their thirties talked far too openly about a very personal subject with ramifications they didn't yet understand. His lawyers, he told her, agreed with him and would reveal to the children only what they needed to know of their inheritances, depending on their age and maturity.

***

Felippe and Lydie set aside at least forty minutes a day to ride at a slow pace on gentle horses around sections of their estate's periphery. Once bathed and dressed, they regularly met in their sitting room and enjoyed an aperitif. Lydie showed her husband any letters received during the day and the couple discussed world and national events reported in New York newspapers. They read mail from friends and from their children in Ontario. That pleasant hour never seemed to be long enough.

A candlelit dinner prepared by one or other of their cooks followed, unless it was a "bistro night," when men and women dressed informally. They relaxed on those evenings, trying to make conversation in French with the encouragement of good wines and much help from Felippe and Lydie. Wives, unless they spoke French well, were not as eager to join the fun as their husbands. They drank much less wine and ate less, although they were full of praise for food that came from Emerance's French kitchen. On August 21, the date of their marriage, whether it be a bistro day or a regular day, everyone toasted one another with champagne.

At the end of the Great War, Felippe and his sons gave generously to Belgian organizations for the rebuilding of cities and towns destroyed in the recent 1914–18 war. Their son, Robert-Gonzalès— who came to be called Robert—and two daughters, Mathilde and Eugènie, went to Belgium to work directly with these and social welfare groups. The three children married, and each presented Lydie and Felippe with two grandchildren, on whom they doted.

***

One afternoon of a beautiful fall day in 1920, when they met in the sitting room on schedule and were alone, Felippe hugged her, kissed her and spoke to her slowly with warm, kind words.

"Dearest, I must remind you that I am now one hundred and one-years-old and love you, and my life with you, as much as ever. When we promised to love one another in spite of swollen ankles or protuberant bellies, we kept the promise, even though neither of us has any such signs of ill-health. However, our elderliness is evident.

"Obviously, *this is* an unpredictable time in both our lives. Our exceptionally strong living bond cannot last forever. I don't know how or when our paradise will end in perpetual separation. The passage of time and the processes of aging will inevitably cause it to happen. Each of us must have the good sense to bravely face what is an entirely normal part of life. I didn't want this permanent separation to happen without my having purposely taken a few minutes to thank you—with all my heart—for being my closest and loving friend. *You* made possible the happiest years of my life.

He hugged and kissed her again. Then he paused, to say kindly, "I didn't want this to be a maudlin scene. I've told you what I wanted to tell you while my mind is healthy."

With tears, Lydie rose from her cushioned armchair, to approach him where he sat on the sofa. She threw her arms around him, addressed him as "my darling, my darling." She kissed him passionately. "My dearest love, I thank *you* for all that *you've* done for our children and for me. I have loved you deeply since we met in the Museum in 1840. That was eighty years ago!

"All but nine of those years we've lived and loved together in a special paradise." Kissing him again, she said, "There are no words to describe how grateful I am to *you* for inviting me, on a sunny summer day, to stroll with you in the garden behind the museum. The lilies are as real today as when we first fell in love. You are my dearest, dearest friend, Felippe—I'm still madly in love with you. You've taught me a great deal, including bravery, so don't worry about me. I'll happily reminisce about the best husband a woman could ever have."

"*Enough*," commanded Felippe softly and with a loving smile. He paused briefly to announce with mock seriousness, "I think I'll have two fingers of Scotch whisky and water as *my* aperitif today. Sweetheart, what will be *your* choice of what doesn't numb your nose?" He drew an unexpected answer. "Darling, I got over that numb nose business a long time ago. I'll *gladly* join you in a jigger of Scotch whisky with water on the side." They toasted one another without a quiver in either's hand.

***

Both died peacefully in their sleep within the same week two years later, at the remarkable ages of 103 and 102. The Fates had been exceptionably kind to them; neither would have wished to continue to live without the other.

They had told their three children to handle their deaths with ultimate simplicity: no funerals, speeches or invocations, and not to traumatize children by allowing them to observe burials of their simple pine coffins. The family cemetery plot was located near the periphery of the acreage Felippe and Lydie owned. Robert and his two brothers-in-law, with help of strong male employees, interred the coffins in the center of the plot.

Mother Lydie had left a simple special request: "Please have a small American flag fly over my grave for a few days. And do the same for father when he, too, ceases to 'breathe the vital air.'" [38]

***

---

[38] Lydie eschewed the word "death." She preferred to use this ancient Greek expression instead.

The three Van Hendryk children, with their spouses, six grown grandchildren and four young great-grandchildren clustered in a garden near the entrance of Grandpa and Grandma's house to celebrate the lives of the two people they loved without reservation. They were, naturally, sad even though Felippe had once asked them not to be. Robert tried to obey his admonition but found he could not. He, alone, was able to recall the day his father and mother married.

"Some kind lady hugged me and asked me never to forget this happy morning because my last name changed when 'Daddy' and mother Lydie stood behind a large bank of flowers and agreed to marry." Robert was a few days older than four on that morning. His remembrance of the event was clear.

Robert informed the other adults of several conversations he had with mother Lydie and father Felippe. They followed their requests to make their burials models of simplicity.

They celebrated the lives of these lovable and loving people with undeniable sadness, but they were not afraid to smile, even to laugh briefly from to time, as they recalled their humorous idiosyncrasies as well as their civility and generosity. It was what Father Felippe and Mother Lydie wanted them to do.

Addendum

Readers have remarked that the unschooled, ignorant Count de Bocarmé seems to speak too properly. I agree but think I know the reason for the anomaly. Without a way to record sounds, it was essential in 1851 that court stenographers be able to copy all spoken words quickly and accurately without ambiguity. Judge Lyon made reference to his "licensed stenographers." Those working in his Mons Court of Assizes probably used something like a method described in 1590. Effectively, it requires a first-class stenographer to have a "gigantic memory" and to have committed himself to "unremitting labor" to know the arbitrarily assigned signs or symbols for "nearly every word in a language." The source of this information is in volume 7, under "Shorthand," of the ninth edition (1889) of the Encyclopedia Britannica.

I do not know for a fact but have heard that, to be licensed, the very best French, English and German stenographer had to demonstrate that he knew "symbols" for at least fifty thousand individual whole words and that he could quickly jot the arbitrarily assigned or personally designed symbols for them. An associated stenographer, who can read the jotted symbols, then spelled the words they stand for into a telegraphic printer with Morse Code. Obviously, he could not spell words as they were misspoken; he would recognize and spell only the *intended proper* word. In no way does this substantially alter the sense of what was said. To the contrary: mispronounced words would become properly "intended" words. (Thus, the count seemed to speak properly). The telegrapher might also correct a few grammatical errors such as confusing word order when entering the words. The rate of his entering words is not rigidly tied to rate of speech as long as there is a jotted record of symbols to copy. Pauses in speech also help him stay abreast of the rate of speech.

Telegraphic printers were in wide use in western European countries during the mid and late nineteenth century, but <u>certainly</u> not in 1590, when stenographers later wrote the words in long hand. There was no nearly immediate available copy.

An intimation that the count enunciated poorly *is* found in the May 28 session of the trial when, within three lines, *mère* (for "mother") is twice incorrectly used when *mari* (for "husband") was the appropriate word. The paragraph is about a husband. Suddenly, it appears correctly spelled as *mari* on the next line. A weak inference is that the stenographer had trouble with the count's pronunciation of the French *mari*; it sounded too much like *mère*. It was the first time the count spoke; the stenographer may have been confounded by the count's poor pronunciation of his native language.